EAST ATLANTA

# EVERWILD

## Also by Neal Shusterman

**Novels**
*Bruiser*
*Challenger Deep*
*Chasing Forgiveness*
*The Dark Side of Nowhere*
*Dry* (with Jarrod Shusterman)

**Dissidents**
*Downsiders*
*The Eyes of Kid Midas*
*Full Tilt*
*The Shadow Club*
*The Shadow Club Rising*
*Speeding Bullet*

**The Accelerati Series**
**(with Eric Elfman)**
*Tesla's Attic*
*Edison's Alley*

**The Antsy Bonano Series**
*The Schwa Was Here*
*Antsy Does Time*
*Ship Out of Luck*

**The Unwind Dystology**
*Unwind*
*UnWholly*
*UnSouled*
*UnDivided*
*UnStrung* (an eBook original)

**The Skinjacker Trilogy**
*Everlost*
*Everwild*
*Everfound*

**The Star Shards Chronicles**
*Scorpion Shards*
*Thief of Souls*
*Shattered Sky*

**The Dark Fusion Series**
*Dreadlocks*
*Red Rider's Hood*
*Duckling Ugly*

**Story Collections**
*Darkness Creeping*
*Kid Heroes*
*MindQuakes*
*MindStorms*
*MindTwisters*
*MindBenders*

**Arc of a Scythe**
*Scythe*
*Thunderhead*
*The Toll*

Visit the author at storyman.com
and Facebook.com/NealShusterman

# EVERWILD

## BOOK 2 OF THE SKINJACKER TRILOGY

# NEAL SHUSTERMAN

**SIMON & SCHUSTER** BFYR

**NEW YORK LONDON TORONTO SYDNEY NEW DELHI**

*For Christine*

## Acknowledgments

I'd like to thank my editors, David Gale and Navah Wolfe, as well as
Justin Chanda, Paul Crichton, Michelle Fadlalla, and everyone at Simon
& Schuster for being so supportive, not just of *Everwild*, but of all my
work. Thanks to Brandi Lomeli for research into crazy things, and for
keeping my life organized. I'd also like to thank my parents for their
constant love and support, as well as my "big sis," Patricia McFall, and
a special thanks to my kids, Brendan, Jarrod, Joelle, and Erin for their
love, inspiration, and valuable critiques throughout the writing process.

 **SIMON & SCHUSTER** BFYR

An imprint of Simon & Schuster Children's Publishing Division
1230 Avenue of the Americas, New York, New York 10020
This book is a work of fiction. Any references to historical events, real people, or real places
are used fictitiously. Other names, characters, places, and events are products of the author's
imagination, and any resemblance to actual events or places or persons, living or dead, is
entirely coincidental.
Text © 2009 by Neal Shusterman
Jacket illustrations © 2020 by Jim Tierney
Jacket design by Lucy Ruth Cummins
All rights reserved, including the right of reproduction in whole or in part in any form.
**SIMON & SCHUSTER** BFYR is a trademark of Simon & Schuster, Inc.
For information about special discounts for bulk purchases, please contact Simon & Schuster
Special Sales at 1-866-506-1949 or business@simonandschuster.com.
The Simon & Schuster Speakers Bureau can bring authors to your live event. For more
information or to book an event, contact the Simon & Schuster Speakers Bureau
at 1-866-248-3049 or visit our website at www.simonspeakers.com.
Also available in a **SIMON & SCHUSTER** BFYR paperback edition
Interior design by Daniel Roode
The text for this book is set in Cochin.
Manufactured in the United States of America
This **SIMON & SCHUSTER** BFYR hardcover edition September 2020
10 9 8 7 6 5 4 3 2 1
The Library of Congress has cataloged the hardcover edition as follows:
Shusterman, Neal.
Everwild / Neal Shusterman.—1st ed.
p. cm.
Summary—Nick, known as the dreaded "chocolate ogre," is trying to find all the children in
Everlost and release them from the limbo they are in, while Mikey and Allie have joined a
band of skinjackers and are putting themselves in danger by visiting the world of the living.
ISBN 978-1-5344-8331-6 (hc)
ISBN 978-1-5344-8330-9 (pbk)
ISBN 978-1-4169-9738-2 (eBook)
[1. Future life—Fiction. 2. Dead—Fiction.] 1. Title.
Series: The Gideon trilogy ; 3
Series: Skinjacker trilogy ; bk. 2
PZ7.S55987 Ew 2009
[Fic] 22
2008051348

# A "Read Me" from Mary Hightower

*Hello, and welcome to Everlost. For new arrivals, I am happy to provide a comprehensive list of everterms and definitions that may help you in your postmortal journey. Naturally I've included my own personal opinions as well, for what list would be complete without the wisdom of someone who knows? Thank you, and I look forward to meeting you very, very soon.*

*Yours most truly,*

*Mary Hightower*

**afterglow:** This is the gentle light that all spirits in Everlost generate. Of course some shine more brightly than others.

**Afterlight:** All residents of Everlost are properly referred to as "Afterlights." To call us ghosts is insulting.

**chime:** To hang one's captives upside down by their ankles from long ropes, allowing them to swing free. As it is impossible to feel physical pain in Everlost, certain evil entities, such as the McGill will chime their prisoners in an attempt to induce long-term boredom.

**chiming chamber:** A place where such unfortunate afterlights are chimed.

**deadspot:** This is a small patch of ground that has crossed from the living world into Everlost. In most cases these spots are just a few feet wide, and mark the place where someone has died; however, in certain instances deadspots can include larger areas.

**dominant reality:** When a building is destroyed, and crosses into Everlost, and a new structure is built in the living world to take its place, which of those buildings is more real? To us in Everlost, the older, "crossed" building is the one we see. Therefore, it is my opinion that Everlost is more real. You can read more about this in my upcoming book *The Living World and Other Myths, as Told by Mary Hightower*.

**ecto-ripping:** One of the criminal arts, as I like to call them. "Ecto-ripping" or "ripping" is the ability to reach into the living world, and rip things out of it, and into Everlost. Avoid ecto-rippers at all costs. Any ecto-ripper sighting should be reported to an authority.

**evercookies:** Certain individuals (whose names I shall not mention) claim that all Chinese fortune cookies cross into Everlost, and if that's not enough, they also insist that every fortune in Everlost is true. I say that these are lies, lies, lies. I advise you to stay away from fortune cookies as if they carry the plague.

**eversight:** We Afterlights can see the living world, but it looks blurry and out of focus to us. Even the colors of the living world are subdued. Only the things and places that have crossed into Everlost appear bright, solid, and clear to us. Such is the nature of eversight.

**everslugs:** You may have discovered a time-worn coin in your pocket when you awoke in Everlost. Throw it away. It's worthless.

**The Everwild:** The unexplored, uncharted, and mostly dangerous regions of Everlost.

**fleshie:** A skinjacker slang term for a living, breathing human being.

**gravity fatigue:** Afterlights are not immune to the force of gravity—it pulls down on us just as it does to the living. Unfortunately, since we sink in the living world, there is always a clear and present danger that we might sink all the way to the center of the earth if we don't keep moving when on living ground. Once one sinks over one's head into the ground, there is usually no hope that that person will ever pull himself back to the surface. We call this gravity fatigue.

**Interlights:** After crossing into Everlost, Afterlights sleep for nine months before awaking in Everlost. During that hibernation period, they are properly referred to as Interlights.

**peel out:** When a skinjacker pulls out of a fleshie, it is sometimes referred to as "peeling out."

**skinjacking:** Another criminal art — perhaps the most useful — if any of the criminal arts can be called useful. Skinjacking is the ability to "possess" a living person, by leaping inside of that person, and taking control of, him or her.

**vapor:** This is the proper way to refer to a gathering of Afterlights. A flock of birds, a gaggle of geese, and a vapor of Afterlights.

# PART ONE

## *A Vapor of Afterlights*

# CHAPTER 1

## *Fresh Havoc*

There were rumors.

Of terrible things, of wonderful things, of events too immense to keep to oneself, and so they were quietly shared from soul to soul, one Afterlight to another, until every Afterlight in Everlost had heard them.

There was the rumor of a beautiful sky witch, who soared across the heavens in a great silver balloon. And there were whispers of a terrible ogre made entirely of chocolate, who lured unsuspecting souls with that rich promising smell, only to cast them down a bottomless pit from which there was no return.

In a world where memories bleach clean from the fabric of time, rumors become more important than that which is actually known. They are the life's blood of the bloodless world that lies between life and death.

On a day much like any other in Everlost, one boy was about to find out if those rumors were true.

His name is unimportant—so unimportant that he himself had forgotten it—and less important still, because in a brief time he will be gone forever.

He had died about two years earlier, and, having lost his way to the light, he slept for nine months, then had woken up in Everlost. The boy was a wanderer, solitary and silent, hiding from others who crossed his path, for fear of what they might do to him. Without camaraderie and friendship to remind him who he was, he forgot his identity more quickly than most.

On the occasions that he did come across packs of other Afterlight kids, he would listen to them from his hiding spot as they shared with each other the rumors of monsters, so he knew as well as any other Afterlight what lay in store for the unwary.

When the boy had first crossed into Everlost, his wanderings had a purpose. He had begun in search of answers, but now he had even forgotten the questions. All that remained was an urge to keep moving, resting only when he came across a deadspot—a solid, bright patch of earth that had, like him, crossed into Everlost. He had learned very quickly that deadspots were unlike the faded, unfocused world of the living, where every footfall pulled you ankle-deep, and threatened to take you all the way down to the center of the earth if you stood still for too long.

On this day, his wanderings had brought him to a field full of deadspots—he had never seen so many in one place . . . but what really caught his attention was the bucket of popcorn. It just sat there on a deadspot, beside a huge Everlost tree, like it had no better place to be.

Somehow, the popcorn had crossed over!

The dead boy had not had the luxury of food since

arriving in Everlost—and just because he didn't need to eat anymore, it didn't mean the cravings ended—so how could he resist that popcorn? It was the largest size, too—the kind you order with big eyes in the movie theater, but can never finish. Even now the corn inside glistened with butter. It seemed too good to be true!

Turns out, it was.

As he stepped onto the deadspot and reached for the tub, he felt a trip wire against his ankle, and in an instant a net pulled up around him, lifting him off the ground. Only after he was fully snared within the net did he realize his mistake.

He had heard of the monster that called itself the McGill, and his soul traps—but he had also heard that the McGill had traveled far away, and was now wreaking fresh havoc across the Atlantic Ocean. So then, who had set this trap? And why?

He struggled to free himself, but it was no use—his only consolation was that the bucket of popcorn was trapped in the net with him, and although half of its contents had spilled onto the ground, half still remained. He savored every single kernel, and when he was done, he waited, and he waited. Day became night, became day over and over, until he lost track of time, and he began to fear that his eternity would be spent strung up in this net. . . . Until he finally heard a faint droning sound—some sort of engine approaching from the north. The sound was echoed from the south—but then, as both sounds grew louder, he realized it wasn't an echo at all. The sounds were different. He was being approached on two sides.

Were these other Afterlights coming for him, or were they monsters? Would he be freed, or would he become the victim of fresh havoc himself? The faint memory of a heart pounded in his ghostly chest, and as the whine of engines grew louder, he waited to see who would reach him first.

# CHAPTER 2

## *The View on High*

M iss Mary, one of our lookouts spotted a trap that's sprung."

"Excellent news! Tell Speedo to bring us down close, but not too close—we don't want to frighten our new friend."

Mary Hightower was in her element this far from the ground. Not so high as the living flew, where even the clouds were so far below, they seemed painted on the earth, but here, in that gap between earth and the heavens, is where she felt at home. She was queen of the *Hindenburg*, and she liked that just fine. The massive silver airship—the largest zeppelin ever built—had gone up in a ball of flames way back in 1937, leaving the living world and crossing into Everlost. Mary, who believed all things happened for a reason, knew why it had exploded: It had crossed into Everlost for her.

The Starboard Promenade, which ran the full length of the passenger compartment, was her plush personal retreat, and her center of operations. Its downward-slanted windows gave her a dramatic view of the ground below: the washed-out hues of the living world, speckled with features both man-made and natural that stood out more boldly than the rest. Those were the places that had crossed into Everlost. Trees and fields, buildings and roads. While Afterlights could still see the living world, it was blurred and faded. Only things and places that had crossed into Everlost appeared bright and in sharp focus. Mary estimated that one in a hundred things that died or were destroyed crossed into Everlost. The universe was very selective in what it chose to keep.

Only now, as she spent her days riding the skies, did she realize she had stayed put for way too long. She had missed so much up in her towers—but then the towers were a citadel against her brother, Mikey—the monster who called himself the McGill. Mikey had been defeated. He was harmless now. And now Mary no longer had to wait for Afterlights to find her. She could go out and find them herself.

"Why are you always looking out of those windows?" Speedo would ask her, when he took a break from piloting the airship. "What do you see?"

"A world of ghosts," she would tell him. Speedo had no idea that the ghosts she spoke of were the so-called living. How insubstantial that world was. Nothing in it lasted, not places, not people. It was a world full of pointless pursuits that always ended the same way. A tunnel, and surrender. *Well, not always,* she thought happily. *Not for everyone.*

"I'd still rather be alive," Speedo would say whenever she spoke of how blessed they were to be here in Everlost.

"If I had lived," Mary would remind him, "I'd be long dead by now . . . and you'd probably be a fat, bald accountant."

Then Speedo would look at his slight physique, dripping wet—always dripping wet in the bathing suit he died in—to reassure himself that he'd never have grown fat and bald, had he lived. But Mary knew better. Adulthood can do the most horrific things to the best of people. Mary much preferred being fifteen forever.

Mary took a moment to gather herself and prepare to greet the new arrival. She would do it personally. It was her way, and it was the least she could do. She would be the first out of the ship—a slender figure in a plush green velvet dress, and with a perfect fall of copper hair, descending the ramp from the impossibly huge hydrogen airship. This is how it was done. With class, with style. The personal touch. All new arrivals would know from the first moment they met her that she loved each and every child in her care and they were safe under her capable protection.

As she left the Starboard Promenade, she passed other children in the common areas of the ship. She had collected forty-seven of them. In her days at the towers, there had been many, many more—but Nick had taken them from her. He had betrayed her, handing each of her children the key to their own undoing. He had placed a coin in each of their hands. The coins! Those horrid little reminders that a true death did await all of them if they were foolish enough to seek it—and just because there was a light at the end of the tunnel, it didn't mean it was something to be desired. Not the way Mary saw it. Heaven might shine bright, but so do flames.

As the ship descended, Mary went to the control car— the ship's bridge which hung from the belly of the giant craft. From there she would have the best view as they descended.

"We should touch down in a few minutes," Speedo told her, as he intently piloted the sleek silver beast. He was one of the few Afterlights to refuse to take a coin on the day Nick betrayed her. That had earned him a special place. A position of trust and responsibility.

"Look at that field." Speedo pointed it out. "Do you see all those deadspots?"

From the air it looked like a hundred random polka dots on the ground.

"There must have been a battle here once," Mary suggested. "Perhaps the Revolutionary War."

There was one Everlost tree, standing on its own deadspot. "The trap is in that tree," Speedo told her as they neared the ground.

It was a grand tree, its leaves full of rich reds and yellows, set apart from the greener summertime trees of the living world. For this tree it would always be the early days of fall, but the leaves would never drop from its branches. Mary wondered what had caused it to cross over. Perhaps lovers had carved their initials in it, and then it was struck by lightning. Perhaps it was planted in someone's memory, but was then cut down. Or maybe it simply soaked up the blood of a fallen soldier, and died years later in a drought. For whatever reason, the tree didn't die entirely. Instead it crossed into Everlost, like so many things that the universe saw fit to preserve.

The foliage of the tree was so dense, they couldn't see the trap, even after they had touched down.

"I'll go first," Mary said. "But I'd like you to come too. I'll need you to free our new friend from the net."

"Of course, Miss Mary." Speedo smiled a smile that was slightly too large for his face.

The ramp was lowered, and Mary stepped from the airship to the earth, keeping the grace of her stride even as her feet sank almost to her ankles in the living world with each step.

But as she got closer to the tree, she saw that something was terribly, terribly wrong. The net had been taken down, and there was no Afterlight inside. All that remained was the empty popcorn tub on the ground—the bait she had left, just as her brother used to—but while the McGill offered his captives slavery, Mary offered them freedom. Or at least her definition of it. But there was no Afterlight in the net to receive her gift today.

"Musta gotten out," Speedo said as he came up behind her.

Mary shook her head. "No one gets out of these nets."

And then a scent came to her from the tree. It was a sweet, heady aroma that filled her with a rich blend of love, swirled with loathing.

The aroma was coming from a brown handprint on the trunk of the tree. A handprint left there to mock her.

"Is that dried blood?" Speedo asked.

"No," she told him, maintaining her poise in spite of the fury that raged within her. "It's chocolate."

In her book *Caution, This Means You*, Mary Hightower says the following about the "evils" of the chocolate one: "Wise Afterlights would do well to heed the many warnings relating to the creature known as the Chocolate Ogre. He is a force of chaos and distress in this world. Indeed, Everlost itself shakes in fury at his terrible misdeeds. If there is justice in this world—and I believe there most certainly is—he will be held accountable when he meets his maker. Should the ogre be seen anywhere near your vicinity, it is best to seek shelter, and immediately report his presence to an authority."

By "authority," one can only assume that Mary means herself.

# CHAPTER 3

## Audience with an Ogre

It was an old steam engine, forged and destroyed in the nineteenth century, but so well-loved by its conductor that it earned a place in Everlost. Of course it could travel only on tracks that no longer existed. Such were the inconveniences of life after life.

A kid with hands much too large for his body, and with a cigarette that never went out dangling from his lip, had freed the boy from Mary's net. Now he gripped the kid's arm a little too hard as he moved him through fields and woods toward the waiting train.

"Whose train is it?" The boy asked in a panic, "What's gonna happen to me?"

"Don't ask stupid questions," said the kid with big hands, "or I'll send you down soon as look at you, I swear I will." Then he pushed the boy up the steps and into a parlor car.

The smell hit him right away.

"Oh, no! No!"

As wonderful as that chocolate smell was, it could

only mean one thing. The rumors were true, and he was doomed.

At the other end of the car sat a figure wearing a tie and a white shirt, although the shirt had become stained with countless brown smudges. So was the rich red carpet. So were the red velvet chairs.

"Don't be afraid," the Chocolate Ogre said—which was always what monsters said when you really should be afraid.

Light poured in from the windows into the frightened boy's eyes, so he couldn't see the face of the ogre clearly, but then the ogre stood and came into the light. All at once everything became clear.

It was as if someone had dipped the entire left half of his face in a fudge bucket. It seemed to ooze right out of his pores—even the color of his left eye had gone chocolate-brown. It was the other half of his face that was the more surprising, for that half did not look monstrous at all. In fact the right side of his face looked like that of an ordinary fifteen-year-old boy.

"Let me go," the terrified Afterlight begged. "I'll do anything you want, just let me go."

"I will," said the Chocolate Ogre. "Even better than letting you go, I'll send you on your way."

That did not sound good, and the boy waited for the bottomless pit to open beneath his feet. But that didn't happen.

"What's your name?" the ogre asked.

It was something the boy had not thought about for a long time. "I'm . . . *me*."

The Chocolate Ogre nodded. "You can't remember. That's okay." Then the ogre held out his hand to shake. "I'm Nick."

The boy looked at the ogre's hand, and didn't know how to respond. It was much cleaner than the other one, which was totally covered in chocolate—but still even his "clean" hand had plenty of stains, probably from touching all the other chocolate-splattered things on the train.

"What's the matter? You didn't expect the 'Chocolate Ogre,' to actually have a name?" His smile made chocolate drip from his cheek and to the darkly stained carpet.

Then the big-handed kid, still standing behind the boy, nudged his shoulder hard. "Shake his hand—you're being rude!"

The boy did as he was told—he shook the ogre's hand, and when he brought his hand back, there was chocolate on it. Even in his fear, that chocolate on his hand looked better to him than the popcorn had.

As if reading his mind, the ogre said, "Go ahead—it's real, and it's just as good as when you were alive."

And although the boy sensed this was a trick—that maybe it was somehow poisoned, or worse—he raised his fingers to his lips, and licked the chocolate off. The ogre was right—it was real and it was good.

The ogre pointed to his face. "The only good thing about it is that I get to share."

"And it's milk chocolate today," said the kid with big hands. "You must be in a good mood."

The Chocolate Ogre shrugged. "Any day I save some-one from Mary is a good day."

This monster was being far too friendly. The boy would have much preferred a fiery temper. At least then he would have known exactly where he stood.

"What are you going to do to me?" he asked.

"I'm not going to do anything. The question is, what are *you* going to do?" He folded his arms. "You crossed over with a coin. Do you remember what happened to it?"

The boy shrugged. "It was just a slug," he said. "I threw it away."

Then the Chocolate Ogre reached into a rusty gray bucket. "Hmm . . . looks like I found it." He pulled a coin out of the bucket and held it out to the boy. "Take it." And when he hesitated, the big-handed kid behind him nudged him again.

The boy took the coin. It did look much like the slug he had tossed when he first arrived.

"Tell me how it feels in your hand," the ogre said.

"It feels warm."

The ogre smiled. "Good. Very good. Now you have a choice. You can keep holding it in your hand . . . or you can put it into your pocket, and save it for another time."

"What happens if I hold it?"

"I really don't know. Maybe you can tell me."

And although the boy had not been this frightened since his first days in Everlost, there was a certain comfort coming from the coin itself. It filled his hand with a relaxing warmth—a sense of peace that was already radiating from his hand to his arm, to his entire spirit. His afterglow—the faint aura of light that every Afterlight radiated—seemed to grow brighter.

Before he could change his mind, he closed his fist on the coin which grew ever warmer in his hand, and in a moment, space itself seemed to split before him, revealing a tunnel. Its walls were blacker than black, but at some impossible distance ahead was a light, as bright as the walls were dark. Why, this wasn't a bottomless pit at all! He had seen this before! Yes! He had seen it the very moment he —

"—Jason!" he shouted joyfully. "My name is Jason!"

The ogre nodded. "Have a safe trip, Jason."

He wanted to thank the Chocolate Ogre, but he found he was already too far away, shooting down the tunnel, finally on his way to where he was going.

A rainbow sparkling of light, a shimmer in the air like heat on a summer road, and the boy was gone.

"They never tell what they see," complained Johnnie-O, cracking his oversized knuckles. "You'd think at least one of them would."

"If you really want to know what they see," said Nick, "then take a coin yourself."

Johnnie-O shifted his shoulders uncomfortably. "Naah," he said, "I'm not done makin' your life miserable."

Nick had to laugh. With all of Johnnie-O's tough-guy attitude, he had turned out to be a solid friend. Of course it hadn't started that way. Johnnie-O was none too happy when Nick showed up with his magic bucket of coins. That bucket, like the fortune cookies, like the coins themselves, was a gift from the unknown places beyond the tunnel — because the bucket was never empty as long as there was a soul who needed a coin. Nick thought he'd have to search far and wide for those coins, and the fact that the bucket would refill itself the moment no one was looking was a sign to Nick that he was doing the right thing.

Johnnie-O had watched as every member of his gang took a coin, and completed their journey out of Everlost. Why Johnnie-O didn't use his own coin is something only he could know—Nick never asked him why—such a decision was too personal to ever question.

*"I'll send you down!"* Johnnie-O had screamed the day his gang took their coins and disappeared. *"Even if I gotta go down to the center of the earth with you, I'll send you down!"* And he had almost done it too. He and Nick had fought and struggled until both were chest deep in the earth. But when Johnnie-O realized he really would go down along with Nick, he backed off, pulled himself out, and let Nick pull himself out as well.

Nick liked to think that, in the end, Johnnie-O realized that giving those kids a ticket out of Everlost was the right thing to do. Nick liked to think Johnnie-O respected him for it. Of course Johnnie-O would never admit that aloud, but the fact that he stayed with Nick, and helped him in his own intimidating way, was proof enough for Nick.

With the boy dispatched to his destination, Nick went up to the train's engine, where a nine-year-old who called himself Choo-choo Charlie stoked the boiler and studied a map that he had drawn himself. Aside from Charlie's map, no one had ever made a record of Everlost's rail lines.

"D'ya think Mary would put my map in one of her books?" Charlie asked.

"Mary won't put anything in her books that doesn't help

Mary," Nick told him. "You'd probably have to draw a map where all roads lead to *her*."

Charlie laughed. "Most of 'em kinda do," he said. "She's got her fingers in everything." Then he got a little quiet. A little scared, maybe. "D'ya think she knows I'm helping you?"

"She'll forgive you," Nick said. "She prides herself on how forgiving she is. She'd even forgive me if I gave up my 'evil ways.' Anyway, you're not 'helping me'—I've hired you, and business is business, right?"

Then Nick handed Charlie a mug full of chocolate. Payment for his services.

"Someday I'm gonna get tired of this stuff," Charlie warned.

"Well," said Nick, "it's all I've got to give."

Charlie shrugged it off. "No worries. I can always trade it for something else."

He was right about that. As awful as Nick's affliction was, in Everlost dripping chocolate was like dripping gold. It was his bad luck to die at fourteen with a chocolate smudge on his face, and as he forgot more and more of his life on earth, that little smudge spread. *In Everlost, we are what we remember,* Mary had once told him. So why did he have to remember that stupid chocolate stain?

Allie—who had died in the same accident as Nick— had never laughed at Nick because of it. And when other kids in Mary's domain had taken to calling him "Hershey," she helped him fight to keep his memories and his name. The thought of Allie saddened him. They had arrived here together, and had journeyed through Everlost together. He had always felt that their fates were somehow intertwined, but they had both gone their separate ways, and Nick never even had the chance to say good-bye. No doubt Allie finally made her way home to find what became of her family. He wondered if she ever took hold of her coin, and completed her journey. He hoped she had, but another, more selfish side of himself hoped that she remained here in Everlost, so he might see her again someday.

"Look," said Charlie, "Mary's already leaving."

Sure enough, Nick could see the *Hindenburg* in the distance, rising up to the sky.

"I should have stayed there by that tree," Nick said. "Then she'd have to face me."

"Wouldn't work," said Johnnie-O. "If she saw you there, she'd never get out of that ship."

Johnnie-O was, right, of course. Still, Nick longed for the moment they came face-to-face. It wasn't just about seeing her frustration—it was about seeing *her*. Being close to her again. In spite of everything, he still loved her. It made no sense to Charlie or Johnnie-O, but it made perfect sense to Nick, because he understood Mary more than she understood herself. She was a victim of her own righteous nature—a slave to the order she tried to impose on Everlost. If he could, Nick would open her eyes to the truth of it, making her see that she was creating far more harm than good. Then, he would be there to comfort her in that moment of revelation, when all she believed about herself crumbled before her. Once she understood what was *truly* right, Nick had to believe she would embrace it, and together they would free as many souls from Everlost as they could.

This was the Mary he loved. The Mary that *could* be.

Each time Nick arrived at one of her traps, and freed one of her snagged souls, he hoped for that moment of confrontation, where her anger would be undermined by the love he knew she felt for him. But she never came forward to face him. Instead, Mary always left without affording him the dignity of a proper slap in the face.

"She's heading northwest," Charlie said. "D'ya want to follow her again?"

"Where are we?" Nick asked.

Charlie looked at his map. "Somewhere in Virginia. East of Richmond."

This was the farthest south they'd ever been—but there were Afterlights who Nick had come across, who spoke of things even farther south than this. Rumors. Things that could not be believed in the living world, but in Everlost, anything was possible. So Mary would not face him—and now he suspected she never would without a full-out war. There was no question her soul traps were all about gathering up an army. *Fine, Mary,* thought Nick. *If that's what you want, then I'll play.*

"Head south."

Charlie shook his head. "Can't. I haven't charted any tracks south of Virginia. Why d'ya wanna go south anyway? Nothing there but the Everwild."

Nick grunted in frustration at the mention of it. "That's all I ever hear! Everwild to the north, Everwild to the west, Everwild to the south—"

"Hey, it's not my fault no one knows what's out there!"

"And to the Afterlights there, *we're* in the Everwild."

Perhaps the living world had finally connected coast-to-coast and around the world, but Everlost was a new frontier. It was just like the days when America was still the New World, and no one knew what breathtaking vistas and unforeseen dangers lay over the next ridge. Perhaps the unknown wouldn't have been so daunting if they had an entire crew—but unlike Mary, Nick hadn't been interested in collecting followers. His job was to get rid of them, which made it hard to maintain more than just the barest of skeleton crews—namely, himself, Charlie, and Johnnie-O. It was time to change all that.

"Come on, Charlie—let's tame the Everwild! We'll chart the rails, and mark the deadspots on the way!"

And although Charlie was reluctant to travel to places unknown, Nick knew he was tempted. There was a certain excitement in breaking away from the familiar, and shattering old routines.

"We'll need to look for a finder who can trade us the paper we'll need to make a new map," said Charlie, "but until then I can scratch the map into the engine bulkhead."

Nick slapped him on the back, leaving an accidental chocolate stain. "Let's get started, then. We'll get to the southern Afterlights before Mary can!"

With the furnace blazing on the memory of coal, the steam engine headed south into a vast unknowable wild.

# CHAPTER 4

## *The Outcast*

O n a warm June afternoon, two finders came to a small-town diner that had burned down many years before. The living world had paved over the spot, and turned it into a parking lot for the bank next door, but in Everlost, the diner remained, its chrome siding shining in the afternoon sun. It was the only building in town that had crossed, and so had become a home to about a dozen Afterlights.

The finders, a boy and a girl, arrived riding a horse. This was unheard of. Well, not entirely unheard of. There were stories about one finder in particular who traveled on the only horse ever known to have crossed into Everlost — and it was said she did travel with a companion, although he never played into the stories much.

As the kids stepped out of the diner, they kept their distance, wanting to, but also afraid to believe that this could be the finder of legend. The cluster of Afterlights were young — and the oldest girl from the diner (who, not surprisingly called herself "Dinah") was their leader. She was ten when she had died, and the thing she remembered about herself more than anything else was that she had long, luxurious hair — so now it trailed behind her like a smooth amber bridal train.

It had been a while since finders had come to town, and their arrival always began with hope, and ended with disappointment. Finders were endlessly searching out objects that crossed into Everlost, bartering and trading the items they found for things of greater value. But nothing much crossed here. The finders usually left with a sneer and didn't come back.

"Sorry," Dinah said to the two, as they got off their horse. "We don't have much to trade. Just this." And she held out a shoelace.

The boy laughed. "The lace crossed, but not the shoe that went with it?"

Dinah shrugged. She expected this reaction. "It's what we've got. If you want it, then give us something in return. If not, then leave." She looked over at the girl, daring to ask what the younger kids in her care were too afraid to ask. "You have a name?"

The girl smiled. "If you want my name, it'll cost you a shoelace."

Dinah pulled the shoelace back, shoving it in her pocket. "A name's not even worth that much here. It's probably made up anyway, like everyone else's."

The girl finder grinned again. "I think I have something to trade for the lace." Then she reached into a saddlebag and pulled out a shimmering ornament that said *Baby's first Christmas*.

All the younger kids oohed and ahhed, but Dinah kept

her stony expression. "That's worth more than a shoelace. And finders don't just give things away."

"Consider it a gift of good will," the girl said, "from Allie the Outcast."

This was the moment Allie loved most. The gasps, and the expressions on their faces. Some would believe she was who she claimed to be, others would have their doubts, but by the time she left, they would all believe—because it was true, and she liked to believe that truth did make itself clear in the end.

The young Afterlights, who had been so standoffish just a moment ago, now crowded around her, bombarding her with questions.

"You're Allie the Outcast?"

"Is it true you can skinjack?"

"Is it true you spit in the face of the Sky Witch?"

"Is it true you charmed the McGill like a snake?"

She glanced at Mikey, who was not at all amused.

"I admit nothing," Allie said with a smirk, which just made them believe it all the more.

Dinah, however was only partially convinced. "All right, if you are who you say you are, then let's see you skinjack." The kids all voiced their nervous approval of the suggestion. "Go on—there's plenty of *fleshies* around." Allie looked around them, and sure enough the moving blurs of the living swept by them on the street, so easy to tune out when one wasn't looking.

"I'm not a circus act," Allie said sternly. "I don't perform on command."

Dinah backed off, then turned her eyes to the other half of the team. "So if she's Allie the Outcast, who are you?"

"My name's Mikey."

Dinah laughed. "Not much of a name for a finder."

"Fine," he said, clenching his fists by his side. "Then I'm the McGill."

But that just made all the other kids laugh too, and Mikey, who had a low threshold when it came to being mocked, stormed away.

Allie still held the ornament out to Dinah, but she didn't accept it. A small boy that had been hiding in Dinah's long trailing hair peered out.

"Please, Dinah . . . can't we keep it?" But Dinah shushed him.

"Do other finders come this way?" Allie asked.

Dinah paused purposefully before answering, perhaps to make it clear that she was in control of the conversation. "Sometimes."

"Well, I'll give you this ornament," Allie said, "if you promise to save all your really good finds for me."

"We promise, Allie," all the little kids said. "We promise." Dinah nodded, reluctantly giving in to the wishes of the others, and took the ornament from Allie.

"You also have to promise one more thing."

Dinah's face hardened. Allie could tell by that look on her face that although she appeared to be no older than ten, she was an old, old soul. "What do I have to promise?"

"That if Mary the Sky Witch ever darkens the sky with her great balloon, you'll hide, and you won't let her take you away."

The kids all looked to Dinah for guidance. "Then who will protect us from the Chocolate Ogre?" Dinah asked. "Who will protect us from the McGill?"

"It looks like you've done a pretty good job yourself," Allie told her. "And besides, there's no reason to fear the McGill or the Chocolate Ogre. Mary's the one you need to worry about."

They all nodded but seemed unconvinced—after all *she* was the Outcast. No matter how starstruck they might be, Allie's advice was suspect.

Dinah gave the ornament to one of the other children. "Hang it on the coatrack," she told him. "It's the closest thing we have to a Christmas tree." Then she turned back to Allie. "We'll keep our promise; we'll save the best finds for you."

It was a satisfactory business deal. She had won the loyalty of many groups of Afterlights. No—not groups—*vapors*, she thought, with a bitter little shake of the head. In one of Mary's annoying little etiquette books, she had insisted that a gathering of Afterlights was properly referred to as "a vapor." A flock of birds, a gaggle of geese, and a vapor of Afterlights. It irritated Allie no end that Mary so effectively determined the language they all used. Allie wouldn't have been surprised if Mary herself had coined the name "Everlost."

Allie found Mikey a street away, stomping on a huge lawn, watching the ripples it created in the living world. He seemed embarrassed to be caught doing something so childlike. Allie tried to hide her smile, because she knew it would embarrass him even more.

"Are we done here?" Mikey asked.

"Yes. Where to next?" Allie made room for him on the horse—letting him ride in front of her, holding the reins. In so many other ways he had taken a backseat to her, the least she could do was allow him the dignity of deciding where their travels would take them.

"I have an idea where we should go," Mikey said. "It's not too far from here."

Allie had learned that being a finder was mostly about luck, and keen skills of observation. Some finders were hearse-chasers. That is to say, they lingered around the dying, hoping they might drop something in Everlost while crossing to the other side. But the best finds were always made quite by accident, and the best trades were made by being shrewd but honest. Even now the horse's makeshift saddlebag was full of crossed items—a crystal doorknob, an empty picture frame, a well-worn teddy bear. In Everlost all these things were treasures.

But locating and trading crossed objects was only part of a finder's job. Their real mystique came from their stories—because while most Afterlights stayed put, finders traveled. They saw more, heard more than others, and spread the tales wherever they went. This is exactly the reason why Allie had decided to become one. When Allie first arrived in Everlost, she had heard tales of monsters and miracles, terror and salvation—but now she had some measure of control over the tales being told. She could spread the word that Mary was the real monster of Everlost and try to set people straight about Nick.

A chocolate ogre? Hah! Nick didn't have an ogreish bone in his body, so to speak. The problem was, Mary was far better at spreading her misinformation. It was much easier for other Afterlights to believe that beauty and virtue went hand in hand.

However, tales of Allie the Outcast were being spread far and wide too. Not all of them were true, of course, but she was developing quite a reputation as Everlost's loose cannon. That got her a certain amount of respect. She could grow used to that.

In fact, she already had.

Cape May: population 4034 in winter, and at least ten times that in the summer. It's the farthest south you can go in New Jersey. Everything after that is water.

Allie stood in front of the town's quaint WELCOME sign, frozen by the sight of it.

"You're sinking," said Mikey, who was still on the horse. Shiloh the horse, having grown accustomed to the strange texture of the living world, kept pulling its hooves out of the ground with a sucking sound, as if it were slowly prancing in place. Allie on the other hand, was already in the ground to her knees.

She reached up, and Mikey helped her out of the ground. "That's it, isn't it?" Mikey asked. "Cape May? I remember you said you lived in Cape May."

"Yes." With all their wanderings, Allie had lost her sense of direction. She had no idea they were this close to her home.

"It's what you wanted, isn't it? To go home?"

"Yes . . . from the very beginning."

Mikey hopped off the horse and stood beside her. "Back

on my ship, I used to watch you look out to shore. You had such a longing to go home. You don't know how close I came to taking you there, even then."

Allie smirked. "And you called yourself a monster."

Mikey was suitably insulted. "I was an excellent monster! The one true monster of Everlost!"

"'Hear your name and tremble.'"

Mikey looked away. "No one trembles anymore."

Allie was mad at herself for mocking him. He didn't deserve that. She touched his face gently. To look at him now, you'd never guess that the fair skinned, blue-eyed boy was once the terrifying McGill, but every once in a while Allie could still see a bit of the beast in him. It was there in the shortness of his temper, and the clumsiness of his hands, as if they were still claws. It was there in the way he approached the world—as if it still owed him something. Yes, the monster still lingered there inside him, but his face was that of a boy, attractive by any standards, if somewhat doleful.

"I like you much better this way."

"Why should I care?" But he smiled, because he *did* care and they both knew it.

*"You must teach me to be human again,"* he had told her, when he first lost his monstrous form. Since then, she had done everything in her power to do so. It was in small moments like these that she caught glimpses of his successful steps back from being a monster. How long ago had that been? As is the way in Everlost, the days had blended until there was no telling. Weeks? Months? Years? Certainly not years!

"So," he asked, "does bringing you home make me more human?"

"Yes, it does."

Even his selflessness was wrapped in self-interest. It would have bothered her, but she knew that he would have done this for her anyway, even if it had no benefit for him. It made him different from his sister, for while Mary pretended to serve others, deep down she was serving no one but herself.

"Just remember—I can't help you if you sink," Mikey said. "You know how it is when you go home—you'll be sinking too fast for me to ever catch you."

"I know." She was well aware of the dangers of going home—not just because of Mary's *Everlost-for-idiots* warnings, but because of Mikey's firsthand account.

Home, he had told her, had a certain gravity to an Afterlight. The ground becomes more and more like quicksand the closer to home one gets. Mikey had told Allie how he and his sister had gone home more than a hundred years ago, shortly after they died. The moment he saw how life had gone on without them, Mikey sunk into the ground in a matter of seconds. Mary had been lucky—somehow she had avoided his fate. She never had to endure that long, slow journey down to the center of the earth.

Mikey, however, had discovered a skill—perhaps the rarest of all Everlost skills. His will was so great that he could force change upon himself—his hands turned to claws, tugging at the earth around him. His memory of flesh was replaced by a full body scar, thick as leather and as pocked as the surface of the moon. He made himself a monster, and as a monster he could rise, fighting the relentless pull of gravity year after year, until the day he broke surface.

But that was all over now. He was Mikey again, and he was slowly growing used to his old self, just as Allie was growing accustomed to Everlost.

Yet through all of their travels, in the back of her mind, Allie knew she had business left undone. Going home had been so important to her when she had first arrived here. But somewhere along the line, it became something best saved for tomorrow, and then the tomorrow after that—but unlike other Afterlights, she did not forget her life on Earth. She did not forget her family, she did not forget her name.

She didn't know why she should be different from others. Not even Mary wrote about such things in her books of questionable information. But then, Allie had powers that other Afterlights didn't possess. Why she and no one else should have these powers was a mystery to her as well. Allie could skinjack. The living might call it "possession," but she much preferred the Everlost term—for she was not a demon taking control of a human being for evil purposes. She merely "borrowed" people, wearing their bodies for a short time—and only when absolutely necessary.

They made their way down the quaint main street of Cape May. The living went about their blurred, muffled business. Cars passed through Allie and Mikey, but they had grown accustomed to the flow of the living world through and around them so they barely noticed it anymore. Not even their horse did.

"Turn left here," Allie told Mikey at the next corner, and as they turned onto the street where she once lived, a sense of dread began to fill that place that ought to be filled with great joy and anticipation. . . .

. . . For what if her father hadn't survived the crash after all?

What if he went down that tunnel into the light in that terrible head-on collision, leaving her mother and sister to mourn for both of them?

"Are you okay?" Mikey knew something was wrong. Perhaps it was the way she sat so stiffly on the horse behind him, or perhaps their spirits had become so in tune, he could sense the things she felt.

"I'm fine."

She also had another reason for her reluctance, and her mind was drawn to her coin. It had been cold in her hand, which meant she was not ready to leave Everlost. She was not ready to move on. Now, as she thought about it, she realized why. She would never be ready for that final journey until she went home, and saw the truth with her own eyes. Her whole Everlost existence had been leading to this—and yet she had stalled for as long as she could.

Because going home meant completion.

Once she learned what had become of her parents, there would be nothing holding her to Everlost. Her coin would grow warm, and although she could resist it at first, she knew she wouldn't be able to resist it for long. She would hold it in her hand, she would make the journey.

And she would lose Mikey.

For this reason, her return to Cape May was both something she longed for, and something she dreaded—but she would not share such private feelings with Mikey.

When they stood on her street, a pang came to her chest. She knew she shouldn't be able to feel pain, but sometimes emotions could coalesce into phantom aches when they were strong enough.

"There it is," she said. "The third house on the right."

Home. Even in the faded tones of Everlost, it looked just the same as she remembered. An unassuming Victorian house, white with blue trim. Her parents had moved to Cape May to capture some rustic charm in a modern world, so they bought an old house with plumbing that rattled, and thin wiring that could never quite grasp the concept of computers and high-voltage appliances. Circuit breakers were constantly popping, and Allie had complained endlessly about it when she was alive. Now she longed for the simple act of turning on a hair drier and plunging the house into darkness.

"Wait here," she told Mikey. "I need to do this alone."

"Fair enough."

She hopped down from the horse, already feeling an uncertainty in the ground beneath her. It felt less like tar, and more like Jell-O just before it sets. She had to move fast.

"Good luck," Mikey said.

She crossed the street toward her home, not looking back at Mikey for fear that she might change her mind—but rushing headlong to her front door was not wise either. With the threat of sinking so very real, she needed someone who could carry her home safely.

Someone like the UPS man.

The brown truck turned onto the street, and stopped at a neighbor's house. The deliveryman pulled a package from the back of the truck, and carried it toward the neighbor's front door. Allie followed him, preparing to make her move before he rang the neighbor's bell.

Skinjacking was not a pleasant sensation. It was like diving into water that was too cold, or stepping into a tub that was too hot. Even though Allie had gotten much better at it, the sudden sensation of flesh, and all that went with it, was always a shock. She took a moment to brace herself, then she stepped inside the UPS man —

*— Three more hours — I should just quit — I can't quit but I wish I could — three more hours — can't quit — wife would be furious — but there's got to be more work out there — I never should have taken this job — three more hours to go —*

The chill of the air, the pumping of a heart, the sudden brightness—*solidness*—of the living world around her. She was in! The volume of his thoughts was painful—like they were being blasted through a megaphone.

*— Three more hours — but wait — wait — I don't feel right — what's this? Who — huh — what — ?*

Allie quickly clamped her spirit down, taking control of his flesh, and at the same instant she forced his unsuspecting consciousness deep down into the limbic system—that primordial part of the human brain where consciousness retreated during the deepest of sleeps. It was easy to put him to sleep; he wasn't all that conscious to begin with.

She turned back to Mikey, but he was invisible now, as she knew he would be. She was seeing through *living* eyes now, seeing only the things that living eyes could see. As long as she stayed inside the delivery man, Everlost would be hidden from her.

Once the initial shock of the skinjack had faded, she took a moment to enjoy it, luxuriating in the warmth of the sun on this warm June day. Even the heaviness of the package in her arms was a fine thing; yet another memory of the wonderful limitations of being alive.

She lingered at the neighbor's door a moment more, then left, taking the package with her to the front door of her own home. Then she stood at her own front door, frozen, just as she had been frozen at the city sign. This was the moment she had waited for. All she had to do was ring the bell. All she had to do was lift her finger—his finger—and do it. Never had a living hand felt so heavy.

Then, to her surprise, the door opened without her ever ringing the bell.

"Hi, is that package for us?"

The woman who opened the door was not her mother. She was a total stranger. She was in her twenties, and had a baby on her hip, who was very excited by the prospect of a large box.

"Just bring it in, and put it by the stairs," the woman said. "Do I have to sign for it?"

"Uh . . . uh . . . It's not for you." Allie cleared her throat, startled by the way she sounded. She could never get used to the masculine timbre of her voice when she cross-jacked. It was one of several troubling things that came with being temporarily male.

"Well, if it's not for us, then who is it for?"

"The Johnson family."

"Who?" she asked, then realized. "Oh, right. We got

things for them every once in a while, once the forwarding order expired."

They had moved—but that could just be her mother and sister, who weren't in the car. She still had no way of knowing if her father had survived.

"Any idea where they went?"

"No," the woman said.

"Wasn't there an accident?" Allie asked. "I heard about it—they lost a daughter."

"I wouldn't know about that. Sorry."

And then Allie asked the big question. "How long have you been living here?"

"Almost three years now."

Allie closed her eyes, and tried to take that in. She had been in Everlost for three years. Unchanged, never aging. Still fourteen. How could so much time have passed?

"Wait a second," the woman said. "Of course, I can't be sure, but I seem to recall something about Memphis. I think that's where they went."

It made sense—her mother had family there . . . but did that mean her father had died in the crash, and her mother had sold the house? There were so many questions still unanswered.

The woman shifted the baby to her other hip, getting impatient. "The neighbors might know more, but then a lot of them are just summer renters."

"Thank you. Sorry to have bothered you."

Then the woman closed the door, to the protests of the baby, who began to wail over the fact that the box was not for him.

Allie went to other homes on the street, but few neighbors were home, and the ones who did come to the door were clueless.

Allie returned to the UPS truck, took one last breath of the flavorful June air, then pulled herself out of the delivery man. Ending a skinjacking was as unpleasant as beginning one, and sometimes a fleshie who fit too well was hard to escape from—especially when she'd stayed inside for a while. Fortunately the UPS man was not one of those. She was able to extricate herself without too much effort, peeling him off like a loose-fitting robe. She suffered a moment of vertigo, and the instinctive panic of spirit separating from flesh. She endured the transition, and when she opened her eyes, the living world had faded to blurred, washed-out hues. She was back in Everlost. Beside her, the deliveryman stumbled for a moment, quickly shook off his confusion, and went to deliver his package to the proper house, never knowing that he had been skinjacked.

"What happened?" Mikey asked, coming up to her. "Were they there? Did you talk to them?"

"They moved to Memphis," she told him, still a bit dazed by it all.

Mikey sighed. "So . . . I suppose that means we're going to Tennessee."

She offered him an apologetic grin that wasn't all that apologetic. It was disheartening to know that her home was no longer hers, and troubling to have so far to go until she could find out the truth. Yet there was relief in it as well . . . because Memphis was far, far away, and that meant she wouldn't be losing Mikey so quickly! Looking at him now, he seemed taller. Majestic. There was a reason for that.

"You're sinking," Mikey said.

Laughing, Allie reached out to him. He took her hand gently but firmly, and eased her out of the ground.

They left, but as they did, Allie couldn't help but look back toward the deliveryman, who was now heading back to his truck. She couldn't deny how much she enjoyed the lingering sensation of flesh. Each time she skinjacked, it felt more and more seductive.

In her book *Caution, This Means You,* Mary Hightower has this to say about the Everwild:

"Finders who survive excursions into the untamed corners of Everlost tell stories of things strange, mystical, and dangerous. Whether or not these stories of the Everwild are true do not matter to the sensible Afterlight, for all sensible Afterlights know that it's best to leave the wild wild, and the Unknown unknown. Venturing beyond one's personal zone of safety is always ill-advised, and can only end in profound unpleasantness."

It is important to note that Mary wrote this before she, herself, took to the skies.

# CHAPTER 5
## Southern Discomfort

Nick had never seen a city with so many deadspots. They were so numerous that they could hardly be called deadspots at all. The city of Atlanta belonged as much to Everlost as it did to the living world. The streets were part cobblestone, part asphalt, part dirt. The night was lit by just as many gas lamps as modern streetlights. Buildings from multiple time periods seemed to occupy the same space, fighting to claim "dominant reality." It made it very clear to Nick that as much as he thought he knew and understood Everlost, he barely knew anything at all.

Their train slowly, cautiously rolled forward on tracks that once carried the Civil War dead. Then, as the train neared the center of Atlanta, the living world road began to fill the train like an asphalt river.

"We're sinking!" shouted Johnnie-O. "We're sinking into the earth! Stop the train!"

"I don't think that's it," said Charlie. "It's more like the street's rising. We're still riding on tracks."

"I have a feeling we're in for a few more surprises," said Nick.

\* \* \*

Long ago, when the battle between locomotive and automobile came to Atlanta, the city was caught in a dilemma. Atlanta, being the chief railroad city of the south, had so many trains, there was simply no room for cars. Then the city planners had a brilliant idea. The words "brilliant" and "city planning" usually don't go together. However, in this instance, the solution was not only brilliant, it was elegant.

Why not build roads *above* the train tracks?

And so by building automobile viaducts above the central railroad gulch, the city of Atlanta was effectively raised almost twenty feet. The first floor of every building was now underground—and second floors became the new ground floors. Then, as cars took over, and rail lines closed down, those old subterranean storefronts were forgotten. Thus was born underground Atlanta—and although modern business interests have turned parts of it into a mall, the real Atlanta underground belongs to Everlost.

The train rolled down the underground street in near darkness, but then the faint, pale blue glow of Afterlights began to fill the street around them. Afterlights were quite literally coming out of the woodwork—not dozens, but hundreds, and, like the buildings around them, these kids were from every era in history. Some held bricks, others metal pipes or bats—but one thing was clear—every single one of them was armed and prepared for a fight.

"*Sticks and stones can't break my bones,*" said Johnnie-O, reciting the familiar Everlost rhyme.

"*But names can always hurt me,*" finished Nick. True

enough, because an Everlost name can define you, and not always for the better. "It's not the sticks and stones I'm worried about," Nick said. "It's that look in their eyes."

Nick could see the intensity of their stares. It was a look that spoke of first strikes against intruders. These kids had a communal instinct for self-preservation that left no room for compassion.

"If they want a fight, they'll get one," said Johnnie-O.

Charlie looked at him, worried, and Nick gripped Charlie's shoulder to ease his mind, leaving behind a brown handprint. Johnnie-O might think with his fists, but Nick knew better than to provoke a fight here. More and more kids flooded the street around them. Then, when it seemed that every Afterlight in Atlanta had come out of hiding, Nick said, "Stop the train."

Charlie turned to him, and Nick swore that his afterglow grew a little pale. "You're kidding, right?"

"Dead serious."

Charlie gripped the brake lever, but made no move to stop the train, for his fear would not allow it. "But look— they're keeping out of our way. If we just keep moving, we'll make it through, doncha think?"

"Who says I want to make it through?"

Charlie shook his head, as if trying to shake off the thought. "You can't be thinking of giving them all coins! There's not enough in the world!"

But that wasn't true; the bucket was never empty. Still, it wouldn't be a good idea to start making kids disappear. The mob would get confused and frightened. The mob would attack. Nick, however, had another reason for making a pit stop here.

"Trust me," Nick said, although he wasn't really sure he trusted himself. Still, Charlie sighed and pulled on the brake. The steam engine came to a wheezing, shuddering halt.

"Now what?" asked Johnnie-O.

Nick reached for the door. "I'll be right back."

Johnnie-O stepped in front of him. "I'm going with you."

"No . . . . Your hands might scare them."

Johnnie-O smirked. "And your face won't?"

He had a point. "Okay," said Nick, "but you've got to lose that scowl. I want you to smile like an idiot. Can you do that?"

Johnnie-O took a deep breath and smiled like the best of idiots. He did it so well, it was scary. Probably scary enough for the kids outside to throw bricks. So Nick pulled Johnnie-O aside and whispered to him. "Actually, I'm more worried about Charlie panicking. It might be a good idea to keep an eye on him."

The grin left Johnnie-O's face, and he nodded, accepting this new security detail. "On second thought," he said loudly, "maybe I'll stay here and keep my buddy Charlie company."

Charlie seemed relieved to know he wasn't being left alone.

Nick opened the door and stepped down from the engine. Around him the Afterlights of Atlanta backed away, cautious and guarded. He didn't know whether they had heard of the so-called Chocolate Ogre, but even if they hadn't, seeing a face such as his gave him a psychological advantage. A kind of authority of the uncanny.

"Who's in charge here?" Nick asked them.

No one answered right away.

"C'mon—a group this big has to have someone in charge."

There were murmurs in the crowd, and then someone spoke, Nick couldn't be sure who it was. "You mean in charge of *us*, or all Atlanta?"

*Interesting,* thought Nick. That meant that there was some sort of structure here. Maybe even a government.

"When I say in charge, I mean in charge," he answered.

The crowd murmured again, and once the murmurs had died down, Nick said, "I'll be waiting." Then he strode back to the train, and prepared for a meeting with the eminent ruler of Atlanta.

They kept Nick waiting in the parlor car for more than an hour. It could have been intentional, or it simply could have taken that long to retrieve the kid in charge. Nick gave them the benefit of the doubt. The kid who finally climbed into the parlor car was a tall and gangly African-American Afterlight, about sixteen or so. The torn, shabby clothes he wore made Nick wonder if perhaps he had been a slave when he was alive, and yet there was a confidence to his stride that bristled with powerful independence. Whatever this boy had been forced to endure in life, he had certainly risen above it here.

He looked Nick over and said, "What's wrong with your face?"

Apparently stories of the Chocolate Ogre had not reached Atlanta after all. He didn't know whether to be grateful or annoyed. Either way, he didn't feel like answering the question. "Please sit down," he said. "Let's talk."

The Afterlight introduced himself as Isaiah. He didn't offer to shake Nick's hand.

"Tell me about Atlanta," Nick said. "How many of you are there?"

Apparently Nick wasn't the only one reluctant to give answers. Isaiah crossed his arms. "First tell me about your train," he said. "I've never seen an Everlost train before."

"My train is my business."

"Well, maybe it won't be your train anymore."

Nick wasn't sure whether this was an actual threat, or just a show of force. He decided to match Isaiah's confidence measure for measure.

"You won't take my train."

"How can you be sure?"

"Because," said Nick, "if you meant to steal it from me, you would have done it already. Besides, you don't strike me as the type. I think you're honorable. I think that's how you got to be in charge here. You probably overthrew some bully, and had everyone's support, because the kids here trusted you."

Isaiah smiled. "I took down a whole lot of bullies, actually." He didn't let the smile linger for long. "Honorable or not, you're trespassing."

"It's not trespassing if we stop the train, and ask for permission to pass." Isaiah was not impressed, so Nick added. "Besides, I have something you need."

"And what might that be?"

"News of the world," Nick told him. "News from the north."

"I didn't think there *was* a north in Everlost," Isaiah said. "And anyway, whatever happens there don't matter to us."

Nick kept silent, waiting for Isaiah's curiosity to kick in. Finally Isaiah said, "What kind of news."

"Have you heard of Mary, the Sky Witch?"

Isaiah shrugged. "Sure I have—but it's just a story, everyone knows it's not true."

"That's where you're wrong." Then Nick told him everything he knew about Mary. How she had kept hundreds of younger kids from finding the light, and leaving Everlost. How Nick had freed them himself, right under her nose . . . and how she was now gathering more Afterlights to mother, to pamper, to trap. This time, however, he had reason to believe that Mary was building herself an army.

"Did you give them coins?" Isaiah asked. "Is that how you freed them?"

"You know about the coins?"

Isaiah nodded. "We all had them once, but lost them, or tossed them. Most of the kids here don't know what they're for, but some of us do." He became thoughtful for a moment. "I'd like to think we'll find them again. When we're truly ready to move on."

"Maybe there's a whole bucketful waiting for you." And that's all Nick said about it. Something told him that freeing the kids of Atlanta was best left for another day.

"There may come a time when everyone in Everlost will have to take sides," Nick told Isaiah. "Can I count on you if I need you?"

"If there's a side to choose, I'll choose it when the time comes," Isaiah said, keeping a stern poker face. "But right now, you can count on me to let you pass through Atlanta safely."

Nick nodded respectfully. "Thank you."

Isaiah prepared to rise, thinking their meeting of the minds was over—but Nick wasn't quite done.

"One more thing," Nick said. "Because I've heard rumors . . . Maybe you could tell me if they're true."

Isaiah smiled. It was unguarded, uncalculated. It was genuine. "So what would you like to know?"

Nick cleared his throat, and tried to figure the best way to word the question. In the end he decided to just be direct.

"What do you know about 'The Ripper'?"

Isaiah's expression was stony. He took a moment before answering as if he had to control some emotion before allowing himself to speak. "I know what they say about him. Not sure if I believe it all, but I don't want to find out."

"Tell me what they say."

Isaiah gripped the arms of his chair as he spoke. "They call him Zach the Ripper. They say he was a bad seed when he was alive, and even worse afterward. Evil to the core, and dumb as a post. They say he hates the living so much, he reaches into the living world and pulls their hearts right out of their bodies."

"Ecto-ripping!" Nick said, not sure whether he was more amazed or horrified.

"They say he can pull anything out of the living world and into Everlost . . . but that kind of ability, it can make a person crazy."

Nick nodded. He had known a spirit called the Haunter.

Ecto-ripping was just one of his powers. He might have been insane, or simply corrupted by his power from the inside out. Regardless, he was darkly evil, and had imprisoned Nick in a brine-filled barrel, where he might have stayed until the end of time, had things been different. The thought of facing another Afterlight like the Haunter made him shiver.

"There's more," Isaiah said, but then he hesitated, as if he was afraid to even speak it aloud. "People say the Ripper can also reach right inside an Afterlight, and pull stuff out, too. And when he does, the wound doesn't heal . . . and whatever he takes . . . it don't grow back."

"That's impossible." Nick knew enough about Everlost to know Afterlight "flesh" wasn't like living flesh at all. Wounds were bloodless, and zipped closed instantly. "You can't *hurt* an Afterlight."

"Maybe it's just a story," said Isaiah. "But maybe not."

Was Nick crazy to be searching for a spirit such as this? Probably. But on the other hand, Mary was building herself an army, and what did he have? Johnnie-O and Charlie? If he were ever to face Mary again, he would need powerful allies by his side to help balance the odds.

Allies . . . and Allie.

He wondered where Allie was now. Of course he wanted to see her again—but he had also spent a lot of time thinking about her skinjacking skill. What an amazing power that was! And terrifying, too. Or at least it *would* be, in the wrong hands. Thank goodness Allie was a decent girl with a conscience—because her skill could really make a difference in a battle against Mary.

But Nick had to admit, with a heavy heart, that there

was no guarantee he'd ever see Allie again. Which meant he had to find other kids with unique powers to stand against Mary.

"Tell me where to find the Ripper," Nick said to Isaiah.

Isaiah sighed, and told Nick where the Ripper was rumored to be. "Like I said, it may just be a story—no guarantee he'll be there."

Then they shook hands. "I hope to see you again," Nick said.

Isaiah couldn't look him in the eye. "You won't," he said. "Because if you find the Ripper, you're never coming back."

# CHAPTER 6
## *Shuttle Diplomacy*

The tracks ended.

They didn't end at the ghost of some grand terminal—they just stopped. Whoever built them must have ripped them out of the living world even before the rail line was completed. Charlie pulled on the brake just in time, and the train squealed to a reluctant stop, just a dozen yards before the tracks vanished. "Lucky I saw it!" Charlie said. "If we went off the end, this whole train woulda sunk, with us still in it."

Charlie etched the end of the line on the map he was making on the engine bulkhead. "There was a spur that went off west, maybe twenty, thirty miles back. We could back her up and see where that track goes. . . ."

"Maybe later," Nick told him, and turned to Johnnie-O. "We'll walk the rest of the way."

Johnnie-O did not seem pleased. "Rest of the way where?"

Nick didn't answer him. "Charlie, you stay with the train." He thought for a moment, then added, "You'll wait for us, right?"

"Sure . . . unless those Atlanta kids show up."

Nick nodded his understanding, and he and Johnnie-O went south, pushing through dense living-world brush that tickled their insides as they walked.

In time they came to a two-lane highway that ran east and west, cutting through the flat, forested Florida terrain. Nick turned east, and they followed the road, which was easier to walk on than the marshy earth.

"Are you ever gonna tell me where we're going?" Johnnie-O finally asked.

Nick didn't look at him. "We follow this road east until we reach the shore."

"Why?" asked Johnnie-O. "You want me to be your bodyguard and all, then I got a right to know why we're doing this."

"I never said you were my bodyguard. If you don't want to come you don't have to."

"Why can't you just answer the question?"

Nick stopped and turned to him, thinking about how much he should say, if anything. "When did you die?" Nick asked him.

"What's that got to do with anything?"

"It just does."

Johnnie-O looked down, shuffling his feet. "I can't exactly remember."

"What *do* you remember?"

Johnnie took some time to rustle up what memories he could. "When I died, *The Whistler* was my favorite radio show," he said.

*Radio*, thought Nick. That would probably place Johnnie-O in the 1930s, maybe '40s.

"The place we're going is part of my history, but part of your future—and anything I tell you will just make you ask more questions that I don't want to answer."

Nick turned and continued walking.

"I'm really starting not to like you," Johnnie-O said. "Not that I ever liked you to begin with." But still he followed Nick east.

Great tragedies have great consequences. They ripple through the fabric of this world and the next. When the loss is too great for either world to bear, Everlost absorbs the shock, like a cushion between the two.

On a sunny Tuesday—for it seems so many awful things happen on a Tuesday—six astronauts and one schoolteacher attempted to pierce the sky. Instead they touched the stars.

Ask anyone who was alive at the time, and they will still remember where they were the moment they heard that the shuttle *Challenger* blew up just seventy-three seconds after lifting off from Cape Canaveral. The shape of that terrible explosion became burned into human consciousness like the shape of the mushroom cloud over Hiroshima.

The world mourned the lives lost, as well as mourning the loss of an idea, for although space flight had always been, and would always be a dangerous endeavor, there was a certain unspoken faith that human ingenuity, and the grace of God, would keep our ascent to the heavens safe. But the universe is nothing if not balanced. For every *Apollo Thirteen*, there would be a *Challenger*. For every miracle, a tragedy.

But look away now from that fiery forked cloud in the sky, for history cannot be undone. Instead look to the Cape, where you will see a spacecraft pointed eternally heavenward, preserved in Everlost, in that perfect moment of glorious anticipation. Its countdown is forever frozen at one second before liftoff, for that is the last moment a launch can be aborted. It is the moment that stands on the edge of hope and doom.

Seven valiant souls got where they were going that morning, and while eternity opened its gates to welcome them, Everlost opened its gates to welcome the majestic vessel that took them where all men have gone before.

"What is that, some kind of castle?" asked Johnnie-O, looking across the lagoon to the towering marvel.

Nick forgave him his ignorance. What would have been the point in trying to explain this earlier? It was best to let him see it for himself. "It's a spaceship."

"Do you think I'm an idiot?"

Nick didn't push the issue; instead he led them both across the narrow causeway to the Cape—a much longer journey than it looked, and as the massive craft loomed before them, Johnnie-O could no longer deny the truth of what it was.

"So it *is* a spaceship!" And then he looked to Nick, both hopefully and doubtfully. "Can we make it go?"

"I don't think that's a good idea," Nick told him. "Anyway, that's not why we're here." And before Johnnie-O could ask any more questions, Nick said, "What do you know about Zach the Ripper?"

Johnnie-O stopped walking and instantly began to sink, but he didn't seem to care. "You're crazy! You're crazier than Mary and the McGill put together!"

"You're probably right."

"If Zach the Ripper is here, then this is the one place in Everlost I *don't* want to be!"

"So go back," Nick told him simply, and kept moving forward. Johnnie-O pulled his feet out of the ground and followed, grumbling all the way.

Like any other Everlost legend, Nick knew there was no telling how much, if anything, about Zach the Ripper was true, but he knew that dealing with a ripper was dangerous business. Isaiah wasn't the first one to speak of Zach the Ripper's ability to inflict permanent damage on an Afterlight. If you were decapitated by Zach the Ripper, you stayed decapitated, and you'd be stuck having to carry your head around in a backpack, or under your arm, or dangling from the end of your hand by your hair. Whether or not you'd feel the pain of it was unknown — for although Afterlights weren't supposed to feel physical pain, all bets were off when it came to an ecto-ripper.

For this reason, Nick was terrified as he approached the great spacecraft, but he didn't show his fear to Johnnie-O. Johnnie-O was scared enough already. Somewhere in the distance, a stray dog in the living world began to bark, but they both ignored it.

"Look at that thing!" Johnnie-O said, staring at the massive craft. "It's just standing there in midair!"

The orbiter and its rocket assembly were indeed floating about a hundred and fifty feet in the air. Nick knew there had once been a launchpad beneath it, but the shuttle launchpad was on tractor treads, and had long since been rolled away.

"It's resting on the memory of a launchpad," Nick told him.

"Wonder what Mary would have to say about that."

Nick put on his best Mary voice. "*In all things postmortem, the stubbornness of memory outweighs the so-called laws of physics. Best to report any antigravitational sightings to an authority.*"

Johnnie-O stared at him. "You're scary."

A closer inspection of the suspended spacecraft revealed that there was a rickety scaffold right beside it, just a few feet wide, and randomly pieced together. It looked more like a vertical beaver dam, stretching up to the engines, and clinging to the craft itself, all the way up to the orbiter's hatch. There was also something else on the huge deadspot beneath the suspended craft. Something that shouldn't be there at all.

"That's . . . a dog. . . ." said Nick.

"Well, I can see that."

But Johnnie-O didn't quite get it. The dog had been barking nonstop for the past few minutes. Nick was used to tuning out barking dogs, just like most other sounds of the living world. But this dog wasn't part of that world. It was here in Everlost. It was barking at *them*.

The dog was some kind of unholy mismatched genetic mutt. Something like Rottweiler, crossed with Pomeranian. It was both huge and annoying at the same time.

"Wait a second!" said Johnnie-O, one beat behind. "That dog's in Everlost!"

The Pomerrott mutt was chained to a spike in the middle of the deadspot. Which meant someone had to put it there. Johnnie-O still couldn't wrap his mind around it. "But . . .

but, there *are* no dogs here. You know what they say, *'All dogs go to heaven,'* right? Right?"

"Not this one. Maybe dog heaven took one look at it and sent it back."

Just then another sound cut between the Pomerrott's barks. It sounded like a loud snapping twig. Nick realized it was a gunshot the same instant the bullet caught him in the eye. It spun him around and knocked him to the ground. Chocolate splattered the underbrush and the Pomerrott barked like there was no tomorrow.

Johnnie-O screamed and ducked for cover. So much for him being a bodyguard. Not that Nick needed protection from bullets. He pushed himself up on all fours, blinked a few times, and the painless "wound" healed itself closed. In a few moments, his eye returned to normal. He had been caught off guard, that's all—in Everlost, a sniper is little more than a nuisance. Still there's nothing fun about being shot in the eye. He looked at the chocolate splattered around him, and wondered whether it had just splattered off of his face or come from inside when the bullet hit him? Were his insides turning to chocolate as well? He tried not to think about it, because thinking about it too much would make it so.

Johnnie-O, quickly remembering his own relative invulnerability, stood up and looked toward the spacecraft looming before them. "Whoever it is, he's going down!"

Nick stood up, hearing the crack of a second shot. This one caught him square in the chest, but since he was ready, he didn't let it throw him off balance. This time he could hear where the shot had come from. Up high. There was a rifle barrel poking out of the ship's hatch, taking aim for a third shot. Nick waited until the fabric of his tie healed closed before he spoke.

"If you're going to shoot at me," Nick shouted, "at least have the guts to come out where I can see you!"

No response but the barking of the dog. Nick strode forward with Johnnie-O right behind, clenching his fists, ready to pound their assailant into pork and beans. A third shot rang out, but missed both of them. Clearly the shooter was losing focus—maybe getting worried that they might reach the scaffold and climb up—which is exactly what Nick planned to do.

Finally a voice called down to them—the voice of a kid—their age, maybe younger.

"Get outta here! Go on! Nobody wants you here!"

"Nobody?" said Nick. "You mean you're not alone?"

"They's a whole buncha us up here. Yeah! A dozen at least. So go on, get lost a'fore we come down and make ya sorry y'got yerselfs kilt in the first place!"

"Prove it," said Nick. "If it's more than just you, let's hear from one of the others."

The kid was quiet for a moment, then said, "I don't gotta prove nuthin'! I gots the gun and you don't!"

He shot again, and the bullet caught Johnnie-O in the shoulder. Quickly, Johnnie-O reached in and pulled out the bullet before the wound zipped closed, then, holding the bullet between his fingers, yelled up at the unseen sniper. "When I get up there, I'm gonna make you eat this!"

"Yeah? Well I'm gonna make Kudzu eat *you*! Go on, Kudzu. Eat 'em up an' spit their chewed-up pieces down there where the sun don't shine 'cept on Sunday."

The second they reached the deadspot beneath the hanging ship, however, the wild Pomerrott pooch whimpered and retreated as far as its chain would allow. So much for Kudzu. Nick grabbed the scaffold and shook it. It rattled like it might fall apart at any second. The thing was made mostly of chair legs, bicycle tires, and balcony railings—basically anything this kid could tie together with bits of string.

"We'll climb up the left side," Nick said. "He won't be able to get a good angle on us that way. Climbing was rough at first, but they quickly got the hang of it. As they passed the orbiter's massive engines, the kid tried to shoot again, but his bullet ricocheted off a rusty bed frame in the scaffold's infrastructure. The bullet's shell casing dropped from above, bouncing off of Johnnie-O's head. "I've never seen bullets come through into Everlost," Johnnie-O said. "At least not on their own. Do you suppose they were ripped?"

Nick decided to keep his opinion to himself—although he was pretty sure that they had found Zach the Ripper.

One more missed shot, and the ripper closed the hatch, shutting himself in. Nick and Johnnie-O continued to climb, trying not to look down.

"If we fall, we'll just land on the deadspot. We'll be okay," said Nick.

"Yeah . . . unless we miss."

"Maybe we can land on Kudzu," suggested Nick, since the dog had begun barking again.

As they neared the top, the scaffold became thinner and harder to climb, until they finally reached the closed cockpit door. The Ripper showed no signs of coming out.

"We'll force our way in!" said Johnnie-O.

"No. It's an airtight hatch—there's no way to get in from the outside."

"So what are we gonna do?" grunted Johnnie-O. "Just let him sit in there? He'll never come out."

Nick looked up toward the orbiter's viewport, but it was out of view. There was no window on the shuttle that could give the Ripper a view of them.

"Ever watch a turtle that has pulled into its shell?" Nick asked Johnnie-O. "How do you get it to come out again?"

Johnnie-O considered it, and understood what Nick was suggesting. The question was how long could the two of them wait right outside that door? How long could they quietly cling to the scaffold?

While Afterlights tended to develop an unnatural patience for the passage of time, it usually accompanied some pleasurable activity. It could be something as simple as jumping rope, or as complex as a chess marathon; it all depended on the person. However, sitting in absolute silence on the top of a scrap-metal scaffold was enough to drive even the most patient Afterlight stir-crazy. Johnnie-O would occasionally open his mouth to ask a question, or just to complain, but Nick always shushed him before the words were spoken. Eventually Kudzu either forgot they were there, or had decided they were part of the scaffold. Either way, he finally stopped barking.

The sun set. The sun rose. The sun slowly crossed the sky, and by noon the next day, the rifle-toting turtle had not come out of his shell. Nick lost none of his resolve, but Johnnie-O was beginning to suspect that the Ripper had either found a coin and evaporated into the next world, or he had decided he was never coming out of his spaceship again.

Then, late in the afternoon, they heard the clunk of metal on metal, and the small, circular hatch began to open. It only opened an inch—just enough for the Ripper to peer out—but an inch was all they needed. Nick wedged his fingers in the opening.

"Grab it! Hurry!"

The Ripper tried to pull the door closed, but Nick's fingers blocked the way. Johnnie-O gripped the edge of the door and pulled with all his might. The hatch swung wide, and they both dove in, tackling the Ripper, who wouldn't stop cursing.

The shuttle's flight deck was cramped, and filled with hard metallic surfaces. It was all very disorienting in vertical liftoff position, with chairs bolted to the "wall" instead of the floor. Dim light spilled in from the darkly tinted viewport, directly overhead, like a skylight.

"Get out!" screamed the Ripper, "This here is my place! MINE!" He struggled with them, but when he saw the size of Johnnie-O's hands, his eyes went wide, and he scrambled away. In that cramped space, however, there wasn't far he could go.

"We're not going to hurt you!" Nick told him.

"Speak for yourself!" said Johnnie-O, trying to reach around a chair for the Ripper, who continued to shift out of reach.

While Johnnie-O and the Ripper played their little cat and mouse, Nick took a moment to gauge the situation. The

Ripper seemed about thirteen. He wore a gray Confederate Army uniform, complete with that odd little hat. There were weapons strewn around the flight deck that the Ripper kept reaching for, but Johnnie-O kept kicking them out of reach. None of those weapons were Civil War issue. There were very modern, very efficient automatic rifles, pistols, and even a submachine gun, along with countless bullets and loaded magazines. This kid may have died during the Civil War, but now he had an entire arsenal of modern military ordinance.

"Leave me be!" the kid shouted, "or I'll ecto-rip yer arms right outta their sockets!"

"I'd like to see you try!" yelled Johnnie-O, finally getting a grip on him. The ripper tried to pull on Johnnie-O's arms, but they were too muscular. So instead the Ripper did something else—something Nick would not have believed if he hadn't seen it with his own eyes. The Ripper reached right through Johnnie-O's face . . . and pulled out his brain.

Johnnie-O froze with the sudden shock of it, and Nick could only stare in disbelief.

A brain.

Right there in the Ripper's hands.

It was just like Isaiah had said.

It didn't look like a real brain; it looked more like a plastic model, with the various lobes labeled in bold lettering—perhaps something Johnnie-O once saw in a classroom somewhere. This was Johnnie-O's *memory* of a brain, and the ripper now held it in his hand like an oversize walnut.

"Aaaaaaah!" wailed Johnnie-O in the kind of abject terror that can only come from seeing your brain held out before you. "Give it back! Give it back!" Painless though it was, there was something fundamentally disturbing about this—not just the fact of seeing one's own brain held up for observation, but to suddenly have one's very consciousness separate and apart from one's body, and yet still tethered as if by some weird wireless connection. For Johnnie-O, the sensation was far worse than pain.

"AAAAAH!" he screamed. "Put it back in! I swear I won't touch you, just put it back in!"

"Maybe I'll just squish it beneath my feet! Squish, squish!"

"Noooo!"

It infuriated Nick to see Johnnie-O helpless and humiliated, so Nick reached for something that might give them a brief balance of power. He found a hand grenade, and held it up to the Ripper.

"Give him back his brain, or I'll pull the pin, and shove this thing in your mouth."

The Ripper laughed at that. "Won't matter!" he said. "If I gets blowed up, I'll just pull back together again, like it was nuthin'!"

"Yes," Nick said with a grin. "In *theory* . . . "

The wider Nick's grin got, the more worried the Ripper became. "Whadaya mean, *theory*?"

"I mean that bullets and cuts are one thing. They heal in seconds, sure . . . but if you're blown to smithereens, how do you know all those smithereens are gonna find one another again?"

Clearly the Ripper had never thought of this.

"You have till the count of three." Nick reached for the pin, ready to pull it. "One . . . two . . . "

"Fine!" The Ripper went over to Johnnie-O, who was now whimpering in a corner, clutching his intensely empty head. "Who needs it?" said the Ripper. "Probably got worms anyway." Then he pushed Johnnie-O's brain right back inside him.

The Ripper then scrambled over the vertically mounted chairs and reached up toward the spacecraft's control panel—then hit a button.

A hatch popped open like a trapdoor right beneath poor Johnnie-O, who was still just recovering from his brain-ripping ordeal, and he plunged through the open hatch into darkness. Nick could hear him tumbling down a tunnel, and crashing into whatever filled the cargo hold of the shuttle.

"Was that really necessary?" shouted Nick.

"You're next!" threatened the Ripper.

Nick was angry enough to pull the pin on the grenade and blow them both to smithereens, but he fought the urge, found a foothold, and climbed toward the Ripper.

"We're just here to talk! Why can't you calm down long enough to listen!"

"I warned you!" said the Ripper, and he reached in through Nick's chest, gripped his grubby hands around Nick's memory of a heart, and tugged.

To the amazement of them both, the Ripper did not get Nick's heart at all. Instead his hand came out covered in chocolate.

It surprised Nick as much as the Ripper, but he tried not to show it.

The Ripper stared at his hand, then at Nick, and for

the first time the cranky Confederate Afterlight was truly frightened. "What . . . *are* you . . . ?"

And although Nick never, *ever* used the words himself, seeing the Ripper's cocoa-coated hand brought home a growing reality he could no longer deny.

"I am the Chocolate Ogre," Nick said. "And you've made me very . . . VERY . . . *MAD*!"

The look of terror on the Ripper's face was the most satisfying thing Nick had seen for a very long time. The Ripper's eyes were locked by Nick's angry gaze, and all the fight drained out of him. There was something about the Ripper's eyes—something about his face that wasn't quite right. Nick wasn't sure what it was, so he filed it away in his mind.

"What are you going to do to me?" the Ripper asked.

"Nothing. If you let my friend go."

Despite his fear of the Chocolate Ogre, the Ripper hesitated . . . but he did quickly glance to a particular green button on the console—a button covered by a clear plastic flap to prevent it from being pressed accidentally.

This, Nick knew, was a "tell." The Ripper's eyes had just given away exactly which button to push that would free Johnnie-O. All Nick had to do was press it. Nick reached up and flipped open the clear plastic cover.

"No! Don't!"

Nick savored the look of terrified helplessness on the Ripper's face for a moment. Then he pressed the green button.

Upon taking up residence in the shuttle many years ago, the Afterlight known as Zach the Ripper had gotten rid of the craft's original payload—a bunch of satellites and experiments that weren't doing anyone in Everlost any good. Besides, the massive cargo hold was the perfect place for the Ripper to store Everlost's finest weapon collection.

The Ripper had weapons and artillery of all kinds. Having developed an intimate knowledge of every military base within a hundred miles, the Ripper knew exactly where to find the best arms, and was highly skilled at ripping items—even heavy, awkward ones—from the living world, and into Everlost.

Living-world news reports regularly told of weapons disappearing. "Military mismanagement," the reports would say, because the rational world demanded rational explanations. The one time an unlucky marine dared to tell the truth of what he saw (a hand that reached in through a hole in space, waved to him, then disappeared with an AK-47 rifle), nobody believed it. The man was sent for psychological evaluation, and then promptly discharged from military service.

The Ripper did not know or care about such consequences. All that mattered was the collection, which filled two thirds of the cargo hold . . . until the day Nick opened the cargo hold doors.

To Johnnie-O, it began as a loud mechanical grinding, echoing in the massive hold around him. He had come down on the piles of weapons, but, still reeling from his brief empty-headed ordeal, he hadn't yet realized the nature of the Ripper's "collection." The cargo hold door opened like a parting curtain, revealing a million-dollar view of the

Atlantic Ocean. Then the pile beneath him began to shift, and that's when he realized he was sitting atop a nasty rats' nest of guns and explosives.

In the flight deck, Nick had, for one crazy instant, thought the cargo door motor was the boosters igniting, and that by hitting the button, he had just blasted them all off into orbit.

"Now you done it!" said the Ripper, hitting the button again and again, but the opening sequence couldn't stop once it started. "Those doors'll swing open wide—and it's all your stupid fault!" He peeked down into the hold, groaning, then ran for the entry hatch. Nick followed. They scurried down the unwieldy scaffold as the craft's huge cargo doors slowly, slowly opened. Once they reached the bottom, and Nick had a view of the cargo hold, he could see that it held a tottering haystack in shades of khaki and gunmetal gray. Gun muzzles and rifle butts stuck out every which way, but far worse than those were the rounded tips and tail fins randomly poking out of the weapon pile.

"Are those . . . bombs?"

"Mortar shells, surface-to-air missiles, smart bombs," the Ripper said, with a hint of pride. "You know—the *good* stuff."

The pile shifted as the doors continued to swing open. Several rifles fell out and toppled to the earth hundreds of feet below. Kudzu jumped out of the way, barking madly. And on top of the pile of weapons sat Johnnie-O, looking a little bit worried.

"Don't move!" screamed Nick.

"Kudzu!" screamed the Ripper. "C'mere, boy!" The dog

came running to the Ripper, its chain clanking on the dead-spot tarmac. The Ripper knelt down and tried to unhook the dog from his chain, while up above, the pile swayed precariously in the wide-open cargo bay of the mystically suspended spacecraft.

"It's okay," Johnnie-O shouted down to Nick. "It's okay, it's not gonna fall."

But he didn't have the view Nick did. Nick could see the shifting of gun muzzles and rifle butts. Everything was starting to slide.

Then Nick thought of something.

"Your coin!" Nick shouted.

Johnnie-O should have had it in his back pocket. So it would be there when he finally felt the urge to move on. Right now would be a good moment to feel that urge—because just as Nick told the Ripper, Everlost physics was not an exact science, and not even Mary had written about what happens to an Afterlight that gets blown up.

"Take your coin!" Nick said. "Hurry!"

"I don't got it! I put it back in the bucket."

"What? Why did you do that?"

"For safekeeping!"

Meanwhile the Ripper was in a panic as he struggled to free Kudzu. Nick went up to him, and the Ripper looked at Nick wild-eyed. "You stay away from my dog!"

Nick ignored him, knelt down, and quickly unhooked the chain from the dog's collar. "Now run!" ordered Nick.

The Ripper didn't need a second invitation. He took off sprinting, putting distance between himself and the tottering stockpile of artillery, with Kudzu at his heels.

"Just jump!" Nick called up to Johnnie-O, but instead of jumping Johnnie-O leaped from the stockpile to the wall of the cargo hold, and found a metal ridge to cling to—but the force of his jump set the mound of guns and explosives toppling. It all began a long cascade, out of the shuttle, to the ground below.

Now Nick was the one in danger, and he ran for cover—afraid to dive into the underbrush of the living world, for fear that diving would take him into the ground, where he'd begin the long, slow sink to the center of the earth. And so he ran as fast as his legs could carry him.

He was barely twenty yards away when the first bomb hit the ground.

One of the basic natural laws that one learns early in Everlost is that things that cross over always do what they were meant to do. Boats float, airships fly, and appliances run even if they're not plugged in. Unfortunately the same thing goes for bombs. They explode—especially bombs that were ecto-ripped, and had no good reason to be in Everlost in the first place.

If anyone had been watching they would have thought the shuttle was lifting off. Flame and smoke blasted from the ground beneath the great spacecraft, expanding as the explosions multiplied and merged into a single massive blast.

Nick was blown off his feet, and sent soaring through the air. Shrapnel tore through him—jagged, burning pieces of metal that left huge Swiss-cheese holes all over his body—and still the explosions grew louder behind him.

He landed, embedding in the living world so deep that

he almost went under. With little more than his head above-ground, it took all his will to push himself out of the earth. Had he been in any deeper, it would have been hopeless, and all his thrashing about would have done nothing but take him farther down. But bit by bit he hauled his shrapnel-blasted body upward. Perhaps the holes helped. Perhaps they made him lighter.

The explosions had stopped by the time he pulled himself out of the ground, and he looked at his own damage. As always the wounds were painless, but that didn't mean the sensation was pleasant. He watched as the wounds healed themselves closed. Even though they were gone, they left a haunting memory of their presence, like the lingering feeling of nightmares.

Nick turned back to the spacecraft to see what was left of it—and of Johnnie-O. To his surprise, the shuttle, the fuel tank, and boosters were all still there suspended in midair, completely undamaged. Perhaps the ship had been designed to withstand such explosions or perhaps its memory was too proud and permanent to ever be troubled by an attempt to take it down, whether intentional or accidental. Of course the same could not be said for the Ripper's rickety scaffold. It was completely gone, which was no surprise. Nick suspected the thing would have fallen if someone had blown on it too hard.

Up in the now-empty cargo hold, Johnnie-O still clung to the inside of the hold, the structure of the shuttle having shielded him from the worst of the blast. Unable to hold on anymore, he slipped and fell, yelling all the way down. He hit the lip of the cargo hold, and bounced off it, tumbling down the tail and careening off the shuttle engines, until landing face-first on the all-too-solid deadspot tarmac, a hundred and fifty feet below the spaceship.

"Johnnie!" yelled Nick, racing to him.

Johnnie-O sat up, dazed. "Am I blown up?"

"No," said Nick, "you're okay."

He looked no worse off than the shuttle itself, except for one thing—the cigarette that had perpetually hung from his lip since the moment he died was now gone—the only part of him incinerated by the explosion. Nick helped him to his feet and decided it was best not to point that out; best to let him discover it for himself once he was in a state of mind to notice.

Then from behind them came a wail of absolute and utter despair.

"My collection!" screamed the Ripper. "Look whatcha done to my collection!"

Nick looked around him; twisted gun barrels and unrecognizable pieces of tortured metal littered the deadspot—and beyond the deadspot even more destroyed weaponry was sinking into the ground of the living world.

"Look whatcha done! Look whatcha done! It's all gone!"

Nick had no sympathy, and stormed up to him. "What kind of idiot keeps a collection of live ammunition and armed bombs?"

"I ain't no idjit," screamed the Ripper. "You're the idjit! I got nuthin' now, thanks to you!"

And that's when Nick realized something.

In truth he had realized it before, only it hadn't fully registered. It was there in the Ripper's eyes, in the shape of the face, and in the lilt of the voice. Nick reached for the Ripper's Confederate cap, trying to pull it off, but of course it didn't come. Just like Nick's own tie, it was a permanent part of the Ripper.

"Get yer hands off!" Zach the Ripper said, slapping Nick's hand away.

But Nick knew this was no "Zach" at all.

"You're a girl!"

The Ripper's eyes narrowed, boldly staring right at him. "You got a problem with that?"

# CHAPTER 7

## *A Fistful of Forever*

I t was not uncommon once war was declared between the North and South for boys to lie about their age so they could serve. Nor was it uncommon for battle-ambitious girls to cut their hair and lie about their gender. Few got away with it, though.

Fourteen year-old Zinnia Kitner was one of those few.

Named after her mother's favorite flower, she had always hated her name—hated the fact that so many Southern girls of their day were named for such passive things as flowers: Violet. Rose. Magnolia. She shortened it to Zin, and allowed only her father to call her Zinnia.

She was not a girl of privilege—no Southern belle. She knew little of fancy things and delicate education. In fact, she had no schooling, and hated the prissy girls of the South's high society. She had no love of slavery, either, but she *did* love her father and brothers who all hated the North.

Then the South seceded from the Union, and war was declared. With her mother long dead, she knew she would be the only Kitner left at home; a Confederate War orphan left in the care of weepy neighbor women who wrung their hands raw in vain attempts to worry their men home.

Zinnia would have none of that. So she cut her hair, and practiced jutting her jaw and shifting her stance so she would look more like her brothers and less like herself. She became Zachariah Kitner. Then, through a combination of the exhaustion and nearsightedness of her recruitment and training officers, she somehow passed for male.

Little did she know she would be stuck passing for a boy for a very, very long time.

She was killed in her first battle, as so many inexperienced soldiers were. A single cannon blast. It was mercifully quick and painless. Zin's trip down the tunnel into the light *should* have been quick and simple; however, halfway there, she was struck by the sudden realization that her father and brothers would have no idea what had happened to her. There are few things that can cause a person to resist the gravity of the light. Thinking about one's self can't do it, because self-centered thoughts are weak when compared to the call of eternity. Thinking of others, however, can be a very powerful thing indeed, and can give a strong-willed person the strength to resist just about anything.

Zin knew what the light was. She knew she had died, and knew there was nothing she could do about that. Going straight into that light would be the easiest thing to do. But she couldn't stop thinking about her family, tormented by her mysterious absence.

And so she stopped falling forward, and found herself lingering at the threshold between the here and hereafter. Then she did something of such incredible audacity, the very universe was both insulted and impressed at the same time.

Zinnia Kitner reached *into* the light, grabbed the tiniest bit of it in her fist, and pulled her hand back again, taking a fraction of the light with her. Then she turned and ran from the light, thus entering Everlost.

What she didn't know was that taking a bit of eternity in her hand would give her a very special power.

Like most Afterlights, the details of her life on earth became hazy, but she did remember the war. For more than a hundred and fifty years she served her part. Collecting weapons gave her a sense of purpose—and woe be to any Afterlight who tried to tell her the war was over—for then what purpose would her existence serve? In spite of her uniform, she never forgot that she was a girl, for she never had a desire to be a boy, only to be treated as one. She still cursed the fact that the hat would not come off and that her hair would not grow—and she hated that they called her "Zach the Ripper." Like the uniform, however, it served a purpose for her, so she lived with it.

That is, until the day the Chocolate Ogre came and stripped everything away.

Zinnia fell to her knees in mourning. There was nothing left, nothing at all. All those years of collecting, and now what was there for her? Kudzu nuzzled up to her, trying to comfort her, but she would not be comforted.

"You've ruined everything. . . ." She would have reached into the fudge-faced kid right then, and ripped him good, if she thought she'd get anything more than chocolate.

Nick chose to keep his distance. He knew any chance for an easy alliance with the Ripper was gone . . . but that didn't mean there couldn't be a reluctant alliance, if he played this right.

"Come on," he said to Johnnie-O, loudly enough for the Ripper to hear. "We came here for nothing. She couldn't be any use in the war."

"That's right," snapped the Ripper. "Get lost!"

Nick turned to go then did a little mental countdown. *One . . . two . . . three . . .*

"What war?" asked the Ripper.

Nick grinned—it was like waiting for thunder after lightning. He turned back to her and looked her over, shaking his head. "Not the one *you're* fighting."

The Ripper looked away, her face betraying an odd mixture of shame and fury. There was a definite sense of craziness in her, but perhaps that could be dealt with. Perhaps it could be refined and directed.

Johnnie-O pulled Nick aside, and spoke to him quietly. "I got this really bad feeling about her," Johnnie-O whispered.

"That's just because she ripped you."

"What if she does it again?"

"I'll make sure she won't."

All the while, Zin kept watching them, trying to hear what they were whispering about.

Nick went back over to her. "After careful consideration," Nick said, "we've decided you're army material."

She looked at Nick warily. "What's my rank?"

"Private first class, in charge of tactical field operations." Nick had made it up on the spot, of course, but it sounded sufficiently impressive to make her consider it.

"Do I get to rip weapons?"

"You'll rip what your superior officers tell you to rip, or

you can go back up in that spaceship and launch yourself into orbit for all I care."

The Ripper scowled at him, but her scowl faded. She turned and looked up at the shuttle. "I tried that once, but it didn't work," she said. "I think they launch it from somewhere else. Someplace that ain't in Everlost yet."

She considered the massive ship for a moment more, then turned back to Nick. "So do I gots to call you 'sir'?"

"Yes," Nick said, figuring it might help keep her in line. "As I am your general, you will address me as sir. This is Mr. Johnnie-O. He's a sir too."

"I'm Zinnia," said the Ripper, "but people call me Zin."

Johnnie-O folded his arms. "I won't shake her hand."

Zin curled her lip in disgust. "I wouldn't shake your hand anyway. Your hands are ugly."

In response Johnnie-O made two even uglier fists.

Nick got between them before it could escalate. "Your first order is to rip something for us."

"She already did rip something," said Johnnie-O. Disgusted, he put his hand to his head, maybe to make sure that his brain was still there.

"I mean something from the *living* world," Nick said.

Zin chuckled. "I thought you'd ask me to do sumpin' hard."

She looked around, then saw a tattered tissue tumbling in the living-world wind. Casually she reached out with her right hand. With a faint shimmering of light, her hand poked a hole into the living world, she grabbed the tissue in midair, and pulled it back through the hole into Everlost. The portal into the living world closed almost instantly.

"Whoa," said Johnnie-O. "Abra-freaking-cadabra!"

She handed the tissue to Nick. "There," she said. "Maybe you can use it to wipe off all that chocolate ailing your face." Then she added, "Sir."

Nick looked at the tissue in his hand, thinking it would take a lot more than a tattered Kleenex to get rid of his particular skin condition. "I'm impressed."

"So you gonna tell me about your war?"

Nick considered how to answer her. "What do you know about Mary, the Sky Witch?"

Zin looked at Nick, then to Johnnie-O, then back to Nick again. "Who?" She looked to Kudzu, as if the dog might know the answer, but Kudzu just wagged his tail.

Nick sighed, pretending to be exasperated, but in truth he was relieved that she had never heard of Mary. It would make educating Zin the Ripper easier.

"Let's go," Nick said. "I'll tell you all about Mary on the way."

Just then, Johnnie-O finally touched his lip and said, "Hey, where's my Camel? What happened to my Camel?"

"What's he talkin' about? I don't see no stinkin' camel."

"My cig, you half-wit tomboy freak!"

Nick ignored their bickering, turning to take one last look at the *Challenger*. Without the rickety scaffold, there was nothing at all to mask the bald-faced fact that the shuttle was fixed in midair, resting on the invisible memory of its launchpad. Memory in Everlost was a far greater force than gravity. It could hold a thousand-ton spacecraft in the air, and could slowly turn a kid to chocolate.

"What'll I do without my Camel?" whined Johnnie-O.

"Maybe Zin can rip you a nicotine patch," said Nick. He had already begun to consider quite a few other things Zin might do with her powers as well—but they were things he wasn't ready to share with anyone—at least not yet.

"I wouldn't rip you the time of day," Zin said to Johnnie-O, and added "sir," as snidely as she could.

"Prob'ly because you can't tell time," Johnnie-O spat back.

Nick tried to keep his laughter to himself. Clearly Johnnie-O and Zin were a match made in heaven, so he let them squawk freely at each another as they set off, leaving behind the great spacecraft that stood in patient anticipation, forever pointing toward the stars.

# PART TWO

## *Dancing with the Deadlies*

In her book *Everything Mary Says Is Wrong*, Allie the Outcast has this to say about the criminal arts:

"Skinjacking, and ecto-ripping, along with all the other so-called 'criminal arts,' are not criminal at all when in the hands of someone with a brain and a conscience. Calling them criminal arts is just one more way Mary Hightower puts a negative spin on things beyond her control."

# CHAPTER 8

## *Treasures of the Flesh*

The living world was habit-forming to a skinjacker. There was no question about that. Allie tried to limit her skinjacking to the times she absolutely had to, but she only had so much self-control. The pull of the living world was hard to resist, and got harder each time she jumped into a fleshie.

The girl she now skinjacked was about her age, maybe a year older, with drab clothes, tight shoes, bad teeth, and acne. She was not someone you'd particularly notice if she suddenly became possessed by a different girl.

Allie had skinjacked her in a music store, and now stood a block away at a newsstand, on the small main street of Abingdon, Virginia. Allie's purpose was research. With all the time that had passed since she had left the living world, she had lost track of things. Who had won the last two World Series? What was the state of global warming? What movies had she missed and what bands were at the top of the charts? This was the reason for today's skinjacking. That's what she told Mikey. That's what she told herself.

So she stood at the newsstand, scouring various

newspapers and magazines, but as she did, she found herself completely uninterested in news of the living world. What interested her more were all the things she could feel in this borrowed body. The consciousness of the girl who owned it had been easily pushed down into mental steerage, leaving Allie to luxuriate in her senses. An unexpected heat wave had rolled into Western Virginia, and the humidity that might have been oppressive to the living, was wonderful to Allie. Feeling the warmth, feeling herself sweat, feeling uncomfortable in a very human way—these were just a few of the many things that Everlost denied her.

And hunger! Allie had no idea how long it had been since this girl had eaten, but she was certainly hungry—her stomach was even growling. She caught the dizzying, yeasty aroma of a bakery a few doors down. A bell jingled as a customer opened the door, and the smell became so intense for a moment, it could have lifted Allie off her feet. She didn't dare go in; how completely wrong would that be to indulge in cookies and pastries? For all she knew the girl was diabetic or had a deathly allergy to nuts. She had to remind herself that skinjacking was a privilege, not a right.

"Are you buying that magazine, miss?" asked the newsstand clerk, "or are you just going to read them all for free?"

Embarrassed, Allie reached into the girl's purse, pulled out a couple of dollars, and bought the tabloid in her hand. Only after she opened the purse did she realize she had opened her own personal treasure box. She gazed in at the trappings of this girl's life. There was a set of keys with a heart-shaped key chain that said "I Love VA." There was lip balm—the kind that smelled like strawberry. There was a pack of tissues to blow her wonderfully stuffy nose—and nestled in the midst of it all: a Snickers bar. It had always been Allie's favorite . . . and after all the girl was hungry. Besides, the candy bar was in her purse already—which meant she must not have some unknown medical issue that would prevent her from eating it. What harm would it do to take a single bite?

*"I shouldn't . . . "*

"Shouldn't what?" asked the news clerk.

Allie hadn't even realized she had spoken aloud. "I'm not talking to you."

The clerk gave her a funny look and Allie walked away. Crossing the street, she found a bus stop bench in the shade, and sat down.

*I've been in this girl for at least fifteen minutes,* she thought. The girl would be frightened once Allie let her have her body back. She'd never know that Allie had been there, but she would certainly miss the time. On the other hand it was only fifteen minutes—and it hadn't been like the girl was doing anything important. She was browsing in a music store, and seemed to be in no great hurry. What was a few more minutes?

Allie pulled out the Snickers bar and slowly ripped the edge then peeled back the paper. The outside layer of chocolate had melted from the heat. It was already getting on her hands and that immediately made her think of Nick—which made her need comfort food all the more.

She raised the Snickers bar to her lips and took that single small bite, feeling her teeth sink into it, feeling the flavor rush over her taste buds. *Life is wasted on the living,* she thought. They take all this for granted. The feel of the weather, the taste of a candy bar, the inconvenience of time, and the nuisance of uncomfortable shoes. To Allie all of these things were wonderful.

Once she had started the Snickers bar, there simply was no way to stop. One bite became two, became three, and soon the entire bar was gone. Now that the deed was done, she felt guilt that almost, but not quite, outweighed the pleasure. She would go back to that newsstand and buy another candy bar for the girl and put it in her purse. That's what she would do.

"Was it good?" said the high-pitched voice of a child.

She turned to see a very young boy and a very old man standing beside her. The boy, who couldn't be any older than three, stared at her with an expression that seemed a little too cold for such a small child. The old man held his cane with a palsy shake and leered at her with a twisted kind of grin. There was something about the two of them that gave her the creeps.

"He asked you a question," said the old man. "Aren't you going to answer him, huh? Huh?"

"Yes," Allie said. "It was good. It was very good."

"Next time," said the little boy, "you should get some milk to wash it down." He held his cold stare for a moment more, then suddenly he burst out laughing and so did the old man. The moment was too odd, too unsettling. Allie could feel gooseflesh bristling on her borrowed body. She excused herself and crossed back to the newsstand, where she bought another Snickers bar, and dropped it in the purse before returning to the music shop. She would leave the girl exactly where she had found her, browsing in the alternative rock section. Only this time the girl would have to make sense of the twenty minutes missing from her life.

Mikey waited. He waited because he had no choice. He couldn't skinjack, and although he could follow Allie, and watch what she did in the living world, he didn't want to. There was something unpleasant about seeing her disappear into someone else's body.

What made it even worse was her choice of hosts. Mikey couldn't understand why she always chose the sorriest-looking fleshies to skinjack. If you could jump into anyone, why not choose someone you'd want to see in the mirror? Unless of course you were a monster, as he had been, and took pride in an unpleasant appearance. Allie, however, was anything but a monster, so her choice of homely hosts baffled him.

*Perhaps I'd understand it if I were more human*, Mikey thought. He had spent so many years as a monster, he was still trying to get the hang of thinking the way humans think again. Considering the feelings of others, holding his temper, digging down to the deepest part of himself to find patience.

He had very little patience when Allie skinjacked. He paced and grumbled, he complained to their sad-eyed horse. He steamed and stewed, and wished he were the McGill again, because it was so much more satisfying to be discontent when he was physically repulsive. Now, according to Allie, he was somewhat cute. He often wondered if she said that to punish him.

"I AM NOT CUTE!" he shouted to the horse. The

horse tossed its head and whinnied like it had just been shown some sort of great kindness. It just irritated Mikey even more. Although he didn't wish to be a monster again, neither did he want a condemnation of cuteness.

He looked to his right hand. It had once been a deformed claw, covered in growths too unpleasant to mention. He had made it that way himself, for he had the power of change. Of course that was before Mary showed him that blasted picture of himself—the memory-in-a-locket that forced him to remember who he was. He turned his hand over, looking at his palm, his fingertips. They glowed with his faint after-glow, but otherwise, they were plain and human, and they hadn't changed since that day he violently and unexpectedly transformed back to his human self.

Forcing change, however, had always been a different matter. It didn't happen in an explosive burst of memory, it was slow, imperceptible. It took weeks to make the smallest of physical changes stick—but no one else he had ever met could do it. Sure, everyone changed over time as they forgot their lives on earth, but Mikey could *choose* how he changed. He could make himself into whatever he wanted.

But not anymore. Ever since becoming his former self, he hadn't physically changed in the least. "It's your fault!" he had told Allie in one of his weaker moments, but Allie had just shrugged it off. "Don't blame me for your morphing issues," she had said—but it *was* her fault in a way . . . because for Mikey to change, he had to truly *want* it. And since Allie liked him just the way he was, he simply didn't want it enough.

But Allie was off skinjacking, wasn't she? She was

practicing her unique talent, so why shouldn't Mikey practice his? And if he changed just a little, at least it would prove that he still could do it! It would prove that being Mikey McGill, the all-American Afterlight, was a choice, and not a sentence. So as he waited for Allie at the edge of the small town, he concentrated on his hand, training his thoughts on forcing some new reality upon himself. It didn't matter what the change was, as long as it happened. He concentrated so hard he could swear the sun dimmed slightly in the sky.

And something happened!

As he stared at his fingers, the skin between them began to grow. He watched in building excitement, as the fingers of his right hand became webbed! True, it was only down at the lowest knuckle, but it had happened—and much faster than ever before. This kind of change would take days to cultivate, when he was the McGill. And it occurred to him that perhaps having been nonhuman for so long, had made him more elastic.

All it took was half an hour away from Allie!

It was that thought that brought his euphoria to a sudden end, because as illuminating as the moment was, it also cast a chilling shadow.

*Does this mean I'll turn back into a monster if I'm not with her?*

Through the space still left between his fingers, he saw Allie, hurrying across the street toward him. The second he saw her, he reflexively hid his hand behind his back. He could have cursed himself for not being more subtle about it.

"We're done here," she said.

"You took way too long!"

She shrugged. "Lots of articles to read." Mikey thought he had gotten off easy, until she asked, "Why are you hiding your hand?"

"I'm not." Still he held it behind his back.

Then she got a troubled look in her eye, perhaps thinking about something she had seen or read during her little skinjacking expedition.

"Let's get out of here," she said. "I don't like this place."

Mikey glanced at the horse—and that's when she grabbed his wrist, pulling his right hand into full view. He grimaced, realizing he had been caught red-handed—or web-handed, as it were . . . But to his surprise the flaps of skin linking his knuckles were gone.

"Hmmm," said Allie. "Nothing. I guess you were telling the truth."

He folded his fingers over hers, interlocking them. "What reason would I have to lie to you?"

Allie squeezed his fingers tighter and smiled. "You're human now; lying is a favorite human pastime."

As they climbed onto the horse, Mikey decided he must be more human than he thought—because not only had he lied, but he had gotten away with it.

The town soon gave way to countryside, and they came across an old rural route that was no longer a part of the living world. Here, Mikey dug his heels into the horse and the horse took off in a cantor that was so much more efficient, something it couldn't do while plodding through that soft stuff that made up the living world. With Allie so close to him on the horse, Mikey wished he could read her mind, for even with her so close behind him, she felt miles away. He was still frustrated by the time she spent skinjacking, but he knew better than to make an argument of it. Allie was the sharpest, most argument-winning girl he had ever met. He knew she would make a convincing case for why she had every right to skinjack whenever she felt like it, and leave him waiting. After all, it wasn't her fault he couldn't do it.

"If I understood how it worked," she had once told him, "don't you think I would teach you?"

Well, maybe she would, and maybe she wouldn't. After all, he had been a monster and who knew if such power in his hands would be a good thing? Now as he rode up and down the hills of Virginia and into Tennessee, he had to admit to himself something he had been avoiding for all their time together. He was very good at being a monster — but as a boy he was mediocre at best.

As it happens, Mikey's sense that Allie was a bit distant was right on target. At that moment, her thoughts were wandering far from the horse they rode. Her mind kept being drawn back to the town they had just left, and the one before that, and the one before that. She was relieved to be away from civilization, and yet in her thoughts, she couldn't leave it all behind, because the taste of the living was becoming too tempting — and it *was* a taste — an inner hunger that was powerful and all-consuming. She felt herself becoming like a vampire, feasting not on blood, but on experience. The silky smooth sensation of flesh. The flavor of other people's lives. Even now she longed to be wrapped in the living — but she could share none of this with Mikey. He wouldn't understand. Empathy was not his strongest point — even the nature of his own feelings were still a mystery to him, so how could Allie expect him to understand hers? And so even though she sat in a close saddleback embrace, a wall had fallen between them. Allie kept her yearning for flesh a secret, certain that she could control it . . . but then it started to rain.

In life, Allie had always loved the rain. When other people would bundle up and pull out their umbrellas, Allie would revel in the feel of the rain against her hair, against her face. "You'll catch your death of cold!" her mother would always tell her, never imagining that Allie would soon catch her death in an entirely different way.

In Everlost, however, rain was different. It washed through you instead of over you, tickling your insides like an itch you couldn't scratch. It was an unpleasant sensation that Allie had never gotten used to.

As a drizzle became a shower, and the shower became a downpour, Allie longed for the feel of it *on* her instead of *in* her. She longed to be wet—not just wet but so completely drenched that the only remedy was a warm fire.

On their travels, they stuck more to rural routes than highways, but the route they now traveled ended at a large lake, with a road continuing to the left and right. They paused for a few moments, and the rain became heavier.

"Which way?" Mikey asked. It was part of Allie's job to check maps when she skinjacked, and navigate their course. She already knew that they needed to go to the left, and yet she said, "I don't know, I'll have to check."

Mikey grunted his disapproval, but Allie ignored him as she dismounted. There was a small boat dock in front of them, and a few hundred yards away, a convenience store and gas station. Needless to say, she had no intention of checking a map. This skinjacking would serve an entirely different purpose, and as Allie made her way toward the convenience store, she hoped she hadn't missed the worst of the rain.

In the store was a tattooed man buying beer. He was a skinjacking possibility, but only as a last resort. The cashier was a tired-looking old woman, whose joints were probably already aching from the weather, and wouldn't appreciate being thrust out into the rain. Allie was beginning to fear she'd have to settle for the tattooed guy, but then a woman hurried inside, wearing one of those hideous plastic rain ponchos the color of a traffic cone.

"Wet enough for ya, Wanda?" said the old woman behind the counter.

"Don't mind it; seen worse," Wanda said.

"I hear ya!"

Allie had no idea what had brought Wanda to a convenience store in this weather, but frankly she didn't care. Allie stepped inside her without a second thought, sliding in smooth and easy.

*—Rolling rolling—how long them dogs been rolling—long enough to give me gas—or worse—I shouldn't go near those things, no sir—*

She experienced the usual moment of disorientation, filled with the static of Wanda's thoughts, and then Allie flipped that mental switch that sent Wanda off to dreamland. Instantly Allie knew why Wanda was here. She was hungry—famished—it seemed fleshies were always hungry, and Allie liked it that way!

Now in complete control of the woman, Allie looked toward the hot dogs rolling on the stainless steel poles of the industrial cooker. She had already been thinking about them, hadn't she?

"I'll have a cheese dog, please," Allie said.

The old woman was happy to oblige. "How's Sam these days?"

"Fine, fine," said Allie—and getting bold, she added, "You know Sam—I can't pry him away from the TV."

The old woman laughed. "So he watches television now?"

"Uh . . . yeah. Well, weekends mostly. You know—the games."

The old woman laughed. "Don't that beat all, a dog that watches sports!"

Allie felt her borrowed face flush, and she decided that less is more when it came to living-world conversation. She thanked the woman for the hot dog, paid with some cash from her purse, and downed the hot dog in three bites. Then she headed outside to the main event.

The rain!

It drummed against her poncho, teasing her, daring her to pull back her hood, and she did, closing her eyes and turning up her face to receive it. In an instant her hair was drenched, and rivers of rain ran down her cheeks. It was all she remembered it was! She opened her mouth and felt the drops on her tongue, but it still wasn't enough, so she grabbed the poncho, and pulled it off, exposing her flower-print blouse to the rain. She was drenched, she was chilled, and it was wonderful!

All caution had been lost in this glorious moment—she didn't care who saw her, or how wet she got. Wanda would not catch her death of cold. She'd be soaked and confused, but in the end, Wanda would have the benefit of that warm fire to dry her off, as she sat beside Sam, the TV-watching dog.

Allie twirled in the rain, laughing, and dizzy. . . . But then, as the rain began to let up, the guilt began to set in. She had used Wanda to satisfy her own selfish desire. How could she have done that? She had to end this now, and get back to Mikey. Somewhere in her rain dance, she had dropped the poncho, and it had blown to the feet of the gas station attendant, a dozen yards away, who picked it up, and came toward her.

"Looks like you dropped this," he said.

"I'm sorry," Allie said. "I got a little carried away."

"Nothing wrong with that. Not at all, not at all." He handed her back the poncho, smiling a lopsided smile that Allie could swear she'd seen before. "Not from around here, are you?" he asked.

Only now did Allie notice that he was just as wet as she, and didn't seem to care. "Yes, I am," Allie said, figuring that Wanda must live nearby.

His smile got wider. More crooked. "Right, right, but I'm not talking about the fleshie," he said. "I'm talking about *you*."

Then his hand thrust out and grabbed Allie's wrist—grabbed it hard. It hurt—maybe more than it should have because it was the first time in a very long time Allie had felt pain. *Fleshie? Did he say fleshie? Then that must mean . . .*

She ripped herself from his grasp, and turned to run, but then found herself running right into a drenched man in a business suit—a man with beady eyes colder than the rain. "First a candy bar, then a hot dog," he said. "Always hungry, aren't you!"

All at once Allie knew where she had seen these two before. It wasn't their faces she recognized—because the faces were different—but their *presence* was the same. This was the old man and the little boy she had run into in the last town. But they had never been a little boy or an old man, any more than she had been the chubby girl eating a snickers bar. They were skinjackers!

The "businessman" pushed her painfully back against the gas pump, jarring loose the nozzle, which clattered to the ground. "Looks like we've finally caught up with Jackin' Jill!"

"I don't know what you're talking about!"

"Don't lie to us!" And his grip on her shoulders got tighter.

Well, they weren't the only ones who could use flesh to their advantage. Pain was a two-way street. She lifted her knee sharply, nailing the "businessman" where it counts. His cold eyes went wide, and he doubled over in pain, yowling. Then, as the "gas station attendant" reached for her, she grabbed the gas hose, and swung the nozzle at his head. It connected with his jaw, spinning him around.

Wasting no time, she peeled herself out of Wanda, returning to Everlost. The two men were on the ground now, and Allie could see the skinjackers inside them beginning to squirm their way out. They must have been spying on her the other day when she jumped into the Snickers girl. If they had been there to watch her skinjack, and saw her peel out, too, it would be easy to follow Allie all the way here, jacking these two men as soon as she took over Wanda.

Well, Wanda and those poor men would have to sort this out for themselves, because Allie wasn't about to stand there and wait to be attacked again. She turned and ran to the dock, where Mikey was waiting.

Mikey, however, was having his own problems. He had hopped off the horse right after Allie had left, and as soon as she was out of view, he began to practice changing again.

It took a minute or two to gain enough focus to do it—especially with the rain, which was an unpleasant distraction. Just as before, he trained all of his attention on his right hand—this time trying to force the growth of a sixth finger. It worked! The finger sprouted right between his thumb and index finger, growing to be just as long as his pinky—but then kept on growing. Soon it was as long as his index finger—and still it didn't stop. *No big deal,* he thought. He just needed to regain his focus. He started this, so he could stop it. But then a seventh finger began to grow next to his pinky—and an eighth sprouted from his palm.

Changing himself, it seemed, was becoming easier and easier. The problem was stopping the process of mutation, and reversing it.

Now the knuckles of his fingers were growing fingers of their own, like branches of a tree. There were too many to count. Beginning to panic, he put all of his focus into reining it in. He looked at his hand, imagining his will to be a relentless wave washing across his many misbegotten fingers. The growth finally slowed and stopped. He sent forth his will in a second wave, hoping—praying—that the extra fingers would shrivel and disappear, for how could he face Allie like this? Slowly the many fingers began to shrink.

So focused was Mikey on his current plight that he never noticed the sudden absence of the horse.

Shiloh the Famous Diving Horse was a loyal, if not entirely intelligent, animal. Only one thing was stronger than its loyalty: its desire to perform the death-defying, crowd-pleasing high dive. This was the creature's grand purpose. It had performed this feat before cheering crowds for most of its life on Atlantic City's Steel Pier, and had continued to do so in Everlost, until the day Mikey McGill climbed on its back to escape a marauding mob.

The steel pier was far away now . . . however, the dock that extended into the lake *looked* very much like a pier. The sight of it filled the horse's spirit. True, there was no high-dive platform. True, there was no tank to land in—but there certainly was water! Although Shiloh's time with Allie and Mikey had been somewhat entertaining, when the chance to perform one final leap presented itself, how could any self-respecting high-diving horse resist?

And so, by the time Mikey had gotten his hand back down to the usual number of fingers, the horse was already barreling at full gallop down the dock.

Mikey ran after it the moment he saw it, but it was no use. By the time he reached the dock, the horse was already nearing the end, and showed no signs of slowing down. Still,

Mikey raced after it, hoping that the creature would come to its senses before hurling itself into oblivion.

The horse, however, was of a single mind. It reached the end of the dock, released a whinny of pure joy, and launched itself gleefully off the end. It hit the water, passed into the lake, and kept plummeting downward. In a moment it hit lake bottom, and passed into the earth, where it began its long journey toward the center of the Earth.

Deep down in its equine mind, the horse knew that there was no return, but that was all right, for it also knew that this was the greatest high dive of all!

Far above, Mikey McGill finally reached the end of the dock, stomping and cursing like a child having a tantrum, nearly sinking through the wood of the pier. The horse was gone without leaving as much as a ripple in the living-world water to mark its passage.

"Mikey!"

And of course this would be the moment Allie would choose to return! Mikey knew she had seen the whole thing—it was there in the panicked look on her face.

"I'll go after it!" Mikey told her. "I'll dive down after it and bring it back!" But even as he said it, he knew it wouldn't work. Yes, he had ridden the horse out of the earth once before, but such a feat required a certain passion he no longer had. The monster within him had been tamed, but domestication came with a cost. Surely he still had the power to pull himself out of the depths, but he doubted he could do it on horseback.

Mikey had no way of knowing that Allie's troubled look had little to do with the horse. She had run from the gas station so quickly, she actually felt out of breath—a sensation that was technically impossible for an Afterlight, and yet still she felt it. When she saw the horse go off the dock, her heart sank. First for the loss of Shiloh, and second, because with him went their only chance for a quick escape.

She tried to get Mikey's attention, but he still blustered like the storm clouds above. "Stupid horse!"

"Forget about that! We've got a bigger problem." She grabbed him and forced him to look at her. "Skinjackers."

"Huh?"

"Two of them! They've been following us—we've got to get out of here!" But as she turned, she realized it was too late. The two skinjackers were at the foot of the dock, stalking toward them. Allie had not seen them in their true form—she had only seen the hosts they had inhabited. In a way it was easier to face them in the living world, where everything was limited by the simple rules of flesh and bone.

Even though she had never actually seen their faces, she knew which was which. The skinjacker to the right was tall and thin, with a puffy, rodentlike face. He had knobby knees and elbows—too knobby, actually—exaggerated like his skewed grin, which practically stretched all the way to his right ear.

"Well, well," he said. "Jackin' Jill has a friend!"

The other skinjacker was in a blue and white football uniform, and his face was little more than a pair of unpleasant eyes in a football helmet. He was big—the kind of kid who was destined to be a linebacker whether he was good at the sport or not. Now, after what must have been a very bad game for him, he was stuck as a permanent linebacker in Everlost. When he spoke, his words came out slurred and slobbery, due to the fact that he also had a mouth guard stuck perpetually between his teeth.

"Wait a shecond," he said. "That'sh not Jackin' Jill!"

"It is! It is!" said the skinny one. "She just made herself look different, that's all!"

"She can't do shumthing like that, can she?"

Allie leaned over to Mikey and whispered in his ear. "We'll run on the count of three."

To which Mikey responded, "I don't run. And neither do you."

He was right about that. But seeing other skinjackers — it had shaken her even more than she realized. "Okay," she said. "We'll fight them." Then she thought about how she had been pushed against the gas pump. "But the football player's mine."

Both Allie and Mikey prepared themselves for the battle, but before it could begin, someone else showed up on the scene. A fleshie came running onto the dock. A teenaged, leather-clad punk with spiky hair that defied the rain. But in an instant the wet spikes resolved into dry curls, and the face became a little less angular. It took a moment for Allie to realize what was happening. A third skinjacker had arrived, and he had just peeled out of his host. He wore a striped T-shirt that was a little too tight for his muscular frame, and he was old by Everlost standards. Seventeen maybe. While the punk-fleshie toddled off in confusion, the third skinjacker grabbed the gangly kid and the football player.

"What do you think you are doing!" he demanded. He

had an accent that Allie couldn't quite place at first.

"It's Jackin' Jill!" said the gangly one, weakly.

"Does she look like Jackin' Jill to you?" the third skin-jacker said. The accent was definitely Eastern European. If Allie had to guess, she would say it was Russian.

The football player wasn't sure whether to shake his head or to nod, so he did a little bit of both. It made him look like a bobblehead doll. "When we shaw her jack the fat girl back in Virginia, we weren't closhe enough to shee her faish."

"Yeah, Yeah," said the other one, "and when she peeled out we had to hang way back, so we still didn't see her face then, either."

The Russian kid heaved a heavy, resigned sigh, then he turned to Allie and Mikey, apologetically. "This is my fault," he said. "When they told me they found a skinjacker, I told them to keep their eyes on you. Now I realize I should have done it myself." He let go of the other two, and took a step forward. "I am Milos—and you have already met Moose and Squirrel."

He threw an angry look at his cohorts, and Moose pushed Squirrel, nearly launching him off the side of the dock. "It was hish fault!" Squirrel pushed him back, but it wasn't nearly as effective.

"You have some nerve spying on us at all!" Mikey said.

"Please, forgive me," Milos said calmly, "but we have had some . . . bad experiences, and they thought you were someone else."

"They attacked me," Allie said. "I had to hurt a couple of fleshies because of them."

Mikey looked at them, furious, and clenched his fists. "They attacked you?"

"I assure you this will not happen again." The third skinjacker turned to Moose and Squirrel. "Your behavior was unacceptable. Apologize!"

The two looked down like kids in the principal's office.

"Sorry," said Squirrel.

"Yeah, shorry," said Moose.

Allie shook her head. "Sometimes sorry's not enough."

"Then," said Milos with a slight bow, "allow me to make it up to you." He held his hand out in an open-palmed gesture, as if he expected Allie to place her hand in his. She didn't.

"You can make it up to us," said Mikey, "by getting lost."

Milos remained calm and smooth. "But have you not longed for the company of other skinjackers?" he asked Mikey. "Surely we can put all this behind us and start again."

Apparently Milos just assumed that Mikey was also a skinjacker. Mikey didn't say anything to correct him, so Allie kept quiet about it as well.

"We're fine on our own," Mikey said.

Although Allie knew they didn't need Milos's help, and certainly had no desire to spend quality time with Moose and Squirrel, there was something enticing about Milos. He was civilized and sane—she could see it in his eyes—curious eyes that were blue, speckled with white, like a sky dotted with clouds. It would be a relief having another skinjacker to talk to—someone who could understand what it was like.

"We're on our way to Memphis," Allie told him, and Mikey looked at her, incredulous.

Milos smiled. "Then allow us to accompany you. At least part of the way."

"No!" said Mikey.

Allie gently took Mikey's hand, holding it to reassure him—and also to make it clear to Milos that the two of them were together in every way that mattered.

"You can travel with us for a little while," Allie said. "I'm Allie. This is Mikey."

Moose gasped. "Allie the Outcasht?"

Mikey grabbed him by his face guard, pulled him close and growled in his face. "That's right. Touch her again and you'll wish you never died."

"Yesh shir," said Moose.

"Now," said Milos, "I suggest we get off this dock before we sink right through it." He gestured for Allie to take the lead, which she did—and although she never let go of Mikey's hand, she couldn't help but appreciate Milos's suave manner. Most of the boys she had met in Everlost were wild to the point of being feral. Allie never considered herself a lady, but for once it was nice to be treated like one.

In her book *Further Reasons for Caution*, Mary Hightower has this to say about roving bands of skinjackers:

"While a single skinjacker is trouble enough, a group of wild skinjackers is a frightening prospect, indeed. These Afterlights caught between two worlds are to be pitied and feared, for the madness of flesh has infected their minds. If word reaches you of skinjackers in your area, it is best for all involved to steer clear of them, and report the sighting to an authority."

# CHAPTER 9
## *Good Stewards*

**W**hile Moose and Squirrel might have been the poster children illustrating Mary's point about "wild skinjackers," they were marginally civilized under Milos's guidance.

"They are not so bad," Milos told Mikey and Allie. "Or should I say, I have seen much worse."

The rain had given way to broken clouds, and they continued to follow the road around the lake. Mikey was sullen, and didn't talk much, and Moose and Squirrel, always lingering a dozen paces behind, snickered over their own private jokes. Milos, however was full of conversation for the newcomers. Allie supposed that, having had no one but Moose and Squirrel to talk to, he was starved for intelligent conversation. Milos told them that they had traveled as a group for several years. The "Deadlies" they called themselves. There were four— Milos, Moose, Squirrel, and a girl they called Jackin' Jill. Jill, however, was gone, and Milos didn't say any more about it. Allie found it all interesting, but Mikey kept making exasperated sounds, as if listening to Milos was like torture.

"Mikey, you're being rude," Allie told him after a particularly loud groan.

"Sorry," said Mikey, although it sounded more like a curse than an apology.

Milos continued the tale of his afterlife, unoffended. As Allie suspected, Milos had come from Russia. "Russian-born, but American-dead," as he put it. His family had moved to America from St. Petersburg. Milos had been hanging out with friends on the roof of his apartment building, and had fallen off.

"It was a stupid way to go," Milos said.

Mikey scoffed. "My sister and I got hit by a train," he said. "We all die in stupid ways, and this is a stupid conversation." He picked up his pace, leaving them, and the conversation, behind. Allie thought to apologize to Milos for Mikey's behavior, but she was tired of making excuses for him. Anyway, Milos was a good sport about it.

"I would have gone into the light if I could," Milos told Allie. "But the light would not take me. It would just keep throwing me back."

This surprised Allie. Not even Mary, in her various volumes on Everlost lore, never mentioned anyone reaching the end of the tunnel, only to be denied admittance.

"Are you sure?" Allie asked. "Maybe you just never reached the light."

"I suppose your friend would say the light didn't like me and spit me out."

Allie laughed. "Well, I suppose you're an acquired taste." She looked toward Mikey. He was twenty yards ahead of them, striding with an impatient pace. His hands were in his pockets, his shoulders high, and he looked to the ground. Even when they were together he seemed to be alone in some fundamental way. It saddened her.

"It's because we are skinjackers," Milos said. "The light won't take us. It would have been the same for you and your friend, had you made it as far as the light." Allie cast her gaze down, wondering how long they could keep secret the fact that Mikey could not skinjack. Then it suddenly struck her what Milos had just said. How major it was—how important it was.

"Milos . . . if skinjackers can't go into the light, then that explains why my coin never gets hot, doesn't it?"

Milos nodded. "I have seen others find passage into the next place, but never skinjackers," he said. "You could say our money is no good."

"So are you saying . . . we'll never leave Everlost?"

"Of coursh we'll leave," said Moose, eavesdropping with Squirrel, right behind them. "We'll leave when we can't Shkinjack anymore."

"Yeah, yeah," said Squirrel. "So we gotta jack when the jackin' is good!"

It had never occurred to Allie that skinjacking could be temporary. "How long?"

"As long as it takes," Milos said.

"As long as what takes?"

Moose and Squirrel looked to each other and laughed, but Milos threw them an angry glance, and they fell silent.

"The length of your natural life span," Milos said. "That is how long you can skinjack."

For Allie this was a revelation. It cast everything in a new light. She had been so worried that she would feel compelled to take her coin and move on after finding her family, but if she was stuck in Everlost for the length of her natural life, then her coin wouldn't work. She wasn't going anywhere. She thought about telling Mikey, but decided to keep it to herself. If he was going to act all antisocial, then there were things he deserved not to know.

"What do you mean by 'the length of our natural lives?'" she asked Milos. "Do you mean the time we would have died if we had died of natural causes?"

Milos gave the slightest of shrugs. "Something like that, yes."

Allie sensed there was more to it, but that was all Milos said on the matter. She would have pushed further, but at that moment, they had come around a bend in the road, and saw the interstate in the distance. "Excellent," Milos said. "From here it will be easy."

He picked up the pace with Moose and Squirrel. As they passed Mikey, Milos gave him a friendly clap on the back, which just made Mikey pull his shoulders in even tighter.

Allie caught up with Mikey. "You could make the best of this," Allie said, "instead of being so unpleasant."

"I don't like this," he grumbled."I don't like *him*. He's much too friendly."

"You lost the right to be a judge of character when you became the McGill."

"So when do I get it back?"

"You don't," Allie told him, intentionally flip. "I do all the judging, and I say Milos's character is acceptable."

Mikey grumbled something under his breath, and Allie nudged him. "You're just mad because he's handsome and charming."

Mikey wouldn't look her in the eye. "Really? I hadn't noticed."

The interstate exit was the only one for miles, and around it were clustered fast food chains, gas stations, and uninviting motels. Cars from dozens of states flowed on and off the interstate in an endless stream.

Milos surveyed the scene, then turned to Moose and Squirrel. "You check the south side of the highway; we shall check the north."

Moose and Squirrel obediently trotted across the highway, ignoring the traffic whooshing through them.

"Would you mind telling us what we're looking for?" asked Mikey.

"Family of five," Milos said, as if it was obvious, "or, if not a family, then five people traveling together."

"I don't understand," said Allie.

Milos looked at her and shook his head. "You have much to learn about skinjacking." He turned to look at the Burger King parking lot in front of them. "We shall skinjack five people in the same car," he explained. "Then we drive to Memphis."

Allie was appalled, and didn't try to hide it. "Is that how you travel? By ripping people out of their lives?"

"This is one way we travel, yes," said Milos, matter-of-factly.

"That's terrible!"

Milos looked at her, a bit stunned by her response. "We do not harm them—and they get their bodies back when we are done."

"Yes, but hundreds of miles away from where they started, never knowing how or why." Allie looked at a family leaving the Burger King. She wondered where they might be going. She wondered what it would be like to be traveling to one place, only to find yourself somewhere else entirely. "People have plans!" Allie insisted. "It's one thing to borrow, it's another to steal."

Milos smiled at her, and crossed his arms. "So Allie the Outcast has a conscience."

Allie couldn't tell whether he was impressed or mocking her.

Mikey, who had been happy to watch them argue, now stepped between them. "Forget it, Allie, let him skinjack whoever he wants—we don't need to go with him." And then Mikey added, quietly so only Allie could hear, "It's not going to work for us anyway, if you know what I mean. . . ."

But Allie found herself too irritated by Milos's smug expression to back down now. "All I'm saying is we have a responsibility. We have to be . . . good stewards."

This time Mikey stepped right in front of her, eclipsing her view of Milos completely. "Let's just go, okay?"

Milos took a step around Mikey, back into her view. "Perhaps my time in Everlost has made me callous," he said. "Maybe we should give more care to those we skinjack. So then, as a good steward, how would you suggest we proceed?"

Allie looked to the interstate. "Let's take the time to find a family of five that's already going to Memphis."

Mikey threw up his hands. "You're forgetting one thing!" he said angrily. "*I can't skinjack!*"

Allie found herself speechless—in her frustration she had ignored the single fact that made their skinjacking jaunt an impossibility. When she turned, she saw Moose and Squirrel standing there dumbstruck as well.

"Did he jusht shay he can't shkinjack?" asked Moose, pointing at Mikey.

Mikey turned on Moose as bitterly as the McGill would have. "What's wrong?" shouted Mikey. "Can't hear through that stinking helmet? Maybe I'll rip it off along with your head and shout down your neck!"

Allie grabbed Mikey's arm and held him firmly. It was enough to ratchet him down to a simmer.

Milos didn't say anything, he just stroked his chin, pondering the change in circumstance.

Squirrel looked at Allie, confused. "So why are you even with him if he can't skinjack, huh, huh?"

"There are more important things than skinjacking," Mikey snapped.

Squirrel shook his head. "No there's not."

Allie was about to launch into a hundred defenses of her relationship with Mikey, but Milos cut her off by saying, "Then we shall walk."

Squirrel looked at him slack-jawed. "But-But—"

"Did he jusht say we're walking?" asked Moose.

"Is there a hurry? No!" said Milos. "And it is a beautiful time of year. I see no problem in walking."

"Yeah, yeah, but what about Jackin' Jill?" said Squirrel. "We still gotta find her and teach her a lesson."

"We will find her when we find her," Milos said. "A few days won't make a difference." Allie couldn't help but notice how he bristled at the mention of her name. Milos then looked to the highway. "We shall travel on the interstate—it will take us straight there."

Squirrel shuffled his feet, and Moose just looked down, slowly shaking his head.

"If you have a problem with this, then leave," Milos said to them sternly. He looked around, then pointed at a car just arriving in the Burger King lot. "There—a man and a woman in a Miata. Be my guest." He gave them an elaborate but annoyed gesture. Moose and Squirrel didn't move.

"No?" said Milos. "Then you will both kindly close your mouths, and accompany our friends to Memphis." He turned his back on them and strode off toward the interstate.

Moose looked at Squirrel, and Squirrel hit him on the helmet. "What are you looking at, huh, huh?" He followed Milos, and Moose lumbered off behind him, all shoulder pads and shame.

Allie turned to Mikey. "Are you coming, or are you just going to stand there and sink?"

"Of course I'm coming." Mikey pulled his feet out of the ground, and the two of them headed off after the others.

"You should thank Milos," Allie said. "He just stood up for you."

But Mikey clearly wasn't in a thanking mood.

Mikey McGill had been in Everlost for a very long time, and had experienced a great many things. He had captained a ship, he had sunk to the center of the earth, and climbed back again, he had been a boy, a monster, and a boy once again. He had amassed a fortune of crossed objects, and had lost that fortune as well. He had endured. Yet through all of it, no experience was as confusing and unreasonable as the experience of love. He had denied for the longest time that he loved Allie. He had told himself their relationship was of no great consequence — that he was merely grateful to her for having saved him from being a monster. He had told himself that their companionship was merely a useful arrangement, while he considered what to do next.

All of these were lies.

The fact was, he loved Allie so intensely it frightened him. There were times when he looked at her that his own afterglow mellowed from pale blue to almost lavender. He realized that love must have its own spectral shade, and wondered if Allie ever noticed it.

His own reaction to Milos caught Mikey off guard. When he was the McGill no one dared challenge Mikey's authority. He ruled supreme. Although things were different since teaming up with Allie, in all this time, no one had penetrated the little circle he and Allie had made. The two of them were always on the move — other Afterlights they met passed in and out of view like the scenery.

Now, however, their circle had become an unpleasant fellowship of five. It wasn't Moose and Squirrel that troubled Mikey. Milos was the threat. Milos, and his easy smile, and his charming accent, and the wispy hint of facial hair that might have been a beard had he lived a year longer. Allie called him charming—and although Mikey knew she had said it just to tease him, it did more than that. It goaded him. It taunted him. Mikey had no idea whether or not Milos was a good spirit, or bad, all he knew was that he hated Milos for simply existing.

For two days as they walked along Interstate 81, and then Interstate 40, nobody skinjacked. This was by Milos's decree—out of respect for Mikey, so he said. By twilight of the second day, Moose and Squirrel were itching for it. Mikey could tell that Allie was too. As they rested on a set of deadspots, beneath what must have been a particularly lethal overpass, Mikey could see Allie's restlessness.

"You weren't like this before," Mikey said to Allie as they sat on a spot a dozen yards away from the others. "You never *needed* to skinjack."

Allie didn't answer right away, but she didn't shrug it off either.

"I've been skinjacking more lately," she finally said, "and the more you skinjack, the more you need to. Don't ask me to explain it, because I can't."

"Do you want to be like them?" he asked her, pointing to Moose and Squirrel, who were twitchy and irritable, like drug addicts needing a fix.

"I'll never be like them," Allie said, although she didn't seem too confident. "And anyway, once we get to Memphis, they'll go their way, and we'll go ours."

"And which way is that?"

Again, Allie didn't have an answer for him. This wasn't like her—Allie tended to have an answer for everything, even if it was wrong.

"Everything's changed now," Allie said, although she didn't say why.

"I know what'll happen," Mikey said. "You'll see your family, and you'll take your coin and go. I know you will."

She sighed. "Trust me, I won't. And anyway, you were the one who brought me to Cape May to find my family, weren't you?"

She was right about that. Mikey shrugged. "So? I was trying to do the right thing. The *human* thing. But maybe I don't want to do the right thing anymore." He couldn't look at her as he said it, and he thought she'd be mad at him and launch into a long speech about the virtues of human compassion and thinking of others before yourself.

But instead she smiled and said, "I'll make you a promise, Mikey. I promise that I'll always be here for you . . . and I promise not to move on . . . until *you* do." Then she leaned over and gave him a gentle kiss on the cheek.

He hoped she didn't notice the slight lavender blush of his afterglow.

Allie had, in fact, noticed the faint color shift in Mikey's afterglow several times before, and although she was usually quite smart about things, she missed all the cues on this one. She simply assumed it was some sort of remnant from his life as the McGill—the equivalent of a living-world scar that ached with changes in the weather. After all they'd been through, she cared for Mikey deeply—not as a boyfriend, though, because that was a living-world concept, and in the living world, boyfriends come and go. A hand held today would be slapping a face tomorrow. Mikey wasn't like a brother to her either. Nick was the one she saw as a brother; connected forever, born into Everlost at the same moment, like ghostly twins.

What was Mikey, then? A soul mate? Perhaps. She couldn't deny there was a sense of comfort in their relationship. They were perfect companions—a good fit for each other. Just being with him gave her a feeling of peace and belonging, but it lacked . . . excitement.

Sure, from time to time, when the moment called for it, she would kiss him, but an Everlost kiss was not the same as a living kiss. There was no heat to it, no beating heart, no adrenaline rush. There can be no way to find oneself breathless when one doesn't really need to breathe. In the end, companions are all two Afterlights can ever be.

And now there was Milos.

Allie could understand why Mikey saw Milos as a threat—and she had to admit she enjoyed teasing Mikey about it—but only because she knew Mikey had nothing to worry about. She had no desire to abandon Mikey for someone else, and certainly not for Milos. So she entered into her friendship with Milos fully believing she had her eyes open and her mind set.

She was very wrong.

# CHAPTER 10

## *Skinjacking for Fun and Profit*

The following morning, Milos suggested a skin-jacking expedition to a nearby roadside café. "No disrespect is meant to you, my friend," he said to Mikey apologetically, "but like it or not, we skinjackers do have needs."

Mikey could see how much Allie perked up at the suggestion. He could also see how much she tried to hide it.

"Yeah, yeah," said Squirrel. "Needs. Like we need to sit inside a nice, juicy fleshie, and enjoy their nice juicy bacon cheeseburger."

"Why should I care if you skinjack?" Mikey said. "Do whatever you want."

Then Milos turned to Allie. "You should join us," he said. "I can see you are in need."

"She doesn't *need* anything," said Mikey.

But Allie said, "I can speak for myself, Mikey." Then she looked at Milos, and said, "Thank you for the invitation, but I'd prefer not to."

This, Mikey knew was a lie—he knew she really did

want to go, but instead she stayed with Mikey as the other three left. It was a good feeling to know she chose to say with him, but that was tempered by how bad he felt to know he was making her suffer.

"Tell ush about Mary the Shky Witsch."

"Yeah, yeah, tell us."

Milos, Moose, and Squirrel had come back from the diner in good spirits. It was dark now and all five of them rested on a deadspot on the highway shoulder. Like Allie, these three other skinjackers enjoyed the act of sleeping— a totally unnecessary thing for an Afterlight. Mikey much preferred nonstop wakefulness—but he had been willing to adhere to a living sleep cycle because that's what Allie preferred. Now he realized it must be a common desire among skinjackers. It was just one more thing making Mikey feel like the odd man out.

"Iz it true the Shky Witsch iz beautiful?"

"Is it true she rides in a giant balloon? Huh, huh?"

Apparently Moose and Squirrel wanted bedtime stories as they sat there in a small circle. There was no campfire, only the gentle light of their afterglows.

"Do we really need to talk about this?" said Mikey.

"Of course not," said Milos. "If you would rather not." But then he added, "I am curious, though. I have never met anyone who knows the Sky Witch or the Chocolate Ogre— and you know both!"

Well, Allie was the one who dropped their names, Mikey decided to let her field the questions.

"So, so you're friends with them?" asked Squirrel.

"The Chocolate Ogre—*Nick*, I mean—is my friend," Allie said.

Moose shook his helmeted head. "Thatsh a bad name for an ogre."

"Nick's NOT an ogre. Or at least I don't think he is—I haven't seen him for a long time," Allie said. "We died in the same car accident."

Both Moose and Squirrel looked over at Milos when she said that. Mikey wondered why, and wondered if Allie noticed.

"Sho what about the Shky Witch?" asked Moose.

"Her name is Mary Hightower," Allie said.

"I know, I know," said Squirrel excitedly. "I seen her books!"

"Her real name is Megan," said Mikey, feeling further and further out of the loop. "Mary's just her middle name." But the others ignored him.

"Don't believe everything you read in those books," Allie said. "She lies and makes stuff up when it suits her."

"She does not have nice things to say about skinjackers," Milos said. "Still, I would like to meet her one day. She seems very . . . intriguing."

"That's not the word I would use," Allie said. "She lures souls in, and traps them in an endless rut, doing the same thing day after day, forever."

"And," added Mikey, "she's my sister."

The others looked at him for a moment, and broke out laughing.

"Yeah, yeah," Squirrel scoffed, "and the McGill is my cousin."

Now Allie burst out laughing, which just made Mikey more annoyed.

"If the McGill was your cousin," Mikey said, "I can guarantee he'd disown you."

Allie reached over and secretly squeezed Mikey's hand, leaving him to wonder what the squeeze meant. Was it a show of affection, or was she trying to tell him he was revealing too much information?

"Now it's your turn," said Allie, changing the subject. "Tell us about Jackin' Jill."

Clearly this was a sore spot with the other skinjackers, because they all looked away. Finally Milos spoke up.

"She and I were very close," he said.

"How close?" Mikey asked, realizing Milos had a nice wound worthy of being prodded and poked.

"Close," was the only answer he gave. "We traveled together, doing jobs for other Afterlights, in exchange for crossed objects."

"Jobs?" asked Allie. "What kinds of jobs?"

"Jobs that could only be accomplished by skinjackers," Milos said. "We would tell family members that their loved one in Everlost was all right. We would pass on some information that they otherwise would have taken to the grave. We would finish their unfinished business in the living world."

"Yeah, yeah," said Squirrel. "There was one kid who was obsessed with finishing his model airplane. So Moose and I skinjacked a couple of neighbor kids and finished it for him."

"And don't forget the time we got hired by that kid in Philly to beat up the fleshie that got him killed."

Milos sighed. "Some tasks were more appropriate for Moose and Squirrel than others."

"Impressive," said Mikey, in spite of himself. The idea of using skinjacking as a profitable skill tickled Mikey where he lived.

"Yeah, yeah—we were very impressive—and we were rich, too," said Squirrel.

Milos nodded. "By Everlost standards. We had quite a collection of crossed objects—and these were not just ordinary items. We had gold and diamonds—our customers would trade us their prized possessions in return for what we could offer. We even had a Porsche."

"No way!" said Allie.

"It's true, it's true," said Squirrel, "but it was a pain in the neck, 'cause it could only drive on roads that don't exist no more."

"Jill would be the one to pass on messages to the living. She was best at convincing the living that the message was real." Milos looked off, caught in the memory. "Then, one day we woke up, and Jill was gone, along with the car and all of our finest things—and she even stole things from the vapor of Afterlights that had taken us in. There were many, and they were all furious."

"Yeah, yeah—they thought *we* had done it. We had to skin-jack our way to safety. Lucky there were some fleshies around."

"Jackin' Jill took everything worth taking," said Moose. "Everything! But we're gonna find her. And when we do . . . " He smashed his fist into his palm.

"I'm sorry," Allie said to Milos, with a level of compassion that made Mikey sick.

"Serves them right!" Mikey said. "It's what you get for being greedy."

Allie threw him a disapproving glare. "You of all people shouldn't talk about greed!"

When she turned her eyes back to Milos they were all sympathetic again, and Mikey just couldn't stand it. He stood up and strode away.

"Where are you going?" Allie asked.

"I don't know," he said. "Maybe I'll catch up with Jackin' Jill."

Allie started after Mikey, but snared herself on a barbed wire fence that, for reasons unknown, had crossed into Everlost. A sharp steel barb tore a deep gash on her arm that felt momentarily weird before it zipped itself closed. By the time she looked up, Mikey was gone.

"Let him go," said Milos, coming up behind her. "Clearly he has . . . what is that expression? 'Skeletons in his closet.'"

"Yeah, and bats in his belfry," Allie said.

Milos looked at her, puzzled. "This expression I do not know."

"Never mind," she said, not wanting to get into it. Mikey's temper tantrums had gotten fewer and further between, but they never went away completely. His moodiness always surfaced in the company of other Afterlights. Social skills were never his strong point. As for "skeletons in his closet," that implied he had secrets Allie didn't know — but she knew all his secrets, didn't she?

"Whatever bee he's got in his bonnet, he'll get over it," Allie said.

Milos smiled. "Bats in belfries, bees in bonnets—this is why I love English."

Allie turned to return to their campsite on the highway, but then Milos said something that stopped her.

"You know . . . I could teach you things."

She slowly turned back to him. "What do you mean?"

Milos sauntered closer to her, hands in his pockets. "If you came skinjacking with us, there are many things I could teach you. Skinjacking is more than just climbing inside fleshies and putting them to sleep."

"If you're talking about your little business of delivering messages to the living, no thank you. I don't want to be a part of . . . of DeadEx."

"This is not what I mean," said Milos, his voice brimming with hushed excitement. "I am talking about the *joy* of it!"

Allie immediately thought to the time she had gone out into the rain. She understood the joy he was talking about, but it was always overshadowed by the guilt she felt stealing moments that weren't hers.

"Have you never dreamed of being someone else?" Milos asked. "Someone rich, or beautiful, or powerful. Have you never longed, if only for a few minutes, to live someone else's life?"

"Of course I have. . . ."

"And yet you do not do it? Why is this?"

"Because it's wrong!"

"Who told you it was wrong? Was it Mikey?"

"No!" said Allie. "I don't need him to tell me the difference between right and wrong."

Milos took a long look at Allie. "Skinjackers are not like

other Afterlights, Allie, and we all must learn to accept this. Because not only are we given this power, but also a powerful hunger to use it."

"A hunger that we should resist!" insisted Allie.

"Resist our nature? Do you not think *that* would be wrong?"

Allie found that Milos was standing just a bit too close, and she took a step back. He was making far too much sense, and it troubled her. She had wanted another skinjacker to talk to — someone who could understand the things she felt. She thought it would be a case of misery-loves-company. She never expected to find a skinjacker who reveled in possessing the living, turning it into an art form. A way of life. What if he was right, and resisting that powerful pull to flesh was the wrong thing for her to do?

"Flesh and bone deserves to be appreciated," Milos said. "Those who have it take it for granted, but not us! We appreciate every breath, every breeze, every beat of the heart. And so, by borrowing their flesh, *we* are the ones who give their bodies the dignity they have lost."

All the reservations that held Allie back — that slapped her down every time she skinjacked — were beginning to feel insignificant, and she was torn. If skinjacking truly was her nature, shouldn't she embrace it?

"Please," said Milos, "let me teach you. Let me show you some of the things I know. I promise you will not be disappointed!"

Allie shook her head, then nodded, but then shook her head again. Finally she settled on telling him, "I'll think about it."

Then she turned and hurried back to the others, for once glad to be in the company of Moose and Squirrel.

It was hard for Afterlights to hide at night. Their afterglow always gave them away. Mikey just wanted some time alone, to brood, maybe sit on a rock, look at the moon, and let all those unpleasant feelings work themselves out, if indeed they ever would. The problem was, the only rock large enough to sit on was living-world, and Mikey had to continually pull himself up out from it. It was annoying.

Then, the last person he wanted to see emerged through a tree trunk, easily finding him by his glow. Mikey wasn't sure whether to stare Milos down or just ignore him. So he did one, then the other.

"Allie is worried about you," Milos said.

"I really don't care," grumbled Mikey.

"This does not surprise me."

"Why is it your business anyway?" Mikey snapped. When Milos had no response to that, Mikey said, "Tell her I'm fine, and I'll come back when I feel like it."

Milos lifted his feet to keep himself from sinking, but didn't leave. He just regarded Mikey with a detached kind of curiosity.

"Why do you hold her back?" Milos asked.

"Excuse me?"

Milos took a step closer. "She could go so much further. She could be so much more. But you—you keep her from using her skills. You are very much an anchor around her neck. This is very selfish."

Mikey came off of his rock to face him. "You don't know what you're talking about!"

But Milos remained calm, and sure of himself. "Is it my words that anger you," he asked, "or is it because you know I speak the truth?"

If there was any hope that Mikey might warm to Milos — maybe even become a reluctant friend, that hope was now gone. "Allie and I . . . Allie and I care for each other. We've been through a lot together — you have no idea!"

"You are right," said Milos, "but I do know that she bears a certain sadness. You must see it."

Yes, of course Mikey had seen it, but he wasn't about to admit it to this skinjacking outsider. "Like I said, you don't know anything."

"You claim to care for her, but I do not see this. If you cared for her, perhaps you would see that your destinies now lie on different paths."

*"Do not anger me!"* Mikey roared. *"I am not to be trifled with!"* And he heard in his own voice a roughness and a rawness he hadn't heard in a long time. Overtones of the McGill.

Milos put his hands up in surrender, as if he were backing down — but Mikey knew this was just another calculated move. "Then pardon me." Milos said, "I meant no disrespect."

"You say that a lot," Mikey pointed out, looking him right in those weirdly distracting speckled eyes. "But I think disrespect is *exactly* what you mean."

"I am only thinking of what is best for Allie," said Milos with a gaze that penetrated uncomfortably deep. "Are you?"

Then he left Mikey alone with his rock, his thoughts, and the moon.

* * *

The next day, they came to the town of Lebanon, Tennessee, and again Milos asked Allie if she wanted to come skinjacking with him. She broached the topic as gently as she could with Mikey.

"There are things he can teach me about skinjacking," Allie told him. "Things that could probably help us."

"Why are you telling me?" Mikey snapped. "If you want to go, then go. Why should I care?"

"I'd feel much better about it if you weren't acting so childish."

"Maybe I don't want you to feel better about it."

Allie clenched her fists and growled in frustration. "I swear, Mikey, sometimes . . . "

"Sometimes what? Sometimes you wonder why you put up with me?"

Allie took a moment to calm herself down. "I know why I put up with you. What I don't understand is why you don't trust *me*."

Mikey looked down and aimlessly kicked the ground. The living world rippled like waves in a pond. "I trust you," he said, his voice a low grumble. "Go learn something useful."

"Thank you." She gave him a gentle peck on the cheek, then went off to join Milos.

Once they were gone, Moose and Squirrel approached him.

"Why don't you come with ush, Mikey?" Moose asked.

"Yeah, yeah," said Squirrel. "Skinjacking can be fun to watch, too. Especially the way we do it."

And although tagging along with the two of them was

the last thing he wanted to do, he went along, because it was better than spending the day thinking of Allie in the company of Milos.

Mikey had to admit, watching Moose and Squirrel skinjack that day was entertaining, in a blood-sport sort of way. They were both ingeniously inventive, and decidedly deranged.

First they skinjacked two older teens who were on their way to summer school, but instead used them to get into an R-rated movie. Then, when they got bored with the movie, they skinjacked two policemen and took their squad car for a joyride, leaving the policemen and the car in a ditch, to wonder how they had gotten there.

Each time they skinjacked, they left their fleshies stuck with whatever bad situation they had created, and walked away scott-free. *Hit-and-run jackers*, he dubbed them.

"We're just having fun," they complained, when Mikey suggested that their activities were depraved. But then, who was he to talk? He had been the McGill—yet even though he had perpetrated a good many mean-spirited, spiteful things, his depravity had a little more class.

Next, Moose and Squirrel went into a bar, got two middle-aged fleshies exceptionally drunk, then peeled out of them just before they were ready to puke.

"No harm, no foul!" said Squirrel. "Right? Right?"

"Yeah," added Moose, "They were gonna do it anyway."

Mikey concluded that these two were the lowest bottom-feeders he'd ever had the misfortune to know. "Does Milos know you're abusing fleshies?"

"Milosh and ush got a 'don't ashk don't tell' polishy," said Moose.

"Yeah, yeah—and anyway, we don't abuse no one—we just play hard, that's all."

Mikey only hoped that when it was finally their turn to go into the light, their pit would be deeper than his.

When Moose and Squirrel skinjacked a couple of nuns, and took them on a shoplifting spree, Mikey decided it was time to call it a day. He crossed through a forest that he hoped would take him back to their makeshift campsite by the highway. The forest had quite a few trees that had crossed into Everlost, and so provided him with spots to rejuvenate, and maybe regain some self-respect. His spirit felt greasy after the way he had spent the day.

There was a house in the woods—a shack, really, but sturdy and cared for. Evidence of ash in the living world suggested it had burned down, but whoever lived there must have loved the place, because it had crossed into Everlost. The sight of it filled Mikey with sorrow. A ghost house with no ghost. What could be sadder? Then he realized why the house bothered him. This shack was him without Allie. Solitary and unvisited. An unknown artifact waiting for eternity to free it from its vigil.

It was at that moment he realized that his spirit was truly human once more. For he no longer remembered how to be alone without being lonely.

In her groundbreaking book on skinjacking *You Don't Know Jack*, Allie the Outcast writes:

"Forget all you've heard about skinjackers; forget the idiotic ramblings of other so-called sources of Everlost information. Skinjackers are just like any other Afterlights. They can be honorable or dishonorable, smart or stupid — it all depends on the individual. There are two things that hold true for all skinjackers, though. The first is a driving, almost instinctive need to skinjack. The second is the overwhelming burden that such a power puts on us. With such a power, the potential exists for incredibly good deeds, and for acts of unthinkable evil. I think it's fortunate for both the living and the dead that most skinjackers are too clueless to do much of either."

# CHAPTER 11

## *Surfing Tennessee*

In her days on the *Sulphur Queen*, Allie had pretended to teach the McGill how to skinjack. Of course her lessons were bogus—skinjacking can't be taught—but it *can* be perfected, and Milos was a master. He could do things Allie had never even thought to do. Things she never dared to do!

At first, he just showed off. They came across a basketball court where a choose-up game was in full swing. He skinjacked the player with the ball, then passed to another player—but Milos got to the other player before the ball did, skinjacked him, and caught his own pass. Allie watched, laughing in spite of herself, as he bounced himself around the court, becoming one player, then another, then another, passing the ball to himself, stealing the ball from himself, shooting and scoring. Allie got dizzy trying to keep track of where and who he was.

By the time he was done, the players were all a bit dazed and confused, not quite sure what had just occurred.

"Jill and I would play many sports together," Milos

told her. "We would jump from player to player—that was always part of the game." The memory brought a smile, but a measure of pain to Milos's expression.

"Did you love her?" Allie dared to ask.

Milos took a few moments before answering. "We came upon a wedding once," he told her. "We skinjacked the bride and groom."

"You didn't!"

"Well, *I* skinjacked the groom, but Jill's legs were cold."

Allie looped that back through her mind. "Do you mean she got cold feet?"

"Yes, she got cold feet. Instead of the bride, she went to hide in the flower girl. That should have told me something, you think?"

"I'm sorry, Milos." Then a silence fell between them that was decidedly awkward.

They made their way to the heart of the town, and found a street fair in full swing taking up all three blocks of Lebanon, Tennessee's main street.

"For your first lesson, I think I will teach you to surf."

Allie laughed. "Well, as the nearest beach is hundreds of miles away, I sincerely doubt that."

"Not that kind of surfing," he told her. Then in a flash he was gone. Allie thought she saw him leaping into a kid eating ice cream, but the kid just continued on.

"Milos?"

"Over here!" His voice was coming from somewhere far away. She looked down the street, and finally caught sight of him — he wasn't skinjacking now, he was just standing in the middle of the street fair, two whole blocks away, waving at her. How on earth had he done that?

Then he vanished again, and a few seconds later, there he was standing right beside her.

"Boo!" he said, and she jumped in spite of herself.

"Did you just . . . *teleport*?"

"More like tele-phoned," Milos answered. "Wires conduct electrical impulses, yes? Well, the living conduct *us*."

"I don't understand."

"I call it soul-surfing. It is a very good way to travel, when there are many people nearby." When Allie first learned to skinjack — before she knew what it was called — she had called it body-surfing. But this feat of relaying oneself across a crowd in seconds — this truly deserved to be called surfing. She wondered if it felt as invigorating as riding a wave. Milos looked around at the modest crowd of the little street fair. "Okay, your turn."

"Wh-what?" Allie sputtered. "I can't do that! I wouldn't know where to start."

"Start with her." Milos pointed to a woman sitting on a bench, reading a newspaper.

"Make as if you mean to skinjack her, but don't take full control. Instead, you must use her to slingshot to the next person, then the next, then the next. Once you get a rhythm, you can work your way to the end of any crowd in seconds."

He climbed into a passing pedestrian, vanished, then a few seconds later appeared across the street.

"Try it!" he called. "From there to here. Short hop."

Allie leaped into the woman on the bench, but lingered too long, and had to peel herself out, which never happened quickly—it was like peeling off a glove. Since Allie didn't immediately put her to sleep, the woman knew something funny was going on. She stood up, looked around, and walked away, unnerved.

Milos had already surfed back and was beside her.

"Well, that didn't work," said Allie.

"Because you took hold. Do not stay long enough to hear the thoughts—just long enough to get a small glimpse through the eyes, then push off."

Allie tried it again with a different person, but still stayed an instant too long, and got drawn in. Milos was patient with her, and encouraging. "Think of Tarzan," he said. "It is like Tarzan swinging on ropes." Then he beat his chest and made a Tarzan yell that made Allie laugh. She tried it again, and the third time was the charm. She began to jump out before she was done jumping in, and it worked! She pushed off from one person to another. Images passed before her like snapshots, but all unrelated and random. Every fleshie was looking in a slightly different direction, and saw things differently. Colors changed, eyesight changed. Each person she surfed was focusing on something different within their field of vision—but now that Allie had the rhythm she could keep herself moving. She began to feel dizzy, and finally took root in a fleshie to stop herself, and—

—*nagging nagging nagging—if she doesn't stop nagging I'll go crazy—nagging nagging nagging—*

She found herself sitting in a restaurant, holding a spoon and looking across the table at a very old woman.

"Harold? Harold? How's the soup, Harold?" the old woman said to her.

Allie, in the body of the woman's elderly husband, tried to speak, but could only burp.

"Too spicy. I knew it!" Then the old woman called for the waitress.

Allie peeled herself out of Harold the Henpecked Husband, and when she was back in Everlost she made her way out into the street. Once outside, she got her bearings, and realized she had crossed the avenue, turned a corner, and had unexpectedly bounced herself into a delicatessen. Milos found her a few moments later.

"What happened?"

"I guess I got lost."

Milos laughed. "It happens. It is hard to keep a sense of direction, yes? You will get better, it just takes practice."

And so they practiced. It got a bit harder once the crowd thinned, but it just served as a challenge to her. She found that if she pushed off hard enough, she could leap from one person to another who was about ten feet away.

"Moose and Squirrel have been doing this for years, and they can not jump that far," Milos told her. "You are, as they say, a natural!"

After a couple of hours Allie was exhausted. She had surfed her way through hundreds of people—some of them several times, and she had begun to recognize the "signature" of their bodies.

"Do they know we're here?" Allie asked Milos. "We're only in them for an instant, but still . . . can they sense us the way we sense them?"

Milos raised his eyebrows. "Do you remember when you were alive," he asked, "and you suddenly forgot what you were about to say?"

"Yes . . . "

Milos smiled. "Perhaps someone was surfing through you."

The thought gave Allie a shiver. Even though she was no longer in flesh, having surfed through so much of it, her spirit held onto some phantom physical feelings. One of those phantom feelings echoed within her when she looked at Milos, and she shivered again. She resisted the urge to move closer to him, and feel his afterglow mingle with hers. It was, after all, just a phantom feeling, easy to dismiss, wasn't it?

"Congratulations," he said gently. "You are one of the Deadlies now. You are one of us." His smile became wider, and that made her all the more uncomfortable. She turned away.

"In any case, soul-surfing is good for crowded places, and big cities," he said. "I can get through a city faster than anything." Then, with a gentle toss of his head, he said, "Although sometimes I prefer to drive if I can skinjack a good-looking man, with a Ferrari."

Allie shook her head, warding off an unpleasant memory. "I tried to jack and drive once. It didn't end well."

Milos puffed out his chest. "So then I do the driving. You ride shot put."

"Shotgun," Allie corrected. His butchered expressions always made her smile, but the smile faded quickly. "I still think it's wrong to skinjack people just for fun."

"What makes fun wrong?" he asked. And when she didn't have an answer for him, Milos said, "What we do is right. It is *natural*—or else why would we be able to do it? If we are skinjackers, we are meant to skinjack."

"We provide a link between Everlost and the living world—perhaps the most important one," Allie insisted. "Maybe we were meant to use it for something important."

"Maybe we were meant to simply enjoy it."

She wanted to argue, but between his easy logic, and his easier smile, she found her argument had no teeth. She looked down to see that, while Milos had continued to shift his feet to keep from sinking, Allie had not, and had sunken into the sidewalk to her ankles. She pulled her feet out, feeling embarrassed that he had caught her ankle-deep.

"In life did you ever do something just for fun?" asked Milos.

"Yes . . ."

"So why not be as you were in life? And if it hurts no one, why is it wrong to enjoy skinjacking? This is what we are."

"No, it's what we *do*!"

"No, Allie, it is what we *are*." Milos gently put his hand on her shoulder. "It is what *you* are."

"So was it fun?" Mikey asked.

Allie shrugged, trying, for his sake, to hide how much she had enjoyed the soul-surfing lesson. "It was tiring. I prefer being me, rather than the crowd. What did you do?"

"I took a walk."

"Through town?" She wondered if he had been downtown, and had seen her with Milos. If she were a fleshie she would have flushed at the thought, then she got mad at herself. She had nothing to feel guilty for.

"I went into the woods," he told her. "There's an oak grove where half the trees have crossed over. And in the middle of it I found a house that crossed over too. It would be a nice place to live. That is . . . if you wanted to."

"We can't 'live,'" she reminded him.

"No, but we could enjoy our existence here. I'm tired of being a finder. I'm tired of moving around. I'm tired of everything."

Allie considered this, noting the slight lavender tinge to his afterglow. Perhaps there was a different meaning for it. "Then maybe you're ready," she said.

"Ready for what?"

"To move on."

What Allie meant as a simple observation hit Mikey like a fist on flesh. He took a step back, reeling from the blow, but tried not to show how deeply it hurt him.

"Maybe I am," he said.

She turned from him. "If you're ready, Mikey, then I won't stop you."

*No, of course you won't,* he wanted to say. *Because then I wouldn't be an anchor around your neck anymore.* But instead he said, "Tell me to stay, and I will . . . "

But Allie shook her head. "That would be selfish of me."

\* \* \*

Once upon a time, Mikey McGill had a bucket of coins. He collected them from every Afterlight he brought to his ship—whether they became a part of his crew, or went to the chiming chamber to hang upside down from their ankles. Why did he take their coins? Because everyone and everything he captured was his property. That's the way he saw things back then. But why did he keep the coins in a bucket, locked safely away? The answer was simple, although he couldn't admit it to himself.

He kept them because he knew.

He knew what the coins were for, just like every Afterlight knows, without ever knowing that they know. It's the memory of a dream lost on waking; it's a name on the tip of your tongue. But if you're an Afterlight, the truth will someday come to you, and you'll realize that you've always known. Sure, for the longest time, the coin was simply standing on its edge in your mind, just a dull metallic sliver, so very hard to see . . . but look again—now it's full and round and shining in your palm. It is your proof of something beyond the Everlost, and your fare to get you there.

Once upon a time, Mikey had a bucket of stolen coins, but now he only had one, and since the moment he admitted to himself what the coin was for—the same moment that Allie made the choice to join him—he was always conscious of that coin in his pocket.

Now it felt heavy, like an entire purse full of coins. All he had to do was pull it out and hold it in his hand. Would it be hot for him now? Would it cause space to part before him, revealing the tunnel to the great beyond, which would suck him out of Everlost, sending him to wherever he was going?

And where was he going?

What if he still hadn't redeemed himself? What if he'd been a monster for so long, he hadn't been able to undo all the dastardly deeds of the McGill?

Well, so what if he hadn't! If that tunnel drew him in, then dropped him into a pit, so be it! He had endured the center of the earth, hadn't he? He could endure *that* place as well.

But he'd be lying if he said he wasn't scared.

He didn't fear anguish—there had been enough of that in his afterlife to last an eternity. He feared . . . nothingness. He feared *being* nothing. And yet, that's exactly how he felt now. Here, among skinjackers, he felt inferior, and that *was* a feeling he could not abide.

No! He would not go down the tunnel with his head hung low. He was once great—he had to remember that. He once inspired fear and respect, but he gave that up for Allie. Because he loved her. And although he still loved her deeply, it wasn't the same as it had been, and he marveled at how love could have so many hidden textures . . . for the feeling that once cushioned his heart now chafed at it.

The five of them walked through most of the night to make up for lost time, then early the next morning, Milos took Allie out for more skinjacking lessons. Today Milos taught her the skills of "justicing," and "terminizing."

Justicing involved skinjacking the incarcerated. There

was a penitentiary halfway between Lebanon and Nashville, and that's where Milos took her.

"I know it is not a romantic place for a date," he had joked.

"Good thing it's not a date," she reminded him.

While the electrified gate of a high-security prison kept the living from escaping, it was little more than an annoyance for an Afterlight. Allie felt the current as she passed through the gate, and it left her with a passing feeling that resembled indigestion, if one could feel indigestion throughout one's entire body.

Once inside the prison, they proceeded to skinjack various prisoners, with the specific goal of determining if they were guilty of the crime they were imprisoned for.

"That's impossible," Allie had told him before they began. "Sure, we can hear their thoughts, but only the things they happen to be thinking about—and if we get too close, they know we're there, and they freak out."

"Ah, but we can control the *direction* of their thoughts," Milos had told her, "without them ever knowing we are there." Then he told her to skinjack one of the milder looking prisoners, and at the same time, think of something that made her feel guilty. Her thoughts immediately went to Mikey, and how bad she felt that he was left alone while the rest of them were out skinjacking—and as those thoughts filled her, she suddenly got flashes from the prisoner. His own guilty conscience told her that, yes, he *did* steal all those social-security checks from helpless elderly men and women.

The moment the confession hit her, Allie peeled herself out, stunned. It took her a few minutes until she was willing to try it again. She tried four more times before it became too much for her. The last prisoner was either innocent, or too hard to read, she wasn't sure.

"Yes," Milos told her. "Guilt is easy, innocence is hard."

"But what's the point of it?" Allie asked. "They're already in prison—what's the point in us knowing they're guilty?"

Milos grinned. "What if the ones we *justice* are not in prison?"

Allie thought about it, and found the idea both compelling and disturbing. "Do you mean diving into random people, and searching their thoughts for crimes?"

"Not necessarily," said Milos. "We could search the minds of people awaiting trial, or perhaps people who are suspected of getting away with the perfect crime. We can find the truth within them, and then make them confess. Have you ever seen a criminal confess to something they might have otherwise gotten away with? Well, maybe they were *justiced* by a skinjacker."

"But isn't that . . . invasion of privacy?"

Milos shrugged. "No more so than a search warrant, and that is perfectly legal. We just search a little deeper."

Although Allie felt conflicted, she had to admit that it *could* be ethical, if there were strict guidelines—such as only searching those who are already under official suspicion. But then, who would decide what the guidelines should be? Every skinjacker would make up their own rules, and not all of them would be as honorable as her.

"This is a good skill to know," Milos explained. "You see, there are those here in Everlost who will pay well to have their killers brought to justice."

"I don't want to be paid."

"Fair enough," Milos said. "Sometimes a good deed is payment enough."

Which led them to the second lesson of the day. *Terminizing.* For this he took her to a hospital in the outskirts of Nashville. Once there, they found several terminally ill patients. Milos amazed Allie by skinjacking one of them — not to take over the patient's body, but simply to make himself known. By the time Milos peeled away, the man had a look on his face like he had been visited by an angel.

"We tell them the truth," Milos explained. "We tell them that there is something more. That after their last heartbeat, the tunnel and the light will come."

"But we don't know what's in the light."

"It does not matter," said Milos. "Most people just want to know that there is something, whatever that something is."

As they went searching for another patient, Allie dared to ask, "So, what's in it for you?"

Milos looked down. "I see," he said sadly. "Everything Milos does must serve Milos."

Allie immediately felt bad she had said anything.

Milos held his pout for a moment more, then it became a mischievous grin. "I ask them to put in a good word for me when they reach the light."

Allie slapped his arm, and he laughed. "Shut up! You do not!" But she was never quite sure if he was joking or serious.

Following Milos's lead, Allie entered a patient, and revealed her presence slowly, so as not to frighten the woman.

Then she spoke of the tunnel and the light. Milos was right—that was all it took to give the woman an overwhelming feeling of peace and comfort. *Thank you!* the woman said in her thoughts. *Oh, thank you!* She didn't know who Allie was, but that didn't matter. It was the message that mattered, not the messenger, and once Allie had peeled away, the feeling of utter peace lingered with her. This was definitely more rewarding than justicing. It was the kind of bedside comfort the living simply could not give. *Perhaps this is the reason we can skinjack,* thought Allie. *To do things like this.*

Allie must have communed with a dozen patients before she felt so exhausted by it, and filled with their gratitude, that she had to stop.

It was getting dark as they left the hospital, and as her mind ran through the miraculous things they did today, she couldn't help but reel from the sheer awe of it. Since the first day she discovered she could skinjack, she had lived in fear of the idea—she had treated it like a nasty little secret, to be used only when absolutely necessary. It kept her from seeing the possibilities!

"Do you realize what we could do?" she told Milos. "Solve the world's greatest crimes, bring peace to the most troubled places on earth. Why, through skinjacking, we could actually change the world!"

Milos found this very amusing. "You wag a finger at me for playing with fleshies, and here you want to change the world!"

"I didn't say I wanted to, just that we *could*."

Then his gaze changed. He was no longer laughing. Now he looked a bit bemused, instead of amused—as if looking at

Allie was like looking at a wonder. The gaze made her feel awkward and she had to look away.

"Perhaps I am too small-minded," Milos said. "This has always been my problem—but now, thanks to you, I will change. I will try to think more . . . globally."

At the time Allie thought he was just humoring her.

*Skinjacking can change the world.*

Only much later would her own words come back to haunt her.

In her book *You Don't Know Jack*, Allie the Outcast makes the following observations:

"Unlike other Afterlights, we have an unfailing memory, and we don't change, since we don't forget who we were. What's more important to remember is that we are more like other Afterlights than we are different—and we must help nonjackers to see this. We straddle two worlds—Everlost and the world of the living. If we wish to be respected and not feared, we must be good ambassadors to both."

# CHAPTER 12

## *Of Monsters and Mullets*

There was no question that Nashville slowed them down, what with so many skinjacking opportunities. Mikey was the only one annoyed by how few miles they were covering. "I thought you wanted to find your family," he reminded Allie.

"I do, but I've waited this long—a couple of days won't make a difference."

She could have told him then about how she'd be stuck in Everlost for a long, long time, so there was no hurry to do anything—but she knew Mikey would ask her a million questions she had no answers to. Like what it meant to be consigned to Everlost for her "natural life," as if the universe knew when she would have died if she hadn't been in the accident. How can a date be assigned to something that will never happen?

An exploration of Nashville had turned up a sizeable vapor of Afterlights in an old burned-out factory that had crossed over. They were friendly but guarded, not trusting of outsiders—least of all a foreigner like Milos. The Nashville Afterlights made room for them in their sizeable deadspot though, and were happy to listen to all their stories of faraway places—and to them, every place was far away.

"So you've all been into the Everwild?" their leader asked—a kid who had blue hair for no reason anyone could fathom.

"Where I come from, *this* is the Everwild," Allie told him, and that made the other kids laugh, thinking she was making a joke.

One kid didn't laugh, though. A bone-thin, sad-eyed kid who was so hunched the other kids just called him Igor. "It's all wild," he said. "No one knows anything about any-where—'cept of course for the Sky Witch."

Both Allie and Mikey shifted uncomfortably at Mary's mention, but neither of them said anything. Neither of them felt like sharing tales of Mary Hightower.

"But the real wild places are to the west," said Igor, and the other kids murmured their agreement. Then he whis-pered, "*Have you felt the wind?*"

"What wind?" asked Mikey.

"We don't feel wind in Everlost," Allie pointed out.

"You'll feel *this* wind," said Igor. "If you're goin' to Memphis you'll feel it sure enough."

Allie looked to Milos, but he just shrugged. "This is as far west as I've ever been."

"Great," grumbled Mikey. "Another problem."

"It's not a problem," said Allie. "It's just wind."

But the looks on the Nashville kids' faces said otherwise.

\* \* \*

While Moose and Squirrel bargained with the Nashville Afterlights, hoping to provide various skinjacking services, Milos invited Allie for another lesson.

"Enough talk of winds and worries," Milos said. "Tonight we have fun."

"If it's an evening of fun, then we should invite Mikey," she said, more of a reprimand than a suggestion—a little jab to remind him that their lessons were serious business.

Milos shrugged. "Of course, of course," he said, sounding a little like Squirrel, "but even if Mikey could skinjack, somehow I do not think he is one to appreciate country music."

Allie studied him, trying to read the mildly mischievous look on Milos's face. "What does country music have to do with skinjacking?"

But Milos only smiled.

Allie went to look for Mikey among the Nashville Afterlights, but he was nowhere to be found.

"Lasht time I shaw him," Moose said, "he wuz leaving the factory by himshelf."

Lately Mikey had been spending more and more time alone. It troubled Allie, but only slightly. Mikey was very good at taking care of himself.

That night, Milos took Allie to Nashville's Grand Ole Opry, where Travis Dix was in concert. There was some country music that Allie loved, and some that she hated—but whether you were a fan of country music or not, everybody loved Travis Dix. Allie's only problem with it was that this felt like a date, and that made her uncomfortable.

Alive, she had always been too busy with sports, student government, and the yearbook to date. Besides, the boys she liked were always out of reach, and the ones who did give her attention always lacked a certain something—such as common sense, or deodorant.

She always assumed there would come a time for her to make boys a priority . . . but death had put a damper on that. Well, she hadn't dated in life, and she wasn't about to start now. She had Mikey as an afterlife companion, and that was enough for her.

"So why are we here?" Allie asked Milos as they passed through the front entrance and into the crowded lobby of the ornate theater. "I hope it's not just to see a concert."

"This way," said Milos. "Come."

She followed him from the lobby into the theater, where, in a few minutes, the show would be starting. Then he led her right up onto the stage. Even though Allie knew that no one could see her, she still felt uncomfortable on a stage, facing an audience of thousands.

"You have practiced soul-surfing, and have gotten better at it," said Milos, "but now, with so many people packed into one place, you can really use it!"

Milos turned to face the audience, and looked up to the highest seats way up in the back of the balcony. The nose-bleed seats, Allie always called them.

"Tell me," said Milos, "how fast can you surf from here to the balcony and back?"

Allie smiled. "Faster than you!" Although she knew it probably wasn't true.

"Then you can try to beat me." Milos squinted up at

the balcony, then pointed. "Do you see the usher at very back?"

Allie looked up to the center aisle between the highest seats. The soft focus and muted colors of the living world made it difficult to see, but she did pick out an usher guiding people to their seats up there. "So he's our target?"

"Yes. The first one to surf all the way up there, tap the usher on the shoulder, and come back to the stage, wins."

"And no cheating!" said Allie.

"How could I cheat?"

"You're not allowed to jump from the orchestra up to the mezzanine—we both have to go out the back of the theater, into the lobby, and surf our way up the stairs."

"Fair enough," said Milos. "Are you ready?"

"Are you?"

"Ready, set, GO!"

Allie took off, making a calculated move, by jumping into a security guard that was a little closer to Milos than to her, figuring that Milos would start with him. Sure enough, Allie felt Milos trying to push his way into the guard, but couldn't because Allie was already there. It put Allie in an early lead.

She went from the guard, to a tall old man, to a short woman with big hair, to a baby, to some guy who Allie could sense didn't want to be there.

She was already out in the lobby, and lingered in the aggravated man just long enough to locate the stairs, before bounding out to the next person. Up the staircase to the mezzanine, person to person, body to body until she reached the balcony. She had no idea where Milos was, and she didn't even know who her host was now—all she could sense was that this person needed to use the bathroom.

She had to get her bearings before she hopped to the next person—she had to spot the usher. Now that she was back in the theater, she was right in front of the steep aisle leading all the way up to the seats that nearly touched the roof. The usher was halfway up that aisle, leading a man to his seat. Allie launched herself out of the full-bladdered fleshie, and surfed through two more people, and right to the man the usher was escorting—

—But she couldn't get in because Milos was already there! He had used her own trick against her! Allie bounced off the man like rubber, and by the time she had skinjacked the next closest person, Milos's fleshie had already tapped the usher on the shoulder.

"Beat you!"

"Not yet!" said Allie, tapping the usher as well.

They left the two bewildered fans and the usher behind. In a moment Allie had surfed herself down the aisle, and out the back doors of the theater again, finding herself on the stairs. Going down, she discovered, was a little trickier than coming up, because everyone was hurrying up the stairs to get to their seats. It was like running down an "up" escalator. She surfed through dozens of people, fighting the current, not lingering for more than an instant in any one person until she was back on the ground floor, and in the theater's main aisle again.

She pushed off in a smooth regular rhythm, relaying herself through various people trying to find their seats, then she surged up onto the stage—and Milos was right beside her, reaching the stage the same moment she did.

"I win!" Allie said.

"No, I win!" said Milos.

"All right, a tie, then."

Milos laughed. "Very good! We both win!"

Allie could not believe how exhilarating this had been. She wanted to do it again and again.

Milos must have read the excitement in her face, because he said, "You see? There are many, many joys to being a skinjacker."

Around them, the house lights began to dim. The audience roared in anticipation, and Allie looked out to the darkening theater, pretending that they were all cheering for her.

"Another game!" she said to Milos. "Hide-and-seek! I'll hide in a fleshie, and you have to find me!"

Milos crossed his arms. "How could I do that? —there are thousands of fleshies here!"

She grinned mischievously. "*I'll* be the one thumbing my nose at Travis Dix!" And before he could respond, she was off, surfing her way through the theater.

Travis Dix took the stage with his band, and the audience cheered. In a moment he was singing his big hit, "Stomp My Heart and Shave my Mullet," and most of the audience was singing along.

*Stomp my heart and shave my mullet*
*All your lies stick in my gullet*
*No more cash is in my wullet*
*Baby, we're through*
*But now I've got a better 'do'*

Allie chose to inhabit a college-age girl in the left mezzanine who was standing and dancing to the song with her friends. Allie carefully balanced herself within the girl, taking physical control of most of her body, but not putting her to sleep. It would be more interesting this way! Keeping her awake would be tricky, but Allie successfully hid in a blind spot of the girl's consciousness, so her presence wouldn't be detected. As soon as Allie took over, the girl's body stopped gyrating, and Allie raised her right hand, putting the tip of her thumb to her nose, and spread out her fingers.

"What are you doing?" asked one of the girl's friends.

The girl, fully awake, and still in control of her mouth said, "I . . . don't know. My thumb is stuck to my nose!"

"Suzie, honestly!" said the friend. "Travis might see you, and then we'll never get backstage!"

Allie silently giggled, and began to waggle her fingers.

"Suzie!"

"I know! I'm trying to stop!" Clearly Suzie had no idea what had possessed her to behave like this. It probably never occurred to her that she actually *was* possessed.

Travis Dix continued to sing. Then, toward the end of the song, a beefy security guard came down the aisle and pointed a flashlight right at Suzie.

*Great*, thought Allie, *now I got the girl into trouble.*

But the guard smiled. "Got you!" the guard yelled, over the blasting music. "Now it's my turn!"

It was Milos!

Allie peeled herself out of Suzie, who shook her head, looked at her hands, and in a few moments, had put the weird incident aside and was dancing to the music again.

Milos was gone, off to find someone to hide in, and Allie counted to ten, then went looking for him.

She found that this game required more than just surfing. She had to jump from person to person to get around, but also had to linger every now and then to get a good view of the different sections of the audience, because in Everlost the crowd was pretty much a blur.

She started with the upper balcony, then worked her way across, then down. There was no sign of Milos, and Allie began to wonder if maybe he wasn't playing fair.

Meanwhile, Travis Dix finished his song, and the crowd roared.

"Hello, Nashville!" he said, and the crowd roared even louder. He waited until the cheers died down before he spoke again. "This song goes out to a very special girl," he announced. "This song is for . . . Allie the Outcast."

Allie snapped her eyes to the stage and watched in disbelief as Travis Dix—*the* Travis Dix—lifted his thumb to his nose, and wiggled his fingers at the audience. To Allie's amazement, the entire audience responded by doing it right back to him!

Allie laughed out loud—a big, booming belly laugh, because now she was in a huge man with a voice that echoed like a bass drum. She skipped out of him and surfed her way back to the stage.

When she got there, Milos was peeling himself out of Travis, who now looked strangely at the audience thumbing their noses at him. Then he looked to his band, shrugged, and began the next song.

Allie couldn't stop laughing. "You win!" she told Milos.

"That was great! No one's ever dedicated a song to me before!"

"Now we shall enjoy the concert," Milos said. "After all, we can have front-row seats," and he gestured to any number of fleshies in the front row, but Allie shook her head. She didn't feel right stealing the concert from fans by putting them to sleep for the entire performance—and keeping a fleshie conscious was bound to be problematic. From where they stood on the stage, Allie could see off into the wings, where a couple of roadies stood, not doing much of anything.

"Those roadies probably travel with the band," Allie said. "They won't care if they sleep through a performance."

"Excellent—but we should switch places a few times—it is never a good idea to stay in the same fleshie for too long."

So they jacked the two roadies, and watched the whole concert from backstage. Then, when it was done, to make their concertgoing experience complete, they jacked a couple of fans in the audience, so they could flow out with the crowd, and enjoy, if only for a few minutes, the charged excitement of the audience around them.

Allie almost gasped as they left the warmth of the theater, and stepped out into the cool night. It was a subtle change, but powerful to an Afterlight, because temperature change meant nothing without flesh to feel it. A gentle breeze blew through the parking lot, and it felt soft and feathery on her arms. She swore she could feel each and every goose bump, and it was wonderful!

"I think you liked this, yes?" said Milos.

She turned, and his fleshie was right next to hers, bringing up a hand, to gently caress Allie's cheek.

Allie was caught off guard. "Don't," she said, taking a step away from him.

"Why not?"

"Well, for one, your fleshie's a girl!"

He shrugged. "So what? Yours is a boy."

Allie looked at herself. Her arms were covered with hair. No wonder the breeze felt so feathery.

"This is just too weird," she said, and peeled herself out. The living world shifted into soft focus, and the breeze now passed through her, so easy to ignore.

Milos peeled out of his fleshie. "I never thought to play hide-and-seek before," he told Allie. "I came here to teach you, and it is you who teaches me!"

"So what's tomorrow's lesson?" she asked.

"Ah," said Milos. "Tomorrow's is the best lesson of all!"

As they left to rejoin the others, Milos held his hand out to her as always, and as always Allie didn't take it, but she couldn't deny that she felt more and more tempted.

While Allie spent her days being tutored by Milos, Mikey spent his time practicing his own skills as well, although he practiced alone. Each day he went off to some secret and solitary deadspot, and there he would spend the day focusing on the one thing he could do better than anyone else. Change. It was the one aspect of his existence that he still had control over—or at least he *could* have control if he practiced enough.

Allie was off with Milos. Fine. He couldn't change that. He couldn't control what they did or said to each other. But he could grow feathers and scales. He could sprout extra arms and legs. He could even grow a rhino horn and moose antlers. And just like skinjacking, changing himself was irresistible—for who can resist their nature?

The transformations were becoming easier and easier to achieve. The hard part was changing back . . . but just as Allie was beginning to master the finer points of skinjacking, Mikey was mastering the art of bringing himself back to normal. It was all a matter of *wanting* to be Mikey McGill more than he wanted to be all those other tweaked and twisted creations. What made it difficult was that, with all the things he could be, he found it harder and harder to *want* to be Mikey McGill.

On the night that Allie and Milos played games at the Grand Ole Opry, Mikey was caught in the act.

He had found a nice sized deadspot—a street that had been torn down to build a freeway overpass. None of the buildings had crossed into Everlost, but someone must have had fond feelings for the street itself, because it had crossed over, along with all the streetlights, which still cast a pale glow all around him. It was careless of him to be practicing his transformations in such a wide-open, brightly lit space. Considering the transformation he was working, he shouldn't have been caught at all, because he quite literally had eyes in the back of his head, among other places. He had been trying to see how many eyeballs he could sprout. He had gotten up to fifty-three—they were popping up all over his body like large blue-eyed chicken pox, and each of them had a unique perspective on the world around him.

When he heard a gasp behind him, every available eye turned toward it, and he saw Squirrel trying to run away.

Wasting no time, Mikey took off after him, turning his

arms and legs into tentacles that he used to fling himself from one lamppost to another, flying right over Squirrel's head, and landing directly in front of him. Mikey gave himself a set of fangs as he snarled, just to addle Squirrel's acorn-size brain even more.

"Please, please don't hurt me," Squirrel whined, which was stupid, because Mikey *couldn't* hurt him. That was the blasted problem with being an Afterlight. He turned one of his tentacles into a jagged green insect claw, and thrust it forward, wedging Squirrel's neck against a lamppost with a clang.

"You didn't see this," Mikey said, pleased at the slithery, inhuman sound of his own voice. "And if you tell anyone you did, I'll use this claw to snap off your useless little head."

Whether or not he could follow through on the threat didn't matter; it was enough to scare Squirrel into absolute obedience.

"Yes, sir," squeaked Squirrel. "I didn't see nothing! I didn't see nothing!"

Mikey forced his claw and tentacles back into arms and legs, then sucked all his eyeballs back into his body, leaving only the standard two to glare at Squirrel. His voice returned to normal. "Now, we'll go back to the others, pretend this never happened, and everyone will be happy."

Squirrel gave a few fast, brain-rattling nods. "Sure, sure, everyone will be happy," and Squirrel ran off, stumbling over his own feet.

Mikey laughed and laughed. The choice to become terrifying—if only for a moment—ensured Squirrel's silence, so it served its purpose. But Mikey could not deny how good it had felt to be a monster once more.

# CHAPTER 13

## Bye-bye, Miss American Pie

Allie couldn't say she particularly enjoyed the company of the Nashville Afterlights. Every vapor of Afterlights was different, and this group was so standoffish—even while attempting to be hospitable—that the time spent with them was awkward at best. It was a relief to leave them behind.

"Nobody trusts skinjackers," Milos commented as they hit the road once more. "Mary Hightower's books make it difficult for us."

"Someday," said Allie, "I'll set everyone straight."

"Someday," said Milos, "I would like to set Mary Hightower straight, personally."

Mikey was silent on the matter. Allie found Mikey to be silent about everything. He had always been somewhat inscrutable, but now he seemed so distant that Allie found walking beside him had become almost painful.

"Talk to me, Mikey," she begged him.

"Why?" he asked. "I've got nothing to say."

"Say anything! It'll make the day go faster."

"No, it won't," he said, glancing ahead of them at

Milos, Moose, and Squirrel. And that was that. Silence returned—and although Allie was tempted to catch up with the others, where at least there was laughter and conversation, she resisted, and hung back with Mikey, but resented it.

At dusk they rested, and both Mikey and Milos disappeared. Allie asked Moose and Squirrel about it. Moose, who had limited peripheral vision out of his helmet, hadn't seen much of anything, but Squirrel had.

"Milos went off that way," he told her, pointing to a neighborhood off the side of the road. "He said he was looking for something."

"What?"

"Didn't say, didn't say—but whatever it was, he said he'd be back soon."

"Did Mikey go with him?"

At the mention of Mikey, Squirrel got even more squirrelly. "Nope, nope—Mikey don't go places with Milos," Squirrel said. "I saw him go off the other way. Don't know what he's doing either—and I don't want to know."

Squirrel looked to Moose with a gaze of dread that even Moose didn't understand.

"Whatsh up with you?" Moose asked.

"Nuthin'," said Squirrel. "Why should anything be up with me? Huh, huh?"

This should have been a further indication to Allie that something was wrong, but her thinking had been confused by so many things lately, denial was the easier path to take.

When Milos returned later that evening, he was all smiles.

"I promised you the best lesson of all tonight," he told Allie. "Are you ready to begin?"

Allie couldn't imagine an evening of skinjacking better than what they had done at the Grand Ole Opry, but she was willing to take a leap of faith. Milos had taught her so much already—not just technique, but acceptance of herself, and what she could do. She was truly learning how to enjoy skinjacking. For better or for worse, it was something she needed to learn.

"Lead the way," she said, and realized she had put out her hand for Milos to take. Milos gave her the biggest smirk she had ever seen him give—and he refused to take her hand. She laughed to mask her own embarrassment that even that little gesture had, for the two of them, become a game—and Milos now had, so to speak, the upper hand.

He took her to a nearby neighborhood—a wealthy western suburb of Nashville, where tract mansions rose from what was once farmland. Everything was winding streets and cul-de-sacs. Allie lost all sense of direction in the moonlight but Milos seemed to know exactly where he was going.

He stopped at a huge house with a rounded driveway that was full of cars. There was music inside, and the sound of a crowd.

"A party?"

"Yes! And we are about to crash it!"

"Interesting," she said, giving him a dubious look. "So is there a name for tonight's lesson?"

Milos thought about it. "I have no name for what we do tonight. Perhaps after the lesson is over, you can tell me what to call it."

They walked right in through the side wall, having no need for the front door, and in an instant, they were in the midst of dozens of teenaged fleshies, doing all those things Allie's parents would have grounded her for when she was alive: drinking, smoking, dancing much too close in clothes that were far too revealing. And, of course, not a single adult was in sight.

"We were all so stupid when we were alive," Allie noted.

"Ah, to be that stupid again." Milos looked around, and pointed to the kitchen. "That way."

The crowd thinned out in the kitchen; there were only about half a dozen kids in there. "There they are!" he said, pointing to a boy, maybe seventeen, talking to a girl about the same age. He wore a shirt that effectively showed off a body in ripped, varsity shape. He was also amazingly easy on the eye.

"Best-looking boy here, yes?"

Allie forced a shrug. "I hadn't noticed."

"And her." He pointed to the girl the boy was talking to. "Miss American Pie."

Allie laughed. The girl was too pretty for her own good. A blond cheerleader type that Allie instantly invented a half-dozen negative fictions about: She must be an airhead, she must be a drunk, she must cheat on tests, she must backstab her friends, and that ridiculous rack *can't* be real.

"Why don't you skinjack her?"

"What possible point could that serve?"

"Listen to teacher," said Milos.

Allie sighed. "Fine, but I'm not going to like it."

But to her surprise, she was wrong. About everything.

She didn't put the girl to sleep. Not at first anyway. First Allie hid behind her consciousness, to get a good sense of her mental landscape. This girl was not any of the things Allie had imagined. She was smart and honest, never held a pom-pom in her life, and the mug of beer on the counter beside her wasn't even hers. Allie found it annoying that this girl didn't fit any of her preconceived notions.

"So, are you going to take the UT-Memphis scholarship?" asked the good-looking boy, "because I think you should. That way you'll be closer to home, right? And—" Suddenly he stopped, and something about him changed. It was very slight—the way he held his shoulders, the angle of his head—and although his eyes were brown, it was as if they were also blue with white speckles at the same time.

Now Allie gently put the girl to sleep, and took full control of her body.

"She looks good on you," Milos said.

"Thanks, I think." Allie looked around. The girl had clear vision, and saw everything in colors a little too vibrant. It figured. "So am I Cinderella at the ball now?"

"That depends. Am I the Prince of Charming?"

"Prince Charming," Allie corrected, then she looked at him sternly. "Do you think I don't know what this is all about?"

He didn't deny it. "Indulge me," he said. "One dance is all I ask."

"Why should I?"

"Out of simple gratitude for all I have taught you."

"No—you lied to me! You said tonight would be a lesson, not a free dance ticket."

"It *is* a lesson," Milos insisted. "Come, look here." He led her to a mirror in a nearby hallway. "Look at yourself," he said. "Before I met you, you would never dare to skinjack someone this beautiful."

The girl in the mirror certainly was stunning. "I never felt I had the right . . . ."

"Why? Do you think so little of yourself that you should only skinjack people less attractive than you are? Why not a girl as beautiful as you?"

Allie couldn't look away from the reflection. "I'm not beautiful. . . ."

"Then I think you don't see yourself clearly. You are on the inside what she is on the outside. And your outside is pretty good too."

Finally she broke away from her reflection and turned to him. "We should give these people back their bodies."

"Yes," agreed Milos, "but first the dance."

He held out his hand to her. She looked at it for the longest time, then she put her hand in his, ending their little cat-and-mouse game. But now a new game had begun.

Milos, in the body of the beautiful young man, led her to the living room, where all the furniture had been pushed aside to create a dance floor. A dozen couples were dancing, and people without partners danced as well to the steady beat. Allie was never much of a dancer, but this girl came furnished with extensive muscle memory when it came to dancing. Allie found herself dancing better than she ever had before, and sweat soon began to bead on her forehead. She had almost forgotten the curious sensation of perspiration!

The song segued into another, and they kept on dancing

through two songs, three, and then the pace slowed. The fourth song was a slow dance, and Allie found herself moving right into it. Milos's arms swept around her, drawing her in, the space between them vanished, and she could smell cologne on his neck. She had to remind herself it was neither his cologne, nor his neck.

It was halfway through the song that Allie realized this girl was in love with this boy. And while the girl's mind and soul might have been asleep, her body was not.

Suddenly the room felt like a sauna, and Allie had to get out.

Pulling away from Milos, she hurried, pushing past the minefield of dancing couples, and out the back door, to an expansive pool deck.

It was cool out here, but there was no escape from the party. People were clowning around in and around the pool. People sat on lounge chairs. One couple sat on the edge of the Jacuzzi, making out.

"Get a room," someone griped.

Although Allie looked away, the lip-locked couple stayed in the corner of her eye, and her gaze kept being drawn to them.

She felt hands slip around her waist. Milos's fleshie. She turned to him, and once more the space between them compressed until they were in that close-dance position again. Milos brushed his hand down her arm, raising gooseflesh all over her borrowed body, until his hand reached hers, and he clasped it.

"Look at me, Allie," he said gently, and so she did. "We break no rules," he said. "These two are already dating. They arrived at the party holding hands."

He touched her face and although she knew it would be wise to back away, she didn't.

"Some feelings are lost to us in Everlost," Milos said. "Some feelings can only be felt in living bodies. Do you understand?"

She did understand, and she was unprepared for it. In life she had never experienced how overwhelming, how strong those feelings could be. How they could confound the most rational of minds.

"And," said Milos, his voice barely a whisper in her ear, "there are things we cannot *do* in Everlost . . . but we can do them here, in these bodies."

Then he leaned in and kissed her. It was profoundly different from an Everlost kiss. An Everlost kiss was about connection, not passion. An Everlost kiss lacked this rudeness, this rawness of flesh, and the insane breathlessness of two hearts pounding faster and faster.

In that instant, Allie forgot who she was, and who she was in. She forgot this was not her body at all. She let the mind of the girl surface, and it began to swim and blend with her own thoughts, until she didn't know whether she was the girl or the intruder.

And for a moment, just for a moment, it felt right. It felt perfect. How could it not be? Their lips separated, and both of them stole a quick breath.

"We could be for each other . . . whatever we need," Milos said.

This time it was Allie moving forward, pressing her lips against his, not wanting this feverish, dizzying sensation to ever end. This body she was in—it shivered with the thrill of it.

"Get a room," shouted the same heckler, but the voice sounded part of another universe.

If Milos had, in that moment, lifted her in those strong, borrowed arms, and carried her off to a quiet place, she would have allowed him to do it, letting herself be swallowed by passion.

But the moment passed, her senses returned, and she pushed him away.

"Milos, no!"

He looked at her, out of breath, eyes barely in control. "Why no?"

She had trouble answering him, and so he kissed her again. She knew if she gave herself over to the kiss one more time, all would be lost. She would gladly be consumed by it. *This is what we are meant to do*, Milos had said. *This is what we are meant to be*. It took every ounce of her will to say—

"Lesson over."

She couldn't bear to pull out of his arms, so instead she peeled out of the beautiful girl, and back into Everlost.

Milos peeled away a moment later, once he realized that Allie was gone.

Allie stood there knowing she had done the right thing, but was still unable to turn and leave. They stood there for the most awkward of moments.

"Now you will say you hated that," Milos said, sheepishly.

Allie shook her head. "No. No, I didn't hate it." And that was the problem.

Beside them, the couple who, after all, really were dating, went back to kissing each other, probably thinking their odd supernatural experience was solely the product of love and hormones. Allie watched them, part of her wishing it could still be her—but realizing that the other half of her wished that the boy could be Mikey.

Only now did she realize that the boy Milos had chosen *did* look just a little bit like Mikey. She wondered if Milos had chosen him for that very reason. What was it he had said? *We could be for each other whatever we need.* She wondered if the girl looked like Jackin' Jill.

"Next time, maybe?" said Milos with an apologetic grin.

"No," said Allie, and took his hands, no longer in passion but in sympathy. "There won't be a next time, Milos."

She could not hate him for this. He hadn't forced her— he hadn't taken advantage. He was just doing what boys do—and he was very good at it.

"Too bad," said Milos. "I could have walked you down the red carpet at the Oscars. I could have danced with you in the White House."

"Now who's thinking too big?"

Milos sighed. "Will you now walk back alone, or may I escort you?"

"Well, since we're both going in the same direction, it would be silly to walk alone."

They returned to the highway together, yet apart. It was a long and painfully awkward walk.

"I'm sorry, Milos," Allie told him, when they were halfway there.

But Milos shook his head. "Please," he said. "I posed a question, and your answer was no. Never be afraid to tell anyone 'no'," he said. "And that includes me."

It didn't make it any easier that he was charming even in defeat. She knew she could have fallen for Milos had Mikey not already been a part of her life, and Milos knew it too. Never before had Allie been put in a position of chosing between two boys. Some girls might like such a game—toying with them, playing one against the other. Allie thought to the times she teased Mikey about Milos, and realized that maybe she had done a little bit of that herself. It made her want to see Mikey all the more.

The one comfort Allie could take from the evening's festivities was that her momentous lapse of reason would go unnoticed and unrecorded. Mikey would never know.

Except that he did.

In fact, he was standing right beside them when they kissed.

# CHAPTER 14

## *Strange Winds*

When Allie and Milos returned to the interstate, Moose and Squirrel were there, but Mikey was nowhere to be seen. Now that Milos's advances had hit a brick wall, he was itching to move on, and didn't appreciate waiting for Mikey.

"It is just like him to make the rest of us wait," Milos said.

"How do you know what he's like?" Allie said, defensively. "You barely even know him."

Milos knew better than to argue the point.

Allie looked around—to the fields across the interstate, and behind her, to the neighborhood they had just come from. She tried to catch a glimpse of Mikey's afterglow, but the moon was too bright; everything seemed to be glowing.

"Wherever he's gone, he couldn't have gone far," Allie told the others. But when Mikey wasn't back by midnight, Allie began to worry.

"What if something happened to him?"

Squirrel stayed silent about it, but Moose—probably following Milos's earlier cue—was annoyed. "Let him catch up with ush."

Milos, on the other hand, had moved past his irritation, and recognized that Mikey's absence was something out of the ordinary. "There will be a sensible explanation," Milos reasoned, "and when he does come back, we can all be suitably angry at him. But for now we will wait."

Allie kept a vigil all night, her mind filling with all the things that could have happened to him. What if the Nashville Afterlights kidnapped him? What if he got caught in one of Mary's stupid soul traps? Yet she knew she was grasping at straws. Those Nashville Afterlights were timid things—and as for soul traps, there was no evidence that Mary had ever been this far west.

When dawn came, and Mikey still hadn't returned, Allie was beside herself. The others kept their distance—not even Milos knew how to handle this. It was in that early morning light that she took special notice of Squirrel. He had nothing to say about the matter all night long—yet he was even more antsy than usual. He kept bouncing his knee and shifting his weight from leg to leg. He wouldn't meet Allie's gaze, and that clinched it. In an instant she had him tried, convicted, and sentenced.

"It was you!" She stormed up to him and pointed an accusing finger. "You did something to him!"

Squirrel's jaw dropped open and he shook his head. "Not me! Not me! I wouldn't do anything to him!" He looked to Moose, who backed away, hoping this plague of guilt wouldn't spread to him, but he was too late.

"It was both of you!" yelled Allie. "I know it just by looking at you!"

Moose's beady eyes seemed to widen within his helmet,

like a cornered opossum. She half expected him to suddenly play dead. "We didn't do anything! Milosh tell her it wazn't ush!" But Milos was not taking sides.

"You're both lying!' Allie screamed at them. "Tell me what you did, or I'll tear you apart with my bare hands!" In that moment, she believed she could do it, and they believed it too.

"We didn't do anything! I swear, I swear!" pleaded Squirrel. "Cross my heart and hope to fry! I'd be afraid to do anything to him, honest!"

And that, coming from Squirrel, just sounded odd. It was just a further indication to Allie that he must be lying.

Finally Milos stepped in. "Afraid of him? Why afraid?"

Squirrel looked to Milos then to Moose, and finally to Allie. "I think . . . I think your friend is some kinda monster." And the expression of horror and hatred that Allie gave him made Squirrel back away. "It's true, it's true! He's got all these eyes—and tentacles. He hides 'em real good, but I know he's got 'em."

"You're LYING!" screamed Allie, and she rushed him. "Take it BACK! You're lying, take it BACK!" She began pushing him, shaking him, hitting him.

It was Milos who pulled her away from Squirrel, and she collapsed, sobbing like she never had in life. Milos tried to comfort her, but she just pushed him away. "He's lying," she said over and over, her voice getting weaker each time she said it. "He's lying. . . ."

"Maybe Squirrel saw something else, and thought it was Mikey," Milos suggested.

"Yeah," said Moose, butting Squirrel in the head with

his helmet. "You alwayz shee things that aren't there!"

"But . . . but—"

Milos put his hand up and silenced him, then he knelt down to Allie, who still wept. "I think . . . we need . . . to consider . . . " He spoke slowly, measuring each word like the tick of a metronome, ". . . that maybe . . . Mikey took his coin . . . and got where he was going."

"He wouldn't do that," said Allie. "No. He wouldn't just leave without saying good-bye."

"Maybe he did not mean to," suggested Milos.

"Yeah, yeah—maybe he took the coin out just to look at it," said Squirrel, "but once that tunnel opens, there's nothing you can do."

Allie still wasn't ready to believe it. "There's got to be another explanation."

Then, after a long silence, Milos said, "Then we will wait."

And so they waited till noon. They waited till sunset. They waited through a second night. Mikey still hadn't returned, and Allie had to face the very real possibility that he never would.

When the sun peeked over the eastern horizon the next morning, Milos finally said, "Come; I said I would get you to Memphis and I will."

Allie shook her head. "I'm not going. I'm staying here."

"Let her stay," said Squirrel. "It's not our problem."

"Shut up!" snapped Milos.

Allie closed her eyes. Things had not gone the way she had planned. In that way Everlost was no different than the living world.

"You must let it go," Milos pleaded with her. "You must get to Memphis."

"Why? Why does it matter?"

Milos sighed. "Because . . . there are things I have not told you."

Allie looked at him, a bit disgusted. "More lessons?"

He shook his head, and spoke in a calm, resigned voice. "No lessons. Because there are some things every skinjacker must learn for themselves. In this I can't help you. I can only point you in the right direction."

Allie wondered if he was just being enigmatic to distract her from thoughts of Mikey or if there was something he was truly hinting at. Either way, Milos was right—she had to move on, because if she stayed here, she would surely let herself sink to the center of the earth.

"All right," she said calmly. "All right, then." She stood, and gathered what fortitude she could. "Without Mikey, we don't have to walk." She looked at the cars whizzing past on the highway. "We can skinjack a family already driving to Memphis, and be there in two hours."

And she hoped that the farther away from here she got, the less it would hurt.

Getting to Memphis took a bit longer than two hours—but not much. First they had to find a car with four passengers at a nearby rest stop, making sure they were heading to or at least passing through Memphis.

Then there was the argument with Moose and Squirrel about how to do it—fully jack the fleshies, or merely hide within them, behind their consciousness, hitching a ride.

"Hiding is for girls," said Squirrel, which just ticked Allie off.

The problem was solved when Moose confessed, "I don't know how to hide—with me itsh all or nothing." Apparently the finer points of skinjacking were beyond Moose.

In the end, it was agreed that they would all just skinjack a family in one fell swoop, put them to sleep, and then wake them up again once they had pulled off the interstate and were safe in some parking lot somewhere. The family would have to deal with inexplicably losing a few hours of their lives, but at least they would be closer to wherever they were going.

Milos drove, while Allie avoided looking in any mirrors, because she really didn't want to be reminded of what she was doing. In the backseat Moose and Squirrel inhabited a pair of six-year-old twins, and wouldn't stop bickering and picking their noses. They were clearly in their element.

They stopped just east of the city, and woke the family after they had parked, peeling out of them, and leaving them to make sense of the sudden time lapse. Allie, however lingered long enough to make her presence known in the woman's mind, telling her that all was well, and not to worry. It was the least she could do.

Immediately upon peeling into Everlost, they felt the wind that the Nashville Afterlights had spoken of. It was a stiff breeze coming from the west. While living-world wind passed through them, barely noticed, this wind did not.

"They said it gets worse the closer we get to the river," Squirrel said.

"I don't like it," said Moose.

Even Milos looked unsettled. "I have heard people say that Everlost ends at the Mississippi River, but I never believed this. Now I think maybe it is true, and this wind is a barrier keeping us back."

"Good thing Memphis is on this side of the river, then," said Allie curtly. She didn't care about the wind. She didn't care about much of anything right now. Mikey's departure had left her numb.

So she was here. She had no address to go by, but she was resourceful. Finding her family might take some time, but she'd be able to do it. She wished that she didn't have to do it alone, but it wasn't Milos's help she wanted. Milos must have know that, because here is where he said his good-bye.

"We'll be heading north," he told her, his voice raised against the whistling wind. "The Afterlights in Nashville heard rumors of a skinjacking girl up in Illinois."

"Jackin' Jill?"

"One can only hope."

Behind them, Moose and Squirrel milled around impatiently, but Milos took his time. "I hope you find your family," he told Allie. "And once you do, you will see things in a whole different light." Then he kissed her hand, and turned to go.

Moose and Squirrel both gave her quick, obligatory waves good-bye. Then the three of them skinjacked some random fleshies, and they were gone.

Later that day, in a Memphis church, Kevin David Barnes, twenty-four, married Rebecca Lynn Danbury, twenty-two.

The groom, a bit scruffy in real life, was quite handsome in his tuxedo, and everyone agreed the bride was the most perfect vision of a bride that anyone had ever seen.

When the minister said those momentous words to conclude the glorious ceremony, Kevin Barnes lifted his new wife's veil to give her that long-awaited kiss. He had no way of knowing that Allie was secretly hiding behind the bride's wild, racing thoughts—not stealing the moment, but lurking within it, hoping to claim the tiniest fraction of it for herself. When the kiss ended, Allie found her spirit bursting into tears. She cried for Mikey, the boy she had lost, for Milos, the boy she had shunned, and she cried because she knew that this moment was someone else's, and she'd never grow to be twenty-two like Rebecca Lynn Danbury. She'd never go to a prom, or walk down the aisle, or be a mother. She was an Afterlight, and Afterlights knew no such things.

Although Allie tried to contain herself, her emotions touched the bride, making her cry as well. And the crowd applauded, so very pleased to see the bride's tears of joy.

In her book *Tips for Taps*, Mary attempts to shed some of her own personal light on Afterlights who suffer from negative emotions.

"Surely sorrow will accompany any Afterlight when they cross from the so-called living world into Everlost—much the way a baby will cry upon being born. This is only natural. However, the healthy Afterlight will quickly put such negative emotions aside, lest they fester into anger or bitterness. I have seen the ravages of bitterness, and it is not pretty.

In Everlost, we have a responsibility to find happiness, and relive that same happiness day after day until eternity finds us filled with joy, and void of anything else whatsoever."

# CHAPTER 15

## *The Flight of Mikey McGill*

Mikey McGill remembered the fateful day he first awoke in Everlost, more than a hundred years ago, when he arrived home with his sister, and realized that they were ghosts. He remembered sinking through the wooden floor, while his sister clung to a bedpost screaming. Neither of them yet understood anything about Everlost, and both were terrified.

But nothing he ever experienced in life, or in death, half compared to what he felt when he saw Milos and Allie kiss.

He had followed them to the party. Until that night, Mikey had resisted the urge to spy on the two of them, but there was only so long he could fight his own curiosity. He kept far behind them, out of view, until seeing them skinjack that disgustingly beautiful couple. Once the two were ensconced in flesh, their eyes would see only the living world, and so Mikey could come right up to them, just inches away, and see it all, without them ever knowing he was there. To Mikey, they now just looked like a living teenage couple, but he knew Milos and Allie were inside them.

He could tell by the way they walked and the things they said to each other.

He was there when Milos asked her to dance, and he witnessed Allie's initial reluctance—which gave him a brief moment of hope . . . but she gave in far too easily, as if her refusal was nothing more than her being coy.

He watched them dance. He watched them dance close, and then he followed them outside to the pool, where it seemed everyone was a couple.

And then they kissed.

The first kiss was horrifying, and the second was devastating—because it wasn't Milos shoving his lips against Allie anymore—the second kiss was Allie kissing him back. This confirmed everything he suspected, everything he feared—and what made Mikey even more furious was that he had trusted her. How could he have been so stupid?

He screamed at them, a primal wordless howl, but they couldn't hear him.

Mikey knew what he would do to Milos once he was back in Everlost—he would push Milos right through that pool deck so hard, he would have made an express trip to the center of the earth, but Mikey knew if he let his fury loose, once he was done with Milos, he would turn his wrath on Allie, and do the same to her. He couldn't let that happen, and so he ran.

He never saw Allie pushing Milos away.

He never heard her tell him "no."

Mikey's grief and rage was unbearable, and yet familiar— so much like the rage that filled him when he commanded the *Sulphur Queen*.

And as he ran, he let his fury transform him.

His rage became red-hot spikes erupting from his skin. His frustration became jagged shark teeth, multiplying row after row, and when his mouth couldn't fit them anymore, it stretched. His jealousy pulled his eyes into narrow glaring slits, and his sorrow hardened his Afterlight skin into a shell as hard as steel.

Spiked armor encased him now, his whole body was like the surface of a medieval mace—but it didn't slow him down. His armored shell thundered with each footfall, setting off seismic ripples in the living world that no one could account for. And, fully encased in that armored exoskeleton, he stormed all the way back to Nashville, right into the factory, and the den of Nashville Afterlights.

When they saw this thing, this horrible miscreation before them, they didn't know what to do. Some scattered, others froze in place, others fell to the ground and covered their heads like the world was ending.

Mikey opened his mouth to speak, but no words came out. Instead, he vomited his entire being out through that gaping mouth, completely turning himself inside out. The armor folded in behind him, and into him, becoming a jagged skeleton within a veiny, sinewy inner self—a mockery of ruined flesh. His whole body was now an open wound.

"*I am the McGill!*" he roared in a ghastly, earthshaking voice. "*I am the McGill! Look upon me and tremble!*"

And they did.

# PART THREE

*The Great White City*

In her book *Everything Mary Says Is Wrong*, Allie the Outcast takes a moment to ponder the hereafter:

"I don't know whether we come to Everlost by accident or by design. Some will say we are abandoned here—lost between the cracks of an unfeeling universe. Others will say we have been selected to be here by an almighty hand, and then they will use that to justify everything they do as God's will.

Whether my ability to skinjack is an accident or intentional, I do know this: I've seen the light at the end of the tunnel, so I know the universe is not cold. I've read the fortunes; they are evidence that we are not alone. And I've seen Afterlights hold their coins, remember who they once were, and finally get where they were going.

I have seen enough to know that there is something beyond Everlost, but the nature of it is just as mysterious here as it is to the living.

So beware those in Everlost who say they know God's will, because they are no different from those who say the universe is soulless and cold. Both are two sides of the same coin, and it's not a coin that will get you anywhere you want to go."

# CHAPTER 16

## Mary's Master Plan

It would be untrue to say that Mary Hightower had, from the very beginning, planned the various things she would soon accomplish, and the many things she would soon attempt. Ideas take root, plans blossom, and old ones wither and die—in Everlost, just as in the living world.

Back in her days at the towers, Mary had dedicated herself to taking stray Afterlights under her wing, and finding for them the one activity that would occupy them until the end of time. She believed this to be a noble calling. Nick, however, had dazzled her children with those abominable coins, then dispatched them all into that mysterious light at the end of the tunnel, from which there is no return.

She could not blame the children, for what child could resist such a mystery? It was all Nick's pigheaded wrong-mindedness, and she marveled at how much damage a single individual could do to her controlled, perfect little universe.

She hated him with a ferocity and passion that was only matched by how much she also loved him—and the endless conflict of those two emotions made it impossible to go back to the way things were before. She supposed in some ways, she owed Nick a debt of gratitude, because if he hadn't freed her children from Everlost, Mary would never have been rousted out of her own pattern; she never would have seen the larger picture, and she never would have cultivated grander plans.

Certainly she would still gather and protect as many Afterlights as she could, but that would soon become a small part of a master blueprint so massive, it would make Mary light-headed every time she was to think of it.

When she came to Chicago, however, the plan was still merely an inkling—a seedling just beginning to sprout something green. She had yet to realize how deep the roots would take, and how large the limbs would grow.

# CHAPTER 17

## *The Death Boss*

Mary allowed her reputation to precede her. In fact, she pushed it ahead of her with a mighty hand. As the *Hindenburg* cut a slow path across the sky, she would send out emissaries ahead of her, with copies of her various books. Then those emissaries would strategically spread stories about her to any Afterlights who would listen—which was just about everyone, for Afterlights all love the telling of stories. Mary's disciples would spread tales of wonder, and proudly tell the stories of Mary's many good deeds. If the stories themselves didn't leave kids gaping in awe, the sight of the massive airship descending from the sky certainly would.

Because Mary had a high regard for honesty, she insisted that they be told only that which was true. Of course she hand chose her emissaries of good will, selecting loyal Afterlights who would portray her in the most favorable light.

Mary's emissaries arrived in Chicago several weeks before she did, and so, by the time the *Hindenburg* came in over Lake Michigan, there was not an Afterlight in all of

Chicago who had not heard her name and didn't wonder if the stories were true.

Mary had Speedo circle the city three times so every Afterlight below would have a clear view of it. Speedo was clearly apprehensive.

"Are you sure you want to do this?" Speedo asked her. He had asked this over and over again, as if asking might get her to change her mind. "There's got to be a reason why the kids we sent out never came back."

"We'll discover the reason soon enough."

On the second loop above the city, Mary decided where they'd set down. It was a city full of deadspots, thanks to the great Chicago fire—but one place stood out. Mary recognized it as the grounds of the 1893 Columbian Exhibition—a giant world's fair. It was more than a mile across—the largest deadspot Mary had ever seen—and even from this height, Mary could see it was quite literally swarming with Afterlights.

"There," said Mary, pointing at the largest square, in the center of the fairgrounds. "That's where we'll set down."

Speedo quaked in his wet bathing suit. "But shouldn't we land somewhere away from the city? Far, far away?"

"No, Speedo," Mary said calmly. "This time, I want to be right in the thick of it."

Their standard operating procedure had always been to settle in less populated areas, set up their various soul traps, then return sometime later to see if the traps had sprung. Then, as the population within the *Hindenburg* grew, she became slightly more daring, setting down in small towns and villages that might have some rudimentary organization to their Afterlight population.

She would address the small gatherings of Afterlights in these towns. Sometimes they would join her, and climb aboard, sometimes not. If they chose not to join her, she would leave them with whatever gifts she could spare, and the nagging feeling that they missed out on something wonderful. By the time she came to Chicago, she had ninety-three Afterlights in her protective care.

"The city's run by a Death Boss!" said Speedo. "That's what he calls himself! A *Death Boss*!"

"Just a rumor," Mary said, although she suspected that the rumor was true. She had heard that he even named himself after the city's most notorious gangster. "Last month you were telling me that Chicago didn't even exist!"

"I didn't say that," said Speedo. "I said that it didn't exist in Everlost."

"And yet now we know that it does," Mary pointed out. "Illumination defeats ignorance every time."

"What if he captures us and turns us into slaves?" pleaded Speedo. "Then what?"

"Dictators who rule with an iron fist are motivated by self-interest," Mary lectured, "and if Pugsy Capone does rule like a dictator, it would not serve his interests to enslave us."

"Are you sure of that?"

Mary sighed. "No," she admitted. "But we're going anyway."

They circled the city a final time, then descended toward the grounds of the Columbian Exhibition.

\* \* \*

The World Columbian Exhibition of 1893 was perhaps the greatest world's fair there had ever been. It filled a full square-mile along the shore of Lake Michigan, and looked more like Ancient Rome than Chicago. Magnificent domed buildings, column-lined courtyards, and glorious fountains stood at the heart of the fair, all of it so alabaster white it became known as the Great White City—blinding in the sun, and glowing mystically by moonlight. These towering colonnades and hallowed halls of industry stood as monuments to the power and permanence of man's creations.

Unfortunately it was all made of cheap plaster, and crumbled like a sandcastle once the fair was over.

However, the loss to the living world was a gift to Everlost. Here in Everlost, the Great White City still claimed the shoreline of Lake Michigan. The gilded Statue of the Republic forever towered resolutely at its heart, and George Ferris's great wheel—the original Ferris wheel—continued to turn relentless circles—still the tallest piece of Chicago to cross into Everlost.

In short, the place was larger than life, but then, so was Mary Hightower, and she orchestrated her arrival with royal style.

The *Hindenburg* settled in the "court of honor," the great courtyard at the heart of the White City, touching down in the reflecting pool that so eerily matched the giant zeppelin in size and shape, it appeared to belong there, fitting like a key in a lock. All around the court of honor, hundreds upon hundreds of Chicago Afterlights gathered to gawk as a ramp descended, and Mary's Afterlights marched out two by two, into the shallow reflecting pool in size order. They then parted, and faced inward, creating a gauntlet; a pathway of Afterlights for Mary to walk between.

They stood at attention, and all waited in silent anticipation. Then Mary emerged, walking slowly, regally, her green velvet dress just brushing the surface of the ankle-deep pool, making her appear to walk on water. She strode to the edge of the reflecting pool and then stopped, waiting patiently for the Chicago Afterlights to dredge up the nerve to approach her. They all looked downtrodden and scared, with circles under their wide eyes that gave them the disconcerting look of zombies—but those eyes weren't empty and mindless, they were full of dread—the first indication that all the rumors about Pugsy Capone were true.

Finally, a young girl, the bravest of these timid Afterlights, approached her and asked, "Are you here to send the Death Boss to hell?"

The question challenged Mary's balance, but only for an instant. She smiled at the girl warmly. "I'm here to help," she said. "Please tell Mr. Capone that Mary Hightower has come to see him."

The girl ran off, and Mary waited patiently, refusing to engage any of the other Afterlights in conversation, because she knew that would challenge Pugsy's power, and she didn't want to do that. Not yet, anyway.

Ten minutes later the girl came back, running as quickly as she had run off.

"His eminence will see you now."

"His eminence!" said Mary. "Isn't that a title reserved for the Pope, and other holy men?"

The girl looked down modestly. "I wouldn't know, your highness."

"You don't have to call me that," Mary said. "You can just call me Miss Mary."

"Yes, Miss Mary," the girl said dutifully, and when she looked up at Mary, she had the slightest hint of a smile—perhaps the first smile she'd had in ages.

She led Mary from the Court of Honor to a huge building labeled TRANSPORTATION. The doorway stood beneath a high golden arch. Apparently the boss of Chicago was receiving her with royal treatment.

"They said to bring you here," said the girl, but she wouldn't step over the threshold into the building.

"They?" asked Mary. "Whom do you mean?"

Suddenly figures emerged from the dark doorway, and hands grabbed her arms more forcefully than she was accustomed to.

"She means us."

They pulled her inside, shut the door in the little girl's face, and Mary was pulled forward into a huge, dimly lit space the size of an airplane hangar by a trio of beefy thugs.

The Hall of Transportation had been stripped of any transportation whatsoever. The towering space was empty except for a single wing-footed statue of Mercury in the center, to which the three thugs chained Mary, and as they closed the shackles around her wrists and ankles, she felt all her hopes fizzle.

"Which one of you buffoons is Pugsy Capone?" Mary snarled, disturbed not only by her situation, but by the viciousness of her own voice. She thought she could find poise in every circumstance. Apparently not.

"The Death Boss has better things to do than deal with prisoners," said the largest of the thugs. It appeared the "Death Boss" chose his personal foot soldiers for their strength, their intimidating faces, and for the clothes they had been wearing when they died. All three of them wore suits. From different time periods, of course, but suits nonetheless. They were all fifteen or so, although they looked older in their suits. The gray-suited thug to her right stepped forward, and recited for her the same thing he probably recited to every Afterlight unlucky enough to stumble into this miserable enclave.

"You are now a subject of Pugsy Capone, and as such, you have no rights beyond the ones Mr. Capone gives you, if any. You will speak only when spoken to, you will perform all tasks given to you. You will cast your eyes to the ground when Mr. Capone or any of us pass. Should you disobey any of these orders, you will be gagged, tied to a cinder block, and hurled out into the living world, where you will sink quickly to the center of the earth. Do you understand these things as they've been explained to you? Do you need anything repeated?"

They waited for Mary's response, but she said nothing, just glared at them, refusing to cast her eyes the slightest bit downward.

The gray-suited thug got right in her face and shouted, "*I said, do you need anything repeated?*"

"No," she finally said. "How long will I be imprisoned here?"

*"No questions!"* he shouted. Then he said, "You'll stay like this as long as he wants you to. Maybe a month, maybe a year, maybe forever."

Speedo had been right—if only she had listened to him. She could only hope that Pugsy Capone would be curious enough to come see her himself—if only to gloat over his victory. A face-to-face encounter could only help her situation.

Mary finally cast her eyes down, and, satisfied, the gray-suited thug stepped back. "Your blimp is now the property of the Death Boss," he said, "and so are all your Afterlights."

Mary tugged at her chains but it did no good. Her miscalculation had not only cost Mary her own freedom, but her children as well. The anguish stabbed as deep as a blade in living flesh, but she would not let it show. Instead, she said with all the defiance she could muster, "It's not a blimp. Any imbecile can tell you it's a rigid airship."

To which the largest of the thugs calmly replied, "It is whatever Pugsy Capone says it is."

Then they left her there to stew in her own intentions, chained to a flying statue that couldn't fly.

Pugsy Capone, Death Boss of Chicago, Lord of the White City, was a very shrewd Afterlight. Shrewd enough to have trapped almost a thousand Afterlights under his "protection." He was a spirit who not only saw afterlife as a competition, but as a competition where points were scored by creating the greatest amount of misery. The thought of dethroning the infamous "Mary Queen of Snots," was the stuff of dreams for him, and had a very high point value, indeed.

However, as Mary had hoped, the thrill of capturing her eventually gave way to his curiosity. It took a while—mainly because he had a new toy: the *Hindenburg*, which he insisted on calling a blimp, and no one dared to correct him—not even Speedo, who was told he'd be sleeping with the magma if he didn't pilot Pugsy anywhere he wanted to go.

It took a week for him to tire of tooling around the airspace above Chicago, and then his thoughts turned to the legendary girl sealed away in the Hall of Transportation. He would not lower himself to go to her; however, he had his three favored foot soldiers bring her to him.

After a week, Mary's spirit had not been broken. It would take more than shackles and solitude to humble Mary Hightower—although there were a few times that she became a bit delirious, and fantasized about Nick putting their battle aside, and barreling into Chicago on his train to rescue her. Her own fantasy infuriated her, because Mary was not, nor would ever be, a damsel in distress.

Finally Pugsy's boys arrived, unshackled her, and led her out into daylight, toward the giant Ferris wheel. She held herself high all the way there. Her presence there drew crowds that were quickly dispersed when the thugs gave them the evil eye.

The Ferris wheel was more than a mere amusement park ride. Its long rectangular gondolas were the size of railroad cars, each one capable of carrying dozens of people to vertigo-inducing heights. The door to the lowermost gondola was open, and Mary was led inside to what must have been the Death Boss's throne room.

The throne was a red leather armchair, and the boy who

sat in it was not at all what Mary expected. Pugsy Capone was a chubby thirteen-year-old in a pinstriped double-breasted suit that was noticeably tight. Mary wondered whether Pugsy immediately decided that since he was stuck wearing the clothes of a gangster, he ought to be one, or if he had simply forgotten who he was, and so defined himself by his attire. Mary suspected he had been in Everlost at least fifty years, by the style of his suit.

It was easy to see how Pugsy had gotten his name. He had unpleasantly bulging eyes, and his nose was pushed up and back, exposing his nostrils, as if he had died while pressing his face up against a window. He looked so much like a pug dog, Mary half expected him to bark.

His thugs took their place behind him, and folded their arms, taking on a posture of invulnerability and arrogance. There was also someone else present—a girl who lurked in a corner, looking on with mild interest. She had waves of unkempt blond hair filled with nettles and thorns, skin so tan it was difficult to determine her race, and a gaudy pendant with a sky-blue gem hanging around her neck. Mary found the girl's cool gaze more disconcerting than Pugsy's bug-eyed glare.

"I'm willing to listen to your pleas of mercy," Pugsy said in a voice that would forever crack between octaves, having not finished changing while he was alive.

"I'm sorry to disappoint you," said Mary, "but you'll be hearing no pleas of mercy from me."

Pugsy shifted uncomfortably in his big armchair.

"What have you done with my children?" Mary asked.

The thug in the gray suit spoke up. "Who said you could ask questions?"

But Pugsy put up his hand to silence him. "I've put them in storage until I decide what to do with them. As for you, I was thinking it might be fun to chain you to the center of the Ferris wheel and watch you go round and round. What do you think?"

Mary fought back her urge to scold him for being such a thoroughly vile little urchin, and instead offered him her kindest smile.

"Come now," she said, "surely the Death Boss of Chicago is above such pettiness. You must realize I'm far more useful as an ally than an ornament."

That gave him pause for thought. If he hadn't realized it before, he was ready to consider it now. Here was the chance Mary had hoped for!

"You've built quite a civilization here in Chicago," Mary told him. "You are to be congratulated."

"Flattery from the Sky Witch! You really must want something from me!" He chuckled softly, and his henchmen took it as their cue to chuckle loudly.

"Do not call me that," she said, forcefully but respectfully. "My name is Mary Hightower, and it is the only name I answer to."

"I know your name," said Pugsy, with an air of disgust in his voice. "So are you gonna tell me why you trespassed on my property?"

"I believe it's best if we discuss matters of importance alone," Mary said. His thugs looked ready to stand their ground, and Mary noticed the girl in the corner smile, perhaps impressed with Mary's boldness.

Pugsy looked to his thugs. "Send us up to the top, and

wait for me on the ground," he told them.

"Yes, boss," they said, ever obedient.

Then he turned to the girl. "Why don't you go skinjack someone, and get today's sports scores."

It was the first thing that Pugsy said that really caught Mary by surprise.

"Whatever you say," said the girl with a toss of her crazy, nettle-nested hair, then she sauntered out behind the three thugs, eyeing Mary all the way.

In a moment the Ferris wheel grinded into motion, and the large car began a long, slow arc up and away.

"You trust a skinjacker?" Mary asked him.

"Sure," said Pugsy, "she comes in very useful—no matter what you say in your books."

"So, you've read my books, then?"

"Only what I could stomach."

"You should attempt to 'stomach' more," Mary suggested. "I've shared all the things I've discovered here—all the things I know."

"Yeah, well I know things too."

Pugsy stood up and went to a window to admire the view. Mary knew he wasn't very tall, but she didn't realize how short and stocky he was until he stood up.

"So now that we're alone, are you gonna tell me why you're here?"

Mary decided to take the direct approach. "I propose an alliance between you and me. A partnership between *equals*."

That made him laugh. "Equals? How do you figure that?" And he gestured out the window at his vast land holdings.

"I have no need to look," she said. "My view from the *Hindenburg* is just as grand as yours."

"Oh," said Pugsy, "but this view is priceless."

Finally Mary looked. They had just crested the peak of the Ferris wheel, and as they began the journey downward, the car next to them came into view. To Mary's horror, it was packed with children—*Mary's* children—every last one of them. They had been packed into that car like sardines. This is what Pugsy meant by "storage."

"It's amazing," said Pugsy. "Afterlights can fit into whatever space you want them to. All ninety-three of yours are in there."

Mary couldn't find words to express her disgust.

"So you see," said Pugsy. "I hold all the chips. You gotta do whatever I say, or they're the ones that'll suffer."

Mary swallowed her urge to slap him silly, and spoke slowly, making sure all her words had time to sink in through his thick skull. "Treating me as an equal will elevate you far more than you can imagine."

"Is that so?" He sneered.

"Yes, it is." Then she put aside all modesty, false or otherwise. "In Everlost I am seen as a queen, an angel, a witch, an enchantress. I did not choose this, of course, but the fact remains that I am the stuff of legend. If you imprison me, you are a mere jail keeper. *But* . . . if you rise to be my equal, you will become legendary as well."

"I already am legendary."

Mary laughed dismissively. "Your infamy does not spread as far as you'd like to believe," she told him. "East of Pittsburgh, and south of Indianapolis, I doubt anyone has ever heard of you. And those who have heard of you, consider you . . . well . . . a gangster. But an alliance with me would legitimize what you've done here."

"And what's in it for you?" Pugsy asked.

Mary had anticipated the question. In this, she chose to be direct as well. "No doubt you've heard of the Chocolate Ogre," Mary said.

"I thought he was made-up."

"No, he's very real. In a single day he could empty Chicago, so that not a single Afterlight remained under your 'protection.'"

"I'd like to see him try," said Pugsy.

"Don't underestimate him; he's very cunning," Mary warned. "But with enough Afterlights, I can defeat him."

She crossed to the other side of the car, giving him time to think about it. As she did, her velvet dress brushed against the back of the red leather armchair. She wondered if it was as comfortable as it looked.

"So . . . " said Pugsy, "you intend to build an army, is that it?"

"Oh, please!" Mary waved away the suggestion. "An army implies a war. I will not have a war . . . but I will protect Everlost from those who might wreak havoc on the order that you and I try to create. No, we won't have an army, but we will have freedom fighters."

They reached the bottom of the wheel, and began to circle up once more.

"Agree to help me bring down the Chocolate Ogre," said Mary, "and I will give my heartfelt, personal blessing to you, as ruler of Chicago, and—dare I say it—with my stamp of approval, you could conceivably spread your reign to the rest of Everlost."

Pugsy was dazzled by the concept. "I'd be the EverBoss!" he said.

Mary tried not to cringe. "If you wish."

As they crested the peak again, they both looked to the next car, where Mary's children peered out, hopelessly cramped and tangled in their rotating cell.

"So," asked Mary, "which will it be? Jailer . . . or Emperor?"

# CHAPTER 18

## *The Interlight Incubator*

A pronouncement was made the following day. All of Pugsy's Afterlights were called out to the Court of Honor to hear it, as were all of Mary's children, who were released from their revolving prison without as much as an apology.

Mary and Pugsy stood side by side at the podium, although he stood on a box so he would appear as tall as her.

"I'm pleased to announce a new alliance between myself and Mary Hightower, Governess of the East," Pugsy told the masses. "This will usher in a new age in Everlost." Then he ordered everyone to celebrate.

There was a feast of crossed food—not all that much to eat, for even in Chicago edible pickings were slim, but it was the idea that counted, and everyone was in good spirits— even the Chicago kids, who, for once, had reason to cheer rather than to despair.

Mary allowed her children to mingle with the Chicago Afterlights, knowing that at the end of the celebration they would happily return to the comfort and routine of the *Hindenburg*.

Pugsy's three henchmen now treated Mary with the utmost respect, and would attempt to stand behind her and fold their arms as they did for Pugsy. Mary would have none of it. She didn't need bodyguards.

"Go practice your intimidation elsewhere," she told them.

"Of course, Miss Mary," they would obsequiously reply, as if being irritatingly polite would win her favor.

The skinjacking girl was a different matter. She moved in Pugsy's inner circle, but seemed immune to his rules. In fact, Mary noticed that Pugsy rarely ordered her to do any-thing, probably for fear that she would say "no." The girl was like a cat, doing as she pleased, knowing she could get away with it.

It was toward the end of the celebration that she sidled up to Mary, to engage her in conversation for the first time.

"It took only two revolutions of the wheel for you to get Pugsy in your pocket," she said. "You must be a witch after all."

"I could say the same about you," said Mary. "You cer-tainly look the part."

The skinjacker fluffed her tangled hair, but not a single nettle fell from it. "Didn't you write *'It's patently wrong to hold an Afterlight responsible for the circumstance of their demise, and one should never make fun of unfortunate clothing and unexpected accessories'*?"

Mary was not pleased to have her own words used against her, but the skinjacker was right. Mary was break-ing one of her own rules of etiquette. She took a moment to compose herself. "I'm sorry if we got off on the wrong foot," Mary said. "You know who I am, but I'm afraid we've never been properly introduced. May I ask your name?"

"I'm Jill," she said. "My friends call me Jackin' Jill."

"Well, Jill," said Mary, "I suspect things will be changing around here. I sincerely hope you do well with change."

Jackin' Jill nodded, but said nothing. Even so, Mary felt that they were both on better ground than when they started. Of course it didn't change her opinion of skinjackers, but if there was to be a shining new world order, everyone would have a part to play.

Mary found that she had free run of the fair. She could explore all places, interact with all of Pugsy's Afterlights—but one place was off-limits. The glass-domed agricultural building. All entrances were perpetually guarded, and when Mary questioned Pugsy about it, he merely said, "It's my business. If you got a problem with it, too bad."

On her third night of freedom, Mary decided it was time to rid Chicago of its secrets. She went to the agricultural building alone, circling it, counting the entrances—five in all—and searching out the guard who looked the least intelligent, and most unhappy in his situation. She found the perfect specimen at the northeast entry.

"Good evening," she said, as she approached. She tried to get past him and through the door without slowing down, but the guard put out his hand and she intentionally bumped into it. It had the desired effect—he looked embarrassed at having touched her.

"What do you think you're doing?" she demanded, as indignantly as she could.

"I'm sorry, Miss Mary," he said, "but no one's allowed to come in here."

"But haven't you heard? Your boss and I have a partnership, which means I have no secrets from him, and he has none from me. Now could you please open the door and let me pass?"

The guard looked uncertain, like this might be a trick question. "I'm sorry, but without a direct order from the Death Boss —"

"Just a few days into our partnership, and our agreement is already being broken," said Mary in an exaggerated huff. "I'll have to take this up with Mr. Capone. What's your name?"

What began as mild awkwardness now turned into sheer terror. "Why do you need to know my name?"

"Never mind," she said, looking him up and down. "I'm sure I can describe you well enough to Mr. Capone."

"But . . . but we're not allowed to let anyone in without a direct order. . . ." His voice had become whiny and pleading. All it took was a silent glare and he caved, not only letting her in, but opening the door, with a bow, and closing it behind her.

She wasn't quite sure what she was expecting to see, but Mary, who had seen just about everything was rarely caught off guard. This was one of those times.

Beneath the crystal dome that once housed a vast variety of plant life, were children — hundreds of them, all asleep and curled up in fetal positions. They were dead, yet not dead. They weren't quite Afterlights, for they didn't have any afterglow.

"What is this place . . . ?" she said, not even realizing she said it aloud.

"We call it the incubator."

She spun to see Jackin' Jill coming up slowly behind her. "I knew you'd find your way in here eventually." Jill looked out over the sleeping children, all lined up in neat little rows. "These are all kids who didn't make it to the light."

Mary found herself stunned into silence. These children were Afterlights still in transition. They were *Interlights*.

"It takes nine months to pass from the living world into Everlost," said Jill. "I thought you'd know that."

"Of course I know that," Mary was finally able to say, "but I've never seen . . . I mean, I've never actually *found* any in this state."

"Is that so?" said Jackin' Jill with a wry grin. "Well, I find them all the time." She wandered among the dead-not-dead Interlight children, and Mary followed. "I find them, then I bring them here. How do you think Pugsy wound up with so many loyal subjects?"

Mary found her quick-mindedness slowed to a crawl by this revelation. Pugsy didn't need soul traps to catch Afterlights—he got them even before they were born into Everlost. Mary knelt to one of the silent children, a boy no older than ten, in a state of perfect peace. There was a number written in chalk on the ground next to him. A date. In fact, each of them had dates written beside them. "The dates each of them died?" asked Mary.

"How could they be," asked Jill, "when all the dates are in the future?"

Mary glanced at several of the dates, but they meant little to her. She didn't keep track of time in the living world.

"Those are the dates that each of them will ripen," Jill said, and Mary realized that was her crude way of saying that these were the dates the children would awaken in Everlost.

"How is it that you can find so many, when I've never found one before they've woken up?"

"Maybe you don't know where to look."

Mary gave her a cold glare. "If you're going to toy with me, then we have nothing more to talk about." Then she turned her back on Jill and wove through the evenly spaced grid of hibernating children.

"It's the amulet," Jill finally admitted. "It glows when something devastating is about to happen. Something like a fatal accident . . . "

Mary turned to Jill, glancing at the blue-gemmed pendant she wore around her neck. It looked like cheap costume jewelry—but Mary was willing to give her the benefit of the doubt. Certainly accidents, and untimely deaths, must set off ripples—not only in the living world, but through all levels of creation. It was possible that an object could resonate with such events—but how could Jill know *specifically* which accidents would result in a child falling short of the light, and into Everlost?

When the truth struck Mary, it struck deeply, as only the truth could.

*"You stop them from reaching the light!"* Mary said, with a

gasp. "You know when and where the accidents will happen—then you wait for them to cross, and you stand in their way!" She looked at the kids on the floor, now caught in an invisible cocoon of transition. "These children weren't coming to Everlost—*you guided them here!*"

She only had to look at Jackin' Jill to know it was true.

Now things truly began to heave and buckle within Mary's soul—a shifting of purpose and design that went down to the core of her being. Finally Mary said:

"What a wonderful thing you've done here!"

Jill, who never seemed fazed by anything, was startled by that.

"Wonderful?" said Jill. "I wouldn't call it wonderful, but it *does* make me very useful to Pugsy."

As Mary looked over at the sleeping Interlights, waiting to be born into eternity, she realized that this was only a beginning, and what seemed so overwhelming just a few moments ago, now seemed like a tiny drop in a giant bucket.

"But don't you see," said Mary. "It *is* wonderful." Mary spread her arms out wide, and spun in a slow circle, feeling as if she was at the center of a gloriously expanding universe. "Look at all these children, Jill! You've saved them all!"

Everything changed for Mary after discovering Jackin' Jill's mysterious ability to keep children from the light. In the right hands, it was a power that was more awe-inspiring than any in Everlost. Mary could not help but feel that it was some kind of divine will that had brought this power to her. Now she saw everything as if refracted through the multifaceted blue topaz in the center of Jill's amulet. The future was sparkling and bright, and as her dreams sailed higher and higher, her sights became more firmly fixed on the western horizon.

She shared all this with Speedo, but he seemed more likely to shove his head in the earth rather than see Mary's big picture.

"If Chicago's not enough for you, we could go south to New Orleans, or north to Canada," Speedo said, pacing the Starboard Promenade. As the ship was moored and grounded—at least temporarily, Speedo had little to occupy his time beyond worrying. "We could even go back to New York."

"You're missing the point!" Mary said, with the most patient exasperation she could muster. "We must challenge the unknown, and the west is Everlost's greatest mystery."

"This isn't like you," Speedo whined. "Stability—*routine*—that's the Mary Hightower I know."

"I will find a peaceful routine for every child in my care," she assured him, "but to build a better Everlost, I must be willing to sacrifice my own routine for the sake of others."

"Build a better Everlost? Everlost is already here—you can't build what's already here."

Mary thought about Jill's incubator, and smiled. "I beg to differ."

Speedo just threw up his hands. It was no use—true, he was the closest Mary had to a confidant, but his thinking was numbingly limited in scope. She longed for someone she could share her revelations with—someone who could not only understand, but see the same vast horizon that she now saw. The future—her future—in fact the entire future of Everlost was spread out before her like a frontier. It wasn't merely her hope to subdue it—she had come to realize it was her destiny. Why else would Jill have come to her? Why else would she have such an urge to move beyond the bounds of the known afterworld?

"With Jill's help, and my guidance, we will save all the children we can, both here and in the west," Mary told Speedo. "And in so doing we will unite Everlost."

"There might not even be a 'west,'" he pointed out.

"Yes, I've heard the stories too," Mary said with a dramatic wave. "A giant cliff that falls off into nowhere. An ocean that pours off the edge of the earth. A wall of fire through which nothing can pass."

"What if one of those things is true? What if they're *all* true?"

"Didn't you tell me the *Hindenburg* made regular trips to Roswell, New Mexico, before it came into your possession—doesn't that prove there is something west of the Mississippi?"

"That's according to the finder who sold it to me—but finders can't be trusted—I know because I was one. He would have said anything to unload this thing!"

Mary sighed. "Let's not put the cart before the horse, shall we? Chicago first, and then we'll see where providence leads us from there. And of course we must not forget the threat of the Chocolate Ogre."

"Nick? He's probably forgotten all about you by now."

Mary bristled at that. "I'm sure he hasn't! And I would prefer that you not call him by his living name. He is the Chocolate Ogre now."

"He was never an ogre, and you know it."

"After what he did, he deserves to be demonized."

Speedo backed down, not up for the battle. "Whatever you say."

Mary studied him closely. "After all this time, are you regretting the choice you made to stay with me?"

"Of course not," Speedo said. "It's just that sometimes . . . sometimes you scare me."

In her book *Order Now, Question Later,* Mary Hightower has this to say about her enemies:

"In Everlost, just as in the living world, there are those who put their own selfish desires ahead of that which is clearly and obviously right. In these cases I have always found such enemies of virtue will eventually destroy themselves if left to their own devices. Although occasionally some assistance might be required."

# CHAPTER 19

## *Eminence Green*

Had there been any outside observers—biographers to mark the afterlife of Megan Mary McGill, better known as Mary Hightower—they would have marveled at how thoroughly she infiltrated Pugsy Capone's rule. How brilliantly, how slyly it was done! Mary, however, would never call herself sly, or even cunning. *Ascendant,* she would call herself. The way cream rises to the top. The way the wise are naturally elevated above the masses. Mary was the *eminence gris*—the shadow power—behind Pugsy's very short-lived "golden era," and while Pugsy had always been very good at tooling people to his own purposes, he himself was not the sharpest tool in the shed. So he never knew that his power was slowly being usurped.

"Your organization needs structure," Mary told him in confidence.

"It works fine the way it is," Pugsy insisted.

"Oh, yes, it does," Mary admitted, but she pointed out how very afraid of him his own subjects were. It was something Pugsy took great pride in, in fact. And so Mary proposed a little test. She asked Pugsy to call in one of his loyal subjects, and order him to perform a simple but time-consuming task. Curious as to where this was going, Pugsy called in a kid whose name he did not remember, and told him to do a head count of the hundred or so Afterlights living in the administration building, and then create a graph, plotting how each of them had died.

"I want it before sunset," Pugsy demanded. "Or else!"

The boy obediently ran off, took the entire day, and returned just as the day settled into twilight. He presented Pugsy with a list and a competent graph, and he cowered until Pugsy nodded his acceptance.

Then Mary asked the same of one of her own children—a boy known as Bedhair—to graph the demise of all ninety-three in her care. The boy took only two hours, and he returned with a list, and not just one graph, but three: a coordinate graph, a bar graph, and a pie chart.

"You cheated!" Pugsy insisted. "He already knew the answers."

"Do you really believe that?" Mary asked in a calm and condescending way. "My children obey my requests because they *want* to, not because they fear what will happen if they fail. Consequently, they perform their tasks better."

It didn't occur to Pugsy that Mary never actually denied that Bedhair already knew the answers.

Mary also discovered that Pugsy did not personally attend to the transitioning Interlights that Jill continued to bring to the agricultural building. He found it beneath him, and left their assimilation to his flunkies. This provided Mary with a great opportunity.

She marked her personal calendar with the date that

every sleeping Interlight would awaken, and made sure she was there to greet them when they did.

"Welcome to Everlost," she would tell the confused, and often frightened, children. "My name is Miss Mary, and you are among friends." Then she would present each of them with a volume of *Tips for Taps*, her definitive book for new arrivals to Everlost—each book painstakingly handwritten by her children on paper scavenged from Pugsy's troves. Grateful for her kindness, these new children would imprint on her like ducklings, ensuring their allegiance, while Pugsy became little more than a distant figure in their minds, a footnote in their world at best.

From Pugsy's point of view, high atop his regal Ferris wheel, nothing had really changed. His subjects still feared him and obeyed his every whim. But now it was merely because Mary allowed it. Only when Mary made it clear that her ambitions stretched beyond Chicago, did he begin to worry about her intentions.

"Tell me what you know about the west," she asked Pugsy one day. "Not what you've heard, but what you know."

"There is no west," he answered curtly. "Everlost ends at the Mississippi River."

"Have you been there?"

"What's it to you?"

"I just assumed that a leader of your stature would want to see it with his own eyes."

Pugsy took the flattery at face value and said, "I did. Once. There's a wind that blows from the other side. A crazy wind. I ordered a dozen Afterlights, one after the other, to cross the Centennial Bridge, but the wind wouldn't let them, and each one of them sunk right through the bridge, into the river."

The thought that he'd order so many Afterlights to their doom didn't sit well with Mary, but she tried not to show it. "Perhaps if you found a bridge that had crossed into Everlost . . . "

"There *are* no Everlost bridges that cross the Mississippi, because there's no Everlost there to cross into, so stop asking stupid questions." He eyed her with suspicion, and Mary realized she had pushed too far.

"Perhaps my next book should be a collaboration," Mary suggested. "I'm sure there are other things you know that I don't."

"And it'll stay that way," said Pugsy, closing the door to further conversation. But, as they say, when God closes a door he opens a window, and in Mary's mind, it was a window facing west.

Jackin' Jill took a close interest in the gradual shift of power. Pugsy was far too busy luxuriating in extravagance to notice it, and although Jill could have sown the seeds of his suspicion, she didn't. Pugsy's life before Mary's arrival had been one of decadent excess, but Mary's superior administrative abilities had made life better for all the Afterlights of Chicago—especially Pugsy. Even the leather armchair that served as his throne was gone, replaced by a gold embroidered settee that a pharaoh might have once used. It was a gift presented to him by Mary as a show of her loyalty to their partnership.

Mary had traded the finest baubles of her own collection for the settee, and yet she had given it away to Pugsy, claiming his armchair for herself. Jill found this very impressive, because she knew exactly what Mary was doing. Pugsy's comfort was worth any cost, because the more comfortable he was, the less he'd be looking in Mary's direction. Jill dreamed that the next partnership would be between her and Mary—that together they would become the most powerful force in Everlost.

On this particular day, Jill carried two fresh sleeping Interlights to the incubator, both thrown over her shoulder like a hunter's kills. The incubator wasn't kept under tight guard anymore. Mary had declared that all Afterlights should be able to see this glorious place, as if it were a hospital nursery. After depositing the sleeping Interlights, Jill went to tell Mary that the incubator was now brimming with almost a hundred and seventy hibernating souls. She found Mary in the *Hindenburg's* Starboard Promenade, talking to another Afterlight—but not just any Afterlight. This one was a handsome skinjacker. A skinjacker by the name of Milos.

Jill tried to hide her shock, but couldn't. She had left Milos and his two miserable cohorts at the hands of an angry mob, and had assumed the mob had sent them on a long, slow trip to the center of the earth. She should have realized that Milos would have found a way out of it. He was so smooth—*too* smooth. Even now he looked at Jill with the suave hint of a gloat, and a grin that hid what must have been hatred, for how could he not hate her after what she had done to him?

"Jill!" said Mary. "I'm glad you're here." She was either oblivious or pretending to be. She was smooth too.

"He's a liar!" Jill blurted out. "Don't listen to a word Milos says. If you have any sense you'll get him off your ship right now!"

Mary showed no signs of heeding her. "What an odd thing to say—I thought you two were friends. At least that's what Milos said."

Jill looked to Milos. The grin never left his face. "We parted under . . . uncertain circumstances," he said. "But Jill, I must say, I am surprised by your . . . how do you say it? 'Unprovoked hostility'."

"Whatever happened between you and Milos, I'm sure you're sensible and mature enough to put it behind you," Mary said. "Just as I've been able to admit how wrong I've been in my assessment of skinjackers, you should be able to resolve your differences. After all, we're all working for the greater good."

Jill was truly speechless, but she tried to salvage the moment. She turned to Milos. "Milos, I'm sorry, let's start fresh." She reached out to shake Milos's hand and he took it, clasping it a bit too hard, making it clear that bygones were not bygones, and that he would have his revenge. Jill squeezed his hand just as hard. Let him try to get back at her. Let him try!

"I really have missed you, Milos. How've you been?"

"Oh, Moose, Squirrel, and I have had some fine adventures, but now we're here. We must spend some time catching up."

Jill glanced to Mary. If she picked up the tension

between Jill and Milos, she didn't care. Or perhaps the tension suited her needs.

"Now, then," said Mary, "I've been bringing Milos up to speed on your amulet, and how you've been using it to rescue children from the light. We now have four skinjackers instead of just one—isn't that splendid? It's been amazing all the things you've been able to accomplish all by yourself, Jill—think of how much more effective you'll be as a team!"

"I can only imagine," said Milos.

If Jill had a stomach, she would have been sick to it.

For Milos, finding Jackin' Jill was nothing compared to finding Mary Hightower. The fact that Jill was unable to ruin things for him was a good sign, and boded well for his future. If success was the best revenge, then his success with Mary would be sweet indeed—and a very bitter pill for Jackin' Jill, who had used him and discarded him.

Moose and Squirrel were still off paying tribute to Pugsy Capone, giving Milos time to follow Jill to the incubator, once his first audience with Mary was done. "I wanted to see your new scam with my own eyes," he told her the moment he knew they were alone. He looked out over the sleeping Interlights. "You've been busy."

"This is no scam," said Jill, practically spewing venom. "And whatever you think you're doing here, it's not going to happen. You'd better leave now if you know what's good for you."

Milos was not troubled in the least. Her threat was empty. He sauntered closer to her, then suddenly thrust his hand forward, grabbing the amulet, pulling it toward him. The chain didn't break, and instead it pulled Jill right to him, by the neck.

"Let go of me!" demanded Jill.

"I remember when I gave you this necklace," he said. "I traded a whole box of Twinkies for it. Do you know what those Twinkies were worth?"

"I said let go!"

This time Milos did, and Jill took a healthy step back from him.

"Does Mary know that your 'magical amulet' is nothing more than blue glass on a fake gold chain?"

Now Jill began to look scared. "Are you going to tell her?"

Milos chose to ignore the question. "What I want to know is how you do it. You obviously cannot see the future, so then how do you know when these deadly accidents will occur?"

Jill looked at him with fuming hatred. "Figure it out for yourself."

"Oh," said Milos, "but I already have."

The hatred in Jill's eyes peaked into desperation, and finally faded to defeat. "What do you want, Milos?"

*Good*, thought Milos. *Now for the bargain.* Few things were more rewarding than blackmailing a criminal. "I will keep your secret," Milos told her, "and in return, you will step back, and allow me to take first position among Mary's skinjackers."

"Mary chooses who she puts in charge."

"Mary will choose me," Milos said with confidence.

"And when she does, you will support it, and accept my leadership." Then he smiled. "Just like old times."

"And if I don't?"

"Then I will tell Mary exactly how you find all these 'new arrivals.'"

Jill looked away, her lips pursing into an angry slit. "Fine. But don't expect me to follow your orders," she said, but Milos knew she would.

Milos left Jill to stew in her own afterglow, returning immediately to Mary, who wanted to brief him on the state of affairs in Chicago. At first she was guarded, but Milos could sense she needed someone to talk to—a new and sympathetic ear. And so he listened, and found everything she had to say fascinating. Perhaps she sensed that, because soon she opened up, sharing things beyond her dealings in Chicago. As stiff as she was, she seemed to relax just the slightest bit.

"It's good to have someone to talk to about these things," she said. "Someone with whom I can see eye to eye."

Milos looked around the Promenade. It said so much about Mary. It was pristine, and spotless. It was full of works of art and furniture that were clearly added by her. The place was as elegant and evolved as Mary herself. There was also a sizeable collection of books in the Promenade. Not just the ones Mary had written, but dozens of others that Mary had acquired. One of those books was out, and sitting on Mary's chair. Milos picked it up, curious. It featured a picture of a suspension bridge under construction. The title was *A History of Civil Engineering*.

"A hobby of yours?" he asked.

Mary took the book from him and set it down. "Every book has something to teach us," she said, "and crucial knowledge at the right time can be a very powerful thing. "Mary gestured for Milos to sit, and so he did, stretching out comfortably on a plush sofa. Mary sat across from him. "Now, if you don't mind, I'd like to know a little bit about your travels."

"What would you like to know?"

"Your friend Moose mentioned that you had an encounter with Allie the Outcast. I would very much like to know about it."

"Allie is of no concern," he told her. "When I last saw her, she was on her way home. It is a serious thing when a skinjacker goes home—you will be the last thing on her mind. Trust me, she is no threat."

Mary shifted her shoulders, the suggestion unnerving her. "Did I say she was a threat?"

"No," admitted Milos, "but she is a friend of the Chocolate Ogre. And he *is* a threat, yes?"

Mary leaned forward, a little too interested. "Did she say anything about him? Anything at all?"

Milos shrugged. "A bit. Very little. She had not seen him for years—since the day on the pier. I understand you were there too."

"I hope you realize that the Ogre must be stopped."

"From doing what?"

"From doing *anything*! He must be brought to justice!"

"And you," asked Milos, "are the judge?"

And then she quoted from one of her own writings. "In

a lawless world, we must illuminate truth with our glow, and create justice by the convictions of our souls."

"So then, you *are* his judge."

"I have seen firsthand the acts of cruelty he's capable of," Mary said. "He sent hundreds of helpless children into the light. He'd send us all there if he had his way."

Milos found he could read her just as easily as one of her books. At least when it came to the subject of the Chocolate Ogre. He tried not to smile as he spoke. "Does he know you're in love with him?"

She snapped him a burning glare, as if the question itself was an attack. "I see you've been listening to smears made against me. Probably from Allie the Outcast."

Milos knew he had to play this very, very carefully. "No, it was only a guess. But believe me," he said earnestly, "I know what it's like to love someone who has betrayed you. And I know how hard it is to move on. But in the end, we must."

They held each other's gazes, and what wasn't spoken at that moment was more important than anything else that was.

Mary was the first to break the gaze. Her eyes drifted to the book sitting on the table beside her. The engineering textbook. She picked it up, and pondered it, rubbing her hand across the surface as if it might sprout forth a genie.

"I will be needing the services of skinjackers, for various missions. *Important* missions. I'll need someone I can trust in charge."

"In that case," said Milos, "I hope I can be of service."

* * *

It was long after dark when he left that night, after hours in Mary's company. There was no question he was dazzled by her. Mary was everything Milos imagined she might be. She had Jill's shrewdness, without the sociopathic streak. She had Allie's high moral integrity, without the naivety that kept Allie devoted to that miserable Mikey McGill. Milos knew his weakness was that he fell in love too easily, which blinded him to the character flaws of the girls he fell for— but finally here was a girl worthy of his attention!

He had already softened her defenses, but truly winning her affections would require a different kind of dance than he was used to. One where all his moves were clear, and his motives transparent. She valued honesty and directness. This he could deliver.

Milos knew he had no choice but to win her over— it was a matter of necessity for him now, because he had already fallen for her—and the only way to survive a force of nature such as Mary Hightower was to make sure that the feeling was mutual.

*If only Mary were a skinjacker,* he thought. *Ah well, one can't have everything.* Besides, if Mary were a skinjacker, she wouldn't have any need for Milos, so perhaps it was better this way.

And she did need him—she said so herself—but there were many levels of need. Milos had had his heart broken one too many times. This time would be different. Somehow he would find a way to be everything Mary needed, as indispensable as air to the living. As permanent as Everlost itself.

# PART FOUR

*Way of the Chocolate Warrior*

In her most recent book, *What You Don't Know Can Most Certainly Hurt You*, Mary Hightower writes:

"It would be untrue to say Everlost is entirely free from illness and disease. Our flesh is gone, but in our beings, seeds of our own doom remain. That which was small will grow. That which was once insignificant can devour us. There are cancers beyond those of our mortal bodies. I consider them punishments for unwholesome deeds and wrongful thinking. The Chocolate Ogre serves as a perfect example, for whose thinking can be more wrong than his, and whose affliction could be more unpleasant?"

# CHAPTER 20
## The Great Train Robbery

A large vapor of Afterlights gathered to watch the festivities in the old train yards of Chattanooga, Tennessee. It was the most exciting thing to happen here in recent memory. It began with the arrival of the Chocolate Ogre, and rumor was that he was going to perform some sort of magic trick.

A team of ten Afterlights, supervised by the Ogre himself, took a rope, and tied it around the waist of a kid in a Confederate Army uniform.

It was, of course, Zinnia.

"Let's not make this a show," Nick told her. "Let's just get this done."

"S'already a show," Zin pointed out, "best milk it for all it's worth."

Zin concentrated and thrust her ripping-hand out of Everlost, and into the living world just as easily as if she were shoving her hand into water. "Ooh" and "ahh" went the crowd. Then, through the tiny portal into the living world, Zin grabbed the rusted coupling of a living-world train car, springing it closed on her forearm, like a bear trap. They had chosen an Amtrak passenger car—an older one, because it was the only uncoupled passenger car they could find.

Once she was sure her arm was firmly snagged in the coupler, she turned to her team. "All right, y'all know the drill. One, two, three, pull!"

The other ten Afterlights behind her began to pull on the rope which was still tied around her waist. Nick watched, but couldn't participate, because these days everything he touched became too slippery to hold on to.

The team of ten strained as they pulled on Zin with all their strength, and with her arm still firmly caught in the coupler, her body lifted off the ground. A living body might have been torn in half by such a thing, but not an Afterlight. Instead, Zin withstood the force, and the solitary train car began to move. Getting it moving was the hard part. Once it was moving, the small hole in space which at first had been just large enough for Zin's hand, now stretched like elastic, until the entire passenger car was moving through the portal, out of the living world, and into Everlost.

The crowd could not contain their excitement as they watched the blurry, faded train car resolve bit by bit into sharp focus, and fill with the bright hues of chrome, rust, and colorful graffiti.

Once the train car was through, the portal collapsed, sealing closed with a pop. The team of haulers dropped their rope, and scattered as the car rolled off onto a side track that no longer existed, rolling toward the last car of the Everlost train.

"Tha's right," complained Zin, as the Amtrak car continued to roll. "Just leave me stuck here to get smashed in the coupler again!"

Nick grinned, and yelled, "That's half the fun, Zin!" Still, he went to free her.

He couldn't move as quickly as he used to—chocolate dripping onto his feet had made them heavy—but fortunately the train wasn't rolling all that fast. He caught up with the rolling car, jumped on the coupler, and used his chocolate-covered left hand to grease the coupler. Zin wriggled her arm free just in time, and they both hopped off just as the Amtrak car hit, and coupled with the last car of the Everlost train, sending a shudder through every coupling down to the engine. The newborn passenger car was now a part of their train, and in the engine, Charlie tooted the whistle to mark their success. The crowd of gawking Afterlights cheered.

"How does it feel to be everyone's hero?" Nick asked Zin.

"I still miss my rocket ship, sir." But Nick could tell she was enjoying the adoration far more than the isolation she had lived in for so many years.

Their train, which had started with just three cars, now had nine—each added by Zin one at a time over the past few weeks. This did not go unnoticed in the living world— although Nick found out quite by accident.

Johnnie-O, who was attempting to teach Zin how to read, made Zin rip various newspapers and magazines from the living world. Johnnie-O, who was now in perpetual nicotine withdrawal, was the world's most impatient teacher, and Zin was the world's most ungrateful student. Every day they would verbally abuse each other for an hour, not much of anything would be learned, and yet the next day, both of them would come back for more.

One day Johnnie-O came to Nick with a copy of *The World Weekly Herald*—a tabloid with questionable news. "I think you'd better read this," Johnnie-O told him. On page two, a headline read SOUTHERN PACIFIC RAILROAD SUES PARALLEL UNIVERSE. The article spoke of train cars gone missing from Southern train yards with no explanation—and a promise by one railroad line to take matters into its own hands . . . but since the headline right next to it read ALIEN BABY DEVOURS AREA 51, Nick really wasn't concerned. Besides, the living world had bigger things to worry about than missing train cars, anyway. And so did Everlost.

Nick had not heard news of Mary Hightower for quite a while, and he couldn't help but worry what kind of mischief she was up to. If Mary had her way, all the world's Afterlights would be trapped in her smothering embrace, and no doubt she was still working toward that end. She had to be stopped at all costs, and Nick had a plan to do it.

That plan depended on Zinnia.

It had been more than a month since wrangling her in at Cape Canaveral.

"I gots no use for you!" she had told Nick and Johnnie-O that first day, as they made their way back through the Florida forests to the train. "But now that ya blowed up my artillery, I gots no use for myself, neither."

Charlie had been waiting with the train, and was more than happy to stay in the conductor's booth rather than have any dealings whatsoever with an ecto-ripper. Johnnie-O, on the other hand, would keep taunting her, until she would rip out some random part of his anatomy, threatening to feed it to Kudzu, and he'd have to chase her to get it back.

Johnnie-O did this so often, Nick was convinced that he actually liked it.

Their first challenge was Atlanta—and Nick knew if he failed there, there'd be little hope after that.

When they rolled back into the Atlanta Underground many weeks ago, the crowd of Afterlights that had been so threatening the first time still came out with their bats and their bricks, but this time it was just for show. They were more curious than anything. Word had gotten around that the Chocolate Ogre was looking for Zach the Ripper, which meant he probably wouldn't be coming back. The fact that he had actually returned elevated him to Monster Supreme in their eyes. Everybody wanted to know what he had found in the Florida Everwilds.

Nick had not planned to reveal Zin right away. He knew the Atlanta Afterlights needed to be prepared. But Zin—to whom common sense was a limp afterthought— made herself known even before the train rolled to a stop. She took one look at the Atlanta kids, then poked her head out of a window, and shouted at them, "If you throw them bricks at me, I swear I'll rip out parts a' ya y'didn't even know ya had! See if I don't!" And then to prove it, she reached over to Johnnie-O and ripped his memory of a spleen, holding it out the window.

"Don't you drop that, ya stupid inbred freak!" yelled Johnnie-O.

Since Johnnie-O had no idea what a spleen looked like, his memory of it more closely resembled a Polish sausage than anything else. Even so, it inspired terror in the crowd. They all dropped their weapons, scattering in abject fear, and yelling, "It's Zach the Ripper! It's Zach the Ripper!"

Johnnie-O pulled her away from the window, retrieving his Polish spleen, but it was too late to stop panic from spreading through the mob.

"Great," Nick groaned. "Why don't you rip out your own brain and give yourself one that works?"

Zin was unfazed. "Yer just mad cuz your chocolate don't scare 'em as much as I do!"

"You had better start listening to me!" Nick put his finger in her face, and, of course, she bit it.

"Sorry, sir," she said, all nasty grin, "but I thought yer hand was one a' them chocolate Easter bunnies."

Johnnie-O let out a guffaw, and Nick glared at him. "Sorry," Johnnie-O said. "It does kinda look like that sometimes."

Nick decided to use a different tack. "Soldier! Your behavior is disgraceful for a sergeant of the Chocolate Brigade."

"Sergeant?" said Zin. "I thought you said I was a private."

"Not anymore." He reached over and painted a chocolate chevron on her sleeve. "You're a sergeant now, and I expect you to act like one."

Zin was overjoyed. "Yes, sir!"

"And if you follow orders and do your job to the best of your ability, you might even make lieutenant."

"Yes, sir! What are my orders, sir?"

Nick had suspected she might be more motivated by responsibility than by threats. "Your orders are not to do *anything* unless I tell you to," he said.

"Good luck," grunted Johnnie-O. Then he asked what rank *he* got to be. Nick told him he was special ops, which suited Johnnie-O just fine.

Five minutes later, Isaiah, the kid who ran Atlanta, showed up, just as Nick knew he would. He barged right onto the train.

"What in the hell do you think you're doing?" he demanded. His sudden appearance and threatening tone of voice set Kudzu barking, and hiding behind Zin. Nick thought about sending Zin away, but decided it was best if she stayed in his sight. Instead he told Johnnie-O to check on Charlie. "He might be in need of some special ops right about now."

Johnnie-O left, but not before matching Isaiah's glare. With Johnnie-O gone, it was no longer three against one, but the tension didn't drop in the slightest.

Isaiah looked at Zin, then back to Nick again. Nick could tell he was afraid, but he hid his fear behind anger. "You take that *thing* and you get it out of Atlanta. Now."

"Who's he calling a thing?" growled Zin.

Nick firmly clasped Zin's shoulder with his chocolate-free hand. "Remember your orders," he said under his breath. Zin bit her lip—literally—as if the only way for her to shut her mouth was to clamp her bottom lip between her teeth.

It was then that Nick realized that Zin was a double whammy. Not only had he brought "Zach the Ripper," but he had brought a Confederate soldier into a city run by a kid who may very well have suffered the life of a slave when he was alive.

"Her name is Zinnia," Nick told him, "and she means you no harm."

"You mean to tell me that *thing* is a girl?"

Zinnia bristled, but kept her mouth shut.

"She's a ripper and she's here to help all of us."

"I don't care what she can do—I don't need help from someone wearin' the gray."

Then Zinnia took a few steps forward. Nick tried to stop her, but she shrugged him off. So much for obeying orders.

"I don't recollect all that much 'bout my life," she said, "but I do know I didn't join the war to protect slavery. I did it to protect my family—and I'd take off this here uniform if I could, but I can't any more than you can take off those torn pants and rope belt. We's all stuck with what we wore, but not with what we were."

Isaiah still looked angry, but he didn't respond. He just waited to see if there was any more to her defense. To Nick's surprise, there was.

"The way I sees it," said Zin, "there ought not to be problems with skin color in Everlost, cuz Afterlights ain't got no skin, technically speakin', right?"

Isaiah nodded. "I'll do you one better than that," he said. "Hold out your arm."

Zinnia held her arm out, and Isaiah held out his right beside hers. "See that?" he said. "Our glow is exactly the same."

"Yeah, how 'bout that!"

"You remember that," said Isaiah, "and maybe I won't have to run you out of town."

"Fair enough," said Zin.

Now that their peace had been made, Isaiah turned to Nick. "So are you just passing through again, or is there something you want from us?"

And that's when the real work began.

# CHAPTER 21

## *Let 'Er Rip*

Winning over the Atlanta Afterlights was a delicate matter, as painstaking, as . . . well . . . the making of chocolate. Too hot and it would burn, too cool, and it would lump. With Isaiah's reluctant permission, Nick introduced Zin to all the Atlanta Afterlights. There were almost four hundred of them. Once more they filled the streets of the Atlanta underground — this time without weapons.

As they gathered, Nick stood patiently with an impatient Zin. Johnnie-O and Charlie provided security, keeping space between them and the curious crowd.

"If things get out of hand, do I got permission to knock some heads?" Johnnie-O asked.

"Absolutely not," Nick told him.

"You're no fun," he grumbled.

When all of Atlanta was there, Isaiah came up to Nick. "Do I introduce you as Nick, Nicholas, or the Chocolate Ogre?"

Nick's instinct was to simply go by Nick, plain and simple — but if Mary was the Sky Witch, how could he hope to be taken seriously if he was just "Nick"?

"Go with the Ogre," he told Isaiah. Mary had invented the name as a smear tactic. Well, it was time he used it to his advantage.

Isaiah raised his hand to get everyone's attention, and in a few moments the murmuring crowd quieted down. "Hey y'all, everybody," he said, in an informal, yet commanding voice. "This here is the Chocolate Ogre, as I'm sure you already know. I've checked him out, and he's okay. He wants to talk to you, so listen up—and don't make him mad, or he'll turn you into chocolate chips or something."

Nick cleared his throat twice. He was nervous, and whenever he was nervous his throat clogged with chocolate.

"Afterlights of Atlanta," Nick began. "I come in friendship . . . and to prove it, I would like to present to you Zinnia the Ripper!"

"Zinnia?" said some kid in the crowd. "Like the flower?"

"Shut yer trap!" said Zin.

Nick pushed on. "I know you've all heard bad things about the ripper—just like you've heard bad things about me. Well, I'm here to set you straight. The ripper's not going to rip anyone's guts out—"

"I could if I wanted to," said Zin, and Kudzu seconded it with a bark and growl.

"Right," Nick said, throwing her a secret scowl. "But the ripper uses her powers for good." Nick took a moment to let that sink in, then he continued. "We all know that there aren't many things that cross into Everlost—and when things do cross, they get picked up by finders, who charge

an arm and a leg for everything. Well, forget about finders—
because if there's something you want, the ripper can get it
for you!"

Nick knew he was sounding like an infomercial, but at
least he had their undivided attention. He glanced to Isaiah,
whose arms were folded, not yet impressed by the show.

"I need a volunteer!" Nick said.

No one came forward at first, then a young girl was
pushed out in front by her friends. She looked terrified.
Johnnie-O escorted her the rest of the way, and she stared
bug-eyed at his huge hand which was gripping her elbow.

"Don't worry," Nick said to the girl quietly, "this is a *good*
thing." Then he spoke loudly enough for the crowd to hear.
"Tell me something you're longing for. Something you truly
feel you deserve, that you've never had here in Everlost."

The girl looked up at him with wide, hopeful eyes. "A
hot fudge sundae?"

Zin laughed. "Y'already got one! He's standing right in
front a' ya!"

Only Charlie and Johnnie-O laughed. Everyone else
was waiting for Nick to turn Zin into a pile of chocolate
chips. Nick turned to Isaiah. "Where in *living* Atlanta could
we find a hot fudge sundae?"

"I know just the place."

Isaiah led them to the World of Coca-Cola, one of
Atlanta's biggest tourist attractions—a veritable cathedral
of carbonated caffeination. Inside was a restaurant that featured all things Coca-Cola—such as ice-cream floats made
with Coke instead of root beer, and Coke syrup sundaes.

The crowd of Afterlights followed Isaiah, Nick, and Zin

right through the outer wall, and into the café. The place was packed with the living—there was a field trip of students all in neon yellow shirts laying siege to the counter, and ice cream was being dished up by four soda jerks who couldn't move fast enough.

"The ripper will now ecto-rip a sundae right before your very eyes!" said Nick, sounding like a carnival barker, and enjoying it.

The crowd of Afterlights all craned their necks to see, and shifted their feet to keep from sinking. The effect was a weird bobbing of several hundred heads.

Nick zeroed in on a silver bowl that had just been filled with three scoops of strawberry ice cream. The soda-jerk was about to douse it in Coke syrup, proving that some combinations really ought to be illegal.

"Quick," he said to Zin, "rip it before it's too late."

Zin shoved her ripping-hand forward into the living world, and the crowd of Afterlights buzzed with excitement. In one smooth move, Zin grabbed the ice-cream bowl, and tugged it out of the living world into Everlost. The soda jerk never saw it happen—and when he emptied his syrup ladle, Coke syrup spilled all over the marble counter. He looked at the counter for a moment in dumb confusion, then he glanced at the other soda jerks and said, "Okay, who's the joker?"

"It just disappeared!" said a living redheaded kid sitting at the counter in front of him. "It disappeared right into thin air! A hand reached out of nowhere and took it!"

"Shut up, Ralphy," said the kid next to him, and that was that. The soda jerk sighed, and made another sundae, not caring enough about the mystery to unravel it.

Zin, with the ripped bowl of ice cream in her hands, held it out to the girl, who was already licking her lips.

"No," said Nick. "Not yet."

Then he held his hand over the ice cream, squeezed his hand into a fist, and dribbled a hefty amount of chocolate over the ice cream.

"Ew!" shouted several voices in the crowd, sounding both delighted and disgusted at the same time.

"There," Nick said. "A hot fudge sundae."

The girl and her friends didn't wait for spoons to be ripped—they devoured it with their hands.

"So," said Isaiah, "the Chocolate Ogre isn't a monster . . . he's a thief."

Nick didn't deny it. He had thought long and hard about what it meant to rip things from the living world, but he ultimately decided that the needs of Everlost outweighed the needs of the living. "Ever hear of Robin Hood?" he said to the crowd, as much as to Isaiah.

"Sure—he robbed from the rich and gave to the poor."

"Well," said Nick, "the living are rich, whether they know it or not. The way I see it, we deserve a small share of the world that was stolen from us."

Isaiah didn't say he agreed, but he didn't disagree, either.

"Okay," said Nick. "Who's next?"

Almost every hand went up, with shouts of "Me! Me! Me!"

Nick turned to Isaiah. "Get me a list of ten reasonable requests, and we'll see what we can do."

* * *

Nick counted on Isaiah to weed out the needy from the greedy, and Nick wasn't disappointed.

"About half of them wanted you to rip them a pet," Isaiah said, when he brought the list of requests to the parlor car. He glanced at Kudzu, who had busied himself licking the chocolate off everything in sight—poison for a living dog, but not a problem for an Afterlight canine.

"I was worried that might happen," Nick said. "What did you tell them?"

"I told them that ripping dogs and cats right out of their lives wouldn't be right."

"I only done it once," Zin told him, glancing at Nick a little sheepishly. "Kudzu here was bein' beaten by his owner. Had to save him from that, and rippin' him was the only way."

Hearing his name, the dog came over, and rolled onto his back, waiting for a belly rub. Isaiah obliged. "Beatin' a dog! You shoulda ripped his owner's heart clear out while you were at it."

"I did!" said Zin. Then she waffled. "Well, I almost did. I mean, I woulda done it, but the dog was watchin'. Couldn't let him see that, could I?"

Kudzu purred like a kitten as Isaiah rubbed his belly. "Sure is one funny-lookin' pooch." Then he stood up and handed Nick the list. "Here you go—ten reasonable requests. Let's see what the girl can do."

The requests that Isaiah passed along were all well-chosen, and although it took some time, they were doable. A saxophone and a guitar for two kids who hadn't played since the day they each crossed over. The sixth Harry Potter book, which, for some reason, was the only one that never crossed into Everlost. A Bible—which often did cross—but the request was for one in Portugese. Zin ripped an art set for a girl who had brushes, but no paint, a big sixty-four box of Crayolas for the younger kids, and a pair of glasses for a kid whose eyesight was as bad in Everlost as it was in life. The remaining requests were for desperately needed sports equipment. Nick was surprised that Isaiah didn't pass along any more food orders, but as it turned out, Isaiah had his reasons.

Once all ten requests had been fulfilled, Isaiah called Nick in for a private meeting. Isaiah's quarters were comfortable but modest, behind an unassuming storefront in Underground Atlanta. He lived no better than any of the kids in his care, although he did have a bit more room. There was a bed that was probably just for show, since most Afterlights—especially leaders—didn't sleep. There was a Formica table from the 1950s, an orange leather sofa probably from the seventies, and several fragile-looking round-backed chairs that looked like something Nick's grandmother might have owned. Nick made a mental note to have Zin rip Isaiah a respectable furniture set.

Nick sat on the sofa, figuring it would be the least likely to be left with permanent chocolate stains, and Isaiah sat across from him in one of the grandma chairs.

"I've let you have your fun," Isaiah said. "Now I want to know what you want from us."

Nick knew there was a fine line between a gift and a bribe. He could only hope that he was still on the right side of that line. "I would have ripped all those things for your Afterlights, without getting anything in return," he told Isaiah. "But you're right—there are a couple of things I'd like to ask you for."

"You can ask," said Isaiah, "but it doesn't mean I'm gonna give."

Nick cleared his throat so that his speech lost that thick chocolatey tone. "First I need information. I need to know about other Afterlights in other towns and cities in the South. I need numbers if you have them, and what those Afterlights are like—are they friends or enemies? Are they easy to deal with, or should they be avoided? You know—that kind of thing."

"Fine," said Isaiah. "I'll tell you what I know about the South." The chair creaked as Isaiah leaned back in it. "But that's not all you want, is it?"

Nick took a moment. This one wouldn't be as easy. He tried to sit up as straight as he could in the low-slung sofa, and looked Isaiah in the eye.

"I'd like fifty of your Afterlights."

Isaiah's expression became so stony, the features of his face actually seemed changed. "They're not for sale," he growled.

"No—that's not what I mean." Nick said. "Mary Hightower is a threat to all of us, and I can guarantee you that she's building an army. Which means I need to build one too. So I'm asking you for fifty volunteers. Only those who want to go—I don't want to force anyone."

Isaiah took his time to think about it. "I don't like it," he said. "I don't like it one bit . . . but I do get the feeling that living under the Sky Witch would be a whole lot worse."

Nick leaned forward. "Will you do it, then? Will you ask for volunteers?"

"If I give it my blessing, you'll get your volunteers," Isaiah said. "But it's gonna take more than 'ten reasonable requests,' from the Ripper to get my blessing."

"All right, then—what?"

What Isaiah asked for was a feast. A Christmas feast for his entire vapor, regardless of the fact that it was the summer. Nick supposed that in a timeless world, each day could be whatever day you wanted it to be.

"Everyone knows how hard it is to find food that's crossed over," Isaiah pointed out. "You saw how they acted when they saw that ice cream. Coulda had a riot if I wasn't there to keep the peace." Isaiah indicated a little jar in the corner that held just one unbroken fortune cookie. "Mostly we get those damn fortune cookies—and when it's a bad fortune, no one'll even eat the crumbs."

"So," asked Nick, who knew more than anyone that every Everlost fortune was true, "was your last fortune a good one, or a bad one?"

Isaiah raised his eyebrows. "At first I thought it was bad, but maybe it's turning halfway decent."

"What did it say?"

Isaiah gave him the slightest hint of a grin. "It said *'Embrace the bittersweet'*."

The feast took some time to arrange, and since all the ripping effort was Zin's, it exhausted her—but she was a trooper.

Nick had her rip a smorgasbord of edible items from dozens upon dozens of restaurants, markets, and homes.

"Why cain't I go to some big ole' banquet hall," Zin asked, "and rip all the food from there?"

"That would be easier," Nick admitted, "but it would also be obnoxious. If we have to steal hundreds of meals from the living, we should spread it out—so that no one feels the cost of what they've lost."

It was obvious that Zin cared little for the living and their loss. The concept of "responsible ripping" was foreign to her. Fortunately, in her many years in Everlost, her designs were never so grand that her ripping created major problems for the living. Unless you count all the missing artillery.

In the end, Zin did what she was told, and asked if this earned her a raise in her military rank. Nick told her a good soldier never asks.

It took three days, working round the clock, to rip enough food to feed the Afterlights of Atlanta, but it was worth the effort. Nick had to admit, when they gathered for the meal, he'd never seen a group of Afterlights so joyful and so content. Whether he got his militia or not, he was glad to have done this.

When all was said and done, and everyone had eaten until they were satisfied, Isaiah asked for volunteers for Nick's army. "Someone's gotta stand up to the Sky Witch," Isaiah told them. "And we gotta do our share."

Nick had asked for fifty—and he ended up with almost eighty—which posed a logistical problem, since the train had only an engine, a parlor car, and a single passenger car.

That's when Zin, to everyone's amazement, had ripped her first train car from the living world.

Isaiah was true to his word, and just before they left, he gave them pretty good intelligence as to where they could find friendly Afterlights, and which ones should probably be avoided. He also gave Nick a word of friendly, heartfelt advice.

"You need to remember who you were," Isaiah told him. "Because more and more you got that mud-pie look about you. There's more chocolate on your shirt—it's even getting into your hair now. I gotta say, it worries me."

"We can't choose what we remember," Nick said, repeating what Mary had once told him, "but I'll try."

"Well, I wish you all the luck in both worlds," Isaiah said. Then, as a gesture of friendship, they put their hands together, and crushed Isaiah's one unbroken fortune cookie between their palms.

Their fortune read, *"Luck is the poorest of strategies."*

While Isaiah might have felt insulted, Nick took this as evidence that he was doing the right thing—preparing for his confrontation with Mary as best he could.

That was more than a month ago. Since leaving Atlanta, Nick and his train had zigzagged from town to town, city to city, on any dead rails that would get them there.

"I'd rip us fresh train tracks," Zin said, "but I can only rip things I can actually move."

The "mud-pie" look that Isaiah had spoken of was even more pronounced than before—so much so that Nick had taken the mirror in the parlor car, and spread his chocolate hand back and forth across it until it was too thick with the stuff to show his reflection. He had work to do, and thinking about himself, well, it was just a distraction.

Based on what Isaiah had told him, they traveled to more than a dozen towns and cities in Georgia and the Carolinas, bringing in volunteers everywhere they went. Zin had become a whiz at dazzling audiences with the items she ripped right before their eyes, and once they were wide-eyed with wonder, Nick offered them a feast without being asked, because if there was one thing that was universal in Everlost, it was the absence of, and the craving for, a good meal.

By the time they reached Chattanooga, Tennessee, and added that ninth train car, Nick's anti-Mary fighting force numbered nearly four hundred.

"It's good to be part of an army again," Zin told Nick, as they headed south toward Birmingham, Alabama. "I've been waitin' halfway to forever for someone to fight."

"We fight because we have to," Nick told her. "We fight because it's the right thing to do, not because we want to."

"Speak for yourself," Zin said. "Everybody's gots their own reasons for the things they do. Alls that matters is that your reasons and mine carry the same flag."

"We don't have a flag," Nick pointed out.

"I could make one."

"Just as long as it's not Confederate."

Zin thought about it. "Whacha say I rip some fabric into Everlost, and come up with sumpin' brand spankin' new?"

"Great—you could be our own Betsy Ross."

To which she replied, "Betsy Ross was a Yankee."

It was a strange thing to build an army when they had no idea where to find the enemy. "I've heard rumors that Mary's gone west," Johnnie-O told Nick. "Maybe even across the Mississippi—but I also hear there's no way to cross the Mississippi, so who knows?"

"D'ya think she's afraid to come this far south?" Charlie asked.

"Mary's not afraid," Nick told him. "But she *is* cautious—which means she'll only come after us when she feels she can't lose." He wondered if she knew where he was right now, and what he was doing.

"What d'ya think's gonna happen when you finally come face-to-face with her?" Charlie asked. It wasn't the first time Nick had been asked that question, and his answer was always the same.

"I don't try to guess at things that haven't happened yet."

But that was a lie. Nick couldn't deny that he had fantasies about their destined meeting. In one fantasy, he would defeat her—but he would show such mercy that Mary would break down in his arms, admit she was wrong about everything—and that admission would heal him, sending every last ounce of chocolate into remission. Then, hand in hand, they would hold their coins and step into the light.

In another version, Mary would win the battle, but be so moved by Nick's valor, and by his passion for freeing the souls she had trapped, that she would finally listen to reason, and allow Afterlights to choose their destinies for themselves. Then together they would lead Everlost into a new age.

All his fantasies ended with him and Mary together one

way or another. This was something he couldn't share with anyone, for how could they trust a leader who was in love with the enemy?

The hundreds of kids who were now under Nick's leadership certainly didn't love Mary. While some of her many writings had dribbled down to the South, fear and awe of the Sky Witch and her magic was much more compelling than the written word. It was their fear of her that made it easier for them to align with the Chocolate Ogre, who, in their eyes, was certainly frightening, but not terrifying. It was a case of the monster you know being better than the monster you don't know. The problem was, their fear of Mary was quick to turn soldiers into army deserters. In a world where ecto-ripping and skinjacking were possible, there was no way to make these kids believe that Mary Hightower had no such powers.

"I only know of two ecto-rippers," Nick tried to point out to a fearful group of enlistees. "There's one called 'the Haunter,' who's inside a barrel at the center of the earth, and then there's Zin, who's one of us. As for skinjackers, I've only ever met one. Her name is Allie, and she's on our side too."

It was the first time Nick had said Allie's name aloud for quite a while. It made him long to see her—to know what had become of her. And as if to answer that longing, one of the kids they had picked up in North Carolina said, "Yeah—Allie the Outcast hates the Sky Witch—she told us so herself."

Nick turned so fast, chocolate flung into the kid's eye. "What do you mean she told you? You saw her? Where?"

"A couple of months ago, in Greensboro," he said. "She

came with this other kid who didn't talk much. I liked her, but the other kid scared us a little."

Nick couldn't contain his excitement. "Tell me everything!" he said. "How was she—how did she look? What was she even doing there?"

Nick sent for the dozen or so kids they picked up in Greensboro, and, pleased to be on the Chocolate Ogre's good side, they were thrilled to give all the information they could. They told Nick all about Allie—how she had become a finder; how she and a boy that Nick could only assume was Mikey McGill rode into town on a horse covered with saddlebags that were packed with crossed items.

"They had good stuff," the Greensboro kids told him, "not junk like most other finders have—and they traded fair. We asked her to show us some skinjacking, but she wouldn't do it."

Then everyone flinched at a loud popping sound, followed by another, then another. Nick already knew that sound. It was Johnnie-O cracking his knuckles. It was always a sign that he was either very anxious, or very excited.

"Y' know . . . " said Johnnie-O, "if we find Allie, we'll have a ripper *and* a skinjacker. With a combination like that, there's a whole lot of things we could do."

But Nick was already miles ahead of him.

"Where was she headed?" Nick asked the Greensboro kids. He didn't expect much of an answer—after all, finders rarely gave away their trade routes. But the boy said quite simply:

"Memphis."

* * *

"How well do you know the rail system west of here?" Nick asked Charlie. He thought Charlie would balk at the question, but Choo-choo Charlie was a tried and true conductor, and seemed ready for a new challenge. By now Charlie had gotten himself enough paper to copy the rail map he had been scratching into the engine bulkhead, and mapping the Everwild rails had become a personal mission for him.

"I know what cities should have a lot of tracks that have crossed over—but there's no way to know till we get there. D'ya mean we're not going to Birmingham?"

"Change of plans," Nick told him. "We're going to Memphis."

"I hear that's where Everlost ends," Charlie pointed out. "The Mississippi River, I mean."

"Well, I guess we'll find out, won't we?"

Then, just before Nick left the engine cab, Charlie pointed to his cheek and said, a little awkwardly, "Uh . . . you got a little spot there."

Nick sighed. "That wasn't even funny the first time, Charlie."

"No," Charlie said, "I mean the *other* side of your face."

Nick reached up and touched his good cheek. His finger came away with a tiny spot of chocolate. He wiped it between his thumb and forefinger until it was smudged away. "Just get us to Memphis."

Nick knew that time was running out for him.

There was no way he could deny it now. It wasn't just the spot on his cheek—little eruptions had begun to pop up all over Nick's body, rising like pimples, oozing chocolate through the fabric of his clothes when they popped. Those tiny brown patches were everywhere, and were beginning to connect like raindrops on concrete, spreading like a relentless rash, to his back, his scalp, and places he didn't even want to think about. His chocolate hand was weak and getting weaker, the fingers almost fusing together. His left eye was always clouded, and losing more and more sight each day. His shirt, which used to look like a white shirt covered with brown stains, was now more brown than white, and the original color of his tie had long since been forgotten. Even his dark pants, which had always hidden the stains, could no longer resist the umber onslaught, and his shoes looked like two piles of brown candle-drippings giving rise to the rest of his body.

Nick knew it was his own memory that was poisoning him — or lack of memory. He had forgotten so much of who he had been in the living world, there was barely anything left of him. His family, his friends, they were all gone from his mind. All he knew for sure was that he had been eating a chocolate bar when he died, and it had smeared on his face. Soon his only memory would be the chocolate, and then what? What would happen when there was nothing else left of him?

He didn't want to think about it. He didn't have *time* to think about it. All that mattered was the task at hand — and only part of that task was building a fighting force. The rest of his plan he kept to himself, because if he told the others what madness he had in mind, he'd have a whole lot more deserters.

Before they left Chattanooga, Zin presented Nick with

the flag she had made, and Nick told Charlie to fly it from the front of the train, for everyone to see. The design was a series of silver stars, in the pattern of the Big Dipper, sewn on a rich brown fabric.

"My papa always said the Big Dipper was there to catch falling stars," Zin said. "Kinda like the way you're here to catch falling souls."

Nick was all choked up, and it wasn't just the chocolate. "You have no idea what this means to me, Zin."

"Does that mean I get to be a lieutenant?"

"Not yet," Nick told her. "But soon. Very soon."

Nick would have hugged her if he thought he could do it without covering her in stains.

# CHAPTER 22

## *Cram That Sucker*

Zin was a good soldier, and proud of it. Being a ripper didn't leave a person with much self-respect, so Zin squeezed all the self-respect she could out of her military service. The Chocolate Ogre was now her general, and she would do her job to the best of her ability. A good soldier follows orders. A good soldier doesn't ask questions. But she couldn't help but wonder about some of the requests the Chocolate Ogre made of her. Particularly the secret ones he called "special projects."

The first request involved an all-day sucker. The kind as big as your face, all colorful and sticky, that gets stuck in your teeth when you bite it, and makes your molars hurt. This sucker had crossed over with a little kid who had probably been working on it since the day he crossed over. The thing was half-eaten, and would stay half-eaten no matter how much the kid licked it.

The Ogre took Zin and the sucker-boy to a candy shop—not an Everlost one, but a living-world shop, where fleshies went about their business buying and selling sweets.

"I want you to rip him a new sucker," the Ogre ordered.

Zin couldn't see why, as this sucker wasn't going anywhere, but she followed orders.

"Yes, sir. A' course, sir."

There was a stand that held suckers like a little metal tree. Zin reached into the living world, and ripped the kid a brand new sucker that was bigger and better than the one he started with. Then she proceeded to rip the old sucker from the boy's hand—something only she could accomplish—and replaced it with the new one. The boy acted like a kid in a candy shop, which, in fact, he was.

But then things started to get weird.

After the boy ran off hopping and skipping with his new sucker, the Ogre pointed to the old one in Zin's hand and said, "Now that he's got a better one, I want you to put this one back."

Zin was confused. "What do you mean 'put it back'?"

"I mean exactly what I said. Rip a hole, and put the sucker back into the living world."

The suggestion just made Zin mad. What, was he stupid? Ripping stuff out was one thing, but putting something back? Whenever Zin ripped, she always kind of felt like a midwife, helping someone give birth. To her, the living world was truly that—a living thing, that could feel everything that happened to it. You don't put back stuff that gets born. "Sir, you can't take sumpin' that crossed into Everlost and shove it back into the living world—that ain't the way it's done."

And then the Ogre asked, "Have you ever tried?"

Zin was about to explain to him just how ripping worked, but her words caught in her throat, because she

realized that she never had tried. The idea of putting something back had never occurred to her. Why should it? It was
all about taking.

"No, I ain't never tried that," said Zin. "But what if put-
tin' sumpin' back is one of them weird scientifical things that
blows up the world?"

"If you blow up the world," the Ogre said, "you can
blame it on me."

Which was good enough for Zin. He was, after all, her
superior officer. If and when she got to the pearly gates, she
could always claim she was following orders.

"Well, all right, then."

She steeled herself, then held the sucker in her ripping
hand, and tried to shove it through, into the living world.

It was not an easy thing. Just opening a hole into the living world was different now that her intentions were different. It was like picking a lock. Then when the portal finally
began to open, the living world resisted.

"It won't work, sir," Zin insisted. "I think the livin' world's
got all the stuff it can stand, and don't want no more."

"Keep trying."

Zin gritted her teeth and doubled her efforts. As she
tried to force that sucker through, she felt a powerful battle
of wills between her and the living world. The question was,
did the world want to keep the sucker out more than Zin
wanted to put it in?

To Zin's surprise, she won the battle: The living world
relented, and took the sucker back. When Zin was done, it
sat on a counter in the candy shop, its bright colors faded
and slightly out of focus, just like everything else in the

living world. Zin pulled her hand back, and shivered.

"You did it!"

"Yeah," said Zin, pleased, yet troubled by this newly discovered power. "I felt like I done something wrong, though . . ."

"It's only wrong if you use it for the wrong things," the Ogre said.

"But the world don't like it, sir."

"Did the world like you ripping when you first started?"

Zin thought back to her earliest days in Everlost. Ripping wasn't easy when she first began. The world held on to stuff like a kid holds on to toys. "No," Zin had to admit. "It was hard at first."

"But the world got used to it, right?"

"I guess . . . "

"It got used to ripping, so it'll get used to . . . *cramming* . . . as well." They both looked at the half-eaten sucker on the living world counter until the candy store cashier noticed it and eyed it with disgust. He then picked it up, and dropped it into the trash.

"I want you to practice this," the Ogre told Zin. "Practice cramming every chance you get, until you can do it as quickly and as smoothly as ripping."

Then Zin asked the million dollar question. "Why?"

"Does there have to be a 'why'?" asked the Ogre. "Isn't knowing the full extent of your powers reason enough?"

But if there was one thing Zin had come to learn and respect about the Ogre, it was his strategy as a general . . . and the fact that everything he did was always a single move in a much larger campaign.

# CHAPTER 23
## *Severance and Blithe*

Doris Meltzer had led a long and productive life. At the age of eighty-three, she knew she didn't have much time left, but she was satisfied with the life she had lived.

For her entire adult life, she wore her wristwatch on her left wrist, but would always glance at her right. She would gently rub it, and convinced herself it was just a nervous habit. The truth of it lay below the threshold of her understanding. At times she touched upon the true meaning of it—at the moment of waking, or the instant before sleep set in—the two places where one's spirit comes closest to Everlost. Never close enough to actually see it, but close enough to sense its existence.

It all began the night of her high school prom. It was a momentous occasion, but not in the way anyone had expected. Her date was a boy named Billy, and she'd had a crush on him since grade school. She had dreams they might be married—and in those days marrying your high school sweetheart was more the norm than the exception.

Billy had just learned to drive and was proud to be

doing it, taking her to the prom under the capable control of his own hands and feet, even if he was driving his father's clunky old DeSoto.

He gave her a wrist corsage of yellow roses.

It was a beautiful thing that matched her lemon chiffon dress. She wore it on her right wrist, and lifted it to her face, inhaling its rich aroma all night long. Even then she knew that, for the rest of her life, when she smelled roses, she would think of this night. She would think of Billy.

The prom was spectacular, as a prom should be. It was after they left that everything went wrong. It wasn't Billy's fault. He had obeyed all the traffic laws, but sometimes none of that matters when someone else has been drinking. Such was the case when a car full of drunken classmates ran a red light at the corner of Severance and Blithe.

Billy never felt a thing.

He was gone before the car stopped flipping. He had sailed instantly down the tunnel and into the light. There were no pit stops in Everlost for him—for at the age of eighteen, the walls of his tunnel were already too thick to allow an unexpected detour. For him, his exit from the living world went exactly as it should.

Doris, however, had a harder time of it, for although she also saw the tunnel, it wasn't her time to make the journey. She was merely an observer, watching him go. She awoke in the hospital days later with her family by her side, all of them thanking God for a million answered prayers. She was alive, and would recover.

As for the corsage, it perished in the crash along with the boy she might have married.

Doris's spine was severed at the L-4 vertebrae, and she never walked again—but in all other aspects she lived a full and exceptionally happy life. She married, had children, and had her own antique business in a time when a woman's place was still considered to be the home.

She had no way of knowing that the corsage of yellow roses didn't entirely perish.

Because of what it meant to the boy who gave it to her, and because of what it meant to Doris, the corsage crossed into Everlost unscathed. Sixty-five years later, it was still as fresh and bright as the evening she wore it.

In fact, it was still right there on her wrist.

It moved with her, unknown and invisible, holding her right wrist in a gentle grasp, secretly giving her comfort when she needed it. This was the cause of that strange urge to look at her wrist, and to caress it, yet she never made the connection.

Then one day, a boy who had half turned to chocolate noticed the corsage.

He was merely passing by when he spotted it. He was out searching for Afterlights to gather, but instead he found the cluster of yellow roses and baby's breath. So vibrant, so bright—it was clearly an artifact of Everlost, and yet it clung to the arm of an old woman in a wheelchair sitting on a porch.

Nick had never seen anything like it. He had always assumed that when items crossed, they fell free from the living world, but here was a corsage that still clung to the hand of its living wearer, even though it existed only in Everlost.

Nick remembered reading about a sort of spirit that

becomes attached to the living. An *incubus* it was called. He had never met or even heard of a spirit like that in Everlost—but this corsage—it was a floral incubus, refusing to leave its beloved host behind.

Refusing, that is, until Nick reached out, and plucked it right off the woman's arm—an easy thing to do, as it was part of Everlost.

Doris knew something had changed the moment it happened, but she couldn't tell what. She wheeled around the porch searching every corner. Surely she had lost something, but what could it be? That's how it was with so many things these days. Half-finished thoughts, forgetting even what she'd forgotten. It was no picnic getting old. She looked to her right wrist, rubbing it, scratching it, wishing the uncanny feeling of loss would just go away.

Meanwhile, in Everlost, Nick went to fetch Zin.

"This corsage crossed into Everlost," he told her. "I think it happened a very long time ago."

"So?" said Zin. "What about it?"

"I'd like you to put it back into the living world."

Zin had been practicing the art of "cramming," as the Ogre had called it, but she sensed that this was a little bit different. She couldn't say why.

She turned the corsage in her hand, put it on her own wrist for a moment, inhaled its rich fragrance—and then it finally struck her why this was different than any of the other things she had crammed back into the living world.

"These flowers are alive. . . ."

She thought she caught a hint of a smile on the clear side of the Ogre's face. "So they are," he said. "Or as alive as anything can be in Everlost. Now I'm ordering you to put that corsage back into the living world."

She instinctively knew that dealing with something "alive" would be a whole new level of cramming.

"I don't know if I can do that, sir." She didn't always remember to call him "sir," but she did whenever she was basically telling him "no."

"You won't know until you try," he told her, because the Ogre never took no for an answer.

They returned to the porch where Nick had seen the woman, but she was no longer there, because the living are rarely so convenient as to remain where you found them. Nick, however, wouldn't rest until he had tracked her down. Although the living appeared blurry to those in Everlost, a woman in a wheelchair wouldn't be too difficult to spot.

Doris was not at home because she had called her teen-age grandson, and asked him to come take her for a walk. She was feeling unsettled. Not quite panicked, but very unsettled.

"Something's missing," she told him.

"I'm sure you'll find it," he said, not for an instant believing that anything was missing at all. Doris's children and grandchildren all thought she was far more senile than she really was, treating everything she said as if it were coming from someplace hopelessly foggy. It annoyed her to no end, and they took her crankiness as further evidence of dementia.

Her grandson rolled her through the streets of the town, and when they came to a corner, she chanced to look up at the street signs.

They were at the corner of Severance and Blithe.

Although she had passed this intersection a thousand times since the accident, the spot was only painful when she paused to think about it, which she rarely did anymore. But today she felt a strange need to pay her respects, and so she had her grandson pause at the corner before crossing.

It was as she sat there, tallying the cost of a single tragic moment, that she felt a strange gripping sensation on her right wrist. She looked down to see that a yellow rose corsage had been slipped onto her hand. Not any corsage, but *the* corsage. She knew nothing of Everlost, or of Zin, who had just successfully crammed it into the living world, and had slipped it onto her hand—but Doris didn't need to know. There was no question in her mind that this was the same corsage. In a sudden moment of intuition, Doris came to realize that the corsage had always been with her, then was briefly taken away, only to be presented back to her fully and completely. All these years it had been unable to live, but unable to die. Now it would do both.

Her grandson didn't notice its appearance—his attention had drifted to two girls his own age farther down the street. He only noticed the corsage once the girls had turned the corner.

"Where did that come from?" he asked once he saw it.

"Billy gave it to me," Doris said honestly. "He gave it to me the night of the prom."

Her grandson glanced momentarily at the trash can on the corner beside them. "Of course he did, Grandma," and he left it at that, making a mental note to keep her wheelchair a little farther away from trash cans.

By nightfall the corsage had begun to wilt, but that was

fine. Doris knew it was the way of all things, and each falling petal was a gentle reminder that soon—maybe tomorrow, maybe next week, maybe next year—her time would come too. The tunnel would open for her, and she would make her journey into the light with a mind as crystal clear as the star-filled evening.

# CHAPTER 24

## *It's a Dog's Life*

Nick could tell there was something wrong in Nashville.

A city this big should have had Afterlights, but there was not a single one to be found. They did find an abandoned Afterlight den—a crossed factory, filled with evidence of Afterlight activity, but not one soul remained.

"Maybe they all found their coins, and got where they were going," Johnnie-O suggested.

"Or maybe they were captured by Mary," Charlie said.

"Or maybe sumpin' worse," said Zin—and by Kudzu's reaction, everyone suspected she might be right. The dog wasn't exactly a bloodhound, but his senses were more acute than human ones—and the second he and Zin got close to the factory, Kudzu began to back off and howl. He wouldn't get near the place.

There was definitely a strange feeling in the air—the residue of some bitter circumstance. It called for a visit from the Sniffer.

The Sniffer was a kid they picked up in Chattanooga, whose sense of smell was so good, he could smell things

that didn't actually have an odor. Like the scent of someone thinking too hard (smells like a burning lampshade) or
the aroma of confusion (smells like rotisserie chicken). One
might think he'd have a monumentally distorted nose, and
yet he didn't. It was a dainty little upturned thing.

"It's not the size of your nose that matters," the Sniffer
often said, "it's how deep your nasal cavity goes," and this
kid was nasal cavity all the way down to his toes. In fact,
when he sneezed, he could splatter an entire room in ecto-
mucus—which was like living mucus, except that it never
dried.

They brought him to the factory and, just like Kudzu,
he wouldn't even go through the door—but at least he was
able to tell them why.

"I smell misery," he said. "The place reeks of it." Then
he pointed southwest, roughly in the direction of Memphis.
"That's the direction the misery went."

"Just our luck," said Zin, still trying to calm down
Kudzu, who had gone from howling to whimpering.

"Whatever it was," Nick said, "let's hope we don't run
into it on the way."

And whatever it was, it was apparently strong enough
to scare the Sniffer off. He deserted Nick's army, having no
desire to follow the misery to Memphis.

Zin just wanted to leave Nashville. Kudzu's reaction
spooked her, and the sooner they were on their way, the better. The Ogre, however, had his own agenda. They lingered
in the city. He said it was because they were still looking for
stray Afterlights, but that was a lie. They stayed because the

Ogre had another secret task for Zin. This was the big one, and looking back, Zin realized this was the task he had been leading up to all along.

They were back at the train, and Zin couldn't find Kudzu. It wasn't unusual for him to explore on his own, but maybe she was smelling a bit of something now too. Something a little skunky. Something that reeked of bad intentions.

She finally found Kudzu in the parlor car—the Chocolate Ogre's private retreat. The dog was licking chocolate from the Ogre's hand.

"Kudzu! Come!" Zin said. The dog reluctantly turned and strolled over to its master.

"Kudzu's been a good companion to you, hasn't he?" the Ogre said.

"The best," answered Zin.

"I know you really care about him . . . and I guess I can understand why you did what you did. Ripping him from an abusive owner, and all."

Zin knelt down and scratched Kudzu's neck. "Had to do it. I saved him from a fate worse than death."

"Maybe you did . . . but that doesn't change the fact that you ripped a living thing out of the living world."

She looked up at the Ogre, who sat in his stained chair. Was it her imagination, or was there more of the brown stuff on him than yesterday?

"Let me ask you something, Zin, because it's important." He leaned forward. "When you ripped Kudzu, did you just rip his spirit, or did you rip the whole dog into Everlost?"

"I guess I ripped everything, sir," Zin said. "I mean it weren't like I ripped his little doggy spirit out of his body or nothin'; I grabbed him, pulled him into Everlost, and there he was. It's not like there was a dead dog left behind when I ripped him here — I ripped him body and soul." Kudzu lay down and rolled over, wanting a tummy rub. Zin obliged, and the dog purred like a kitten. "He didn't sleep for nine months, neither, on accounta he never officially died."

"So . . . " said the Ogre, "somehow, he was flesh until you pulled him here . . . and now he's not."

"That's right — he's an Afterlight just like any of us. He don't grow old, he don't get sick, he don't change, and he got the glow."

"Still, by taking him you did something very wrong."

Zin didn't like the direction this conversation was going. "No more wrong than anything else I done," she said defensively. "No worse than any of the things *you* made me to do," and then she added "sir," a little snidely.

"It *is* worse, and I think you know that."

"Well, that there's water under the bridge. Nuthin' I can do about that now."

And the Ogre quietly said, "Yes, there is."

Zin didn't want to hear this. "C'mon, Kudzu, let's go." She practically lifted the dog to his feet and headed for the door.

"Come back here," said the Ogre. And when she didn't, he said, "That's an order!"

She stopped just short of the door, and spun back to him. "You can order me around all you want, but you can't do nuthin' to Kudzu — he's my dog, not yours!"

"If you want to set things straight in the hereafter," the Ogre said calmly, "then you need to put Kudzu back in the living world—just like you did to those flowers the other day."

"No!" She didn't even bother saying "sir," this time.

"It's the right thing to do, and you know it."

"If I put him back, he'll have no place to go!" she pleaded.

"He will if you find him a good family."

"If I put him back, he'll die!"

"But not until he lives the full length of a dog's life."

Zin found herself screaming into the Ogre's face, but he stayed calm, which just made her even madder. "*Why're you asking me to do this?*"

He didn't answer her. Instead he said, sternly, "I am your commanding officer, and your orders are to find a good home for Kudzu . . . and then you are to use your powers to put him in it."

"*You can ask me from here till doomsday, I won't do it!*"

He was quiet for a second. Then he said, "If you do it, I'll put you in charge of an entire regiment of soldiers."

The Ogre had just put his nasty, sticky little finger on her button, and Zin was disgusted with herself to know how easily her buttons could be pushed.

"How many's in a regiment?" she asked.

Zin hated this more than anything, but she couldn't deny that the Ogre, curse his Hershey's hide, was absolutely right. She had no business ripping a living dog into Everlost. And the story she gave—the one about saving him from an owner who beat him? It was a flat-out lie. Kudzu had a good life with a family that was so sweet and caring, it had made

Zin sick. This was before she went off to be a hermit, when she still believed she could linger with the living, and pretend she could be one of them, even though they never knew she was there. She stayed with that family for more than a month, sitting with them at the dinner table, ripping bits of food off their plates. She sat in their playroom, ripping toys and watching the brother and sister fight, blaming each other for the missing playthings.

The dog sensed her presence. Not entirely, but just enough for it to act edgy whenever Zin was in the room. Then the dog warmed to her. It would come near to where she was standing, and roll over, waiting to be scratched on the belly. So Zin would use her ripping hand to reach in and do it. When her hand came back with dog hair on it, she got the idea. If dog hair could come through, then why not the whole dog?

That family never knew what happened to their beloved pet. Probably figured coyotes got him or something. And now Zin had herself a much needed friend. She even changed his name. Since she was named after a flower, she named him after another plant. She chose the fast-growing kudzu, because of the way the dog had grown on her. She didn't even remember his real name anymore.

But that was a story she couldn't tell, because she knew in her heart how shameful it was. Well, what goes around comes around to bite you in the butt, and now it was time to make things right. But she didn't have to like it.

She did what the Ogre told her to do: She found a family. Not just any family, but one that was like the one Kudzu had come from. She found a wealthy family with two little kids, and Zin watched them long enough to know they were good people. She sat with them at dinner, ripping herself some corn on the cob when no one was looking. Then, when she was absolutely sure this was the right home, she went to get Kudzu and the Ogre.

Distant thunder rolled, low and ominous as they approached the house. Dark clouds filled the Eastern horizon. Zin felt much the same on the inside.

"Looks like they already have a dog," the Ogre said, as they stepped into the family's backyard. There was a dog-house in the yard, and two big bags of dried dog food leaned up against it.

"*I* put that there," Zin told him. She had ripped the doghouse and the food from a nearby pet store, and had crammed it all into the backyard earlier in the day. The family had seen it and was understandably confused. The children were convinced that this was all some sort of surprise — that somebody was about to give them a dog, and the parents tried to figure which friend or relative might do something like this.

"I hadda prepare them," Zin told the Ogre. "Because, if a dog just showed up in their yard, they'd probably just take him to the pound. But if he shows up along with all this other stuff, they'll know he's not just a stray. They'll know that someone meant to put him here, even if they don't know who."

"Good thinking," said the Ogre.

The family was inside now, maybe making calls to see who was playing pooch games with them. Zin held Kudzu for the longest time. He might have been a smart dog, but he had no idea what was coming.

"Maybe it won't work," Zin said. "A dog's not like a bunch of stupid flowers. Maybe something this big—this *alive*—can't get through."

"Maybe not, but there's only one way to know for sure."

She knew the Ogre would say that.

Zin spoke to Kudzu in hushed tones, saying all the things you say to someone when you know you're never going to see him again. Then finally the Ogre said, "It's time."

Zin grabbed Kudzu by the scruff of his neck with her ripping hand. "Sorry, boy," and she began to push him forward.

Cramming, which had been so hard at first, had become easier, just as the Ogre had said it would—but nothing could make *this* easy. It wasn't like picking a lock, it was like breaking into Fort Knox.

And to make it even worse, Kudzu began to whine and resist the second the portal began to open. "Help me!" Zin said, straining to force Kudzu forward. Now the Ogre pushed along with her, both of them straining with all their might. His snout was through, then his head, then his front legs. Kudzu let loose a mournful howl, the portal stretched around his haunches, and with a final push he was through, the portal healed closed, and Zin and the Ogre fell back, knocked down by the shock wave of the sealing portal.

Kudzu darted back and forth on the grass in front of them, confused and confounded by the change.

"Look!" the Ogre said. "He has no afterglow! Do you see? *Do you see?*"

Kudzu was back in the living world! The browns of his fur were paler and out of focus, and his body was true flesh and bone. He leaped this way and that, searching for Zin, barking frantically. Some faint sense must have told him she was still there, but he couldn't find her and never would.

"He's alive!" the Ogre said, like some mad scientist. "*He's alive!*"

"I'm sorry, boy," Zin whimpered, "I'm so, so sorry. . . ." But she knew Kudzu couldn't hear her.

The family, hearing the barking dog, came out to the yard, and although it took a few minutes, it was the kids who won Kudzu over. They put their arms around his frightened neck.

"What's your name, boy?" the girl asked.

"It's Kudzu!" shouted Zin, but no one heard.

Thunder rolled, a little closer than before. The parents looked up at the threatening sky, and the boy said, "Let's call him Storm!"

And that finally closed the circle—because Zin suddenly remembered that Storm was his real name.

In a few moments, the dog's barks became whimpers, which soon gave way to nervous panting. It wasn't long until Kudzu/Storm lay down and rolled over, angling for a belly rub, which his new family was more than happy to provide.

Zin turned to the Ogre. "I hate you," she said, and she meant it with every bit of her being.

"You can hate me all you want," he told her. "But you've just shown your loyalty by putting your orders ahead of your personal feelings. That kind of loyalty is rewarded . . . lieutenant."

Then he reached forward with his chocolate-covered hand, and painted a fresh brown chevron on the sleeve of her uniform. Then he said something that put it all into focus for Zin, making her admire him almost as much as she hated him.

"I want you to remember what it took to push Kudzu into the living world," the Chocolate Ogre told her, "because very soon, that's exactly what you'll be doing to Mary Hightower."

# PART FIVE

*The Skinjacker Revelations*

In *Tips for Taps*, chapter 5, entitled "What You Don't Remember Can't Hurt You," Mary Hightower writes:

"Memory is a strange thing in Everlost. The Afterlight mind is like a toy box in a toddler's room. If a precious memory is taken out of the box to be pawed and fondled, chances are it won't get back into the box. Consequently the only way to hold on to a memory in Everlost is never to think about it."

# CHAPTER 25

## *Lair of the Cat Woman*

When it came to memory, Mary's observations didn't hold true for skinjackers. Unlike Nick, Allie never forgot her last name. It was Johnson.

With such a common last name, however, locating her parents in Memphis was not an easy matter. Her parents' names were Adam and Andrea, so naturally they chose *A* names for their daughters. There were ten Adams, two Andreas, and more than a hundred A. Johnsons in the Memphis area. She had already determined that both their cell phone numbers had been disconnected, so Allie would have to skinjack someone, and start making cold calls.

It had to be done by skinjacking—she already knew that. She didn't know whether or not the "gravity" of home would apply here, but she didn't want to take the chance. Showing up at her family's new house and witnessing their lives moving forward without her might turn the ground to quicksand just as standing on her old doorstep had.

Besides, she had another compelling reason to skinjack. The Everlost wind. It was uncanny, and maddening—a gale force that only Afterlights could feel blasting off the Mississippi River. Five miles east of Memphis, where she and Milos had parted company, the wind was just a breeze, but the closer one came to the river, the more powerful the wind grew—and since Memphis rested right on the river's east bank, there was no way to escape it.

Allie skinjacked a tourist walking toward the river to see what this was all about. From within a fleshie, there seemed to be nothing unusual at all. The river appeared normal . . . but then she made the mistake of peeling out of the tourist right by the riverbank. The wind caught her like a hurricane, whistling in her ears, scrambling her thoughts. She struggled against it, but in the end it lifted her off her feet, and tumbled her head over heels through building after building, until she was far enough away to find her balance again. In this city—and presumably anyplace on the east bank of the Mississippi—the only way to resist the wind was to skinjack.

Therefore negotiating Memphis required her to skinjack on a regular basis. It was a challenge, because Allie had never stayed fleshbound for long periods of time. The longest had been the recent drive with Milos, Moose, and Squirrel as they drove to Memphis in the bodies of a family. That had taken just a few hours, and Allie found that peeling out had been like trying to take off a wetsuit that was two sizes too small.

The task of finding and approaching her family would require a very specific kind of host, but who to choose? There were so many variables, Allie had to create herself a checklist of all the things that her host should, and should not be.

*1) It had to be someone her parents would invite inside.*

If she skinjacked a deliveryman, as she had done when she approached her old house in New Jersey, it wouldn't be good enough. With a deliveryman as her host, any encounter would be brief, and only over the threshold of the front door. What she needed was not just a way to get the door open, but a way to get through it.

*2) It had to be someone they would feel comfortable talking with about the accident.*

When she finally got inside their new home, she didn't want to talk about the weather and current events, she wanted to know how it all played out, and somehow give her parents, her sister, and maybe herself, some comfort and closure.

*3) It had to be someone who would not be missed for multiple skinjackings.*

If Allie was to use someone's body as a base of operations, it would be a nuisance if that person had a demanding job or a whole lot of personal responsibilities.

*4) It had to be someone who would not notice the lost time themselves.*

A suspicious fleshie was the worst kind of host. Best to choose someone who wouldn't be aware that something unusual was going on—or at least could come up with a logical explanation for the missing time.

With all these things to consider, Allie was undecided for days, shuttling from person to person, hiding within them, observing them, thinking she had the perfect host, but then changing her mind. Allie finally settled on a woman who lived alone, except for a multitude of cats that came and went through a pet door. By Allie's observations, the woman's life was simple, and predictable. Tending to the cats, watching TV, crocheting, taking an afternoon nap. No one bothered her, and she bothered no one else. She was the perfect host for a long-term project.

When the woman lay down for her nap at two o'clock the following afternoon, Allie skinjacked her, and her detective work began. The first few phone calls determined that none of the Adams and Andreas listed were her parents, so she went on to the countless A. Johnsons. The idea that one of her parents' live voices could be at the other end of any phone call made her borrowed heart race, but mostly she got answering machines, which was a relief each time. That first day all she did was make calls, but not a single A. Johnson had been her mother or her father, and what few Memphis relatives she knew by name must have been unlisted too.

After three hours of unsuccessful phone calls, Allie began to doubt everything. What if the people in New Jersey were wrong, and her parents didn't come to Memphis? What if her father died in the accident after all? Allie began to despair, and her own emotional turmoil began to wake the woman.

Losing control of a fleshie was like slipping on wet ice — once you lost control, it was hard to get it back, and Allie was slip-sliding like crazy. The woman awoke, took over her own body, and Allie quickly hid behind the woman's thoughts — which, without proper preparation, was like hiding behind window curtains. Now there was only a slim veil between her consciousness and Allie's — any powerful thought would reveal her presence, so she tried not to think at all.

*—My my my—half past five long nap—my my my—how did I get into the kitchen—my my my—I didn't leave that phone book out did I—my my my—*

Allie knew peeling out of the woman wouldn't be easy, having been in her for more than three hours, but she didn't want to linger inside her either. She peeled out while the woman was distracted, tending to the cats—but after three whole hours, this wasn't like peeling off a wet suit, it was more like ripping off a Band-Aid. It was sharp and shocking. The woman gasped and fell back into a chair, her hand on her chest. Then, when the woman caught her breath, she went around the house checking that all the locks were secure, as if she sensed an intruder. So much for not raising suspicion.

Now Allie was back in the wind—not strong enough to knock her off her feet, but disorienting nonetheless. She skinjacked someone driving through the neighborhood, then when she got to a more crowded street, she soul-surfed from car to car, until she was far enough away from the river that the wind was bearable. She spent the night knees-to-chest on a roadside deadspot the size of a basketball, considering what her next move should be.

It was somewhere around midnight that it struck Allie how amazingly stupid she had been! Her investigative technique was stuck in "Nancy Drew" mode, which might have been fine when the cat woman was her age, but not in this day and age. Allie should have been much more forward-thinking. This, after all, was the age of information. Why would anyone need a phone book when you had e-mail addresses?

Allie returned the following day to discover that the cat woman was cutting-edge. In her spare room, she had a laptop that picked up a neighbor's wireless network. Of course her Internet favorites list contained things like the Crocheting Club of America, but it was good to know that even the hopelessly old-fashioned and questionably batty could still be Web-savvy.

Now Allie had a plan. She waited until the woman took her afternoon nap, jacked her the instant the woman's head hit the pillow, and went straight for the laptop.

First Allie created a new e-mail address: catwomanjacker@ yahoo.com. The question was, why would the cat woman have a reason to e-mail Allie's parents? Allie had the perfect solution. The cat woman bore a slight resemblance to Mrs. Wintuck, one of Allie's old teachers. Of course the hair was the wrong color and a little too straight, but that could be dealt with. Allie felt confident that this woman could pass for Mrs. Wintuck—at least when it came to her parents. So she composed an e-mail using both of her parents' e-mail addresses as recipients, marking it "urgent."

Mr. and Mrs. Johnson: I'm not sure if you'll remember me—my name is Sarah Wintuck, I was your daughter Allie's fourth-grade teacher. Having left New Jersey myself several years ago, I never heard about what happened to her until recently. I'm so terribly sorry. My heart goes out to you. I will be visiting Memphis all this week, and would love the opportunity to meet with you.

Allie thought for a moment, then added:

I have some fond memories of your daughter that I know she would have wanted me to share with you.

Sincerely,
Sarah Wintuck

Now there was nothing to do but wait.

Within five minutes the mailer-daemon sent back her father's e-mail as "undeliverable" and "nonexistent."

Allie's heart sank in the old woman's chest as she stared numbly at the screen. It was her mother who had relatives in Memphis. Could it be that her father died in the crash? She tried to dismiss the notion and see the glass as half-full. Her mother's e-mail was not bounced back. That was a positive sign.

She waited for a response from her mother, filling her time by tending to all those mewling cats who kept jumping up on the table, competing for her attention. By six o'clock no response had come, and Allie knew she couldn't stay much longer. She lay down on the bed, peeled out of the woman, and the shock of it jarred the woman awake. The cat woman bolted up in bed, then once more chastised herself for sleeping the day away, and checked all the locks again.

The next day when the cat woman lay down for her nap, she set her alarm clock for one hour. It did no good, because the moment Allie skinjacked her, she turned the alarm off.

There was a single e-mail waiting for catwomanjacker@ yahoo.com.

Allie felt the woman's body become lightheaded in nervous anticipation. She took slow, deep breaths, waited until the wave of dizziness passed, then Allie opened the e-mail.

Mrs. Wintuck: Thank you for your note. It would be wonderful to catch up with you. Anytime after five, any day this week would be fine. Perhaps you could come over for dinner. The address is 42 Springdale Street—let me know if you need directions, and when you'd like to stop by.

Sincerely,

Andrea Johnson

Allie pushed away from the computer so quickly, she nearly fell over backward in the chair. A cat jumped up on the laptop, opening several random windows. It must have hit the reply button as well, because the top window was an empty reply, just waiting for Allie to fill in the words.

Allie told her mother she would be there at six thirty tonight.

Then she went out to buy hair color and a curling iron.

# CHAPTER 26

## *Home*

The house did not look like a home her family should live in—but then, no home that didn't include Allie would seem right. As she approached the front door, she double-checked her dowdy clothes, and her newly styled hair—now auburn instead of the salt-and-pepper it had been. If she didn't know better, she really would think she was her fourth-grade teacher.

She stood at the front door for what felt like forever, reaching for the doorbell, then pulling her finger back, reaching, then pulling back, until finally she pulled back a little too late, and succeeded in ringing the bell anyway.

Footsteps from inside. The door opening. A familiar face. A little careworn, a little tired, but Allie still knew that face. After three years Allie was standing in front of her mother.

"Mrs. Wintuck, I'm glad you could make it."

Allie had to keep from hurling herself into her mother's arms. She had to remember she had a role to play. She was Allie pretending to be a cat woman pretending to be a teacher from New Jersey.

"Please, call me Sarah," Allie said, and stepped into the house. The foyer opened right into the living room. All their old furniture was there, with a few new additions.

"Make yourself comfortable," her mother said. "Would you like something to drink?"

"Some water would be nice."

Her mother went off to get some water, and Allie went to work looking around the room, searching for any sign that her father was still part of this picture, but there was so much to take in, she didn't even know what she should be looking for. He was in photographs, but then so was she. A high school graduation picture sat on the mantel. It hadn't even occurred to Allie that her sister, April, would now be away at college. While time had stopped for Allie, everyone else's lives had moved on.

"I've ordered Chinese food," her mother said, coming back from the kitchen with some bottled water. "I hope you don't mind; I didn't get home from work in time to cook."

"That's perfectly all right, I'm just glad to be here."

"We're glad to have you."

*We!* Her mother said *we!* "So . . . your husband . . . "

"He's picking up the food on the way home. He should be here soon."

Allie practically collapsed into the sofa, full of sweet relief. So he had survived! If nothing else came from this meeting, at least she would have that! But then—what if it was a *new* husband? What if her mother had remarried? A sister in college, a new house—a lot can happen in three years. She had to know.

"Was he . . . badly injured in the accident? I hope not."

Allie clenched her toes, preparing for the worst of all possible news. Then her mother said.

"It was a difficult rehabilitation, but he pulled through."

Allie released her breath, not even realizing she had been holding it. She felt her face flush with relief. Her mother took it for thirst, and sat across from her, pouring the bottled water into a glass for her. As Allie reached for the glass, she saw that her hand—the cat woman's hand—was trembling, so Allie took the glass with her other hand instead.

"I must say, I was surprised to get your e-mail," her mother said.

"As soon as I heard you were here in Memphis, I knew I had to contact you. You know, Allie was one of my favorite students."

Her mother smiled slimly. "Really."

Allie searched her memory for a poignant moment to share. "I remember for Mother's Day, we had a poem that each student was supposed to paste into a card they were making—but Allie insisted on writing her own poem—and when it was done, half the class wanted to use her poem instead of the original one!"

Her mother looked at her incredulously. "I still have that card. And you're telling me you remember that?"

Actually, Allie remembered the poem itself, but realized that reciting it might be just a little too weird. "As I said, she was a favorite student."

"What else do you remember?" her mother asked. The tone of the question seemed just a little bit off. Allie didn't think much of it at the time.

"I remember . . . I remember one day she came to

school sad, because you and she had a fight that morning. Something about a neighborhood boy you didn't want her to spend time with. She never told you, but she was sorry— and you were right, he turned out to be a real creep."

Her mother furrowed her eyebrows. "That wasn't in fourth grade."

*How stupid!* thought Allie. *Of course it wasn't.* Allie found herself getting increasingly nervous, and as she did, that hand kept trembling more and more. "No, it wasn't," Allie said. "But sometimes Allie would confide in me, even years after she had left my class."

Whoo! Lucky save. Allie lifted the water to her mouth, and noticed that both her hands were trembling now.

"Are you all right?"

"Yes, yes, fine. Not to worry." Then the glass slipped from her hand and shattered on the hardwood floor. It was the blasted cat woman! Allie was losing control. How long had she been in her body now? Three hours? Four? Quickly she bent over to pick up the broken glass, but her hands were shaking too much. "How clumsy of me!"

"Don't worry, I'll take care of it."

Now they were both on their knees picking up the broken glass, and when Allie looked to her mother, Allie found herself suddenly hissing through gritted teeth.

*"Help me—she's stolen my body!"*

Her mother just stared at her, not sure how to react. "What did you say?"

Allie was slipping on the ice again. The cat woman was not only awake, but she knew! Allie had to remain in control at all costs. She grappled with the woman inside her mind, forcing her down, and said, her voice a strange warble. "You'll have to forgive me. I'm prone to sudden outbursts. Tourette's Syndrome, you know. Some days are better than others."

Then came the blessed sound of a phone ringing.

"I should get that," Allie's mother said, a little coolly. "Leave the glass, I'll take care of it."

She crossed the room to pick up the phone, while Allie buried her face in her hands.

*Stay out of this!* she silently told the cat woman. *You'll get your stupid body back!*

*— Who are you? What do you want from me? —*

*It's not your business!* Allie bore down and pushed her deep again.

Her mother was on the phone now. Allie now sat on her shaking hands, and forced a fake smile as her mother turned back to her.

"Yes . . . I see . . . " her mother said into the phone. "Is that so? . . . Don't worry, I'll take care of it. . . . I said don't worry . . . I know . . . me, too."

She hung up, and came back toward Allie, but she didn't sit down. "That was my husband," she said. "He just got off the phone with Sarah Wintuck, who's still teaching fourth grade in Cape May, New Jersey."

The slippery ice beneath Allie's feet became the edge of a glacier calving into the sea. She was in freefall now, and deep inside her the cat woman was screaming to be released.

"I don't know who you are, but I want you to leave," her mother said coldly.

"I . . . I just . . . " But what could she say? What could

she tell her that would make any sense? "I have a message from your daughter!"

The hatred in her mother's eyes was so potent, Allie had to look away. "I want you out of my house!" she said. "Now!" And she didn't wait for her to leave. She grabbed Allie by her skinny cat woman arm, and pulled her toward the door. In a moment she was over the threshold again, outside the door, about to be hurled out of her parents' lives.

"Please!" Allie said.

*"Help me!"* shouted the cat woman.

"You think I don't know about you people!" said her mother. "You prey on people's hopes, telling them what they want to hear, and then you rob them blind! Well, you picked the wrong family to scam!"

Her mother's hand was on the door, ready to slam it, and Allie couldn't allow that. She had to say something to make her understand.

"They were arguing about the radio!"

And it stopped her mother cold. "What did you say?"

"When the accident happened, they were arguing about the radio—he turned it down, and she turned it back up. But it wasn't his fault! She wants you both to know that the accident wasn't his fault!"

Her mother's expression went from shock to horror to fury in the span of a single second, and then she said in a voice lethal with venom, *"Whoever you are, I hope you rot in hell!"* She slammed the door so hard it almost broke the jamb, and Allie could hear her bursting into tears on the other side.

Allie ran from the house, tears filling her own eyes, her

whole body shaking, the cat woman fighting to get out, and there was a pain deep in her back, spreading down her arms.

This wasn't the way it was supposed to happen. She was supposed to bring comfort to her parents, not anguish.

—*Let me go!*—screamed the cat woman, and Allie refused, taking out all her anger on her. If the woman had only stayed asleep—if she had only stayed quiet, Allie would have talked her way out of this. Things would have gone differently if she didn't have to fight the cat woman for control.

*This is your fault!* Allie screamed in her thoughts as she ran. *You couldn't just let me do this! You couldn't just let it be!* They were on a busy street now—a commercial street full of shops restaurants and cars. Plenty of people to skinjack. Allie tried to peel out, disgusted with the cat woman and her body—but she couldn't do it. She tugged and twisted, but it was as if she was glued to the cat woman's frame. She had stayed inside her too long!

—*Get out of me!*—

*I'm trying!*

The pain in her back was moving to her chest. It was intense, and it was hard to breathe. She shouldn't have run so fast. Not in this body. It suddenly dawned on her that the cat woman was having a heart attack—Allie had given her a heart attack, and now she was stuck with her in this feeble failing body!

—*what have you done to me?*—the cat woman wailed.

It wasn't supposed to happen this way.

She stumbled in the front door of a restaurant.

—*what have you done?*—

*Shut up! I'll get us out of this,* Allie told her.

The maître d' looked at her in alarm. "Help me!" she said. It was all she could do to get the words out. "Heart." Restaurants did have emergency kits, didn't they?

The Maitre d' looked like a deer in headlights, then he glanced down at his reservation book as if the solution might be written there. He was useless.

Allie, with pain getting worse by the second, and darkness closing in around her, spied an electrical outlet on the wall. They used electricity to restart a failing heart, right? She grabbed a knife from a table, crumbled to her knees, and shoved the tip of the knife into the socket.

The electric shock sent Allie flying. She seemed to burst apart in all directions, and pull back together a dozen yards away. She fell to the ground and began to sink into the living world. She was herself again, and back in Everlost!

She stood, and turned to the cat woman being helped up to a sitting position. She looked bad, but not as bad as Allie thought she would. A waiter took her pulse, and seemed satisfied. Silverware in a socket wasn't the best way to jumpstart a heart, but at least it had worked.

"She stole me," the cat woman muttered. "She stole me. . . ."

"Just relax," the waiter said. "You're going to be fine."

Half the people in the restaurant had already dialed 911, and the wail of an approaching ambulance could already be heard. It was out of her hands now, so she soul-surfed out of the restaurant, into a passing car, then another, then another, and didn't stop until she was miles away.

* * *

The joy of seeing her mother should have been enough to take away the sting of her reaction. After all, how could her mother react any other way? How could she trust a strange woman who had not only lied to her about her identity, but seemed to know secrets that no one but Allie could have known? Of course she would have been horrified!

But that didn't make it hurt any less. The fact that she had nearly killed a woman barely even registered in Allie's mind. All that mattered to her was home. She still hadn't seen her father—but she knew this craving for home was even deeper than that, because, like skinjacking itself, a little taste of home was not enough. Against all reason, she hungered for it. She needed more than just closure, she needed connection. Coming here was a mistake, but now that she had opened this Pandora's box, it couldn't be closed. The only way to close the lid was to step inside and pull the lid down like the lid of a coffin.

# CHAPTER 27

## *Skinjacker's Lullaby*

That night, Allie fell to what may have been the lowest point of her afterlife when she skinjacked a seven-year-old boy at one in the morning.

It had to be someone lighter and more nimble than her, because the only way into her parents' new home was to climb in through an upstairs window. She didn't know what she would do once she got in, all she knew was that she had to get in, and keep getting in until she could make her parents understand that she was not gone, she was right here, and wouldn't be going anywhere anytime soon.

There was a tree in the front yard, and open windows upstairs. Her parents always kept the upstairs windows open on summer nights. The tree was a live oak—a knobby thing, with a double trunk full of random twisting limbs. It was a climbing tree—and although the limb leaning closest to the house was a slim one, Allie reasoned that a child who weighed less than fifty pounds wouldn't break the limb.

She trespassed in neighborhood homes, and finally found the perfect specimen a few blocks away. She didn't have to put the boy to sleep, because he was already in the deep kind of slumber that only young children can reach. She easily seized control, slipped on a pair of velcro Spider-Man shoes, and went downstairs and out into the night.

The moon was a scant sliver in the sky, a scimitar edge that seemed to slice the clouds that crossed its path. The streets were deserted, and no lights were on in Allie's parents' house. This boy was no stranger to climbing trees. Allie knew it the second she scuttled up the trunk. She relied on the boy's muscle memory to take her higher until she was on the branch that stretched toward the house and the open upstairs window. She climbed out toward the edge of the branch, and just as she reached toward the window the branch began to break.

Allie gripped on to the window ledge for all she was worth, and the boy hit the side of the house with a thunk. Had she been in her own body, she would not have been able to cling to the ledge, but there's a reason why small children can climb to high places. His body was so light, she was able to pull herself up, then, holding on with one hand, she thrust the other through the window screen, and tore the screen loose. It tumbled down into the yard, and Allie hauled herself through the window, into a bedroom.

By now a light had come on in the hallway—she could see it underneath the closed door—and she heard footsteps moving hurriedly toward the room, so she scrambled underneath the bed just as the door opened. From under the bed, she could see two bare feet entering the room. The feet of a man. Her father. He flicked on a light and the room around the bed became much too bright for comfort. Allie pulled herself as deep under the bed as she could get. Although

Allie was wildly out of breath, and spiked with adrenaline, she slowed her breathing to make it as quiet as possible, and she watched her father's feet as he moved around the bed to the window. Allie could feel the boy's heart beating as far up as her eyeballs now, making her vision blurred and veiny with each beat.

"What was it?" said her mother, who was now standing at the threshold.

"Nothing," her father said. "The tree knocked down a window screen, that's all."

"I told you we should have had it trimmed." Then she added, "Are you sure that's all it was?"

"Come look for yourself."

Her mother crossed to the window. Allie heard the window being pulled closed. "I'm sorry," her mother said. "After that woman today, I'm a little spooked."

"There are crazies everywhere. But if it'll make you feel better, I'll see about getting that alarm system."

Her parents left the room, turning off the lights and closing the door. In a few moments Allie heard the complaint of springs as they climbed back into bed. Allie remained frozen for ten minutes, just in case they decided to come back in. Then finally she came out from under the bed and looked around. With nothing but a distant streetlight shining through the curtains, everything was cast in shades of gray. Even so, Allie recognized exactly what this room was.

This was her bedroom.

Or at least the Memphis version of it. It had been her bed she was hiding under, with her covers spread across it. There was the desk where she had once labored over homework, and on the walls were posters of bands whose music she hadn't heard for three years. It was like a museum. A shrine to her memory. What on earth had possessed her parents to do this? It would be one thing to keep her room in the old house, but to recreate it here? She didn't know what to think.

She reached out and took a teddy bear from a shelf. Allie secretly loved fluffy things, but being a nonfluffy girl, she never kept her stuffed animals the way nature intended; she always tweaked them somehow. This one was "Winnie the Punk," with Sharpie-drawn tattoos on his fur, and a safety pin through his eyebrow. The bear seemed larger than she remembered, but then she realized that it wasn't larger, she was just in a smaller body.

Allie clutched the bear to her chest, and felt herself becoming emotional. She blamed it on the boy's physiology — after all, little kids are quick to turn on the waterworks — but who was she kidding? These tears were all hers. She sat down, and let the tears flow gently and quietly.

Why had she come back here? Did she really think she could just walk into her parents house in the body of this boy, and talk to them? And yet she was already angling on ways to return tomorrow — perhaps in the body of someone selling alarm systems. Would that be her life now? Returning each day in a different body, pretending to be someone else, just so she could be near her parents?

She curled up on the bed clutching the bear — a remnant of a life that was lost. Then something happened that she wasn't expecting. She should have realized it could happen, because, after all, it was the middle of the night, and she was in the body of a small, exhausted child. As she held tightly on to the bear, her thoughts began to swim together, and in an instant, without warning, Allie fell asleep.

Allie awoke at 7:45 in the morning.

Unfortunately the boy she was skinjacking had woken up at 7:41. It's amazing what can happen within the span of four minutes.

"It's all right, don't worry—it will all be all right. We'll get you back home."

It was her mother's voice. She was in her mother's arms. They were rocking back and forth. She was out of breath, her vision was blurry, her chest was heaving, and a God-awful wailing sound was coming out of her. Allie's whole body was shivering with the force of her own sobs. What was going on here? Where was she? *Who* was she?

"I wanna go home," she heard a child's voice say. It was all nasal and stuffy so it came out *"I wadda go hobe."* Then she realized it was her own mouth speaking those words. All at once it came back to her—she was in the body of a boy she had skinjacked. She was in her parents' home, in her own room. Her mother was holding her, her father was standing nearby, phone in hand.

"I wadda go hobe!" the boy wailed again—he had no idea how he had gotten here. Then Allie realized a moment too late that she wasn't hiding behind his consciousness—she was out there in the open, right in the middle of his mind. Now that she was awake, the boy knew she was there, and he screamed in terror.

"Who are you?" the boy wailed. "Go away! Go away!

Get out of here!" Allie's mother backed off, thinking he was talking to her. "I don't want you here! Get out of me!"

This was a bad situation that was only getting worse. The best Allie could hope for now was damage control. She struggled to seize the boy's body, and send him back to dreamland, but now that he knew she was there, he didn't go easily. He went kicking and screaming all the way, until finally his thoughts fell in upon themselves and he was unconscious.

Allie was in control, but the boy's body was still full of fear and heaving with sobs. She looked to her father who was holding the phone in one hand, and in his other hand . . . in his other hand . . .

. . . *he had no other hand.*

His left arm now ended just past the elbow. As Allie tried to process this, she saw that his left hand was shifting the phone in his palm, preparing to dial with his thumb. He was poised over the 9 button.

Calling 911 was definitely not part of Allie's damage control.

"You're calling the police?" Allie screeched, using the boy's wild state to her advantage. "I don't want the police! I don't I don't I don't!" She screamed as loudly as she could, and her father looked helpless.

"Put down the phone, Adam!" her mother ordered.

"All right, all right!" He dropped it on the desk like it was about to explode. "There, I've put it down."

Allie stopped screaming, and took a minute to calm the boy's body down, allowing her mother to hold her. Allie hugged her back, and took more comfort from it than her mother could possibly know. The convulsive sobs eased until they were nothing more than shallow sniffles. "Can you tell us your name?" Allie's father asked.

Allie did know his name, because if there's one thing that little kids fill every thought with, it's their identity.

"Danny," she said. "Danny Rozelli."

"Well, Danny," said Allie's mom, "I think you did a little bit of sleepwalking last night."

"Yeah," said Allie, "sleepwalking, yeah." She was always impressed by her mother's ability to be logical against all reason.

"Could you tell us where you live?" Allie's father asked.

She knew where Danny Rozelli lived, but wasn't ready to share that information, so she shook her head, and said, "Something street."

Her parents sighed in unison.

Allie looked at the stump of her father's arm. There were indentations in the skin that must have been from a prosthetic arm, but of course he hadn't had time to put it on before finding little Danny Rozelli screaming in their dead daughter's bed.

"How'd that happen?" Allie asked, realizing that a seven-year-old's lack of tact was an asset now.

Her father hesitated for a moment, then he said, "Car accident."

"Ouch."

"Yeah. Ouch."

Her father also had a scar on his forehead and cheek. So the accident had taken his right arm, and left him with scars. None of it was pleasant, but it could have been a whole lot worse. Then again, it *was* worse, because they had also lost a daughter.

Allie longed to tell them that they hadn't lost her at all — that she was right here in front of them, but she couldn't find a way to do that as the cat woman, and she couldn't as Danny Rozelli, either.

"Do you know your phone number, at least?" her mother asked. "We really should let someone know you're here — your parents must be worried sick."

Allie didn't have much sympathy for parents who would eventually get their child back. She didn't know the number anyway, and that was fine. She was finally here with her own parents, and they were treating her with love and kindness. This was the closest thing she might ever have to true family time with them.

"I'm hungry," she said. "Can I have something to eat?"

Her parents glanced to each other, her mother threw her gaze to the phone, her father nodded and he left the room. It didn't take a genius to figure out that he was going to call the police from another room. Allie thought of throwing another hissy fit, but realized she couldn't stall the inevitable much longer. She would make the best of the time she had.

"Can I have Apple Jacks?" she asked. "Apple Jacks in strawberry milk?"

She could have sworn her mother turned a previously unknown shade of pale.

"Never mind," said Allie. "You probably don't have that."

"Actually," said her mother, "we do."

Her father rejoined them in the kitchen, giving a secret nod to his wife. He must have made the call. Allie figured they had about five minutes before the police arrived.

Allie savored every spoonful of her cereal while her parents sat with her at the kitchen table. She tried to trick herself into believing this was just a regular family breakfast.

"Sorry if they're a little stale," her mother said.

"No," said Allie, "they're fine."

"Our daughter liked Apple Jacks," her father said. "She liked them with strawberry milk, too."

"A lot of kids do," Allie told him—although she didn't know anyone else who ate them that way. She dipped the spoon into the pink milk and let the last applejack float in like a lone life preserver.

"More, please."

Her mother poured a second bowl. Allie pushed down the orange cereal circles with the back of her spoon, coating them with milk.

"I guess that was your daughter's room I was in, huh?"

Her mother nodded, but didn't meet her eyes.

"Something happened to her, didn't it?"

"Yes, Danny, something did," her father answered.

"You don't have to talk about it," Allie said, realizing this was going too far.

"No, that's okay—it was a long time ago," he said.

*Not that long*, Allie wanted to say, but instead she said, "I'll bet she loved you very much."

She should have left it there, but she could see a police cruiser pulling up to the curb outside, and then a second one. If she was going to do this, she had to do it now.

"Sometimes people go away," Allie told them. "They don't mean to, but they can't help it. It's nobody's fault. I'll bet if she could, she'd want to tell you that it's okay—that *she's* okay. I mean, people die, but that doesn't always mean they're gone."

Then her mother and father looked to each other, then back to Danny Rozelli with moist eyes, and her mother said, "Allie's not dead."

Allie grinned. It was so like her parents to see things that way. "Of course she's not. As long as you remember her, I guess she'll never really be dead."

"No," her father said. "We mean that she's still alive."

Allie slowly lowered her spoon into the bowl, staring at them. "Excuse me?"

"She's just asleep, Danny," her father said. "She's been asleep for a long, long time."

# CHAPTER 28

## *The Sleep of the Dead*

Comatose.

Nonresponsive.

Persistent vegetative state.

All complicated words used by medical specialists to label a patient who remains unconscious. You would think that the labels mean something—that doctors know exactly what's going on in the brain of a comatose patient. But the truth is, nobody really knows anything. A coma can actually mean a whole range of things, but at its heart, all it really means is that someone simply won't wake up.

Allie Johnson had suffered internal injuries and severe head trauma in a head-on collision. She flew through the windshield, into another boy who was on his way through his own windshield. Nick was, of course, killed instantly, but Allie was quite a fighter. Her heart continued to beat. It was beating as they rushed her to an emergency room. It was beating as they hooked her to a dozen different life-support machines. It was beating as they worked on her on an operating table for five hours to repair her massive wounds, and it was still beating after all the operations were done.

Thanks to medical science, and a body that simply would not give up, Allie did not die. Although her wounds were severe, her damaged body eventually healed, and her brain still showed a hint of basic brainwave pattern, proving that she was not entirely brain-dead. Brain-dead would have been easy. It would have given everyone a reason to just throw in the towel. But now Allie's parents were both blessed, and cursed, with the smallest fraction of hope.

"I won't try to sugarcoat this for you," the doctor had told her parents several weeks into Allie's coma. "She could wake up tomorrow, she could wake up next month, next year, or she might never wake up at all—and even if she does, there's a good chance she won't be the girl you remember. Her brain might be too damaged for higher cognitive functions—right now we just don't know." Then, in that compassionate yet heartless way that doctors have, he told Allie's distraught parents this: "For your sake, I hope she either wakes up the same girl you knew, or dies very quickly."

But neither of those two things happened. And now in a hospital somewhere, in a room somewhere, in a bed somewhere, Allie Johnson lies asleep unable to wake up . . .

. . . because her soul is in Everlost.

In her book, *You Don't Know Jack*, Allie the Outcast gives this as her final word on skinjacking:

"There is a truth about skinjacking that I can't tell you, because it's not my place. I don't have the right. It's the reason why we can skinjack, why we don't forget things, and why we're different from every other Afterlight in Everlost. It's a truth that all skinjackers must learn for themselves—and if you are a skinjacker, then you *will* learn it, because the more you skinjack, the more you are driven toward it, like a salmon fighting a current to the head of a stream. I can only hope that once you do know the truth, you find the courage to face it."

# CHAPTER 29

## *Teed for Two*

Little Danny Rozelli was having a bad day. It began with waking up in a strange house, and now many hours later, things weren't getting any better. He was talking to himself, twisting and turning in bed—everything short of spinning his head around and vomiting pea soup. In the olden days, people would have said the boy was possessed, but modern science knew better. Danny was just sick. Very, very sick.

"Get out of me!"

*—I can't!—*

"Get out of me!"

*—Just calm down!—*

"Mom! Make her get out of me!"

*— Will you stop saying things like that out loud! They already think you've gone crazy!—*

Danny Rozelli was a willful little kid, who was still too teed off to be reasonable. He had already discovered the trick of thinking out loud. It gave him more power over his own body—it helped him to stay in control. Unfortunately, when you think out loud, people can hear you.

"Danny, honey, it's all right—everything's going to be all right." But clearly Danny's mother didn't believe this, because she turned to her husband and cried, "What do we do? What do we do?"

Allie fought against the boy, and regained control of his body long enough to say, "Nothing's wrong with me. Everything's fine," but Danny fought back, his body went into convulsions, and he wailed, "Make her LEAVE!"

It was all Allie's fault. If she hadn't fallen asleep in his body, and skinjacked him for seven whole hours, none of this would have happened.

She should have tried to peel out of him the second she woke up that morning in her parents' house, but no, instead she asked her parents to feed her, and over a bowl of Apple Jacks they told her that she was still alive.

*Alive!*

The news was such a sudden shock that it not only echoed in her own mind, it also woke Danny up, and he began fighting his way to the surface. She tried to run, but when she opened the front door, she ran right into the policeman standing there. In a second even more police cruisers were showing up—one of them bearing a distraught couple, who had woken up two blocks away to find their son missing. When Allie's father had called 911, the police had apparently put two and two together, and raced Danny's parents over for a family reunion.

At the time, Allie was still reeling from her own revelation. *She was alive.* Did that mean she could live again? Could she—dare she even think it—could she skinjack *herself*?

Oblivious to what was going on, Danny's parents had smothered him with kisses, and the police had questioned Allie's parents as to how on earth the boy had turned up there. Allie didn't want to fight Danny, and once they were in the police cruiser, driving away, she tried over and over again to peel herself out of the boy. His body stiffened, his back arched, his eyes bulged, but Allie could not get out of his body, and his parents became more and more concerned with their son's strange behavior. As the police car pulled into the Rozelli's driveway, Allie finally realized the true cost of skinjacking someone for too long. She was now a permanent resident in Danny Rozelli's body.

But the worst was yet to come.

It was the element of surprise that gave a skinjacker the advantage. A person didn't know how to defend themselves against a skinjacking, or how to fight to retain control of his or her own body—especially against a seasoned skinjacker like Allie. But fleshies learn quickly. Each time Danny's spirit surfaced, he was stronger, more able to fight Allie from the inside out, and now, half a day later, the two of them were still battling at sunset, with neither one getting the upper hand. They were two evenly-matched spirits sealed into a single body, and it looked like they were going to stay that way for good.

"I'm fine!" Allie insisted, in control of Danny's mouth. "I'm fine, really." Unfortunately Danny had control of the rest of his head, and began banging it against the wall.

His mother began to wail, his father grabbed him and restrained him, and Allie withdrew, trying to figure out a new approach to this unhappy situation.

She pulled way back, allowing Danny to have full control of himself, but not so far back that he could force her to sleep—for he had figured out that trick too. She waited as his body relaxed, his breathing slowed, and his father, who was still restraining him, loosened his grip.

"It's all right, Danny," he said. "We're going to get you help. I promise."

Danny, tears in his eyes, nodded. Allie waited a minute more, then pushed her thoughts forward in a faint whisper.

*—Danny, please listen to me—*

*No!* he thought back to her. *No, no, no!* But at least now he wasn't shouting it out loud.

*—Bad things will happen if you don't listen to me—*

He didn't answer her right away. Then he thought, *What kind of bad things?*

*—They'll take you away from your parents and put you in a hospital—*

*No! My parents won't let anyone do that!*

*—What do you think they mean when they said they'll get you help?—*

Danny didn't respond to that. Good. He was finally seeing reason.

*—I didn't mean to get stuck in here, Danny, but I did, and we have to make the best of it. Now we have to be friends until I can figure out how to get out—*

*I don't want to be your friend! You're a girl! I don't want a girl in my head!*

*Great,* thought Allie, *that's what I get for skinjacking a seven-year-old.*

*I heard that!*

And now not even her thoughts were private. This was going to take a lot of getting used to.

*—Think of me as your guardian angel, Danny—*

*You're an angel?*

*—Yes, I am—*she told him, seizing onto the one idea that might make this whole thing work, *—and if you want things to be okay, you have to pretend like it already is okay. You have to pretend like I'm not here—*And then she made a decision. *—I promise not to take over your body without your permission . . . if you promise to calm down and act normal—*

*Okay,* thought Danny, *but if you start making me do girly things . . .*

"Danny, honey, talk to me," said his mother. "Tell me what's wrong."

Danny took a deep breath, and said, "Nothing, Mom. I'm okay now. I was . . . I was having a bad dream, but it went away."

His mother hugged him. Allie was impressed that he pulled it off. *—Very good—*thought Allie. *—They'll probably still take you to see doctors, but if you act normal, everything will be okay—*

*Will they give me shots?*

*—I don't think so—*

*Good,* thought Danny, and then he asked her, *Will you help me with my homework sometimes?*

*Sure,* thought Allie. *Why not.* She tried to tell herself that she'd be okay with this—being a backseat driver to a second-grader, but the reality of it filled her with despair. Everlost was gone—she couldn't see it anymore, couldn't feel it. It was invisible to her, just as it was to Danny, or any other fleshie. She knew her body was out there somewhere, but she had no idea where to find it—and even if she did, she was still stuck inside this kid. Good going, Allie.

*Don't be sad, Allie.*

And so, for Danny's sake, she tried not to be.

# CHAPTER 30

## A Place on the Mantel

Five hundred miles northeast of Memphis, another skinjacker paced in the *Hindenburg*'s Starboard Promenade.

"Patience, Milos," Mary said. "Patience is what we need right now."

"But why must I spend my days running petty skin-jacking errands for Pugsy Capone? That is work for Moose and Squirrel, not for me!"

Mary took his hand. "You're doing it as a favor for me."

"Yes, but there is so much more I could do for you, if you let me! Please! Give me a task—something you think is impossible, and I will do it. I wish to show you how useful I can be for you." More than useful, Milos knew he needed to be indispensable—otherwise how would she ever see him as an equal?

"By serving, and keeping an eye on Pugsy, it frees Jill to catch crossing souls. She's bringing in two and three a day, thanks to you!"

"I could bring you more! And I do not need an amulet to do it!" Milos held her gaze for a moment, then paced away, realizing he had just opened a can of ants. Or was it worms? He could never get these English expressions correct.

"Is that so?" said Mary, slowly sauntering up to him. "And how might you accomplish that?"

He was so tempted to tell Mary the truth—he owed no loyalty to Jill after what she had done to him. He could tell Mary that Jill wasn't just catching souls as they crossed— no, her role was much more active than that—much more "hands-on." He wondered how Jill did the deed. Did she use a weapon, or did she do it with her fleshie's bare hands? The more Milos thought about it, the less he wanted to know.

"How would you save the children with no amulet to guide you?" Mary pressed. "Tell me, I'd like to know."

If he told Mary, he suspected it wouldn't just turn her against Jill—it would poison her against all skinjackers. If he brought down Jill, he'd bring down himself as well. It wasn't for Jill's sake that he kept her secret.

"Never mind," said Milos, deflating. "But I do wish you would let me do something special for you. Something that might truly earn your trust."

"I trust everyone until I'm given a reason not to," Mary told him, which was nice in theory, but ridiculous in practice— so Milos gave her a teasing grin.

"And how many reasons do I give you so far?"

Mary tried to suppress a smile, but failed miserably. "I've lost count."

"Well," said Milos, "maybe I am after something more than trust." He let the thought linger for a moment, then gave a slight, but courteous bow. "Now if you will excuse me, I have to get Pugsy some sports scores."

He turned to go, but Mary wasn't quite done with him yet.

"You asked for an impossible task," she said. "Perhaps I can give you one."

Milos turned back to her, watching as she strode across the Promenade, peering down out of the angled windows, looking at the Afterlights in the court of honor. The children here now played games. The same games, day after day after day. "Things have certainly gotten better here since my arrival," she told Milos, "but Pugsy is really more of a hindrance than a help, don't you agree?"

Milos, who had no love of the Death Boss, said, "Of course I do."

"Well then, I want you to . . . talk . . . to Pugsy. I want you to persuade him to leave Chicago. Forever."

"I do not think this is possible," Milos told her. "He will never leave Chicago of his own free will."

Mary shrugged and raised her eyebrows. "Well, you said you wanted an impossible task; there it is."

Milos considered it. "Persuade him, you say . . . "

"I'm certainly not suggesting anything unseemly. . . ."

"Of course not. You would never do such a thing." Milos came to the window beside her, "And if I succeed?"

"If you succeed," said Mary, "and Pugsy ceases to be a problem, you'll have better things to do than fetch his sports scores." Then she smiled. It wasn't her usual warm, welcoming smile. This time it seemed steeped in intrigue and design. "Tell me, have you ever been to the West, Milos?"

"No," he answered. "I have heard stories of skinjackers

who jacked their way across the Mississippi, but they never returned. Are you planning an expedition?"

"If you accomplish the impossible," Mary told him. "Perhaps I will too."

Milos gently took her hand. "It is a pleasure to be in your service, Miss Hightower, Governess of the East, and soon to be West." Then he raised her hand to his lips and gently kissed the silken, glowing back of her hand. He knew he was being too bold, and if ever there was a moment she would throw him out, this would be it, but instead she slowly withdrew her hand, and said, "You, Milos, could be very dangerous."

To which he replied, "Is that an observation, or a request?"

That brought forth a laugh, but no answer. Perhaps because she was still undecided.


That night Pugsy Capone dined on lobster. There was always lobster, or steak, or good old Chicago Pizza since Mary became a part of his establishment. Her children diligently ventured out into the living world in search of crossed food, and her relationships with some fairly well-known finders resulted in a trade surplus that kept Pugsy in the pink. Whatever he wanted, it was available. Even his own Chicago Afterlights were following suit, becoming busy bees, instead of lazy oafs.

"I've been thinking of declaring myself boss over Indianapolis, and then spreading East to Ohio," he had told Mary. "Whadaya think?"

"It sounds visionary," Mary had told him. "Stretch as far east as you like."

While he had been reluctant to join with her at first, he had to admit that they were an unstoppable team. The future was looking brighter than ever before. So when he was approached by Moose, who told him that a truck had arrived full of tributes and gifts from the Indianapolis Afterlights, foul play was the last thing he suspected.

As he crossed the midway with Moose, it didn't trouble him that his trio of bodyguards were nowhere to be found. He had come to rely on them less and less since security, and a need for six-fisted intimidation, had become less of a priority. He was caught off guard by the sack that was thrust over his head, and before he knew what was happening, his hands and feet were tied, and he was carried off.

He was dumped some time later on a wooden floor that creaked beneath him, and when the bag was ripped from his face, he was looking up at three Afterlights glowing in the dark night: It was the new skinjackers. All three of them.

"What do you think you're doing?" Pugsy shouted.

Milos was way too calm. "We are having a meeting. I am so glad you could come."

As Milos was a Ruskie, Pugsy hated him on principal. It was Mary who had convinced him that Milos could be trusted. Well, Mary would get an earful for this!

He tried to stand but his legs were tied too tightly. "All three of you have just bought yourself a place on the mantel." Which was one of Pugsy's pet expressions for a trip to the center of the earth—along with "earning core time" and "sleeping with the magma."

"Look around you, and think again," said Milos. Pugsy glanced around, and instantly knew exactly where he was. This was what he affectionately called "the submarine terminal." It was an Everlost dock on Lake Michigan where he would dispatch unwanted Afterlights into the "dirty deep," yet another pet name for the center of the earth. In fact, right now, there were three others bound and gagged, with cinder blocks tied to their ankles. He would have thought the work was done by his bodyguards. Except that they *were* his bodyguards. Now Pugsy began to worry.

"Tell me," said Milos, "how many are the Afterlights you have thrown from this dock?"

"I don't know," said Pugsy nervously. "I don't keep count."

"Guess."

"Throw him off! Throw him off!" shrieked Squirrel, but Milos threw him a gaze that shut him up.

"I said guess."

"Uh, maybe, a hundred? Two hundred?"

"Just as I thought." Milos nodded to the other two, and they lifted up one of Pugsy's boys, then tossed him off the dock.

"No!" screamed Pugsy.

Then Milos knelt down to him. "I have grown tired of you," he said. "So I am now inviting you to leave Chicago. I am inviting you to leave alone, and to leave now."

"What are you, nuts?"

Milos nodded to the others again, and they sent the

second of Pugsy's bodyguards off to the dirty deep.

"You have thirty seconds to accept my invitation."

"Mary!" said Pugsy. "Go get Mary! She'll negotiate for me. She'll give you whatever you want!"

The other two laughed, and Milos whispered to him, "Mary is the reason we are all here on this fine evening." He signaled the other two, and they hurled Pugsy's last bodyguard off for serious core time. Then they dragged a cinder block to Pugsy, and tied it around his ankles.

"Okay, okay, okay, I see you mean business! So I'll tell you what. You can untie me, and I'll leave, just like you asked. I'll leave right now and I'll never come back. Okay? Just like you asked, okay?"

Milos gave Pugsy a satisfied smile. Then he said, "I'm sorry, but I cannot hear you."

"What?"

"You have ten seconds."

"I said I'll leave! I'll *leave!*"

"Sorry, your answer must be in Russian."

"I don't speak Russian!"

"Five seconds."

"I'll leave-ski Chicago-ski!"

"Time's up." He nodded to Moose and Squirrel. "Goodbye, Pugsy."

"Nooooooo!"

Pugsy was lighter than the other three, so he flew much farther before hitting the lake. He quickly plunged through the living-world water, as thin to him as air, and then passed into the lake bed, toward his place on — or rather *in* — the mantel. As he sunk deeper and deeper into the earth, he could only hope that when he reached the center, he wouldn't come across anyone he sent there himself.

The following day, all the Afterlights of Chicago were called for a town meeting—the first such meeting since Pugsy announced his partnership with Mary some weeks ago. Now Mary stood on the same balcony, looking out over the crowd. This time, however, Pugsy was absent. Instead she stood with Speedo beside her. Milos was there, too, but he lingered in the background, along with a silently aggravated Jackin' Jill.

"You shouldn't be up here at all," Jill told Milos. "I earned the right to be here, but what have you done?"

"Not much," Milos told her. "Just what was necessary."

She was unimpressed. "Where's Pugsy?" asked Jill, glancing around. "He's never late when he calls a town meeting."

"Pugsy did not call it," Milos said casually.

At the front of the balcony Mary looked down on the crowd. Speedo, having been a finder, was still intimidated by large vapors of Afterlights. Finders were usually hunted down by such mobs, accused of unfair trading. It didn't help that he was eternally in a wet bathing suit, displaying a bare belly in a pasty shade of pale. He could never get used to being Mary's right-hand man—and he suspected she was now grooming Milos for the position. Speedo, who had no desire for power beyond the horsepower of an airship engine, would be more than happy to slip into the background when the time came—and he hoped it came soon.

"Look at all of them," said Mary. "It hardly seems

appropriate to call them a 'vapor of Afterlights' anymore."

"More like an entire cloud," suggested Speedo.

"A cumulus!" said Mary, delighted with herself. "A cumulus of Afterlights!"

Their numbers had indeed grown. A census upon Mary's arrival revealed there to be 783 Afterlights in Chicago, including the ones she brought with her. But once word got out that Mary had settled in for an extended stay, stray Afterlights began to wander in to the Columbian Exhibition grounds—more each day. Those, plus the new arrivals waking into Everlost for the first time, brought their numbers close to a thousand now.

Nick had stolen from her more than a thousand souls. Now she had them back, and with Pugsy gone, she didn't have to share them with anyone. This was truly a day for celebration.

"Afterlights of Chicago," she announced to the crowd. "It is with the utmost of mixed feelings that I must announce that Pugsy Capone has chosen to leave us."

The crowd murmured in excitement, mingled with doubt.

"He has decided to travel, and has taken a permanent leave of absence. I'm sure you all join me in wishing him everything he deserves, wherever his journey takes him."

It began as a smattering of applause, that grew into cheers, as the crowd realized exactly what Mary was telling them.

"As Pugsy will not be coming back, I am pleased to accept the position as Governess of Chicago."

The cheers reached a fever pitch. "Listen to them, Speedo!" Mary whispered. "Do you see how happy they are to finally be freed!"

"Where did Pugsy go?" Speedo asked her.

"Milos was so kind as to convince him to leave." She turned back to give Milos a much-earned smile. "It's probably best if we don't know the details, don't you agree?"

Mary turned back to the crowd and resumed addressing them. "Since my arrival, there have been many changes here, and there will be many more to come. My goal is to bring your quality of death to the highest possible level. Many of you have found your own "special activity" to make each and every day your personal perfect day. For those of you still searching, my door is always open. I pledge to help you in every way I can."

The crowd seemed a bit less enthusiastic at the prospect of a gloriously repetitive eternity, but that was all right. They would come to see the wisdom of Mary's way. They always did.

Milos was called for an audience with Mary in her Promenade. He assumed it was a private audience. Milos already knew she spoke to no one else as candidly as she spoke to him. He had to believe that it meant something. That *he* meant something.

He came with a chilled bottle of champagne that he found in Pugsy's wine cellar mixed in with all the bottles of root beer, and two champagne flutes. When he arrived, however, he found the audience was anything but private.

"Milos, I'm glad you're here," Mary said, not even

noticing the champagne. Speedo was there, and there was another Afterlight as well—one who Milos had never seen before. He sat in the red leather armchair—the one that used to be Pugsy's—and Mary was offering him candy from her private stash.

"He's one of Mary's long-distance scouts," Speedo explained, "and he just got back." Apparently he was an important player in Mary's war against "the forces of dark chocolate," as she liked to call it.

The boy then tilted his head back, opened his mouth, and closed his eyes. The others, who knew what was coming, ducked, just as the boy released an earth-shaking sneeze. Milos was the only one caught unawares, and was splattered with more unspeakable ecto-stuff than ought to be allowed in any universe.

"I'm sorry, Milos," said Mary. "I should have warned you. But every talent comes with its own stumbling block, and the Sniffer is no exception." She turned to the boy. "You really should cover your mouth when you sneeze."

"I know, but I always forget."

Speedo rose from the chair he had hidden behind, and threw a rag to Milos to clean himself, but it was much too small to do the job.

Mary was not bothered by the deluge—she would have someone clean it later. What mattered was the news the Sniffer brought back with him. And what news it was! "How marvelous! How absolutely marvelous!" she said after he told her what he had learned. It was exactly the information she needed. She now knew not only Nick's location, but the size of his vapor, and where he was going.

And as for this "Ripper" he seemed to have acquired, how much damage could she do, really? The ripper was just one against a thousand.

Mary stood up, her plan already taking shape in her mind. She would see Nick again, and she would see him soon . . . but it would be on her terms.

"Well, if the Chocolate Ogre has gone to Memphis to find Allie the Outcast, I think we should meet him there. A thousand of ours—against four hundred of his!"

Milos just stood there, a little shell-shocked by the sudden shift of direction. It was the first time she noticed he held a bottle of . . . was that champagne?

Speedo, as always, was wary. "You had a thousand last time . . . and you know what happened."

The memory only made Mary more determined. "Last time he went behind my back. So this time, we'll sneak behind his!"

"There's one more thing," the Sniffer said. "I smelled something . . . nasty . . . that was also moving toward Memphis. I'm not sure what it was, but if I didn't know better, I'd think it was the McGill."

It caught Mary off guard. She felt her afterglow sputter liked a burner low on gas. She hoped no one saw it. "The McGill no longer exists," she proclaimed. "In fact, he never did. Speedo! Make a note that I should point out the nonexistence of the McGill in my next book."

"Yes, Miss Mary."

And then she turned to Milos. He still stood there dripping with the Sniffer's unpleasantness. Even so, she found she wanted to embrace him, but restrained herself. "Milos,

I asked you to be patient, and now your patience will be rewarded." Then she went to her bookshelf. "We will defeat the Ogre in Memphis, and from there we will begin our crusade to unite the East and the West." Mary ran her finger over the book spines, then pulled out the heavy volume on Civil Engineering.

Milos was amused. "Don't tell me—you wish me to build a bridge in your honor!"

"Not exactly." She held it out to him. "I want you to study this—because in this book are the blueprints for every bridge that crosses the Mississippi River."

"Yes, but these are all living-world bridges," Milos pointed out. "They are of no use to us."

Mary put the book firmly into his hands. "Come now, Milos," she said with a smile that, on anyone else but Mary Hightower, might be called wicked, "I think you're much smarter than that."

She sent Milos to clean up, and requested she meet him in the non-slimed Portside Promenade, on the opposite side of the ship, when he was done.

Milos was still reeling from this change in circumstance. All of them leaving Chicago, a war with the Chocolate Ogre, and the possibility of Allie being brought into the mix. But then this might not be a bad thing. This battle could provide him an opportunity to make himself truly indispensable to Mary. And what if Milos could bring Allie in—even if only as a prisoner? That would certainly win him huge points.

The Portside Promenade was a mirror image of the Starboard promenade, except that it still had the airship's original furniture. Mary told him she was planning to gut it, and turn it into a playroom for the younger children, but hadn't gotten around to it yet.

When Milos arrived, all squeaky-clean, Mary had already opened the champagne, and poured two glasses.

"I never usually consume spirits," Mary told him, "but I suppose we have a lot to celebrate."

Milos hesitated. "Consume spirits?"

"Drink alcohol," Mary explained. "What on earth did you think I meant?"

Milos just chuckled in his own embarrassment, which seemed to please her.

"Let's toast," she said. "What shall we toast to?"

"To the Governess of the East, and soon to be West," suggested Milos. "The beautiful catcher of lost souls."

Mary's thoughts seemed to darken when he said it, but she clinked glasses anyway. She took a sip, put her glass down, and strode away from him.

"Is something wrong?"

She paused, looking out of the window. "Saving the children of the world is not always an easy thing," she said. "But the end does justify the means, wouldn't you agree?"

"Sometimes, yes." Milos cautiously moved closer to her.

She still looked out of the window, a convenient way to avoid his gaze. "There's much work to do, but before we begin, there's something you need to know, and something I need to find out."

Then she offered him a confession.

"As much as I despise stepping out into the course of living events, there are times it must be done," she told him. "There is an appliance store not too far from here. In it are many of those television machines, and they often display the news of the day." She began to rub her arms as if she was cold. "I was there, in search of something in particular, and I found it. There was a report of a dreadful car accident — a terrible thing. Witnesses claimed that the driver actually swerved to hit pedestrians, but the driver claims to have no memory of it whatsoever. Imagine that."

Milos took a nervous sip of his champagne. "Strange things do happen in the living world."

"Yes, they do," agreed Mary. "But I don't think it was an accident at all. And I don't think the driver was himself that day."

Milos withheld his opinion. "And . . . were any lives lost?"

"What a curious expression. How can a life be lost when you know exactly where it is?" Mary said. "Two children did leave the world of the living, if that's what you mean. The news was kind enough to show their photographs, but I had already seen their faces. Jill had brought them both into the incubator earlier that day. Of course they were asleep, but I still recognized them."

Finally she turned to him. "You knew, didn't you? Don't lie to me, Milos."

"I am truly sorry," was all Milos dared to say.

"Sorry that I found out, or sorry you didn't tell me that Jill's amulet was fake?"

He looked at the bubbles in his champagne, feeling all his hope begin to extinguish. Milos had no idea what Mary would do now. Would she throw him out? Would she have both him and Jill hurled off the pier to join Pugsy? *Directness and honesty*, thought Milos. *That's what Mary respects.* And so rather than wasting his breath trying to spin things to his favor, he simply told her the truth.

"I was afraid to tell you. I thought you might blame all skinjackers for what Jill was doing. I feared that you might send us away. That you might send *me* away. But I'm not like Jill. . . ."

And instead of throwing him out, Mary tapped her champagne glass very gently to his and said, "Do you really think I am so shortsighted as to let you go, Milos?" He didn't think he was supposed to answer, so he didn't. "It does change things, though," she said. "Since we don't have to wait for accidents, I can increase Jill's quota."

"Increase . . . Jill's quota?" Milos was stunned.

"The more opportunities we have to save innocent children from the living world, the better, don't you agree?"

As Mary's words tumbled through Milos's mind, he knew there were two sides to which they could fall. The side of terror, or the side of wonder. He also instinctively knew that the choice he made now would define his entire afterlife—it was, in fact, the very focal point of his existence. Milos had always considered himself a good person at heart. Admittedly, he leaned toward serving his own best interests, but in an enlightened way—always in a way that helped others even as it helped himself.

"Milos, are you all right? Did you hear me?"

Terror or wonder? To which side would it fall? He still wasn't sure, yet he forced a smile, and took a step closer. "You never cease to amaze me," he said, which was true.

"I understand that skinjackers can't skinjack forever,"

Mary said, "and that Jill has been skinjacking much longer than you."

"Jill has been in Everlost for more than twenty years, I have been here for four," he told her. "I do not think she will be able to skinjack for much longer."

She looked at him a bit differently than before, as if she were searching his eyes, and Milos held the gaze, hoping she would find whatever she was looking for. "I know you're not like Jill," she said, "but there may come a time that I will need you to do what she does. . . ." They were standing close now. Close enough to be deep within each other's afterglow.

"If I asked you to, Milos, would you do it for me?"

He knew the question was coming, but he didn't want to believe she would ask it. There was no more hiding behind a gentle gaze and inscrutable eyes. He needed to make a choice. What Mary called "saving innocent children," would be called something very different in the living world. It would be called murder. Would he do that for Mary? Should he? His own words came back to him. *"You should never be afraid to tell anyone 'no',"* he had once told Allie—but if he said no to Mary, he would lose everything. He would lose *her.* Losing Mary was not an option for Milos, and once he realized that—once he realized what he *truly* wanted, the choice became clear.

"Would you do it, Milos? Would you do it if I asked?"

He took Mary's hand, and his afterglow blushed lavender. "Yes," he told her. "I would do anything for you."

# PART SIX

## *City of the Dead*

In her book *Order First, Question Later*, Mary Hightower offers us her personal insights on the art of war:

"To bring about order in a chaotic world, one must, on occasion, resort to large-scale conflict. Weaponry and the size of one's army are certainly factors—but far more important are brains and righteous convictions. In the living world it seems right-thinking people are often trampled beneath the filthy boots of impure ideas. However, I like to believe that, at least in Everlost, good will triumph over evil."

# CHAPTER 31

## *On the Banks of Eternity*

The city of Memphis is gone.

This once great river city—the very center of civi-lization—now lies in ruins, eternally buried by time and river silt. That is to say, the *Egyptian* city of Memphis, capital of ancient Egypt when that kingdom was at its height, over 3,000 years ago. The great palaces have crumbled, and the towering stone obelisks, once wonders of the upper and lower Nile, have fallen like trees, and now lay hidden beneath farmland.

Across the Nile river from Memphis, on its western bank, was the necropolis: the city of the dead, containing the tombs and burial chambers of Egypt. It seems all cultures respect the awesome and mystical nature of a great river—how it can divide life from death, here from there, known from unknown.

No one has ever accused Memphis, Tennessee, of being the center of civilization, although it does have its moments. It, too, lies on a great dividing river—a gateway to the West. At least it's a gateway in the living world. In Everlost, however, it is a city of relentless wind, and marks an inexplicable barrier to the

West . . . which makes it interesting to note that Memphis, Egypt, was also known as *Ineb-hedj* or "the White Wall."

To the living world, the kingdoms of Egypt are ancient history—because in the living world, even that which is considered permanent is always proven to be temporary. To the living, eternity is a concept, not a reality—and yet they know it exists.

The living do not see eternity, just as they don't see Everlost, but they sense both in ways that they don't even know. They don't feel the Everlost barrier set across the Mississippi River, and yet no one had ever dared to draw city boundaries that straddle both sides of its waters. The living do not see Afterlights, and yet everyone has had times when they've felt a presence near them—sometimes comforting, sometimes not—but always strong enough to make one turn around and look over one's shoulder.

Look behind you now.

Do you feel in your heart a slight hastening of its beat, and a powerful sense that something momentous is about to happen?

. . . Perhaps, then, this is the hour that Mary Hightower takes to the sky with a thousand Afterlights heading toward Memphis.

. . . Perhaps this is the moment that Nick, the Chocolate Ogre, arrives in that same city in search of Allie, only to find that he has no idea where to look.

. . . Perhaps this is the very instant that a monster called the McGill arrives there as well, aching to ease his pain by sharing his misery—not only with his new minions, but with anyone he can.

. . . And perhaps you can sense, in some small twisting loop of your gut, the convergence of the wrong, of the right, and of the woefully misguided. If you do, then pay sharp attention to the moment you wake, and the moment you fall asleep. . . . For maybe then you will know, without a shadow of a doubt, which is which.

# CHAPTER 32

## *The Low Approach*

Nick had no idea that this day would lead him right into a vortex—and not just any vortex, but one of the most dangerous ones Everlost had to offer. All he knew was that nothing was going according to plan. The moment Nick had heard Allie was in Memphis, he was convinced that he was destined to find her. He was certain that he would arrive, and there she would be. How foolish. Did he expect her to be standing there in the middle of Beale Street waiting for him?

He had teams search the city for days, battling that soul-numbing wind, but they didn't find a single Afterlight in Memphis, or a single clue as to Allie's whereabouts.

A scout had returned from St. Louis, claiming the Mississippi wind was no better in that city. He spoke of rumors that Mary Hightower was farther north. Michigan, perhaps, or Illinois. Charlie, who wanted to map more of the Midwest rails, was urging him to head north, but Nick wouldn't have it. They could face Mary without Allie, but having Allie there simply felt . . . right. The sum of the parts would be greater than the whole. It would make them complete. It would make *him* complete.

"Allie the Outcast is here!" he told his restless troops. "I can feel it." And he could. That connection, forged the moment they were born into Everlost, told him that she was right under his nose, if only he knew where to look. "Keep searching!" he told them, sounding more like an Ogre by the minute.

Then, on their sixth day in Memphis, Johnnie-O approached him with some news.

"She's coming," Johnnie-O said. By the tone of his voice, and the look on his face, and the way he cracked his knuckles, Nick knew he didn't mean Allie. "Somehow Mary knew we were here!"

Nick stood from his chair. It was getting increasingly harder for him to rise, and as he walked forward, he dragged his feet, leaving chocolate skid marks on the ground.

"How close is she?" Nick asked.

Johnnie-O cracked a knuckle, the sound as penetrating as a sonar ping.

"Stop that," Nick said. "For all we know she has a kid with big enough ears to hear that a hundred miles away."

"Sorry." Johnnie-O looked deeply worried, and he was not an Afterlight who was easily intimidated.

"How close is she?" Nick asked again.

"You're not gonna like it," Johnnie-O said.

"Just tell me."

Johnnie-O let his large hands fall limp by his side. "She's already in the city. Less than two miles away."

Nick stared at him incredulously. How could that be? Everywhere they went, they sent scouts out for ten miles in all directions, searching the skies for the *Hindenburg*. If there was one thing Mary Hightower could not do in an airship, it was sneak up on them. "How could she get so close?"

"I think maybe we were all looking too high," said Johnnie-O, nervously cracking his knuckles again.

Two miles away, a hundred Afterlights holding ropes heaved themselves forward, dragging behind them a giant airship. Inch by inch it moved, its belly practically crawling across the ground.

Mary had been unconvinced that the western wind was the obstacle others claimed it was. Still, she had Speedo conduct the airship due south from Chicago, and didn't turn west until they were over Tennessee airspace. As Memphis had begun to loom in the distance, their airspeed slowed, and the airship's rudder strained hopelessly to keep them on a western course. When it became clear they would get no closer by air, Mary had Speedo set the ship down, and arranged for an alternate method of propulsion.

A hundred Afterlights were chosen for the team that would pull the *Hindenburg* forward toward Memphis, straining against an increasingly powerful wind. It was amazing how a ship that was supposed to be lighter than air could feel heavier to drag than a stone obelisk.

Fortunately, obstacles in the living world were not obstacles at all, for the airship passed through living forests and buildings—and although it was difficult for the team of pullers to struggle for traction in the bog of the living world, Mary's children always did what they were told.

Within the airship, the rest of Mary's kids filled the rigid aluminum frame, resting on catwalks, finding space between the huge hydrogen bladders. Mary had briefed them personally on their part in the upcoming mission, and now an air of excitement filled the hollow spaces of the giant craft, like the static electricity that brought the airship to Everlost in the first place.

She had left behind a dozen of her most well-trained followers in Chicago to tend to the sleeping Interlights—more than two hundred of them when she left. She didn't know when she would return to Chicago, but when she did, there would be a fine community of Afterlights, all brought up with the benefit of her teachings.

As the grounded airship crawled toward Memphis, Mary tried to quell her own anticipation by taking the most frightened of her children to her in the Starboard Promenade, and telling them whatever comforting stories she could remember from the living world. Fairy tales with endings she tweaked toward the positive. Happily-ever-afters fabricated where none existed before. Still, the children were on edge.

"What if the Ogre attacks us before we get there?" one of her children asked.

"He won't," Mary told him, for as much as Mary wanted the world to think that Nick was a ruthless monster, she knew he was not. He would try diplomacy before waging an all-out war. In fact her whole strategy counted on it.

At noon, she could see from her windows that the airship was no longer laboring forward, for the many Afterlights straining to drag it had reached an impasse against the wind. This was as far as they would go . . . which meant the time had come to finally make an opening gesture to Nick. A letter—which she wrote and rewrote until she was sure it was just right. She crafted it to make sure he could read nothing between the lines. It would not reveal the feelings she still had for him—mainly because she couldn't be sure he still felt the same way for her. And besides, after today, those feelings would no longer matter.

Once the letter was ready, she sealed it with old-fashioned sealing wax stamped with an *M*, then she called for one of her fastest runners.

"I need a brave messenger," Mary told her. "Can I count on you?"

The girl nodded enthusiastically, thrilled to be able to please her.

"I need you to go to the Ogre's train as quickly as you can—Speedo will tell you the way—and bring the Ogre this letter. You must hand it to the Ogre personally, and to no one else."

The girl no longer looked enthusiastic but terrified, so Mary put a gentle hand on her shoulder. "The Ogre is a terrible creature to be sure—but this letter will keep you under my protection. As long as you are brave and true, and do not accept *anything* the Ogre offers, I promise you will remain safe."

"Yes, Miss Mary."

After the girl was gone, Mary took some time to revel in her plan, and to mourn over it as well, because much would be lost today. Milos and the skinjackers were already out in the world, using their talents, and manifesting their own destinies on her behalf. The trap had been set for Nick, and all that remained was to spring it.

"I'll set out on foot," Mary told Speedo. "You know what to do while I'm gone."

Speedo didn't look pleased. "Why do you have to go alone?"

"An entourage will invite suspicion," Mary answered. "I know what I'm doing."

"Do you? I agree it's a good idea to meet with him on neutral ground—but why meet him at a vortex? Aren't vortexes dangerous?"

"*Vortices*," corrected Mary, "are only dangerous if one doesn't understand the danger, and I do. We have reliable information on the Memphis vortex, and it is exactly what we need."

She turned away from Speedo then, for she knew her face gave away certain emotions she preferred to keep to herself. She comforted herself with thoughts of her larger purpose in Everlost. All those chosen to lead were asked to make painful sacrifices to prove themselves worthy. And today Mary would sacrifice her love.

In her book *Caution, This Means You*, Mary Hightower devotes the following bullet point to vortices.

"Vortices are both the bane and blessing of Everlost. On the positive side, unexpected objects have been known to cross into Everlost through one vortex or another. However, on a less pleasant note, vortices will affect Afterlights in very undesirable ways. If you suspect that you've come across a vortex, it is best to steer clear of it, and report it to an authority."

# CHAPTER 33
## *Suspicious Minds*

In the varied and multilayered quilt of creation, one might say that vortices are the points where the surface is attached to the lining. In other words, a vortex is a spot that exists both in Everlost and the living world simultaneously.

Who can say what creates them? Perhaps it is the constant attention of the living that does it—for all vortices exist in spots that are the focus of human scrutiny. The living, of course, have only the slightest clue about the supernatural nature of these black holes of consciousness. Rare sightings of Afterlights, visible only in infrared light, perhaps—or recorded Afterlight voices that can only be heard at twenty times the normal volume. Odd smells, or unexpected chills—but nothing more than that.

In Everlost, however, the effect of a vortex can be immense.

Any Afterlight that steps on the pitcher's mound in old Yankee Stadium will be sent flying toward home plate at 107 miles per hour—the speed at which Billy Wagner threw the world's fastest pitch on that very spot. Any

Afterlight that stands directly beneath the Capitol dome in Washington, DC, will suffer the simultaneous bombardment of every speech ever delivered in Congress and the House of Representatives, causing instant and irreversible insanity. And any Afterlight that enters any Department of Motor Vehicles in the western world will discover that time doesn't just stop, it ceases to exist entirely.

The Memphis vortex is a unique one, because it affects every Afterlight differently. One boy, for instance, had walked in on a dare. His most prominent feature was a sizeable Afro that was his pride and joy—even larger in Everlost than it had been when he was alive. He stepped into the vortex, and ten minutes later rolled out as a six-foot furball with eyes.

An Afterlight girl so self-conscious about her braces that they had already doubled in size in her mouth, stumbled into the vortex to satisfy her own curiosity. When she left, she found her entire head encased in wires, brackets, and gum-bands.

And then there was the Afterlight who was somewhat sensitive to odors. He passed through the vortex, and emerged with a supernaturally acute sense of smell, along with highly irritable sinuses.

The Memphis vortex is a place of excess. That is to say, whatever you bring in with you, you leave with tenfold.

While in Everlost it is known as *the Intolerable Nexus of Extremes*, the living have a different name for it.

The living call it Graceland.

The Mississippi wind kept most Afterlights away from Memphis, so only a few Afterlights knew of the strange and curious properties of Graceland, and the rumors faded

the farther one got from the place. Mary Hightower, however, was now privy to firsthand information. After hearing
the Sniffer's account of his own personal experience there,
Mary concluded, with both excitement and remorse, that
this was the place she must meet Nick. In fact, she believed
it was the *destined* place for their meeting, chosen, perhaps,
by the Almighty himself.

Mary had no fear of the vortex, because the way she
saw it, she could not be any more right than she already was.

*Dearest Nick,*

*It appears our paths cross again. While I detest the very idea
of putting my children at risk, I will defend what I know to
be true. It would be foolish of you to battle us, however. I
have more than two hundred loyal Afterlights —certainly
we outnumber you.*

*I propose a meeting at a neutral location. I have been advised
that the mansion at Graceland is a comfortable place for
such a meeting. I will be there waiting for you today at five
o'clock P.M. I feel confident we will be able to either resolve
our differences, or reach an acceptable compromise.*

*Most humbly yours,*

*Miss Mary Hightower*

The girl who had brought the note looked terrified. Nick
smiled to ease her fear, but he knew his smile no longer

appeared comforting. Most of it flowed into a dark dripping frown which made the girl back away into Johnnie-O, who stood behind her. Used to be kids were more frightened by Johnnie-O and his power-knuckles than they were of Nick.

"Thank you," Nick told her. Then he reached for the bucket, which he still kept close, and with his good hand he pulled out a coin. "As payment for bringing me this message, I'm going to offer you a reward." He turned the coin in his fingers. "Do you know what this is?"

"Mary says it's evil."

"Do you believe that?"

"Yes," said the girl quickly. Then after a moment. "I don't know . . . " She regarded it for a moment more, clearly tempted. Then she asked, "What will you do to me if I don't take it?"

"Nothing," said Nick. "Just because I'm offering it to you doesn't mean you have to take it." He was surprised by the question, but he supposed he shouldn't be. The lies that Mary must have told her children about him were woven so deeply into their minds, it would take more than a chocolate smile to win them over.

"I'm not supposed to take anything from you, sir."

"I understand. Go back to Mary and tell her the Chocolate Ogre says yes. I'll meet her."

The girl left as quickly as she could, and Nick showed the note to Johnnie-O.

"Two hundred Afterlights?" said Johnnie-O. "If all she has are two hundred, we outnumber her two to one! We could take them on right now!" He pounded his fist into his palm. "Sneak attack!"

"We could, but we won't. This is about freeing, not fighting—never forget that."

"Yeah, but you got an army back there waiting to bust some heads."

"We're in Everlost," Nick reminded him. "Heads don't bust." But Johnnie-O still wasn't satisfied. Nick sighed. "You'll have your fight," Nick admitted—as much to himself as to Johnnie-O. "Mary's got them so brainwashed, they'll fight us rather than take their coins."

"Then we'll force 'em" said Johnnie-O. "We'll make 'em take their coins, and if they don't, we'll push 'em down into the dirt. Good riddance!"

A surge of anger raged through Nick, and for a moment his chocolate ran as dark as licorice. He grabbed Johnnie-O by the shirt, and his voice became a deep liquid roar. *"That's not the way we do things around here!"*

Johnnie-O was not intimidated. "You're the one who wanted an army," he said. "What did you think an army was for?"

Johnnie-O's point struck deep. The idea of gathering a fighting force was one thing—but actually using it was another. Nick might have been a good leader, but he was no warlord.

His anger faded, and he let his chocolate arm slip from Johnnie-O's shirt, leaving behind a nasty brown stain in the middle of his chest.

"Once Mary's defeated, we'll free the ones we can," Nick said.

"And if they won't take their coins?" Johnnie-O asked.

"Then we take them as prisoners of war," Nick told him.

Johnnie-O nodded, but his expression was still one of worry. "Y'know . . . you can't fight her if you love her." All this time it had been an unspoken rule that they never spoke of Nick's feelings toward Mary. But maybe Johnnie-O was right to bring it up.

"I fought her before, and I won," Nick reminded him.

"Yes, but this time, she'll be ready."

Nick closed his eyes, and searched for something in himself more sturdy than chocolate. "So will I."

The note from Mary had come shortly after noon, but it was more than an hour before Nick called for Zin. He wanted some solitude, some silence so he could find a sense of resolve, but the Mississippi wind whistled over the train, making it difficult to feel anything but uneasy.

His good intentions had become like the chocolate devouring him—sweet and rich, but also muddy and debilitating. He had become too much of a good thing. Now he sat with a full bucket of coins that could free countless Afterlights, but how many had he freed since he began to build his army? None. He began to wonder how much different he was from Mary after all.

"So, is this it, then?" Zin asked, as she stepped up into the parlor car. "Do we got our date with the devil today?"

"Sit down," Nick told her.

"I prefer not to, sir," she said. "Ain't no chair clean enough in this train car."

And she was right, so he didn't force her. "Mary has

called for a meeting. We'll take a team with us, but once we get there, you and I will go in alone," he told her. "Bring paper—I'll tell her you're there to write up a treaty."

"Johnnie-O's been teachin' me readin' but we haven't got to writin' yet."

"That doesn't matter—because when I give the word, you're going to drop everything, and cram Mary like there's no tomorrow."

Nick had played it out dozens of different ways until he saw the whole thing clearly in his mind. He would be there with Mary, engaged in a polite, but guarded conversation of diplomacy. He would string her along until he felt the moment was right, then he would make his move.

*I have a gift for you,* he would tell her. *The finest gift in the universe, and it's all for you.* He would step forward, and he would kiss her. A final kiss. Then Zin would grab her, and begin to push, until Mary was thrust through to the other side, into the living world, just as Zin had done to Kudzu. Mary would be alive, with nothing but the clothes on her back, and the sweet taste of chocolate on her lips.

*I will not only save Everlost from you, but I will save you from yourself. I will give you the precious gift of life, Mary. Because I love you.*

"What if I can't do it, sir?" said Zin. "Crammin' Kudzu was near impossible, and a person's bigger than a dog."

He put his good hand on her shoulder. "Your whole afterlife has been leading to this," he told her. "I have every faith in you, Zin."

# CHAPTER 34

## *Poolside Rendezvous*

Several of Nick's scouts had gone down Danny Rozelli's street, and one even walked right through the boy, but they were looking for a teenage Afterlight girl, not a live seven-year-old boy. A needle in a haystack didn't come close.

Within Danny Rozelli were two sets of thoughts, two minds, two histories, and with each day it was getting harder and harder for Danny and Allie to recall whose memories were whose. Now they both fell asleep at the same moment, awoke at the same moment, and when they dreamed, they dreamed as one.

It was late August, and the school year had just started. Life was slipping into a regular routine. Allie tried to imagine growing up, and growing old as a lifelong tenant in someone else's body. Would there come a time when she could accept life as the other half of Danny Rozelli? In these two weeks they had learned each other's rhythms and patterns like Siamese twins, and were quickly adapting to a life for two in a single body.

And what of her own body? It was lying somewhere in

any one of a dozen hospitals—and that was just if she was in Memphis. She tried calling a few, but never got very far.

"Honey, why don't you put your mama on the phone?" the receptionists would invariably say. It was hard to get respect as a seven-year-old.

*—This is not who I wanted to be*—Allie thought.

*—Me neither*—Danny thought right back at her, but both of their protests were getting weaker every day. They were becoming resigned to a shared existence.

Then the pool cleaners came.

They came the same day that Mary arrived in Memphis and sent her letter to Nick, but Allie had no way of knowing that, or anything else that went on in Everlost. As long as she was stuck in a living body, all she could see was the living world.

Late that afternoon, Allie and Danny were out in the yard playing handball against a side wall. It was one of the benefits of their particular condition; there was always someone to play with. Allie would hit the ball, then pull back, letting Danny take his turn. They had become skilled at switching back and forth at will. Neither fought for control anymore. It was like riding a tandem bike.

Allie scored a point.

"Aw! No fair!" Danny said.

*—Quiet*—Allie thought to him—*your mother will hear you talking to yourself*—

But when they looked up, it wasn't his mother standing there, instead it was a man holding a blue pole with a net on the end, and a second man a few feet behind him.

*—It's okay*—Danny told Allie—*It's just the pool guys*—

The head pool guy was a middle-aged man with a frayed baseball cap and beard stubble. His assistant was a punk with skull tattoos and a limp mohawk on the verge of surrender.

"Hi, Curtis! Hi, Chainsaw," said Danny, brightly. "Pool's real dirty. S'got lots of leaves and bugs today."

"Guess we'll have to see about that," said Curtis, but neither man moved. Chainsaw glanced at the house, where Danny's mom could be heard talking on the phone, completely engrossed in her conversation.

"C'mon, I'll show you," Danny said. He led them to the pool, and pointed at one of the drains. "See—it's all clogged."

But the pool guys weren't here for a service call today.

"I wish to talk to Allie now," Curtis said.

Danny recoiled out of shock, pulling far back inside himself like a kid finding strangers at the front door. Allie pushed forward to fill the void. She could feel Danny's heartbeat instantly begin to race. He wanted to run—he wanted to tear into the house, but Allie didn't let him. Maybe she should have, but she didn't let him go.

"Who is this?" she asked.

Curtis smiled, and Allie instantly knew. It was hard to see him behind the beer belly and beard stubble, but she knew.

"Milos?"

"So you *are* in there!" He looked down at her with a furrowed unibrow. "I thought you went home. Is this . . . home for you?"

"What do you think? Does it look like I'm back in my

own body?" And she couldn't help but add, "This might not have happened if you would have told me that skinjackers' bodies are all still alive!"

*—Who is that, Allie? That's not Curtis! I don't like this!—*

*—Just let me handle this, Danny—*

Allie looked over at Chainsaw, noticing the way he shifted from one foot to the other, looking around like ninjas might leap out and attack him at any moment. "And that's Squirrel, I presume."

"C'mon, c'mon," Squirrel said. "We found her, now let's just get out of here."

"How did you even find me?"

"A friend of ours. He was able to sniff you out." Milos took a good look her, and shook Curtis's head. "So much you did not know about skinjacking. If you had just stayed with us . . . "

"Fine! Tell me 'I told you so' all you want—but if you know a way out of this, tell me!"

"Shhh." Milos glanced to the house, where Danny's mother threw occasional glances out of the window. "Do not look suspicious," he said. "Act like you're playing."

Allie found a rusted toy car in the nearby grass, then knelt down and began to run it along the concrete edge of the pool deck, while Milos moved the net back and forth in the water, pretending to clean it.

"As it happens, I do know a way to free you."

"You do?" Her excitement made the boy's body jump with joy. "Thank you, Milos, thank you! I'll owe you for this."

To which Milos said calmly, "Yes . . . you will."

Allie's excitement took a slightly sour turn. She became guarded, and a little worried. Yes, she would owe him, and she already knew that Milos didn't do anything for free.

"I have come a long way, and at great peril," he told her. "If I free you, there is something I want in return."

"Like what?"

"If I free you," he said slowly, "then you will owe me your loyalty and your commitment. You must, therefore, follow my orders. You must do whatever I ask you to do, for as long as I ask you to do it."

Allie was speechless. She didn't know whether to be horrified or amused. "Have you lost your mind?" she told him. "I won't be your slave! The answer is no!"

"Do not misunderstand," said Milos, still moving the pool net in a pointless figure eight. "I have a higher purpose now, and I am giving you this opportunity to be a part of it. You should not throw it away so lightly."

Allie looked toward Squirrel, who nervously brushed his hand over his bad mohawk. "C'mon, Milos," he whined. "We can't stay here—she won't like it! She won't like it!"

"Quiet!" growled Milos.

"What do you mean 'she'?" Allie asked Squirrel. "What 'she' are you talking about?"

Milos fumed at Squirrel, and Squirrel seemed to shrivel. Even the skull tattoos on his fleshie appeared to cringe.

Milos sighed, then gave her the full story. She almost wished he hadn't. "There is only one force in Everlost worth aligning with," Milos told her. "You know of whom I speak. She has ideas . . . she has vision . . . and so do I."

Allie was shocked, but not entirely surprised. Milos was

all about jockeying for higher position. It made perfect sense that he would set his sights on Mary.

"You once told me that skinjacking can change the world," Milos said. "Well, Mary Hightower has envisioned a way to do that, and I am a part of her plan. You should be too."

"I won't have anything to do with Mary Hightower," she told him.

"How can you be so naive?" Milos said, a little too loudly. "Who do you think can help you? Your friend the Ogre? I can assure you that Mary will defeat him, if she has not done so already."

"Yeah, yeah!" said Squirrel, chuckling as he imagined it. "I'll bet she's gettin' him real good there at Graceland."

Allie snapped her eyes to Squirrel. *Nick was here in Memphis? Now?*

Milos was even more angry at Squirrel than before. "Go clean the pool!" he snapped.

Squirrel grabbed the equipment clumsily, and moved down to the other end of the pool, looking guilty.

So Nick was here in Memphis, and Mary had planned some sort of ambush. Allie had to warn him, but how? She couldn't even see Everlost as long as she was stuck in the boy—how could she warn Nick if she couldn't even see him?

"Danny?" called his mother. "Danny, are you okay out there?" She peered out of the screen door, the phone still to her ear.

"S'all right, Mom," Allie said, just as Danny would. "I was just telling Curtis about all the bugs in the drain."

"You let them work, Danny. Don't be a pest!" Then she

retreated back into the house, satisfied that everything was under control.

"One year," said Milos. "One year with us, and then you will be free to go. That is my offer."

Allie was about to tell him exactly where he could go, with or without a coin to get him there, but then she thought about Danny. Even now he was hiding behind her, listening to everything, but not understanding any of it.

*—There's an ogre? What kind of ogre? Is he bad?—*

It had only taken two weeks for her to know this boy better than any other human being, and she couldn't help but care about him. In any other situation, her refusal to give in to Milos's demands would mark her integrity and self-respect, but here it would mark nothing but selfishness . . . because by refusing Milos, she'd be condemning Danny to share his life with an uninvited spirit. The only way to free Danny was to accept Milos' offer.

"C'mon, c'mon—we gotta go!" nagged Squirrel. "Jill and Moose are waiting at the bridge!"

Milos ignored him. "This is the last time I ask you. Do you wish to be free or not?"

Allie took a deep breath and closed her eyes. But they weren't her eyes to close, were they? As much as she hated it, there was only one answer she could give. "Yes," she told him. "If you can get me out of here, then the answer is yes. I'll do whatever you want."

Milos smiled. "Very good. Now tell the boy to come out."

Danny retreated even further behind Allie's thoughts.

*It's all right, Danny,* Allie told him. *He won't hurt you. I promise.*

Danny timidly came forward, taking control of himself once more. Milos must have recognized the transition, because his own expression changed—no longer the sharp, piercing gaze he had shown Allie, but the inviting, disarming gaze meant for a child.

"What do you want?" Danny asked, his voice shaky.

"I just want to help." Milos looked at the pool, then back to Danny, kneeling down to his level. "Tell me, do you know how to swim?"

Danny shook his head. "No. My daddy tried to teach me, but I didn't learn good. Next summer for sure!"

"Very good," said Milos. "Then this will be easy."

And without warning he reached out, grabbed Danny with both hands, and threw him into the deep end of the pool.

Mary Hightower's warnings against skinjackers were all so much hot air—nothing but empty worries—that is, until she had skinjackers in her own employ. That's when she realized how powerful and dangerous skinjackers could be. Such power in the wrong hands could be devastating—which was the reason why she desperately needed Allie the Outcast either reformed or neutralized.

Milos had offered to find Allie in Memphis, and take care of it personally.

"If you can do it, then do it," Mary had told Milos, "but don't let it distract you from your mission. There is no margin for error."

"We shall find her quickly, and get back to the river in time to help Jill and Moose," he had said. "I promise I will not disappoint you."

It was his idea to have the Sniffer seek Allie out. Mary was impressed by his quick thinking and resourcefulness. She had once told Pugsy Capone that they were a team, but that was just a means to an end. This partnership with Milos was very different, and he kept proving himself time and time again to be a worthy counterpart. In time, Mary dared to hope that someday he might even take Nick's place in her heart.

"I know you won't disappoint me," she had told Milos. "In fact, I expect I'll be pleasantly surprised by you again."

*—Swim, Danny!—*

*—I can't!—*

*—Just move your arms and legs!—*

*—But it's not working!—*

*—It's not that hard—*

*—I don't know how!—*

As they floundered in the pool, Allie seized control, but the same muscle memory that had worked in her favor before now failed her miserably. The same body that was so adept at climbing trees could not perform the motions that would keep it afloat. Danny couldn't swim . . . which meant Allie couldn't swim either.

Panicked, Danny drew water deep into his lungs as he went down. They looked up to see through the shimmering water, Milos and Moose just standing there in the bodies of the pool men, watching. Waiting for them to drown.

This was Milos's plan! Allie should have realized it. There was only one way to separate a soul that's bound to a body. She should have known!

*—I'm scared—*cried Danny.

*—I'll save you!—*Allie told him*—Somehow I'll save you!—*
She had promised that Milos wouldn't hurt him, and he did.
She was an accomplice to this, whether she liked it or not.

Another gasp of water. Their arms thrashed as their
body sank. Angry squirms of darkness bore in from the edge
of their vision. Danny's heart pounded, screaming for oxy-
gen to power it. Their chest felt like it would explode. Allie
could not remember such awful pain.

*—Help us! Somebody help us!—*

The living world closed in . . . then it went away . . . the
pain faded . . . and for the second time, Allie Johnson died.

She felt herself leaving Danny's body—not peeling out,
but more like evaporating. She was herself again, back in
Everlost, and sinking quickly through the bottom of the pool,
into the earth, while Danny's body settled against the blue-
painted steel of the pool floor. The moment Danny came to
rest, a circular patch spread out beneath his body, bright
and solid. A deadspot was born. Quickly Allie grabbed for
it, pulling herself onto it. She reached for Danny's body, but
now that she was an Afterlight again, her hand passed right
through.

Suddenly there was commotion in the water. Bubbles,
and a billowing flowered blouse. A woman in the water,
frantically diving down, grabbing at the boy's body. Danny's
mother!

Allie reached her hand toward the woman, and was
immediately swept up, drawn inside her, skinjacking her.

The woman was crazed beyond belief, her body in a full
panic state—which is exactly what was needed, for although

she was not a strong woman, she could swim, and with all that adrenaline in her, she could swim for two. Allie took over her body completely, and set herself to the task of saving Danny.

She fought her way to the surface, pulling Danny with her. He was sandbag-heavy, a limp, dead weight. She broke surface to find that all hell had broken loose. Allie could instantly tell that Milos and Moose had left their hosts, because Curtis was on his knees screaming at the top of his lungs, and ripping his hair out of his head. Chainsaw was in enough control of his senses to leap into the pool to help her.

"I got him, Mrs. Rozelli!" With one hand he hurled Danny out of the pool, and climbed out after him. "I can do this! I know CPR!" Chainsaw began chest compressions on the boy as Allie, still within Mrs. Rozelli, climbed out of the water. Chainsaw valiantly fought to resuscitate the little boy, but it was no use. Danny was dead. His soul was long gone.

Or was it?

Allie peeled out of Mrs. Rozelli, and back into Everlost, where she could see Milos and Moose still standing there, observing everything.

"Welcome back to Everlost!" Milos said cheerfully. "I knew it would work!"

Allie could not believe he could be so casual about the terrible thing he had just done. Somehow Mary had changed him. Like everything else she touched, Mary had turned him rancid.

In the living world, Mrs. Rozelli fell to her knees, dazed

and terrified. She wailed so loudly, it rang out as clearly in Everlost as in the living world.

"C'mon, kid!" cried Chainsaw, struggling to revive the boy, knowing he was dead, but not willing to stop, for he couldn't face the woman's anguish. And behind him the other poolman dug his nails into his scalp and tore himself apart, his mind shattered from the awful thing Milos had made him do.

But in Everlost, there was a sight that none of the living could see.

Allie turned to the pool, and saw Danny's spirit! He was floating in midair just above the surface of the water. He was staring in wonder at something that Allie couldn't see, and a bright, unearthly light painted his face. He reached out toward the source of that light.

"No, Danny!" screamed Allie.

"It's so bright. . . ."

"Don't go down the tunnel!" Allie shouted to him. "Don't go to the light!"

"But it wants me to," Danny said, confused. "I think I'm supposed to. . . ."

"No! You're not! None of this is supposed to happen!"

Finally Chainsaw gave up trying to resuscitate the boy, and buried his face in his hands, sobbing. "I'm sorry. I'm so, so sorry. . . ."

Allie summoned her most commanding voice.

*"Danny, look at me!"* she demanded. *"Look at me NOW!"*

Finally Danny's spirit turned to her. "Allie?" And the moment he saw her, the light on his face vanished and he dropped into the pool.

Allie was close enough to grab him. She pulled him out, and into her arms. He looked at her with lazy eyes. "So that's what you look like," he said and yawned.

Behind them, above the cries of the living, came a voice far more pleased with this heart-rending moment than he should be.

"Well done!" said Milos, practically beaming. "Very well done, Allie!"

"Yeah, yeah," said Squirrel, "I'll bet she did that even better than Jackin' Jill."

"Congratulations," Milos said. "You have just brought a new soul into Everlost. Whatever you did to Mary in the past, she will forgive you now."

"I don't want her forgiveness."

"You may not want it, but you will need it," Milos said, very seriously. "Otherwise she will destroy you, and I do not wish to see that."

Danny's eyes rolled as he looked at Allie. "I'm so tired," Danny said.

Allie realized what would happen next. "Stay awake, Danny!"

"But I'm so sleepy. Just let me rest."

"Whatever you do, don't fall asleep!" Because she knew the moment he did, he would lapse into nine months of hibernation. If he fell asleep, he would become an Afterlight. But he wasn't one yet—he had no afterglow—which meant he was not entirely gone from the living world. . . .

Allie knew what she had to do. Without wasting an instant, she took Danny's soul and thrust him forward, plunging him back into his own lifeless body.

The effect was instantaneous. The moment Danny was plunged back into himself, his body heaved, and he coughed up an explosion of water. The dead boy came back to life.

Allie's scream of joy and relief could only be matched by his mother's. She tried to grab him, but Chainsaw held her back with a strong arm. "Give him time."

Chainsaw rolled him over on his side, and Danny coughed up more water, as if he had the entire pool in his lungs. He coughed, coughed some more, then his eyes opened. His mother took him into her arms against Chainsaw's warnings.

"I'm tired, Mom."

But that was okay. It was all right for him to be tired now. Chainsaw went over to Curtis, shaking him, screaming at him in fury for what he had done, but Curtis's mind was entirely gone. He would be the victim of all this, but Allie could not save him. She had saved Danny; she couldn't save everyone.

She turned to Milos, who was surprised, and maybe a little impressed, by what she had done for Danny.

"Always the good Somalian," he said.

"That's 'good Samaritan.'"

"Why does it matter?" Then he held out his hand to her. "Now we go."

Allie didn't move. "Do you think I would ever come with you after what you just did?"

"You gave me your word."

"Then call me a liar."

Milos signaled to Squirrel who began to circle behind

her. "I do not wish to take you by force," Milos said, "but if I have to, I will."

"You'll have to catch me first."

Allie ran, while behind her Mrs. Rozelli said a quiet, thankful prayer as she carried her little boy into their home, and the deadspot at the bottom of the pool faded away into nothing.

# CHAPTER 35

## Allie-Allie-Oxen-Free

The Union Avenue Bridge was narrow, always crowded, and nowhere near as efficient as the two interstate bridges that carried the bulk of the city's traffic over the Mississippi into Arkansas. It was the oldest bridge in Memphis, first built for the transcontinental railroad, but it had been modified years ago to add lanes for automobile traffic on either side of the train trestle.

Reports of its crumbling structure were occasionally seen on the inner pages of the *Memphis Daily News*, but there were always more immediate things for the living to worry about—like who killed the beauty queen, and who fathered the rock diva's baby.

Still, the Union Avenue Bridge was an accident waiting to happen. Of course some accidents need to be helped along.

While Milos was "freeing" Allie from Danny Rozelli's body, Jackin' Jill waited with Moose on the bridge—an impossible feat for most other Afterlights, who would be blown into the river by the Everlost wind—but Jill and Moose were safely packed into two fleshies. They might have looked suspicious just standing around on the bridge, but their fleshies were road workers, and road workers have been known to just stand around on a regular basis.

"What if Milos and Squirrel don't come?" Moose asked.

"We can do this without them," Jill told him, annoyed by Milos's absence, and further irritated by her own fleshie's bad teeth and chewing tobacco breath.

A freight train blared its horn, and rattled down the bridge's central trestle between the east- and westbound lanes of snarled traffic. It startled Jill, and she gagged on her fleshie's chew. She had half a mind just to hurl him off the bridge, and find another fleshie—but that would definitely draw unwanted attention.

A police car stopped on the bridge beside them, and the officer lowered his window. Moose looked panicked, and Jill told him to go fiddle with some traffic cones.

"Everything okay here?" the officer asked. "Need us to divert traffic?"

Jill adjusted her hard hat. "Naah, just filling in a pothole. We'll be done soon enough."

Once he was gone, Jill glanced down at the gym bag at her feet. Moose, idiot that he was, had left the zipper open. It was just luck that the cop hadn't seen the explosives. All that effort to skinjack a demolition engineer just to get them— how stupid would it be if their fleshies got busted here on the bridge? They couldn't afford a slipup, and every minute they waited made it more likely they'd get caught.

"Forget about Milos and Squirrel," Jill finally said. "We'll do this without them."

Jill would take care of the bridge, and Mary would know that Milos was a no-show. Maybe then Jill could squirm her way out from underneath Milos's thumb.

A few miles away, Allie raced from the Rozelli backyard. There was no one in range for her to skinjack, so she had to rely on her own speed, hoping that her will was strong enough to propel her faster than Milos. Twice she felt him grab at her, and twice she shook him off. Then she finally reached a crowded rush hour street, filled with plenty of people and plenty of cars. She could jack to her heart's content. This would be the Grand Ole Opry all over again, soul-surfing as quickly as she could, playing hide-and-seek in fleshies, hoping she had learned enough from Milos's lessons to beat him at his own game.

She leaped blindly into a car moving through the intersection, grabbing the driver, swinging off of him, and hurling herself into a car moving in the other direction. She grabbed hold of a passenger in that car, then pushed off again, leaping into the air, this time catching a passing truck driver. She bounced from one vehicle to another, playing a human shell game. She was sure Squirrel couldn't keep up, but Milos was another matter. She knew he was surfing just as deftly as her, so Allie surfed random and wild, until landing in the passenger seat of an SUV, diving deep inside a fleshie.

*—Late—late—we're always late—it's not my fault—it's his fault—it's always his fault—why do we always have to be late—*

Allie wedged herself behind the woman's thoughts, digging in, certain that she had lost Milos three or four fleshies ago. She could hide here until she was far enough away to peel out and not be noticed.

Then the driver, a bald man with bad skin, turned to her and said, "Be sensible, Allie. All this fuss is getting you nowhere."

He let go of the wheel and grabbed Allie with both hands. Allie struggled, and the car veered off the road.

"Watch out!"

Horns blared, the car jumped the curb, flattened a mailbox, and rammed into the corner of a restaurant. Airbags blossomed from almost every angle, cushioning the two fleshies, but Milos and Allie were hurled out of their hosts, and into the crowded restaurant they had crashed into.

Now everything depended on how quick Allie's reflexes were. Before she even hit the ground she reached out and grabbed someone—a waiter, still shielding his face from the crashing plate glass window. His thoughts were loud and panicked.

*—what the—who the—how the—whoa is that a car—am I alive—yes—am I hurt—no—okay keep calm—keep calm—keep calm—*

Allie hid within him, silent and still. Everyone jumped up and scurried deeper into the restaurant to get away from the accident—everyone except for a single woman who stood there scanning the room with eagle eyes. It was Milos.

"Come out, come out whoever you are," said the eagle-eye woman. "Ollie-ollie-axen-flee."

How stupid, thought Allie, if she gave herself away by correcting Milos's English. She lingered in the waiter, not taking him over, otherwise Milos might notice. She just hid inside him as he tried to herd diners out the door.

"This way, c'mon, everything's going to be fine. Is anyone hurt?"

Milos walked right past, and the second his eagle-eye fleshie was looking the other way, Allie left the waiter, hitched a ride in an exiting diner, then raced down the back alley. Finding herself on another street, she hopped into a man in a mustang who was fiddling with his radio—

*—Hate this song—hate that song even more—there's never a good station—and this song's even worse—*

She took control, floored the accelerator, and headed toward the highway. Once she was sure she had lost Milos, she took a moment to consider her next move. There was really only one place she could go. Nick was here in Memphis and he was in danger. She had to help him. She let the driver surface just long enough to scan his mind for directions to Graceland.

*—what's happening—what's going on—who—who are you— —oh shut up!—*

Allie found what she needed, and put him back to sleep.

She was already heading in the right direction. Traffic was moving, and the Graceland exit came up in just a few minutes. Once she was on Elvis Presley Boulevard, traffic slowed, and it was faster to surf than drive. She launched out of Mr. Mustang, to another driver, and another, jumping two and three cars at a time when she could. Milos would know where she was going—but if she was lucky, maybe she could get there first.

She surfed her way down the boulevard, until there, between convenience stores and gas stations, stood a mansion on a hill, completely out of place on the ugly urban street. Allie could tell there was something very odd about the place. It seemed to shift in and out of phase. It shimmered like a mirage in unsteady double vision, as if she were seeing two Gracelands—one in Everlost, and one in the living world, both competing for dominance.

Was this a vortex? She had heard about them, but had never actually seen one.

All at once she realized that there were Afterlights standing in front of the Graceland mansion. If they were Mary's children, then she was already too late!

There was no way in without alerting those Afterlights to her presence, which meant she would have to skinjack her way in. She hurried into the nearby visitor's center, looking for a suitable fleshie. Tourists meandered around, fingering gift-shop trinkets. It was a quarter to five, and the last tourist tram of the day was about to ride up the short path to the mansion. She launched forward, surfing every fleshie in her path, building momentum. The tour bus door had closed, but that didn't matter, she could launch right through the door, into the driver. She reached the last person between her and the bus, then bounded forward in a high arc toward it—but halfway there she smashed into another Afterlight, and he brought her down to the ground.

She was sure it was Milos—it had to be! Yet it wasn't. It was someone else—some*thing* else.

"Gotcha!" it said.

This kid was all wrong in every way. He had an ear

where an eye should be, and an eye instead of a nose. His cheeks were at different heights, and his mouth was entirely upside down. It was as if someone had been playing Evil Mr. Potato Head with his face.

"Who are you? Let me go!"

There were more of them now. A dozen of them, and they were still coming out of the woodwork, grabbing her, keeping her from moving. Every one of them had skewed features, but no two were exactly alike. *Picassoids*, Allie decided to call them, because they looked like something Pablo Picasso might have painted on a very, very bad day.

"Don't let her skinjack!" shouted the Picassoid in charge, who had blue hair that was somehow familiar.

"You have to let me go!" she shouted, while behind her, the tour bus left for the mansion.

"I don't think so," their leader said. "We've been looking everywhere for you, Miss Allie."

She had to talk her way out of this, and she thought she knew just the thing. "Are you Mary's children? I'm here to help her," Allie said. "I've seen the error of my ways, and I'm here to beg for forgiveness—now LET ME GO!"

The Picassoids looked to one another, then back to Allie. "We don't work for the Sky Witch," the blue-haired Picassoid said. "We serve a monster. The one true monster of Everlost."

Allie did not like the sound of that. "What monster do you mean?"

Then he gave her an unpleasant upside-down smile. "We serve the McGill."

\*\*\*

Mikey McGill was not blessed with good timing.

In life he would get his knuckles rapped repeatedly for looking at his neighbor's paper at precisely the moment the schoolmaster would look at him. He jumped in front of a speeding train at precisely the wrong moment, sending him and his sister to Everlost—and even in Everlost, he had chosen to spy on Allie at precisely the moment she had kissed Milos.

Naturally it would follow that he would capture Allie at the worst possible moment in this, or any other, universe.

His new minions—the Afterlights he had picked up in Nashville—feared him, and obeyed his commands, but that wasn't enough. He made them pledge themselves to him, but that still wasn't enough. He twisted and tweaked their faces using his talent of change to change them, but none of this could fill the hole inside him. Allie was the only one who could fill it, and so he followed her to Memphis. Since he was convinced he would never win Allie back, he decided the next best thing was to steal her away.

The Picassoids brought Allie to Mikey in an old-fashioned paddy wagon—a cell on wheels that had crossed into Everlost, God knows when.

When Mikey saw them approaching with Allie in the cage, he felt a heart begin to swell in his chest, threatening to transform his entire body into a bloody beating thing. He allowed his bad emotions to overwhelm the good, forced his heart back down his throat, and he strode forward encased in the same armor that had grown the day he ran away. Every step shook the ground as he approached her. Then, when he was right in front of her, he spilled himself through his open mouth, turning inside out, revealing the horrible thing he had become.

"Look at me!" he demanded. *"Look at me."* Although he didn't have to say it, because she was already looking. He wanted her to scream, he wanted her to cry, he wanted her to feel the misery of what she had done to him . . . but she did not react the way he expected. He sprouted himself an extra eye so he could read her more clearly.

"Mikey!" she grabbed the bars, peering through at him, not repulsed, not averting her eyes in the least. "Mikey! You didn't leave! You're still here!"

There was a good reason why Mikey, even with an extra eye, couldn't read Allie. That was because Allie found her emotions were such a strange mix, they all blended together into something unidentifiable. There was incredible joy in knowing that Mikey hadn't left Everlost, but confusion as to why he had turned into this nasty-looking thing. Rather than being horrified, she found herself impressed by it and deeply saddened at the same time. She knew him well enough now to know that his shell was merely that: a mask that he used to express the things he couldn't put into words. Was this, then, the manifestation of what he had been feeling? She couldn't deny that Mikey had been sullen and subdued while he was locked into simple human form—and although she never wanted to see him as a monster again, there were parts of the monster she missed. The truth was, Mikey was boring when he was beautiful.

But what was she thinking? None of this mattered at the moment. Nick was in danger! She had to save Nick!

"Mikey, listen to me!"

"No, *you* listen to ME!" He didn't care what she had to say. She would not rob him of this moment! He reached into a fold in his awful body that had once been a pocket, and he pulled out a coin. *"You chose Milos over me!"* Then he grabbed Allie's hand. *"If I can't have you, then no one will!"* and he placed the coin firmly in her palm, closing her fingers around it. He was determined to stay silent as she vanished into the light, but he couldn't stop himself from saying the words he could never before say out loud.

"I love you, Allie. . . ."

Then he waited for her to get where she was going.

He waited.

And he waited.

But Allie's eyes did not grow wide with cosmic wonder. The light of infinity did not shine on her face. She did not disappear in a rainbow twinkling of light. She stood there mesmerized—dazzled by his heartfelt confession, but she did not vanish. Then, she squeezed his hand firmly, but lovingly, and said:

"Mikey, we need to talk."

He let go of her hand, not knowing what to do, because he had not seen anything beyond this moment. The way he imagined it, Allie would be gone, he would wallow forever in the misery of it, and that would be that. But instead, Allie gave the coin back to him. "It doesn't work for skinjackers," she said. "There's a lot I have to tell you, but now's not the time. You have to let me go now. I have to help Nick."

Mikey turned his transformed hand back to the hand of a boy and gently took the coin. "It doesn't work for me, either. So neither of us is ready."

Allie looked at his humanized hand, surprised. "How did you do that?"

"I can do a lot of things," Mikey said, and to prove it, he took on his normal boyish face once more, on the body of the monster. Allie was amazed.

"You can change at will?"

"You have a power," said Mikey, "and so do I."

"Why didn't you tell me?"

"I thought you hated the monster."

"You were never the monster you pretend to be, Mikey. Not then, and not now."

"I am if I want to be. I am *whatever* I want to be."

Allie shook her head and smiled. "Then I love all the things you choose to be, because beneath it all, you're still Mikey McGill."

Mikey took a step back. Was she trying to trick him into freeing her? "But . . . but you love Milos. . . ."

Allie laughed. "Is that what you think? Is that why you left?"

"I saw you kiss him. . . ."

She gasped at the realization that he had seen the kiss. But then she said, "Mikey, you are such an idiot." Then she looked him in the eye and said, "*You're* the one I love."

Mikey found his ears starting to grow larger all by themselves—as if by doubling his hearing it would help him to understand. "Prove it."

"Okay, fine!" Allie said. "Give me your worst. The most horrible thing you can imagine—but do it quickly!"

And so Mikey dug inside himself to find the worst of all his feelings, the worst of all his fears, the very worst of himself. Then he pushed forth a face so hideous his followers turned their eyes away in terror. A face that could melt the living, or at the very least turn them to stone. A face so God-awful it defied the ability of any language to describe.

And yet Allie not only looked at him, but she reached out through the bars, pulled the horrible head to hers, and she kissed him.

The kiss was the definition of perfect. True, it lacked the heat, the passion, the breathlessness of the living-world kiss she had given Milos, but this had something greater. More than a flash of fire, it had an unbreakable, perhaps eternal bond of connection. Mikey had transformed back into himself by the end of the kiss, and the moment their lips parted he knew, as he should have known long, long ago, that no one—not Milos, not another Afterlight, not anyone in any world—could ever come between him and Allie, from now until the day they met their maker.

"Now please, Mikey. *Please* let me go help Nick."

Suddenly Mikey felt naked and exposed before her, so he stepped back and pulled himself in, folding into his armor shell. Then he bore down and forced his armor to dissolve. It was harder than changing his features, harder than growing an arm or an eye or a tentacle, but he did it, and promised himself he would never grow the armor again.

He turned to his followers who looked at him with shock and surprise.

"Hey—you're not the McGill," said one of them. Mikey considered turning himself horrible just to scare the kid into line, but he decided he didn't want to. He could be whatever he wanted to be, but there were many more parts he wanted to play beyond that of a monster. So instead of fangs, he sprouted himself a pair of tall white ears. "No, I'm the Easter Bunny," he told them. "Now free Allie from that cage!"

And they were all so bewildered that they hopped right to it.

# CHAPTER 36

## *The Intolerable Nexus of Extremes*

Graceland had a faint but perpetual smell of peanut butter and bananas.

"Even better now with chocolate," offered Zin, as she and Nick stepped inside.

From the moment Nick arrived, he knew there was something odd about the world-famous tourist attraction. The floors were both soft and solid at the same time, and everywhere he looked Nick saw double. He wanted to chalk it up to his own failing vision, but he knew it was more than that.

"What is this, some sorta funhouse?" asked Zin, but Nick suspected there was no fun to be had for anyone but the tourists. *This is a vortex*, Nick realized. He sensed it would be wise to leave, but he said he would meet Mary here, and he wouldn't go back on his word.

He had come with a team of Afterlights, but told them to wait outside, as he went in with Zin. They moved through rooms that alternated between elegant and absurd, and the air was filled with the faint echoes of a thousand parties. Of course, all the living heard was "Love Me Tender" pumped in through the speaker system, but they were beginning to notice an uncanny aroma of chocolate.

Toward the back of the mansion, Nick and Zin found the infamous Jungle Room, full of leopard- and zebra-skin furniture and green shag carpeting—not just on the floor, but on the ceiling, too. There they waited for Mary.

Nick didn't feel well at all, and this was troubling, because you couldn't feel sick in Everlost. Yet there was a fever burning within him, rising from the deepest part of his soul, radiating out.

Zin nervously doodled on her prop notepad to pass the time. "What if she don't come?"

"She'll come," said Nick.

When all the clocks in the house struck five, and Mary hadn't arrived, Nick began to worry. Mary was never late, and with each passing minute Nick felt worse.

"She's not comin'" said Zin. "Let's get outta this place, it gives me the creeps."

"She'll be here."

Nick's fever peaked, and then it finally broke. He began to sweat, but as he tried to wipe it away, he realized it wasn't perspiration he was sweating. It was chocolate.

*Please let her come soon*, he thought.


Nick had arrived twenty minutes early. Mary arrived ten minutes late.

She approached Graceland alone with no outward fear, but she could not deny that inwardly she was terrified. Not fear of Graceland, but fear of her own reaction when she saw Nick. *The plan*, she thought, *stick to the plan*. Speedo had his part, Milos and the skinjackers had theirs, and so did she. Mary comforted herself in knowing that she had the moral high ground over Nick, which meant that if there was any justice in the universe, she would be properly rewarded for her efforts today.

Twenty of Nick's Afterlights stood outside the Graceland mansion, looking at the troublesome way it shifted in and out of focus. As Mary approached, they parted, staring at her in awe and in fear, but she only smiled at them.

"Take heart," she told them. "Whatever your worries, I promise things will be better for you from now on." Then she walked into the vortex.

The overall decor of the mansion did not suit Mary's tastes. The last dwindling groups of tourists moved about the place on guided tours. Mary ignored them, and followed the scent of chocolate to a garish African-themed room, where she found Nick waiting. She had to fight the urge to run to him, shake him, hug him, hit him. No! She had to maintain a cool distance, or she would never be able to bear the burden of this critical hour.

Then she realized Nick wasn't alone. A grungy Afterlight in a Confederate uniform stood beside him, notepad in hand, holding the pencil the way a monkey might hold a spoon. Mary wasn't fooled. She knew about the Ripper. In fact, this was one of the reasons Mary had come alone. Nick's sense of honor would put him at a distinct disadvantage, for he would never have the Ripper attack a lone, defenseless girl. She hoped.

Nick stood when he saw her, and she took a good look at him. It was as she suspected: the chocolate had spread, consuming his thoughts, and thus his body. Calling him "the Chocolate Ogre" had done its damage, and now it had become a self-fulfilling prophecy. Most of him was covered in it now. Only an arm and a third of his face remained clear, but the skin was already turning moist and darkening. It was the effect of the vortex. All she had to do was stall and she would defeat him without lifting a finger. *You brought this on yourself, Nick,* she wanted to say, but couldn't bring herself to do it.

"Hello, Mary."

"Hello, Nick."

She still loved him deeply, but as she looked at him now, she recoiled, feeling her love curdle into pity. Seeing him this decrepit state allowed her to tell herself that Nick was gone, and all that remained was the Chocolate Ogre—a creature that needed to be put out of its misery.

It was easier now to keep her distance. "What shall we say to each other, Nick?"

"How about 'good to see you'?" he said, his voice raspy and thick. Barely human. He coughed a thick, liquid rattle.

"Yes," said Mary. "And it *is* good to see you. Truly." Mary could feel the effect of the vortex herself, but she knew she would not have to endure it as long as Nick. That's why she came late. Yet its effect was different on her. She did not feel weighed down, but enlightened. She actually felt stronger.

"I've missed you," Nick said.

"Have you? Is that why you continue to be a thorn in my side? Are you a little boy with a crush, seeking attention?" His chocolate oozed a little darker. Mary sighed. "I've missed you, too," she admitted.

Nick shrugged, a little bit awkward in the moment. "I'd reach out and hold you, but I might dirty your perfect dress."

Mary sadly shook her head. "It shouldn't be this way between us, Nick. Why must you rally against me so?"

"The same reason you fight me. Just like you, I have to do what I believe is right, and freeing kids from this place is the right thing to do."

"We are here to build Everlost, not to empty it!"

"How can you be so smart, and so wrong?"

Mary closed her eyes, resigned that there would be no last-minute salvation for Nick. He would never see things her way.

"Coming here tonight," she said, "was the first 'right thing' you've done in a long time."

Nick shifted, and she could see his left shoulder sag, beginning to lose human shape. She wanted to look away, but instead she watched it happen, because she knew witnessing this was part of her personal penance for having trusted Nick in the first place.

"If you have a peace proposal, let's hear it," said Nick, his voice sounding less human by the moment.

Mary shook her head. "There is no proposal," she told him. "I will not compromise my integrity for you. Every Afterlight in Everlost deserves the peace and comfort that I have to give. I will not sacrifice a single one for a treaty with you."

"Then why are we here?"

Mary smiled in grim triumph. "To accept your unconditional surrender, of course. Right now my children are storming your train, and taking your army prisoner. There will be no one for you to return to, Nick. I've already won."

From where Nick stood, Mary was just as beautiful, just as powerful as she ever was—perhaps even more so—for it seemed this place magnified both her beauty and her powerful presence. But in a moment she would deflate. A little boy with a crush—is that what she thought? Now he took guilty pleasure in the look of despair that would soon be filling that beautiful face.

"Your children are going to have a surprise," he told her. "You have two hundred Afterlights, I have four hundred. My army will capture them, hand them coins, and for a second time 'your children' will be set free—but thank you for sending them to the train. It makes it easier that way."

Mary's reaction was not what Nick expected. She tossed back her hair, and shifted her shoulders in proud defiance.

"Oh, but Nick, I think you misunderstood. As I said, I have more than two hundred Afterlights, and I didn't lie." Then she smiled a terrible smile. "I have a thousand. That's certainly more than two hundred, isn't it?"

As the words hit him, and he realized what it meant, his own will began to collapse. She had a thousand souls. She would handily defeat his army. Now the pressure inside of him—the pressure he had been holding back since stepping into the vortex—could no longer be held. He felt a dam inside him rupture. His vision blurred and went dark. He felt everything begin to dissolve as the last bit of him gave in to the sickly-sweet cancer. What began as a small stain on his face was now all that remained of him.

"Now, sir?" asked Zin. "Should I do it now?"

Yes, that was it! Although he might not have his victory against her children, maybe he could still have his victory against her.

*I give you a gift, Mary,* he tried to say, just as he did in his fantasy, but he could no longer speak the words, for his mouth could only make a moaning sound like a cave in the wind. Before his thoughts could become too muddled, he sent Zin forward. *"Now,"* he tried to say—and she must have understood, because Zin lunged toward Mary, grabbed her by the shoulders, and began to push.

Mary had thought she had a contingency for everything.

In her mind the Ripper was a minor threat. A nuisance at best. *Let the Ripper steal whatever she wants from me,* Mary thought. *I'll survive.* But the moment the Ripper began to push, Mary realized that she had miscalculated. There was a tingling in the back of her head unlike anything she had ever felt before. It moved down across her face to her shoulders as the ripper pushed her backward. What was happening to her? The Ripper wasn't ripping at all!

Mary opened her mouth and gasped—*she actually gasped*, drawing in a breath of air like a living, breathing person would, and then it finally dawned on her exactly what the Ripper was doing. She was pushing Mary into the living world! How could that be? Was such a thing possible? She didn't want to find out—so she fought back. Grabbing this horrible child, Mary tried to pull herself back into Everlost.

Zin had never felt so strong.

She knew it was the vortex helping her—the vortex had made opening a portal into the living world as easy as slicing butter, and Mary was sliding on through . . . until Mary began to fight back. As strong as Graceland made Zin, its effect on Mary was even more intense. Mary's greatest asset had always been the sheer force of her will. Now her will was horribly amplified—and Mary did NOT want to be alive!

*"This will not happen,"* Mary asserted, her voice loud and echoing in both worlds. *"I will not be forced out."*

The commanding sound of Mary's voice sucked away Zin's strength. Mary was halfway into the real world, but she dug her heels in, and each time she spoke, Zin felt weaker.

*"I will not be forced out of Everlost!"* Inch by inch Mary pulled herself back through the portal.

*"I will not be beaten by a by a sniveling, illiterate fool!"*

"Help!" Zin cried to Nick. "Sir! I need your help!"

But Nick was not himself. He was barely anything at all. He was a lumbering boneless mass. His fingers were dissolving until there was not enough of him to reach out, until there was not enough of him to know why he'd even want to.

"Help me!" Zin cried.

*What is this all about?* thought Nick. *Why am I here? What's happening? I have to stop and think.* So he crawled away into a corner, leaving bits of him behind as he went.

"I can't do this alone!" yelled Zin

*What is that commotion over there? It has to stop so I can think. If only I can clear my mind, I'll know why I'm here. I'll know who I am.*

And so the dissolving spirit closed its eyes, and melted into a corner, spiraling down into the bittersweet darkness of its own thoughts, trying to find something to grasp on to that wasn't chocolate. In a moment he was gone, and a layer of chocolate slowly spilled out across the floor like a lava flow, burying the green shag carpet.

Nick had lost. And now Zin was losing, too.

Mary had pulled herself back through the portal into Everlost, and although Zin still grabbed at her, trying to push, it was useless. There was no way she could fight against the monumental force of Mary Hightower's overwhelming presence. Mary pulled the last of her head through, and behind her the portal began to close. She grabbed Zin by the front of her uniform.

*"You will be rehabilitated,"* Mary bellowed, her will still magnified. *"You will learn to use your powers for good. You will learn to use them for ME."*

Mary took a step forward, but something snagged in her hair. She tried to pull free, but whatever it was pulled back—hard enough make her chin jut upward—and all of a sudden she felt that tingling sensation in her head again. She began to lose her balance, falling backward, and in front of her, the ripper lunged at her once more.

Allie had soul-surfed her way back to Graceland as quickly as she could, but it wasn't fast enough. She arrived too late to save Nick, but she could not let herself mourn what had happened to him. The only way she could help him now was to finish the job he'd begun. She didn't understand what was going on until Mary had pulled herself back into Everlost from the living world. Had Mary been alive? As in flesh-and-blood alive? Well, at least the top half of her had been.

This kid in the gray uniform had done it somehow—but now the hole into the living world was closing.

Neither of them had seen Allie lurking there. Good. Quickly she skinjacked a female security guard coming into the room.

From a living world point of view, the Jungle Room seemed perfectly normal—except for an overpowering smell of chocolate, and a shrinking hole in midair the size of a grapefruit. Through that hole Allie could see the back of Mary's head. So Allie took her fleshie and reached through the hole into Everlost, grabbing Mary's hair, and she began to tug with all her might.

As she pulled, Mary fought like a shark on the end of a line, but she had lost her balance. Allie pulled again.

*"Let me GO!"* Mary demanded. Her will was almost strong enough to send Allie flying away from her, so Allie twisted her hand, making sure her fingers were snagged and knotted in Mary's long copper hair, unable to be freed no matter how Mary worked against her. Then Allie added her other hand as well, pulling on her hair like it was a tug-of-war.

There were two of them working against Mary now, Allie pulling, and Zin pushing, but it still wasn't enough. Then suddenly there was a third hand in Mary's hair, and a hand pulling on her chin, and two hands grabbed her by the armpits—yet somehow all those hands were Allie's. She had skinjacked a guard—but two tourists had come into the room as well, and Allie was now seeing things through three different sets of eyes.

The Intolerable Nexus of Extremes had a different

effect on every Afterlight, and now Allie wasn't just skin-jacking a single person, she was skinjacking three at the same time—and all three of them had a single purpose: to pull Mary Hightower out of Everlost, and into the world of the living!

*"This will not happen!"*

But for all her will, for all her fury, Mary could not fight that many foes. As the tingling passed through her chest, her waist, and down her legs, she knew that there was no stopping this. But if she was going, she was not going alone! She grabbed onto the Ripper, with hands as tight as claws, and pulled on her. Both of them slid through into the living world.

Zin was so focused on pushing Mary, she had no idea what had happened to her until she finally let go and looked around. The strange double-vision view of Graceland was gone. The chocolate flood was gone. Mary stood across the room in shock. One tourist suddenly fainted, and the other tourist screamed at the top of her lungs and ran up the stairs. The guard who had first helped Zin, now stared at Mary in disbelief.

Zin turned around to see the portal shrink down to nothing and vanish. She reached out a hand and tried to create a fresh portal back to Everlost, but the living have no such powers. She was no longer a ripper, she was just a living human girl. She knew, not just because of what she saw—and not just because it hurt when she pinched herself. She knew, because, for the first time in a hundred and fifty years, her cap fell off her head, and tumbled to the ground.

"What have you done?" Mary glared at her with such

raw hatred, it chilled Zin's newly formed blood. So Zin ran, and didn't stop running until she was far from Graceland.

Allie had released two of her fleshies, one fainting in shock, the other screaming as she ran, but Allie held on to the guard, keeping a close eye on Mary. Mary's hair was wild, her green dress wrinkled, and she was out of breath from the ordeal. Mary Hightower, out of breath! What a wonderful concept! Allie couldn't contain her smile.

A tour guide raced down, responding to all the commotion. He didn't even see the tourist who had passed out behind a zebra-skin couch. "What's going on here, Candace?"

"Don't worry," said Allie, feeling authoritative in her guard uniform. "I'll take care of this. Go find out what that woman was screaming about."

"Who are you?" Mary demanded once the tour guide was gone.

"Don't you recognize me, Mary? It's your good friend Allie the Outcast—although it looks like you're the one who's out-cast now." Then Allie realized something with far too much glee. "Now that you're here—alive and all—there's something I've wanted to do for a very long time." Then Allie reached back, curled her fleshie's right hand into a fist, and swung it toward Mary with all her might.

This was one strong fleshie!

The punch connected with Mary's eye so hard, that Mary's entire body spun around, and she collapsed into a leopard chair. Allie's knuckles hurt, but it was a good kind of pain.

"My eye!" wailed Mary. "Oh! My eye."

It was the first pain Megan Mary McGill had felt in more than a hundred years. She brought her hands to her face, but it hurt to even touch it. She felt she would die from the pain, and she wished that she would, so she could be free from this horribly limited body. *I'm alive,* Mary thought. *Heaven help me, I'm alive!* There was no greater hell for Mary than to be bound to a flesh-filled hell on earth.

Allie prepared to peel back into Everlost, but before she could, a man grabbed her by the throat, and pushed her against the wall. It was the tourist who had fainted.

"I should never have freed you! So much trouble you have become!"

Milos! He had found her, but he was too late.

"Before you strangle this poor fleshie," Allie said, "why don't you have a look at your fearless leader."

Milos turned to see Mary, and he was stunned.

"Milos? Milos, is that you in there?" Mary, her eye already starting to swell, stood and gathered what composure she could. "This is only a small setback. You have to go through with the plan—nothing has changed."

Milos just stared at her, still trying to take it in. "But . . . but look at you . . . everything has changed. . . ."

"No!" insisted Mary. "You'll have to take care of my children for a while, but I'll work this out! I will! I'll work it out!"

Allie knew she should have taken this moment to escape, but watching Mary Hightower sink into absolute desperation was mesmerizing.

"I can still work from this side!" Mary insisted.

"I think you fool yourself," said Milos.

"No! I can make this work, I know I can. Please, Milos," and Mary fell to her knees—a gesture so foreign for her, Allie could only stare. "Please don't leave me like this! I'm begging you, Milos! Please don't leave me!" There were tears on her face now—real human tears.

Milos reached out his fleshie's hand, and wiped away her tears. "Your children do need you," Milos said thoughtfully. "We will see. . . ."

Then he whispered something in Mary's ear that Allie couldn't hear. Whatever he said, it calmed Mary down. She nodded a glum acceptance. Then Milos turned to Allie and she realized she had waited too long.

Allie could leap to another fleshie, and run, but there were none in the room other than the ones she and Milos had already skinjacked. Then suddenly something occurred to Allie.

*Mary was now a fleshie. . . .*

Did she dare do it? Did she dare skinjack Mary Hightower, the self-appointed Queen of Everlost? Of course! In fact she couldn't resist! As Milos came at her, she leaped from the guard, and directly into the flesh of Mary Hightower.

Mary knew the instant it happened.

She could feel Allie picking through her brain. She felt herself infected by this filthy, filthy girl. "GET OUT!" Mary demanded—and even though she was no longer an Afterlight, the force of her will was still strong enough to hit Allie like a mortar blast. Allie recoiled, and was ejected out of her—but not before seeing the depths of Mary's mind— and what she saw there, the plans, the schemes, the terrible things that would happen if Mary had her way—it was like witnessing Armageddon itself. And what made it all the more horrifying was that Mary truly believed it was all in the service of good. More than ever, Allie knew that Mary must be stopped!

But the force of her expulsion from Mary's body had rattled her and made her weak—weak enough for Milos to grab her. They were both back in Everlost now. She was looking at him—not a fleshie, but Milos himself—and his expression was stone.

"You have made life very interesting, haven't you?"

Allie tried to pull free, but she was too weak now.

"You're not going anywhere but with me," Milos told her. "In case you forgot, you made me a promise, and you're going to keep it." Then he pulled her out of Graceland, and she didn't have the strength to resist.

# CHAPTER 37

## *Sky Refugees*

Johnnie-O sat facing Charlie in the Starboard Promenade of the *Hindenburg*, a bucket of coins between them.

"You go first," said Johnnie-O.

"No, you go first," echoed Charlie.

"No, *you* go first!"

"No, *you!*"

How they got here was a mixture of failure, triumph, and luck.

While Mary Hightower had made her way to Graceland for her momentous meeting with the Chocolate Ogre, her children attacked the train.

Johnnie-O took charge, ready for the fight. "Bring 'em down or push 'em down," he told the army. Any enemy that couldn't be captured would be sent to the center of the earth. Then he went out into the battle swinging his heavy fists. Charlie, who was not much of a fighter, followed behind him, carrying the bucket of coins, and wearing a gardening glove on his hand to protect himself from the coins' power. Maybe Nick wanted to give these kids a choice, but Johnnie-O and

Charlie were determined to send as many of them as possible into the light, whether they liked it or not.

Johnnie-O grabbed one Afterlight after another, dragging them to Charlie, who would put a coin into their palms, and force their fists closed around it. They all had the same reaction, a look of terrified surprise that was quickly replaced by an expression of utter peace before they disappeared in a twinkling of light. Johnnie-O didn't like the peace part of it. There was no satisfaction for him in making his enemies content, but as long as they vanished from his sight, he didn't complain.

Ten minutes into the battle, however, Johnnie-O began to worry. Mary's children just kept coming and soon it became clear to Johnnie-O what their objective was. The train.

"Keep them back!" he ordered. "Don't let them near the train." But there were simply too many of them. Johnnie-O and Charlie had dispatched at least fifty or sixty with coins, but there were hundreds more. The Sky Witch had tricked them!

"Take coins," he told the others. "Everyone, take coins and put them into their hands. Do it!" But that backfired miserably, because every kid who grabbed a coin from the bucket couldn't resist the urge to grasp the coin themselves, and vanish. They were losing more of their own than the enemy.

It was over in less than twenty minutes. Their entire fighting force was backed up against the train, hands in the air, and the train itself had been captured. It took four Afterlights to hold Johnnie-O down. Then, as he struggled to break free, he felt a drop of water on his forehead, then another, then another and when he looked up, he saw a wet kid in a wetter bathing suit looking down at him. Water dripped into Johnnie-O's eye from a little silver key dangling around the kid's neck.

"The Sniffer told us all about you, Johnnie-O," the wet kid said. "Mary was even looking for a punching bag, to give you something to do until the end of time, but she never did find one. Guess you'll just have to shadowbox," which was a nasty thing to say, since Afterlights didn't cast shadows.

Johnnie-O wasn't about to be defeated by a kid in a bathing suit, so he fought himself free from the Afterlights holding him. "Dry up!" he told the wet kid, which was an equally nasty thing to say, because he couldn't. Then Johnnie-O pushed him out of the way, and ran to Charlie, who was sitting on the bucket of coins, hands behind his head and surrounded by a cluster of Mary's kids. Johnnie-O pushed his way in, pulled Charlie up, and grabbed the bucket, swinging it like a weapon.

"C'mon!" he said to Charlie, and they both ran.

Mary's forces had captured the Chocolate Ogre's army and they had taken his train—but there was still one more means of transportation available for someone with the nerve to take it.

The *Hindenburg* was not too difficult to find, as it was taller than anything around it. There were still dozens of Mary's Afterlights holding it down with ropes, keeping it from being torn away by the brutal wind.

"There's a whole bunch of them, and only two of us," Charlie said. "I don't like those odds."

But Johnnie-O realized something Charlie didn't. These Afterlights couldn't fight, because they already had their hands full. If it took this many of them to hold the airship down, how many would have to be taken off the job until the ship would tear free?

They wasted no time. Johnnie-O pulled them from the ropes, and Charlie slapped coins into their hands one after another. They had dispatched more than ten of them by the time the others figured out what was happening. They all panicked, and began to let go of the ropes. The airship began to lurch.

"Let's go!" Johnnie-O said. They raced toward the *Hindenburg*. The ramp was dragging across the ground, beginning to rise into the air. They leaped on, and pulled themselves inside.

The airship's nose lifted higher as it caught more of the Everlost wind. Some Afterlights still dangled from the ropes, but they had the good sense to let go, and the zeppelin took to the sky, twisting and turning out of control, at the mercy of the wind. It was just the two of them in the giant craft. They hadn't been able to save the train, or Nick's army, but at least they saved the bucket of coins.

"Can you fly this thing?" Johnnie-O asked Charlie.

"No," he answered, "but I got plenty of time to learn, doncha think?"

They fumbled their way through corridors until finally finding the bridge, and that's when they realized there was a problem.

There was a bar across the door, and that bar was held in place by a huge padlock.

"Where's the key?" asked Charlie. "There's got to be a key."

Johnnie-O knew exactly where the key was, because he had seen it dangling above his face dripping water into his eye.

"D'ya think we could break it?" asked Charlie. "Those fists of yours can do it, right?"

And although Johnnie-O tried, he knew it was no use. This was an Everlost door, and an Everlost padlock. Once something crossed into Everlost, it didn't break. Ever.

The airship rose into the clouds, slowly spinning like a weather vane as it blew eastward.

"This was a bad idea," said Charlie.

"Shut up," said Johnnie-O. "Just shut up."

So now Johnnie-O sat facing Charlie in the Starboard Promenade of the *Hindenburg*, a bucket of coins between them.

"You go first," said Johnnie-O.

"No, you go first," echoed Charlie.

"No, *you* go first!"

"No, *you!*"

But neither one was willing to take a coin. Instead they both stared at each other as the *Hindenburg* drifted across the sky, each wondering who would be the first to blink.

# CHAPTER 38

## *Last Train Out of Memphis*

Milos raced as fast as he could with Allie, staying away from the living, just in case Allie found strength enough to skinjack and escape. He had no idea whether Mary's force had captured the train. If they hadn't, Allie would be a bargaining chip. If they had, Allie would be a valuable prisoner.

"I saw her thoughts, Milos," Allie said weakly, as he pulled her along. "You can't go through with this! Mary hasn't told you everything! You don't know what she plans to do!"

But he was already overwhelmed with things to think about, and didn't need this. He was confused, and more than a little bit scared about what would happen now—and that just made him angry. "Quiet," he told her, "or I might just have to push you into the ground myself to silence you."

"Do it," said Allie. "I'd rather be there than have any part of Mary's plan."

"It's not her plan anymore," he told her. "It's mine."

They came through into a clearing, where the train rested on dead rails. Milos spotted Speedo right away, shouting frantic orders. The airship's ground team had just arrived, which meant the *Hindenburg* had been cast off.

They had captured the train, and Mary's plan had proceeded without her.

The entirety of the Ogre's army had been squeezed into the last train car. It had been Mary's idea—something she learned from Pugsy. "Afterlights can fit wherever you put them," she had said, and she was right—there were hundreds of them in that car: faces, hands, feet, and elbows pressed against the windows. It was a kind of purgatory until they came around to Mary's way of thinking.

When Speedo saw Milos, he looked worried. "Why aren't you with Jill at the bridge?" Then, when he saw Allie, his afterglow began to falter. "Something went wrong, didn't it? What went wrong?"

"Lock this one up somewhere special," Milos told Speedo, "but be careful—she's clever," and regaining some of his suave composure, he winked at Allie. "A little too clever for her own good—but maybe she can be, as Mary says, 'rehabilitated.'"

"Mary's not back yet," Speedo said. "We can't go till she gets here."

Milos hesitated for a moment. There was no easy way to tell Speedo the truth. "Mary will not be coming back," Milos said. "I am sorry."

"You mean . . . the Ogre defeated her?"

"The Ogre is gone," said Milos. "They are both gone."

Speedo was shell-shocked. He wanted to know everything, but there was no time, and Milos wasn't quite ready to share. "All we can do now," said Milos, "is to finish what she started."

"But how are we supposed to go on without her?"

"Oh, I think Mary will always be with us," Milos told him. "We can be certain of that."

Speedo had Allie strapped to the very front of the train, facing forward, and Milos allowed it.

"I was thinking something a little more comfortable," Milos said. "But this will do just fine."

"I am not a figurehead on a ship!" insisted Allie.

"Today you are," Milos told her calmly. "You took away Mary from her children. They would prefer that you were tied in a bag, and sent to the center of the earth, but I told them no. I told them that we must show you compassion, the way Mary would. Hate me all you want, but I just saved you."

"Forgive me if I don't thank you," Allie snapped.

Then Milos got close to her, and said, "I can forgive you for everything . . . except for taking her away from me. I will not forgive you for that."

Then he went to tend to Mary's masses, leaving Allie lashed to the front of the train, with a better view than anyone else of the path ahead.

The train had come to the end of its tracks as it reached the river. It could go no farther, for the trestle that ran down the center of the Union Avenue Bridge was very much a part of the living world. There were no Everlost bridges that crossed the mighty Mississippi.

The train waited as Moose, Squirrel, and Jackin' Jill arrived and came on board.

"You must be Allie the Outcast," Jill said, as she passed the front of the train. Then, glancing casually at the way Allie was all trussed up, she said, "Cute."

Allie suspected what was about to happen, but wanted to believe that it wouldn't. She held on to that hope until she saw and heard the explosions.

The first detonations took out the bridge's eastern tower, then its western tower blew just a few seconds later. Girders tore apart like confetti and flew in all directions. The rail trestle gave way, the traffic lanes collapsed, and the entire bridge plunged into the river, taking dozens of cars with it.

As Allie watched, wailing in the anguish of this terrible scene, the thoughts that she had dug out of Mary's mind came back to her.

*Some will be sent into the light before this day is done, but their sacrifice will pave the way for the many thousands we will save.*

*Thousands,* Mary had thought. *And even then, that's only a start.*

And so the bridge came down, killing all those who were on it . . . but out of the smoke of its destruction, a memory of the bridge materialized, as solid and as real as anything else in Everlost. The Union Avenue Bridge had crossed into their world.

Although the wind would not allow anyone to cross the Mississippi by foot, by boat, or even by airship, a steam engine could beat that wind. All it needed were tracks.

Allie, still strapped to the front of the train, was the first to inch out over the bridge as the train pulled forward, challenging the Everlost wind with the brute force of its engine. It roared at full steam, and although the wind struggled to hold it back, it was no match for such a powerful machine.

In just a few minutes the train crossed the river, rolled onto a dead rail line on the river's far side, and chugged forward with Allie unwillingly leading the way into the vast Western unknown.

# CHAPTER 39

## *At the Moment of Madness*

Everyone living in Memphis remembers where they were when the Union Avenue Bridge was taken down. The evidence pointed to unlikely suspects — a few road workers seen on the bridge, and a demolitions expert with no history of violent crime. A half dozen radical groups tried to take credit, making the truth even more difficult to ferret out. All that was known for sure was that somebody intentionally brought the beloved landmark down, taking the lives of close to fifty people.

At the moment of the disaster, a redheaded girl in a green velvet dress was seen watching the bridge collapse from Martyr Park, which overlooked the river. Witnesses noted something strange in her demeanor. She showed no sign of surprise, nor concern for the many people losing their lives before her eyes. Rumors had already begun to spread that she was a terrorist, or that she was a ghost, or that she never really existed at all. Mysterious sightings of the girl in green were being reported everywhere, and she was quickly becoming a local legend. A green velvet dress would be a popular Halloween costume for redheaded girls in Memphis this year.

At the moment of the disaster, another girl several miles away, wearing a very authentic Confederate uniform, was caught trying to steal a chicken right off a supermarket rotisserie. In the commotion of the blast, as shoppers ran out into the street to find out what had happened, the girl had thought no one would be looking, so she could take what she pleased. However, the store's manager was more concerned with criminal activity in his market than with death and destruction elsewhere. The girl made a big fuss about being caught, but became respectful when a uniformed police officer arrived on the scene.

As it turned out, the girl was a strange case. She claimed to have no family, no home, and she didn't match any children in the national database of kids reported missing.

"You have to have some family somewhere," the officer insisted as he let her eat the stolen chicken.

"Nope, ain't got no family a-tall," she said, in an accent from a place so Southern-deep, you could get the bends coming up from it. "Nope, no family," she said. ". . . a'course I *do* got a dog. . . ."

The officer concluded that, under the circumstances, finding that dog was as good a place as any to start.

At the moment of the disaster, Mikey McGill finally arrived at Graceland to find a handful of Afterlights in distress, not knowing what they should do. They had come with the Chocolate Ogre—but the Ogre had gone into the vortex, never came out, and no one was brave enough to go in after him.

"What about Allie?" Mikey asked. "What happened to Allie?"

They told him that a girl fitting her description was taken hostage by another Afterlight—a tall, dark-haired boy with strange speckled eyes. By the time word came down that the bridge had been blown, and that an Everlost train had taken Mary's followers across the river, Mikey knew he was too late. Allie would be a prisoner on that train, and the train was long gone.

Mikey raced to the bridge, and although it was solid beneath his feet, he was not a steam engine. No matter what form he changed himself into, he could not overcome the wind. He couldn't cross that bridge to rescue Allie.

And at the moment of the disaster, a bubble surfaced on the chocolate-covered floor of the Jungle Room, jarred into being by the rumble of the blast. The bubble rose to the surface, searching for consciousness, and settled back down again, unable to find it.

# CHAPTER 40

## *The Changeling and the Golem*

Mikey McGill had certain realities to face.

Allie was gone, the bridge was uncrossable, and Nick had disappeared into a vortex. Were it not for his own selfish intervention, Allie might have arrived in time to save Nick—and maybe she wouldn't have been taken hostage. Had Mikey not been so captivated by his own misery, perhaps she would have been here with him right now, instead of on a train heading west.

Now he had a choice. He could rage in fury at his own pigheaded stupidity, and wallow in self-loathing—that would certainly be the easy, familiar thing to do—or, he could, for once, choose to do something useful.

Later that night, he returned to his minions, and called them to him one by one. He then carefully rearranged their distorted, twisted faces, bringing them back to normal, and, when he could, made them a little better-looking than when they started.

"I release you from my service, now and forever," he told them. "Now go home."

They lingered just long enough to be sure he really

meant it, then they headed back for Nashville.

Once they were gone, Mikey made his way back to Graceland, where the dozen or so of Nick's Afterlights still kept a vigil, not knowing what to do. Mikey told them to go as well.

"We can't just leave," they said.

"Yes, you can," Mikey told them. "Go back to wherever you came from. Tell stories to your friends about the Ogre, only don't call him that. Call him by his name. Nick."

Reluctantly they left. Then, after they had all gone, Mikey turned and strode straight into the vortex.

Mikey began to feel the effects of it right away—a shifting inside of himself like the rumbling stomach of the living, but this feeling was all over his body. He followed the overpowering smell of chocolate to the Jungle Room where a layer of the stuff, about an inch thick, covered the entire floor.

Even before he stepped into the room, he began to change. He grew fingers from his knees, and nostrils in his armpits. The fingers turned to flowers and his eyes slid down to his elbows. He had no control over what Graceland was doing to him and he could see what it had already done to Nick. He had no idea whether a vortex was a living thing, or just a thing, but he knew he couldn't fight it, and so he didn't try. He gave in, letting it turn him into a creature in constant flux. He had a mission here, and as long as he could remember that mission, the vortex could not destroy him.

He got down on his knees and began to work. When his arms turned to tentacles, he used them. When they turned to flippers he used them. When he had no appendages at all, he waited until he sprouted something new. He worked, training his mind entirely on his task.

It took more than an hour, and when he emerged, he was wholly unrecognizable. Changes came so quickly now, he did not become any one thing entirely before changing to something else. Yet somehow he made it out the front door rolling, squirming, crawling—and he pulled with him a very heavy trash can—since the vortex existed in both worlds, he was able to pull it like any other Everlost artifact. It said "recyclables only," but he had removed the cans and bottles it had held, and now it was full of rich, creamy fudge—the kind that melts in your mouth—but he had no intentions of eating it.

Now that he was out on the porch, beyond the outer edge of the vortex, he sat down trying to slow the changes that swept through his body. He was changing once each second, but he concentrated, trying to make each form last, until the changes were coming once every five seconds. Then he took control, defining the changes as they came, choosing the forms he would assume.

Only one problem remained now. He could no longer remember his original form. Was he a creature with arms or with wings? Did he walk on all fours or did he have eight legs? Was he a creature more at home in water than land? Did he have a tail?

He found that trying to remember himself was impossible, so he tried to remember someone else. Her. Allie. *Allie*... He could see her face clearly in his mind, then tried to see himself through her eyes. It was by finding her that Mikey found himself.

One by one he pushed forth arms and legs, drew in any stray horns, and made his unsightly spider spinneret shrink into standard human hind-quarters. By and by he became who he was: the irascible, short-tempered, imperfect, but occasionally heroic Mikey McGill.

Once he was done, and he was sure his form would stick, he dragged the trash can from Graceland, and found a deadspot on the stone path of a nearby park. It was late now—long past midnight, but he did not care about the time. He webbed his fingers, effectively turning his hands into shovels, and began to scoop out the fudge, creating a pile on the ground. The stuff had hardened in the cool night to be the consistency of clay. That made it easier to work with. From the lump before him, he began to fashion a figure. A head, shoulders, a torso, arms, and legs. If he could rearrange the features of other Afterlights, surely he could shape an entire being from scratch as long as he had the raw materials.

There is an ancient story about a rabbi who, desperate to protect his village from destroyers, created a man out of earthen clay. He put into it all the care, all the hope, all the faith that he could muster. He danced around it, called on the secret name of God, and thus willed his clay creation to life, and it walked the earth. A golem. A creature not quite alive, but not quite dead.

Mikey was no rabbi, did absolutely no dancing, and rather than mud, he worked in a mixture of sugar, butter, and the brown ground powder of a rainforest bean—but like his sister, Mikey had a will that could move the universe.

When he was done, the chocolate golem was not much to look at. Its shape was roughly human, but it was little more than a mound on the ground. Its face had no features, but Mikey hoped that wouldn't matter.

It was early dawn now. The sun was threatening the eastern horizon.

Mikey put the finishing touches on the golem. He scraped a line for its mouth; and above it, pressed his thumbs in, creating indentations for its eyes; then beneath the eyes, he shaped a small bump of a nose. He poked two holes for ears, and then put his lips close to one of the holes and whispered,

"*Wake up . . .* "

A moment passed. Then a moment more. And then two eyelids rose, revealing a pair of eyes that were the same shade of brown. The golem blinked, then blinked again.

"Am I?" said the golem. "Am I?"

"Are you what?"

"Am I . . . here?"

"Yes," said Mikey, "you are. Do you know your name?"

The golem looked at him blankly. "Do I have a name?"

"Yes. Your name is Nick."

"My name is . . . Nick."

"Say it again," urged Mikey.

"My name is Nick!"

The holes on the side of the golem's head grew into actual ears. The slit that was its mouth became a pair of lips.

"My name is Nick!" the golem said again, and sat itself up. "Is your name Nick?"

"No. I'm Mikey."

"Mikey McGill!" said the golem, pleased with itself. Its shapeless body took on human curves. Its lump of a nose spread with two nostrils.

"What do you remember?"

"I don't know," said the golem. He looked around, then said. "Allie!" And suddenly his mittenlike hand divided into fingers and a thumb. He looked at them curiously.

"Yes! Yes, Allie!" said Mikey.

"But . . . but what's an Allie?" asked the golem.

Mikey sighed. This wasn't going to be easy, this wasn't going to be quick, but in Everlost, time was a plentiful thing.

"Allie's a friend," Mikey told him, "and you and I have to help her."

The golem stood, then walked, and when Mikey felt confident that the golem was sure-footed enough, he led them both west, toward the Mississippi, until they could no longer fight the wind.

There was no way they could cross the bridge, there was no way they could forge the river. . . .

. . . But there was another way to get to the other side.

Now, as they stood in place, they both began to sink into the living world. The golem looked down, to see his brown ankles had already disappeared into the earth. "We sink if we don't keep moving!" he said. "I remember now!"

"Good," said Mikey. "Keep on remembering."

They were up to their knees now, but Mikey made no move to pull himself out, and so neither did the chocolate golem.

"Hold on to me," Mikey told him. "Hold on to me tight, and whatever you do, don't let go."

The golem did as he was told, but as they sunk to their

waists, he said, "I don't think this is a good idea."

"It's all right," said Mikey. "We're just taking a trip."

"Where are we going?"

"We're going under the river, coming up on the other side. And then we're heading west to find Allie." Mikey forced his feet and his hands to grow into long, jagged claws, just perfect for moving through the earth. He had once clawed his way back from the center of the earth, he had to believe he could do this!

The wind still blew strong and relentless, but it did not penetrate the earth. Soon they had sunk to their chests.

"I'm scared," said the golem.

"So am I, Nick." But then Mikey thought about Allie, and came to understand that there was another feeling in him far more powerful than fear. A feeling that made his afterglow turn lavender. He held on to that feeling as he sank to his shoulders, and kept on going. Then, in spite of everything, he began to smile. So much of his existence in Everlost had been full of despair. Despair, and a fear of losing what he had. But Allie was not lost, she was just there across the river, waiting for him to find her. Nick was not lost either—not entirely.

It was then that Mikey McGill realized something. It must have been his sister who first called this place Everlost, because by naming it so, it stripped away all hope except for a faith in her, and the "safety" she could provide. Well, Mary was wrong on all counts, because *nothing* in Everlost was lost forever, if one had the courage to search for it.

Mikey held tightly on to this shining truth as he and the golem sunk into the earth. Then with all the force of his heart, his mind, and his soul, Mikey McGill began to dig.

# EP|LOGUE

## *Requiem for the Living*

On a bench in a train station in the city of Little Rock, Arkansas, sat a girl who made the ticket agent nervous.

She had arrived early in the morning, presumably to wait for someone to arrive on the train, but few passenger trains came through Little Rock's Union Station—in fact it was more of an office building now than anything else. The ticket agent called security, and the two security guards on duty eyed her from a distance.

"A nut job," concluded the older man, but the younger guard was not so jaded. He had just turned twenty, and was new to the job. He still saw the best in people. "Maybe she's just waiting for the Texas Eagle."

"That train's not due for hours," said the older guard. "I'm tellin' ya—she's a wacko. Sooner or later there'll be a 'tell' that gives it away—you watch!"

The girl did not have the look of the various and sundry crazies that frequented the nation's train stations. She was well-dressed—in fact, overdressed in a emerald-green satin gown. True, her red hair looked a bit disheveled, but she was neither talking to herself or engaging in questionable activities—although sitting for hours in a train station was, in and of itself, questionable.

She was hard not to notice. What with that shimmering gown, she was the only bright spot in the dreary station, and it drew the younger guard's attention all morning long, until he finally approached her. She was as beautiful up close as she was from a distance, although some discoloration around one eye attested to some sort of trouble.

"Are you all right, Miss?" he asked. "Can I help you with anything?"

"No," she said cheerily. "I'm just waiting for a friend."

"The train isn't due to arrive for another six hours—and with that bridge down in Memphis, everything's been rerouted, so it's bound to be late. Wouldn't you rather come back later?"

"My friend is not necessarily arriving by train," she informed him.

"Oh." Since he didn't quite know how to respond to that, he just let her be, convincing the other guard not to evict her for loitering. It occurred to him that this girl fit the description of a woman wanted for questioning in the bridge disaster, but there was no way it could have been her. This girl was far too young and innocent to be involved in that kind of thing.

She was still there at noon, and was beginning to get fidgety. The young guard had realized she had not eaten—in fact, she didn't even have a purse or wallet of any kind, so he bought her a bagel at the station café, and gave it to her.

"On the house," he said.

"Why, thank you!"

"Are you sure I can't help you?" he asked. "Maybe we could call your friend."

"I'm afraid he has no telephone." And clearly neither did she.

She ate her bagel slowly, with a grace rarely seen in these days of fast food and stuffed faces. If she was still here when his shift ended, he thought he might offer to buy her dinner—if only to watch the graceful way she dined.

As the day wore on, she became more and more unsettled, and her behavior became such that the older guard crossed his arms and said, "See, I told you so!" But again, the younger guard convinced him to leave the poor girl alone. "She's all yours," the older man said as he left at the end of his shift.

At about four in the afternoon, the girl began to walk around the station with increasing impatience, zeroing in on anyone who lingered alone for too long, and the guard began to truly feel for her.

"Is it you?" she asked a man who stood reading a newspaper.

"Pardon me, I thought you were someone else," she said to a worker fixing a vending machine. "*Are* you someone else?"

These were all "tells" to be sure, and now that she was up and about, there was one more thing to give away the fact that things weren't quite right. It was her dress. It was beautiful, it was elegant, and it still had a price tag hanging from the back.

***

The living world had not been kind to Mary Hightower in the week she had been in it. Resilient and adaptive though she was, there were simply some situations she was unprepared for. It wasn't only that her sensibilities were suited to a kinder, more genteel time, but she had also forgotten the endless inconveniences of the human body.

First there was the weakness brought on by hunger and thirst, which nearly caused her to faint several times during her first few days alive. The need for nourishment was an ever-present nuisance. She abhorred theft of any kind, so she hoped simple human compassion might sustain her. She was appalled at how few people were willing to share their food with her when asked politely. In the end she had to resort to taking food from abandoned plates after the diners had left—and even then she was constantly shooed away by heartless restauranteurs.

She quickly became disgusted with bodily functions as well, but discovered that ignoring them was not a good idea—and then there was this awful business of body odor. In Everlost she always smelled faintly of lilacs and wildflowers— just like the fields around her on the day she died. Well, the living body did not smell at all floral, and although she had worn the same green velvet dress for more than a hundred years, in just a few days it had become so dirty and so foul-smelling that people would keep their distance from her.

Over the week, as she traveled west, she had come across several men who appeared gallant, and willing to help her—such as the man who purchased for her the lovely dress she now wore. However there was nothing gentlemanly about them at all. In fact, they turned mean when she didn't return their affection, and left her.

*Well,* she thought, *at least I have my self-respect, and a new dress.*

On the night before her arrival in Little Rock, she bathed herself in a fountain to wash off the stench of living, and groomed her hair with a brush she had found in a drainage ditch.

*"Meet me in one week's time,"* Milos had whispered to her on that terrible day in Graceland. *"One week's time, at the train station in Little Rock."*

No matter what she was forced to endure during this terrible week, she was determined to look her best for Milos.

She knew he would be skinjacking, so there'd be no way to spot him in advance. All she could do was wait. So that's what she did. She waited all morning, and all afternoon. But as the day wore on, and the sun began to set, she became increasingly worried. What if Milos wasn't coming? What if he had changed his mind? What if she was now truly stuck in the living world? And what if this nightmare of a week became her whole future? She imagined herself aging, her body corrupting with decay. What had she done to deserve such an unspeakable punishment?

A train came, people boarded, people left, and it moved on. It was long after dark now, and Milos had not come. She buried her head in her hands and wept.

"Listen, Miss . . . I'm sorry your friend didn't show. . . ."

She looked up to see that nosy young security guard again. She gathered what little poise she could, and pulled a few stray strands of hair back from her face. "It's fine," she said. "Really it is." She looked at the large station clock, which showed half-past nine. They were the only ones left in the station now.

"I'm sorry," he said, "but the building's closing."

Mary blotted her eyes, as he sat down beside her. "You must work very long hours," she said. "You've been here since this morning."

He offered her an apologetic shrug. "Actually my shift ended a while ago. But I was worried about you, so I stayed."

Then he reached around to the back of her neck. "You know you left the price tag on."

"Did I? I hadn't noticed."

"Might as well be a 'kick me' sign. May I?"

"Please."

He reached into his pocket. "I got this off a trouble-maker the other day. He was trying to shoplift cigarettes." And he produced a large switchblade. He reached behind her and cut off the tag.

"Thank you."

Then he offered her his hand. "My name is Roberto, but my friends call me Beto."

"A pleasure to meet you, Beto. My name is—" She hesitated, then said, "My name is Megan. Megan McGill."

"Listen," said Beto, "since we're closing and all, maybe you might like to go get something to eat."

Mary sighed. So here it was again; a young man pretending to be a gentleman. Was it too much to hope that he could be sincere?

"Yes," Mary said. "I would like that. I would like that very much."

Neal Shusterman

She wiped away the last of her tears and they left—but before they reached the door, he stopped, as if perhaps he had changed his mind.

"Is everything all right?"

"Yes," said Beto. "I thought I had forgotten my keys, but they're right here." He jingled them in his pocket.

"Oh—so we're taking your car. . . ."

"Got to," he said with a chuckle. "Already missed the train."

Mary wondered how wise it was to get into a stranger's car, but decided unless she wanted to walk these empty downtown streets alone, she had little choice.

"A city can be a scary place at night," said Beto, as they stepped out into the cool night. "But this neighborhood looks worse than it is." Then he added, "Besides, you have your own personal security guard."

Mary laughed at that, if only to make the moment less awkward.

"This way," he said, leading her down an alley. "The parking lot is in the back."

He took her hand, and she chose not to resist.

"So what are you hungry for, Mary? Chinese food, maybe? A burger?"

"Food is food," she said. "Anything is fine."

It wasn't until they were halfway down the alley that she realized, and stopped cold.

*She had told him her name was Megan . . . not Mary.*

A distant streetlight at the end of the alley lit half of his face, but from this angle his eyes were in shadow, so she couldn't be sure.

"Milos?"

Then he smiled. "I was wondering how long it would take for you to figure it out!"

"But . . . how long?"

"Do you remember when he stopped to check his keys?"

Milos laughed, and Mary launched herself into his arms. She simply couldn't stop herself, and in return, he held on to her with arms strong and unfailing.

"You came back for me! You came back!"

"How could I not? Your children need you," he said. "*I* need you too."

Milos went on to tell her about their week west of the Mississippi. The train traveled slowly, stopping at every town they came across, but they hadn't found a single Afterlight. There were dubious sightings of creatures that seemed part animal, part human, but that may just have been the overactive imaginations of the younger children.

"I've been thinking about what you said," Milos told her. "How you might be able to work from this side. It will be difficult, but it might work. Even alive, you can give comfort to your children. Of course you won't be able to see them, but they can see you."

"Is anyone with you right now?" Mary asked.

Milos shook his head. "No. We're all alone in both worlds."

"Good!" And then she did something she never had done in Everlost. She kissed him. She kissed him so long and so hard that he had to back away to catch his breath. She knew it was partially the weakness of her flesh that made her do it, but she also knew it was necessary to seal the bond between them. He had come back for her. He didn't have to, he didn't need to—he could have chosen to rule her children alone, yet he didn't. Mary knew what he wanted; he wanted to take Nick's place in her heart. The least she could do was make him think that he had achieved that goal—and who knows, maybe someday he would. But for now, she would do him the service of telling him what he wanted to hear.

"You are very special to me, Milos," she told him. "You are every bit my equal, and I'm glad we found each other."

Even in the stark slanted light, she could see that he was blushing. "So then . . . shall I spend some time with you in this body?"

"No," Mary told him. "I've spent enough time in this body." In fact, she realized, it had been more than enough. She did not want to endure another day in the dread place called the living world. This week had been horrible—but in a way, it had been a gift to her. It made her realize just how desperately all the people who suffered from life needed to be freed from it. She would free every single one of them if she could—and maybe someday soon she'd be in a position to do it. Not just a hundred, or a thousand, but all of them! She would not rest until no one on earth was left alive.

Of course, just as with bringing down the bridge, it would take planning and precision to bring an end to the world of flesh once and for all, and allow Everlost to take its place . . . but if it was ever to happen, then it had to start today. Not with a thousand souls, but with one.

"I want you to do something for me, Milos," Mary said. "There's a switchblade in your pocket. . . ."

Milos reached into Beto's pocket, pulled it out, and opened it. The blade caught the glare of the streetlight at the end of the alley, casting a long, sharp shadow against the brick wall.

"I don't belong in the living world, Milos. I belong in Everlost. I belong with you."

When Milos realized what she was suggesting, his hand began to shake, and she gently touched it to steady it.

"Are you . . . sure about this?"

"More sure than anything."

"But you will go into the light."

"No—because you'll catch me, and stop me."

"But then you will fall asleep. You will sleep and you won't wake up for nine months. . . ."

"And you'll protect me while I'm sleeping, won't you, Milos?"

Milos took a slow, deep breath, then he nodded. "Yes, I will," he finally told her. "And I promise I will be waiting for you when you awake."

"I believe you," Mary told him. "I trust you." But then something troubling occurred to her.

Milos must have read it in her eyes, because he said, "Do not worry about this fleshie. He was kind to you, and so I will make certain that your body of flesh is never found, and he will never know what he has done."

Mary smiled. "You think of everything, don't you?"

"It is something I learned from you."

Milos looked to both ends of the alley to make sure they were unobserved, before lowering the blade to her chest. It still quivered in his hand, so he tightened his grip until the blade was still.

Then in that lonely alley in the living world, Megan Mary McGill put her arms over Milos's shoulders, feeling the steel tip of the blade lightly pierce her new satin gown, just barely touching the skin above her heart. She looked into his eyes until she could see Milos behind the face of the security guard, and then she commanded in a powerful, impassioned whisper:

" . . . Bring me home, my love. . . ."